THE HEIR OF ATARGATIS

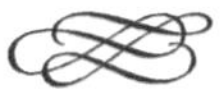

A.G. WHITT

For my mother,
Who spent endless hours with me creating this world.

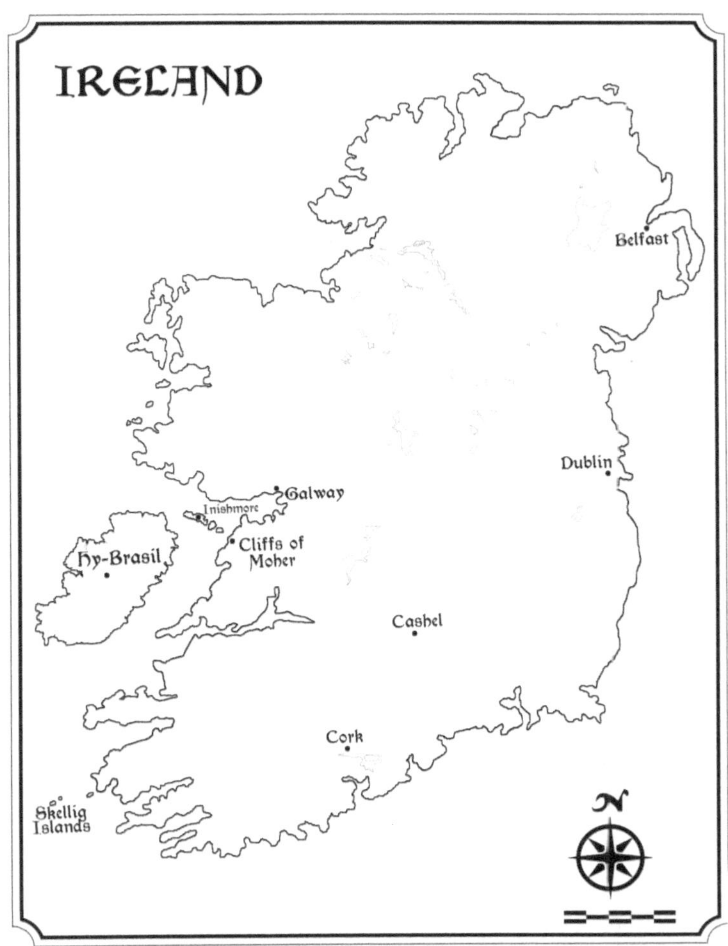

IRELAND
Belfast
Dublin
Galway
Inishmore
Cliffs of
Moher
Hy-Brasil
Cashel
Cork
Skellig
Islands
N

PART I
LAND WALKER

MEMORIES

Marianne's office had an infuriatingly loud, outdated grandfather clock that stood in the corner like a watchful eye, reminding me of the exact minutes I had left to forcibly open my soul to the stranger across the chipped coffee table. After all, that's all a therapist is—a complete stranger to whom you pay a handsome sum of money to give you advice that you may or may not take, because it may or may not be any good.

Even I could admit, however, that a candidate such as myself ought to be here. Aside from the general nature of my perfectionism that had plagued my internal monologue for the majority of my childhood, the more recent events in my past had led to more than one friend suggesting I attempt to find solace in the remedial treatment of therapy. I reluctantly agreed, and was humbly surprised to find that this coping mechanism was an annoyingly perfect fit for my needs.

"Jasmine?" came the familiar voice across the room.

"Sorry," I said faintly, my voice trailing off as my gaze refused to leave the popcorn ceiling. "I missed what you said."

Marianne pushed her thick-framed purple glasses up the

bridge of her nose in the way my friend Marissa used to do-I wondered if she still did-when she was either nervous or impatient. I guessed Marianne's movement may have been prompted by a mixture of those two emotions, should therapists be allowed to grow impatient. I thought not, considering their livelihood seemed to be entirely reliant on the willingness of stubborn individuals to drive the success of their own sessions.

"I asked if you were ready to tell me about the accident," she said in a voice that was so steady it was nearly robotic. As my employer's generous insurance plan did not cover these meetings of ours, I thought by the third go around I might as well get to the point for my own wallet's sake.

"Sure," I said with a loud sigh. I had run through it over a dozen times in my head in the past year...what was the harm in saying it out loud? I proceeded to tell her of the abysmally traumatizing day that had occurred nearly a year ago.

IT HAD BEEN A BRIGHT, September day in Tampa with the slightest breeze-the kind of pleasant weather that inspires the masses to romanticize living in the sunshine state. I had suspiciously punctual lunch plans with my two best friends at the time-Marissa and Kristen-neither of whom were ever known to be timely. This first of many residual clues led me to believe that a surprise was coming, but of course I had already known what it was.

I had had my finger sized only a month prior, and with my twenty-eighth birthday just around the corner, Matt had happened to run out for a mysterious errand with no estimated time of return on a morning that simply made sense for it to be *the* day. He was never great at lying, no matter how small the matter may have been. It was one of the reasons I was sure I wanted to marry him.

"Can you please not ruin something for once?" came a shrill

voice from the kitchen. "You are the only person I know who hates surprises."

The tall, graceful figure of Kristen appeared in the doorframe of the bathroom and she leaned against it, her mouth turned down in a weak attempt at a scowl. Her eyes darted around the room in search of someone else to scold as I had made it clear I was a useless target. Marissa, who had been curling the back of my hair for me, shrugged in resignation.

"We tried," she said simply, plugging her nose as she drenched my head in hairspray.

"I don't hate them!" I said defensively. Unable to stop myself, I added under my breath, "I just always know when they're coming."

I shrugged with an air of superiority that was not lost on the others and Kristen let out a loud cluck of disapproval.

As if in defiance of my statement, there came an authoritative knock at the apartment door that made all three of us jump. Both Kristen and Marissa grinned with satisfaction as I peered around the corner with curiosity.

"I *know* you didn't see this one coming," Kristen sang loftily as she strode across the vast living room, her sheet of white blonde hair bouncing in her wake.

The warm, glowing sunlight of the late morning streamed through the floor-to-ceiling windows, casting a faint shimmer of gold onto the dark wood that moved in symphony with waves dancing in the bay below.

"Look who's here!" Kristen sang as she threw open the door.

She was right, I had not seen this part coming. On the other side of the door stood my best friend from childhood, Kiana Hardy. Breaking into a wide grin upon seeing my expression of shock, she leapt through the doorframe and pulled me into a rib-crushing hug. Although it was customary for me to refrain from these types of physical embraces, my disbelief kept me rooted to the spot.

"Wow, she never lets us hug her like that," Kristen remarked with a smirk.

I laughed as I felt tears brimming in my eyes, looking between Kristen and Marissa who wore the triumphant smiles of two people who had pulled off the impossible.

"Surprise!" Marissa said happily.

"I can't believe you're here!" I exclaimed, shaking Kiana's shoulders as confusion and excitement caused me to stumble over my words. "What about school, what about-"

Kiana gave a grand wave of clanking silver and gold on her wrists, dismissing my concerns.

"Law school will be there when I get back. It's just a weekend." She stood on her tiptoes and peered over my shoulder. "Are you going to invite me in or what?"

"Of course, may I also get your bags, ma'am?"

I stepped back across the threshold and bowed my friend inside with mock formality. Her jaw dropped as the vast floor plan of sleek modernity was revealed behind me and I turned bright red.

"So *this* is what it's like to be engaged to a doctor, huh?" she said, punching me in the arm playfully.

I let out a loud laugh that sounded more like a nervous bark as I had no witty response prepared for my friend of nearly two decades. I knew I was lucky, and I was grateful for it.

"I'm really happy for you," she said sincerely, still shaking her head in admiration. "For the engagement, for everything."

"Well, I'm not engaged yet," I said, finding amusement in the fact that my oldest friend would not bother with pretenses in the way my newer friends did. She knew me too well.

"Are you *both* incapable of a surprise!" Marissa exclaimed, rounding the corner.

She greeted Kiana with a warm hug that was sincere, despite the exaggerated eye roll that accompanied it.

"I don't think anyone should be truly shocked about a decision like this," I said. "It's too important."

"Jasmine, forever the mind of reason in a world of fools," Kiana praised with judicious sarcasm.

"Save that for the toast," remarked Kristen.

Marissa pushed her glasses up the bridge of her nose.

"But really, how did you know it was today?" she feigned mere curiosity, but I could see the flicker of frustration in her eyes. "I thought we did a great job of keeping at least *the day* a secret."

Not wanting to hurt her feelings, I softened.

"You did!" I caught the knowing glances of the other two from behind Marissa's back and suppressed a laugh. "No, really, it was Matt who gave it away. He left before I had even opened my eyes this morning."

"Let's get going," said Kristen, looking down at her watch.

My doorman Ivan greeted me in the same manner he always did, waving goodbye with a jovial smile on his face that always made my mornings brighter.

"Goodbye, *Miss* Jasmine," he said happily, placing emphasis on my title as if the next time he addressed me it would be something different.

We pushed through the revolving doors that deposited the three of us right in the heart of Water Street, already buzzing with the lunch rush of a perfect Saturday afternoon.

"I miss the sun," groaned Kiana as she closed her eyelids and let her head fall backward.

Although she had spent the last two years in D.C. for law school, Kiana had spent undergrad in Miami and the long term plan was for her to return to any part of Florida as soon as she could. The other three of us had had much less of a focus on intense academics, completing our bachelor's degrees at the University of Central Florida.

We made our way through the active farmer's market on Water Street, dodging dogs and their owners who carefully balanced lattes in one hand and fresh vegetables in the other. There was live music coming from somewhere, and everyone had evidently had the same idea as ourselves when it came to taking advantage of the rare weather for the season.

At last we reached the restaurant, a cozy lunch spot positioned right at the edge of the action. There was a large table just inside by the window that had a bottle of champagne nestled in a French chiller, and the hostess sat me directly next to it. I glanced up and saw there was a piano that had certainly not been there the last time I had dined, and I smiled. Of course, Matt would be incorporating his most impressive talent into the proposal. I always said he was a gifted pianist with a beautiful voice who had simply happened to fall into the medical profession in order to pay the bills.

A number of empty chairs were situated around the table and I counted in my head. There would be one for Matt of course, as well two more for his parents that lived just on the other side of the bridge in St. Pete. The other was likely for Christian, Kristen's boyfriend, who was also Matt's best friend. Marissa's fiancé would not be joining of course as he was at his brother's bachelor party in Arizona this weekend.

I looked hopefully at the remaining chair…but no. My father was in Sweden at least until the end of the semester, and I knew he would likely stay to finish the year. In fact, he was enjoying his new post as a graduate professor of marine biology at the University of Stockholm so wholly that I thought he may never leave at all. The next time we had planned to see one another was not until Christmas.

While most would agree that Florida would be the preferable climate in December in comparison to Sweden, Matt and I had excitedly booked our tickets the moment the invitation was extended. The Christmas markets of Scandinavia were on both of our bucket lists, and Stockholm's Gamla Stan had been my screensaver for over a year.

"How are you feeling?" whispered Marissa, her kind blue eyes looking up at me through her frames.

She rested a hand on my upturned palm, warming the thin silver scar that never seemed to lose its sensitivity no matter how many years passed.

"I am so excited for you," she said, beaming at me.

"Me too," said Kristen, taking a deep gulp of champagne. "Even though you ruined the surprise. I'll let it slide."

We all laughed, and I never asked about the last chair. I didn't want to get my hopes up.

A glass of champagne warmly buzzing in my stomach, I looked around happily, observing the street shoppers through the wide window. No one had yet sat down at the piano, and I imagined Matt's fingers gracing the keys with the natural, effortless rhythm that all artists seem to have.

"Would you ladies like to order some cocktails while you wait?"

I started at the sound of our server's voice. The young girl looked at us expectantly, eyeing the empty chairs nervously.

"Sure," Kristen said distractedly, looking at her watch and frowning. "They're certainly running late, aren't they?" she mumbled.

I opted for a glass of white wine rather than a cocktail, wanting to ensure that the upcoming moment would be crystal clear. I watched as the server shuffled away, looking behind her as she went.

"I've seen the ring, by the way," Kristen blurted out suddenly, eyeing me while I absentmindedly rubbed my fourth finger on my left hand. "It's stunning."

"Kristen!" Marissa scolded.

"What?" Kristen replied, finishing off the last of the champagne as she gestured to the remaining seats with a flourish. "She knows already!"

Kiana rolled her eyes and pulled me into a conversation

regarding engagement party locations, color schemes, and other matters I had hardly wrapped my head around. I felt oddly displaced, recalling suddenly that I had not heard from Matt since the morning. Terrible at keeping secrets as he was, I thought it unusual for him to not have shared even a semblance of an alibi by now.

"I'm going to give them a call," said Kristen abruptly, excusing herself from the table. "I'll be right back."

Her long legs took only a few steps before she disappeared through the revolving door and into the busy street.

I sat back in my chair, catching a glimpse of our server (whom I now knew to be named Katie) talking nervously to her coworkers. They all took turns glancing back at our table, and I suddenly became painfully aware of how crowded the restaurant was in addition to the long line of potential diners waiting outside. Feeling guilty for holding them up, I pressed everyone to make their decisions on food. Without consulting the others, I signaled to Katie that we were ready to order.

She began to make her way over, but was cut off by Kristen who had returned quicker than I expected. To my surprise, my friend ushered the server aside hurriedly and turned her back to us. I wondered if it had something to do with the proposal and thought I should look away, but my curiosity got the better of me. I continued to watch them, a growing sense of unease in the pit of my stomach for a reason I couldn't explain.

"What's that about?" asked Kiana.

"I dunno."

I saw Katie slowly place her hands over her mouth in response to something Kristen had said, and the manager rushed over to join them. Even from afar, the general air of profuse apology from the waitstaff was obvious, though I could not see a reason that rendered it necessary based on our positive experience thus far.

The manager snapped his fingers, sending a young woman

who had been sitting near the doorway speeding toward the piano. She sat down and began to play at a soft volume that complimented the atmosphere of a pleasant brunch. Kristen returned to the table, pale and expressionless.

"Kristen, what was that about?" asked Marissa in a whisper, eyes wide with confusion.

Kiana looked at her expectantly and I began to sink backward in my seat, instinctively knowing that something was deeply wrong.

Kristen ignored them both and looked straight at me. Whether she delivered the message in the best way or not is irrelevant. I cannot say how I would have done it myself.

"Jazz, I-" she began, and her voice faltered.

The sound of the piano seemed to grow louder in my ears as my stomach turned over in expectation of dread. Kristen then did something entirely uncharacteristic-she reached for my hand and grasped it tightly between hers. I jumped slightly at her touch.

"I went to call Matt-but it was Christian who answered," she said. "There's been a horrific accident on the water."

The words did not seem to compute in my brain.

"An accident," I repeated bluntly, my body numbing along with my thoughts. "What do you mean?"

She looked at me with desperation that alarmed me. I had never seen Kristen lost for words.

"Matt, he was with your dad-he had flown in from Stockholm," she said in a rush, her words pouring over into one another.

"Raj?" I said, hearing my own voice as if it were coming from someone else-someone who was very far away. "M-my dad's here?"

She nodded but ignored me, continuing to speak her blubbering words as if her story could not pause or she wouldn't be able to finish it.

"They were bringing the boat over from St. Pete since we were going to take it out afterward, and they were just out in the bay when…"

She told me the rest, but I didn't need to hear it. A dark tunnel was closing in on me, leaving me with nothing but a tiny circle of clarity that allowed me to see Kristen's face saying words that could not be true. I was underwater-the voices of my friends were crying out in confusion muffled by a gigantic wave of realization that started to pull me under.

"Are they dead?" I asked.

They were the only words I could find. Harsh and terrible as they were both to hear and say, it was the sole combination that would get me the only answer I needed to know. The other details did not matter.

"My dad and Matt," I said flatly. "They're both dead, aren't they?"

"Oh, Jasmine… I-yes."

WHEN AT LAST I finally looked up from my shoes, Marianne's expression was unreadable, and I was grateful for it. It was the pity from others that weakened my ability to isolate the pain in the dormant part of my mind where I had tucked it away. When I was left with just the truth of my own words rather than the reactions of others, I could handle what had happened. Most of the time, anyway.

"And that was a year ago?" Marianne asked matter-of-factly, as if she were simply plotting the points of my life onto a timeline for the sake of a works cited page.

"Just about," I said, glancing at the calendar she hung on her wall-reminding me again how insufferably antiquated her lifestyle was-and saw it was turned to September of the following year.

"Labor Day weekend," she observed.

"Which isn't a holiday in Sweden, obviously," I said, my gaze returning to my sneakers. "So that made it all the more shocking that Raj would've been able to escape for a weekend to surprise me so early in the term."

For the hundredth time, I cursed his selflessness. I wished his flight had gotten delayed, or canceled altogether…anything for an extra few moments that would have altered the events in the slightest way. But Marianne and I had already covered that sentiment in my previous sessions. I could not change the past.

"Maybe we can talk about your father," Marianne suggested. "If talking about Matt isn't helpful right now."

Again, I appreciated her approach. I had made it very clear from our first session that the topic of Matt beyond the facts of what had happened would be off-limits for a while. I knew at some point or another she would find a way to manipulate me into divulging more information considering it was her job, but that day wouldn't be today.

"Sure," I said, feeling a sudden (and rare) surge of willingness to cooperate. "What about Raj?"

I had mostly referred to my father by his nickname rather than "dad" since I was roughly sixteen years old. I assumed it must be a habit that kids with single parents develop as they get older. He never seemed to mind, in any case.

"Well, anything, Jasmine," Marianne said, shrugging in an attempt of informality. "Do you have any particularly favorite memories? Sometimes those are a good place to start."

Of course I had endless amounts of fond memories to choose from. My father had been a brilliant man and even as a child, I knew I was lucky to have him. He really had done the best he could, raising a child-a girl, nonetheless-by himself while balancing his career as a college professor that wanted to drag him all over the world. I looked up at Marianne who was waiting expectantly with a kind smile on her face.

"Yes," I said, clearing my throat. "I wouldn't call it a favorite singular memory, necessarily. But the few years we spent in Portugal were the happiest times of my life."

Marianne leaned back in her chair and propped one purple pant leg on top of the other. She tossed her arm on top of the sofa in expectation. "I'd love to hear about it."

I HAD JUST TURNED eleven when my father got the offer at the University of Porto. Before he pivoted to studying the science of the seas, he had been an absolute fanatic for space exploration and the science of the sky.

Raj had been given the chance of a lifetime with a temporary (though the term was ambiguous) assignment in the Astronomy department, teaching a graduate course on the Origin and Evolution of Stars and Planets. The Centro de Astrofísica da Universidade do Porto was not only the largest astronomy program in the country of Portugal, but was one of the best in the world.

Portugal was immediately home to me. I was young, so I picked up the language more quickly than my father did (to his utmost frustration). I've lost a good amount of it by now, due to years of being out of practice, but I remember I used to order in Portuguese at restaurants and translate directions for him when we would go on road trips.

Of course Lisbon was the grand capital, but Porto was magical. The rich historical buildings were the first of their kind that I had ever seen and set the course for my mad desire to travel the world-a hobby that my wanderlust father was all too willing to encourage. Outside of the city there was even more beauty to behold-from the striking cliffs of the Algarve in the summer to the luxurious tropics of the Azores. We kept extremely busy with domestic travel that year.

And of course as anyone can expect of an academic who spent his time researching, discussing theory, and smoking cigars, Raj discovered his deep appreciation for port during that time. I was too young to care for the products of them back then, but the rolling vineyards of the Duoro Valley were charming to me all the same. With the University of Porto situated right smack in the middle of the city, I was gradually allowed on miniature outings by myself or with the few friends I had made at school. The added bonus of the world's most beautiful bookshop, Livraria Lello, being directly next to my father's office at the university gave me plenty to explore while he was grading papers. Tourists needed to buy tickets, but I somehow always found a way to slip inside undetected.

"I REALLY LOVED IT THERE," I said to Marianne. "I wanted to stay forever."

I rubbed the deep scar in the palm of my left hand absently, the light catching the straight line of iridescence that seemed to glow like a moonstone in perpetuity as I remembered the day I got it. I decided it was a safe enough memory to share with Marianne, since we were on the topic of Raj.

THE STRANGE SCAR originated from the day my father had taken myself and one of his top graduate students, Liam Brennan, out on the water.

Raj had already begun his extracurricular studies of the ocean given our proximity to it, and he was fascinated with the marine life of Iberia. When he heard there would be prime visibility of Jupiter off the western coast, he jumped at the opportunity to combine his current studies with his love of the sea. The university actually deemed it a research project-making the prize for being the top student in Professor Atarga's class that semester a field exploration off the coast during the Jupiter event.

It had not surprised Raj in the slightest that Liam Brennan, the lad from Ireland and one of his only foreign students, had risen to the challenge. He had always been the brightest in the program. Without a son of his own, Raj had a soft spot for Liam as he, too, was far from home in the Iberian Peninsula.

Additionally, my father had always been fascinated by the history of Ireland because his first love (my mother) had been Irish. In fact, *Raj* was a nickname coined by her. His actual name, Faraj, simply didn't roll off of her Gaelic tongue in the way it was supposed to sound. But he liked it, so the name stuck. Personally, I had never heard him called anything else. Since we spent most of my childhood in America, I guess it had been easier that way. I had heard the story of my mother's mispronunciation many times, but it still made me grin.

"FAH-RAJ," my father had said to her. She was a beautiful girl with red hair that was so dark it looked like a cup of mulled wine. Her eyes twinkled as she looked up at him.

"Fuh-rahhh," she said, her accent undoubtedly exaggerated by the third martini swaying dangerously in her hand.

He caught her wrist and took a sip off the top to save it from splashing onto her shoes. They were graduate students at Cambridge in their final year, and somehow had never met until that night.

"Almost," he said. "But a little less emphasis on-"

She pressed a finger to his lips. "I'll just call ye Raj, if that's alright with ye."

"Alright," he said, laughing. "Then you're Annie to me, because I can't pronounce yours either."

"HE WAS GOING to take me to Ireland one day you know," I said quietly. "We were going to go and research my... well, *her* family history."

That story had been one of the very few I had ever heard

about my mother, because the truth was that Raj barely knew her. I often thought he was embarrassed by that, so I never pressed him on the subject.

"Your mother was Irish?" Marianne asked, her brow raising in interest. "What was she like?"

I shrugged. "I dunno. Having me was not…on purpose," I said awkwardly. "And then she was gone."

'Gone', meaning she left him. And me.

I sat quietly after saying the words out loud. I never really thought about her, but when I did, it struck me how it made me feel. Like a whole half of my history was inexplicable. There was so much to be learned when you didn't know your mother. But I was grateful that I had known at least *one* of my parents.

I hoped Marianne wouldn't press for more regarding how the abandonment of the mysterious Annie had impacted my self esteem or some bullshit like that. After all, I didn't have much to tell. I had no idea where the woman was, and I was too old now to take it personally.

My therapist must have determined that one dead parent was enough for her to work with for now, and she left it alone. She smiled and urged me to continue my original story.

"You were talking about your boat day with Raj."

"That's right."

LIAM HAD MET us at the docks, and I (being an only child of eleven years old who desperately longed for a sibling) was clinging to the grad student like a monkey. He had brought along his telescope, but Raj assured us there would be little need for it other than for extreme detail. It turned out he was right, and the planet shone above us brighter than I could have ever imagined, piercing the night with its godly glow that left no debate as to who was the ruler of the sky.

"Incredible," my father breathed.

I watched him as he looked up in wonder, the imperfectly round silver disk mesmerizing him as it spun at a speed incapable of detection by the human eye. To us, it was completely still.

After several moments of observing my father and Liam silently dumbstruck by their view of the planet, I, like most other children, had grown restless. I sat at the edge of the small boat, watching the dark waves lap sleepily at the sides as the lights from the shore twinkled in unison. My eyes began to droop, but I would not allow myself to fall asleep. After all, I had begged to come along as I always did with my father's expeditions. To fall asleep was to admit defeat, and so I busied myself with counting the gentle waves as the boat caught them.

"One, two, three..." I yawned. "Four, seven..."

Just as I began to doze off, a faint glimmer in the ocean caught my eye. I immediately turned around and directed my gaze upward, assuming it was the reflection of the planet or other stars on the surface of the water.

But it wasn't. I rose to my knees and grasped the edge of the boat, peering over into the waves. I saw it again. There was a distinctive, bright glimmer of silver that seemed to be just below the surface. Was it a fish?

No, it was moving much too slowly. I reached a hand instinctively toward it and then immediately pulled away as the flicker of light became solid, emitting a strange glow that radiated like a small, bright moon beneath the waves.

'It's a strange rock, or maybe a jewel,' I thought, fascinated. If I could only reach it...

Before I could process what was happening, an unexpectedly strong wave crashed into the boat and I lost my fragile balance. My grip was slick with salt water and I tumbled into the black waves with a splash.

I then made the critical mistake of opening my eyes underwater as I desperately kicked my feet in search of the surface. The salty sting was unbearable, but I fought to keep them open to get a sense of my surroundings.

Fear began to overcome me as I could not determine which way was up from beneath the nighttime waves. The water was ice cold and impenetrable in the darkness, leaving me blind in my pursuit for air. Surely my father would have heard the splash and would be after me at any moment. Why had I been so close to the edge of the boat?

A flash of silver shot past me like a bullet, leaving a trace of pearlescent bubbles in its wake. I looked frantically for the source of the moonstone glow, but my eyes were so narrowly slanted in pain that I could barely see my own hands.

Without warning, I felt a sudden, agonizing pain in my left palm and my eyes shot wide open. I froze as I caught a glimpse of what looked horribly like a sickly pale human hand reaching for me in the darkness. I shut my eyes and at last felt the relief of a strong, more welcome hand yanking me forcefully out of the water and into the temperate night air.

"Jasmine what on earth!" my father screeched from behind Liam, who was holding me out of the water by the scruff of the neck like a puppy. His other hand was quickly wrapping my tiny frame in a massive towel while I shivered. I shook violently. Not from the cold, but in fear.

"Dad, I'm sorry, I-" I began, tears streaming down my face.

Liam passed me into my father's arms and he pressed me into his chest where the tears began to flow uncontrollably. The pain in my hand was still throbbing, but the shock was worse.

"Oh honey," he said with a suppressed sob. "Are you alright?"

"Yes, I'm okay," I said shakily. "I just fell."

"It's okay, it's okay," Raj said, speaking more to himself than me as the reassurance in his voice wavered.

He saw the blood on my hand and motioned over my head for Liam to get the first aid. The student returned with it at once.

"I got it, Professor," he said, his thick Irish accent cracking ever so slightly as he had been just as worried as my father. Raj nodded appreciatively and rocked me gently back and forth while Liam held my hand. "Easy does it, now."

I looked at him and felt embarrassed, knowing I had already been a burden to the grown-ups even *before* falling off the boat. I may have been young, but I had always been self aware.

"Sorry," I repeated, casting my eyes downward and into my hands as Liam poured a disinfectant onto my palm that made me wince.

"It's nothing but a small scratch," he said assuredly as my father looked on in alarm. "See? It already seems to have stopped."

My father frowned at the cut as he brought it under the light. "Seems really deep to have stopped bleeding so quickly," he murmured. "But you're tough, aren't you, Jazz?"

I smiled weakly as my father set me down and went to pull up the anchor. We had clearly reached the end of our trip. Liam began to dress my wound, whistling quietly to distract me from the pain. This measure proved unnecessary as it had already subsided substantially. He went to place a gauze bandage around it and paused.

"You may be returning to school with quite the battle scar," he said to me. I noticed his voice was oddly distant.

He examined my hand closely and my curiosity caused me to do the same. I understood his intrigue at once-the scrape on my hand appeared to exude the same faint glow that I had seen in the water. Where there should have been a red line of blood, there was instead a bright white gash that I somehow knew (even in that moment) would never go away.

"Is everything alright?" Raj called from the other end of the boat.

Liam nodded, reluctantly peeling his gaze from my hand.
"All's well."

As I watched him cover the last of the scar with the bandage, I thought that explaining *why* I had been drawn to the edge in the first place might make me look less foolish.

"I was diving for a gem," I said. My father being at the helm, Liam was the only one who heard me.

"A gem?" he asked absently, putting away the supplies as the boat began to turn back toward the shore. "Perhaps a pirate's treasure gone astray."

"No," I grumbled. Desperate to make amends for my clumsy behavior, I continued. "I saw this bright, shiny looking thing in the water-so I reached for it. And then it scratched me."

Liam's back was to me, but I saw his shoulders stiffen.

"What do you mean?" he asked, a hint of something I could not read in his voice as he knelt in front of me to listen. "What scratched you?"

I shrugged in answer.

"I thought it was a fish at first. But then it tried to grab me." My voice trailed off as I heard how silly it sounded.

"Well, you've been very brave," Liam said with a smile, patting my hand.

"And I still have the scar to this day," I concluded. I held up the palm in question for Marianne to see, the silvery glow visible even in the fluorescence of her sterile office.

She smiled, plainly intrigued more by the memory I chose rather than the nature of the scar itself.

"Aside from the injury, it sounds like this was just one of many exciting adventures with your father," she mused. "And he certainly enjoyed bringing you along with him."

"He must have," I acknowledged. "He took me everywhere with him, even after that. Probably a lot of places that weren't quite suitable for a child."

She smirked at this, the corners of her eyes crinkling into a smile.

"And what about Liam Brennan?" Marianne asked. "You've mentioned him before. He was a close family friend for years after that, is that right?"

I nodded and smiled, recalling the role Liam Brennan had played in our lives. From Raj's top grad student, to his mentee, to eventually even my godfather despite him not meeting me until I was eleven. He was part of our family.

"That's right," I said. "Liam went on to be a Professor himself back in Ireland. Now he's at Trinity College, no less. He and his wife have spent at least three holidays with us since those days."

My smile faded and I gulped as I remembered the phone call I had received from Professor Brennan following the accident. Given the time difference, he had accidentally called me in the early hours of the morning, but of course I was already wide awake. In fact, I hadn't slept that night at all. It had been one of those torturous occasions where my mind had alternated between night terrors and insomnia, accompanied by the eternal cold sweat of despair that often envelops a grieving person like a suffocating shadow.

"Jasmine? Are you alright?" came the voice on the other line. "I was devastated to hear."

Professor Brennan's voice cracked, and I wondered who had told him the news. I had certainly not been able to do it. Not yet.

"I'm okay," I managed to choke out. A long silence had followed, as neither of us had much to say.

"If you need anything at all, Jazz, you know Bridget and I are always here for you. You need only say the word."

"I know," I said in reply, wondering how on earth Professor Brennan and his wife, all the way in Dublin, could be of any help to me at all. Nevertheless, I *did* appreciate the sentiment.

Liam had then regrettably missed Raj's funeral due to a medical emergency with his own child who was barely three years old, which garnered a thousand apologies from his side and a million pardons from my own.

"He will feel you there," I had said with certainty. "Don't worry."

"WE'RE MAKING EXCELLENT PROGRESS, JASMINE," said Marianne, her gaze softening to a genuine smile that was impossible not to return. I realized then that I had spoken for the majority of our appointment, which was certainly a first.

"Thanks," I murmured.

But the progress, I knew, was confined to the walls of her prehistoric office. It was only for now-while I discussed my father to a woman whose professional duty it was to make me feel better-that I could acknowledge the tragedy that had befallen me. The moment I left the sanctity of therapy, I would be faced with the reality that no one else cared about those memories, and I was very alone.

CHAPTER 2

AN UNCOMFORTABLE REUNION

By the time I returned to my apartment, it was already dark.

The city lights outside of my high-rise flooded the living room with Water Street's fluorescence, deeming my own light switch unnecessary. The floor-to-ceiling windows were once more illuminated with the buzz of a thousand lives more interesting than mine, and I pulled back the curtains to get lost (as I had many times before) in the lives of the strangers wandering the street below.

After the accident, I had refused to leave the refuge of the home I had just moved into with Matt, thinking the fewer disruptions, the better. After all, we had barely lived there a month, and half of my things were still in boxes.

Unfortunately, remaining in my building had had just the opposite effect from what I intended. I had been incredibly lonely, with the ghost of my old life haunting me at every turn. The concrete ceilings and dark wood floors that I had once loved for their modernity now felt cold and unfamiliar. The walls remained blank and the tables were empty aside from a lone picture of myself and Matt from our trip to Prague sitting on my desk. The kitchen was also sparse as I rarely cooked for myself anymore. Matt had been the chef of the house.

I showered and opened the fridge, seeking scraps for dinner like a subway rat. Although I rarely finished an entire meal, I had enough self awareness to at least go through the motions of eating. I found some frozen vegetable lasagna that looked decent enough. I popped it in the microwave and sat on the couch, uncorking a bottle of Cabernet.

My phone was lying face down on the coffee table in airplane mode, a habit I had started to employ after working hours for the sake of being left undisturbed. After flipping through my streaming apps for over thirty minutes, I ultimately landed on the ritualistic comfort of watching the local evening news. Mindless.

Sometime during the weather forecast, there was a harsh knock on the door that made me jump.

"Who is it?" I asked, my voice shaking.

I did not expect visitors, and I certainly had never given my neighbors the impression that stopping by unannounced would be welcomed.

"It's us," said a voice I had not heard in many months, though it was entirely familiar. It was Marissa.

The sense of surprise wore off almost instantly and was replaced by rising irritation that my time of seclusion was being interrupted. I stood up and flipped the lights on, knowing I had already given myself away for being at home.

"One minute!" I called.

The next wave of emotions brought embarrassed panic as I attempted to brighten my appearance in the mirror. I was met with the reflection of an undeniable recluse-eyes overcast with a permanent haze of dishevelment that was quite unlike the original version of myself.

Deciding it was useless to attempt to freshen up in seconds, I opened the door to two friends who looked much more put together than myself. They were certainly dressed to go out and be seen, while I had barely dragged my blanket across the floor.

"Did we have plans?" I asked in a confused voice, staring at the figures of Kristen and Marissa in the doorframe.

"No," said Kristen, her blonde hair swishing in its tightly pulled ponytail. "We just came from happy hour at the place below your building. The happy hour that *you* blew off."

"I didn't blow anything off," I said defensively, my annoyance rising at my being pestered in the threshold of my own door.

As was customary of Kristen, she ignored my warning tone and pushed me further.

"Right, well you turn your phone off every day so you probably missed the group chat where we planned this on Monday," she continued. "It's Friday."

"I saw that," I lied. "But I never said I could make it."

I knew I had certainly become antisocial, but to be called *unreliable* was simply not fair.

"Oh really? Had other big plans tonight?" she said, eyeing Blair Waldorf's paused face on the flatscreen and the now half empty bottle of wine on the side table.

"I-" I began, but my voice faded. I was too tired to argue.

Marissa emerged quietly from behind Kristen's tall frame with a sheepish smile, interjecting as she always did when she sensed tension.

"Can we come in?"

I yielded to my kindest friend and swung the door open. I couldn't be harsh with Marissa.

As they stepped inside, I became suddenly uncomfortably aware of how barren my place was. It was essentially exactly the same as the first time they had ever seen it nearly a year ago. That day seemed so far away.

"Love what you've done with the place," said Kristen sarcastically.

Marissa shot her a warning look, but I was unbothered. I had been acquainted with Kristen long enough to know that she was incapable of delicacy in the wake of uncomfortable situations-it was one of the very few personality traits that we had in common.

The difference between us was, I chose to be as quiet as possible unless my commentary was explicitly solicited, while Kristen's approach of choice was to be an asshole.

Marissa was more refined, keeping her thoughts to herself as she discreetly observed my barren lodgings. However, her gaze lingered on my throat where the engagement ring Matt would have given me still hung from a thin silver chain. The four-carat cushion-cut diamond was freshly polished even though it would never be on my finger. My friends had all cringed at the idea when I suggested wearing it in this way, but I could not bear to part with it. I knew it was time to take it off, but I didn't want to.

"So how have you been?" she asked shakily as Kristen continued to snoop around behind me.

I shifted uncomfortably, knowing there was an ulterior motive for their impromptu visit. But whatever it was, I knew it wasn't malicious. They *were* trying to help. They had been for several months. It was *me* that had created this miserable divide between us, and I felt that I couldn't reverse it now.

"I'm okay," I finally said in a small voice.

I noticed Kristen had toned down her usually white blonde hair to a warm honey, and Marissa had cut at least an inch off of her own auburn locks. I supposed I hadn't seen them in a longer while than I thought.

"Jazz," Marissa said tentatively, following me into the kitchen as I swept my wine off the table and began to search for a glass. I hoped they hadn't connected the dots that I had been drinking it straight from the bottle.

She pushed her glasses up her nose and took a deep breath before continuing.

"I don't want to be insensitive but-"

"Something has to change," Kristen said abruptly. "I mean. You cannot continue to live like this…"

Her voice actually softened with pity at the end, making it worse.

My back still facing my friends, I closed my eyes tightly, afraid to turn around and meet their gaze. I felt the familiar, dull tears brimming from deep within and I steadied myself by grasping the marble countertop.

I had learned that there comes a point in the grieving process where crying is so exhausting that the tears don't come easily anymore. Sometimes being angry is easier.

"Living like *what*, exactly?" I burst out suddenly, making them both jump. "I'm working out every day, my apartment is spotlessly clean. I'm not out partying until two AM-I'm here! At home!"

They were momentarily speechless and I took advantage of the silence to continue my tirade.

"You two act like I'm in need of some kind of intervention. I promise you, I'm not!"

I must have looked even worse than I sounded, judging from the identical expressions of horror on both of their faces.

Marissa spoke first.

"Jasmine," she said seriously. "This isn't healthy. You don't leave your house. You are working out until you puke. And then you don't eat." She pointed to the wine bottle. "I mean, I know that's your dinner."

"And your apartment being spotless is because you live like a serial killer with no possessions," Kristen added flatly.

At that, I couldn't stop myself from letting out a small laugh despite the suffocating atmosphere that surrounded us. Marissa rolled her eyes but smiled begrudgingly as well.

Tensions momentarily eased, I looked back at my two friends as I leaned against the cold countertop with arms folded across my chest. Though they communicated it in their own ways, I knew they were both severely worried about me. And I *did* feel guilty for the distress I was causing them.

"Well," I said in a small voice. "I *have* been going to therapy."

They both brightened at this.

"I'm so glad, Jazz!" said Marissa sincerely. "I promise it helps."

I shrugged, recalling my session with Marianne from the afternoon in a new, pessimistic light. What exactly had I accomplished today by rehashing a memory with my father? A memory in which I had caused him anguish and distress, for that matter. I rubbed my scar absently, biting my lip. The picture of Matt on my desk suddenly seemed to mock me, and I slapped it downward in a swift, forceful motion that again took my friends by surprise. I needed to stop doing that.

"Sorry," I said, noticing their alarm. "I just-I can't look."

"I know," said Marissa softly. The pity in her eyes was excruciating. I looked away from her again.

Ever since the day Matt had passed, I had found it increasingly difficult to spend time with either of the friends that stood across from me. Especially Kristen. No matter what I did, I always saw her, in tunnel vision, confirming my worst fears and subsequently ripping my entire world apart.

I knew it was foolish and unfair, but a tiny part of me actually hated her for it. I couldn't help it. She tried to catch my gaze and I avoided it, ultimately turning completely around and facing the window like a cornered, pouting child. The bay below was sparkling in the moonlight, casting an eerie glow of dancing waves onto my cold floors. I would probably have thought it beautiful in the old days.

"Well, we have an idea we want to run by you," Kristen said finally, joining me at the window.

I glanced up and saw Marissa was hovering in the background, evidently not wanting to crowd me. I had always appreciated her respect for personal space.

"What's that?" I asked dully.

Kristen raised an eyebrow at me and spoke slowly. "Something fun," she said cautiously.

This time Marissa spoke up.

"We know you wanted to go with your dad and Matt one day but…" she began, her voice trailing off in uncertainty. Always the meeker of the two, she deferred to Kristen who gave her an encouraging nudge.

"We want to go on a trip," Kristen finished for her. "To Ireland. All of us."

The words hung in the air, stagnant for a moment before Marissa rushed to clarify them.

"We know you were always curious about your mom's heritage," she explained. "And while we don't have academic credentials or research abilities like your dad had, we think even just learning about your roots might be…" she trailed off but I finished her sentence for her.

"Might be good for me," I said, touched by their thoughtfulness.

I let the silence linger once more as I didn't know what to say quite yet. Thoughts of actually attempting track down my mother were certainly not appealing, but I *would* like to learn more about Irish culture in general…

Kristen had anticipated my hesitation and jumped in.

"We know you're happiest when you're out seeing the world."

She was right. Having barely left my apartment in the last year, I definitely missed traveling. I crossed my arms and slowly paced the room, feeling their eyes boring into my back. I *had* always desperately wanted to go to Ireland. The castles, the cliffs, the natural beauty… it seemed such an enchanting place.

"Ireland," I repeated, nodding my head. Then I stopped, my hands suddenly growing cold with fear. "I really shouldn't take time off right now."

"Oh it's not even your busy season yet," said Kristen dismissively, thwarting my only real argument. "You can easily get away with a week off."

She was right again. It truly wouldn't get too hectic until late October, and it was barely the end of August. Having done nothing but thrown myself into work and unhealthy routines for the past eleven months, I certainly had the vacation days to spare.

"What about the weather right now?" I said, certain that September in Ireland was dreadfully cold and wet. I had seen enough National Geographic specials to know that it was not the ideal time to visit the country.

"Please, like that's ever stopped you before," Kristen rebutted again, and I couldn't help but smile, remembering my old Christmas plans in Stockholm that had never come to fruition. It was true, I was hardly ever deterred by the weather.

"So…?" said Marissa in a small voice, rocking back and forth on her heels in anticipation.

My iceberg of my self pity began to melt away as I saw how sincere they were. Moreover, neither of them cared for educational travel in the way that I did, so I had to at least appreciate the selflessness of their gesture.

"*Kiana's* even agreed to come," Kristen said with emphasis, clearly having saved what she thought would be the most enticing selling point for last. But at this news, my smile actually flickered.

I had not seen Kiana since the day it had all happened, but not because she hadn't tried. Thinking that while Tampa had been desperately lonely, the cold darkness of Washington D.C. was certainly not the place I had wanted to mourn. She had offered to come to me more than once, but I had already begun to spiral into my antisocial behaviors and made up countless excuses. I couldn't tell whether she bought them or not.

Either way, I realized that Kiana was likely unaware of how steeply I had declined over the past year. It was easy enough for me to check in over the phone and pretend everything was okay, but I knew my physical appearance would not hide what had become of me. I pictured the disappointment on my best friend's face when she saw my sickly pallor and alarming weight loss. There was something different about causing Kiana to worry versus my other friends. She was after all, the closest thing I had left to family.

"Jazz, what do you think?" asked Marissa eagerly.

Ultimately, the pull of wanderlust was stronger than my fear of Kiana's impression of me. I would have time to figure it out. Maybe eat a few square meals in between now and then.

"Okay, I'll go," I said.

Without warning, I was engulfed in a crushing hug by Marissa. She pulled away almost instantly and I noticed (with horror) that her eyes were brimming with tears. I smiled weakly and looked at Kristen who had a smug grin plastered across her own face.

"I knew you couldn't say no to a *trip*," she said, slapping me on the back. "So off we go to the great Emerald Isle!"

* * *

THE NEXT FEW weeks passed in a blur as I turned all of my focus to planning the upcoming trip in detail. Marianne was of course thrilled with my decision to go, and my last session with her was the day before our departure.

"I'm expecting this trip to provide just the type of healing that you need," she said warmly. "You have some excellent friends."

"I know," I said. "I just wish Matt could be there with me."

I told her about the night Raj, Matt and I had decided we'd all go to Ireland together one day. Matt's general infectious personality coupled with my father's lack of a son made them the perfect pair, and I knew how lucky I was to truly look forward to the times we all got together.

It hadn't occurred to me back then that Raj might have

intended to use that trip as an opportunity to actually *look* for my mother. I still doubted it even as I reflected upon it-he wasn't the hopeless romantic type. He was merely a scholar, curious about anything and everything he could learn about a foreign culture.

"THERE WILL BE an element of academic research in regards to your mother's mysterious family heritage," Raj had said, carefully wording the sentence so as not to arouse any sour feelings I might have had. I had told him countless times I didn't care, but he was delicate, nonetheless.

"But we will certainly need to find time for the pubs as well. How else do you think we'll convince Matt to come along?"

Matt laughed in his usual intoxicating way, his blue eyes twinkling with good humor.

"That's where you're wrong, Raj," he said, wagging his finger. "More of a whiskey guy myself. It's the Jameson distillery I'm interested in."

"An American wasting away in the Jameson distillery. Imagine that!" my father said, pouring out a glass of port for each of them.

(Somewhat) unbeknownst to me, that had also been the very evening in which Matt had asked Raj for my hand in marriage. I had heard the story later, by way of a teary retelling from his best friend, Christian, at Matt's own funeral. I wished Raj or Matt had had the chance to tell me instead.

"Jasmine's presence in my life enriches all things that make me happy," Matt had said, without a hint of anything but sincerity in his eyes. "I want to spend the rest of my time on earth making sure she has the life of her dreams, because she's already given me mine. Will you let me do that?"

A single tear fell down Raj's cheek as he nodded with the deep contentment of a father who knows his daughter is in good hands.

"I'll be honored to call you my son," he said with finality.

I came back outside to the teary scene which both men had covered up seamlessly (or so they thought) in fits of coughs and the loud clearing of throats. I chose not to acknowledge it as I had enough sense to know that some moments are best left unspoiled.

We ultimately agreed that the Ireland trip would need to be delayed due to Raj's next post in Stockholm, where he swore he'd only spend a single semester. Matt and I both knew better and neither of us held our breaths for flights to Dublin in the near future.

I LEFT Marianne's office and returned to my apartment that night hoping that I had left no stone unturned in my search for exciting activities to cram into a week long itinerary. I knew our trip was not nearly long enough, but I figured we could at least tackle the southern portion of the country. Northern Ireland would have to wait until next time. I also hoped my employer never chose to look through anyone's search history, as mine was rampant with scratched itineraries and travel blogs rather than any actual work.

Despite my natural resistance to relinquishing any power of planning to others, I had begrudgingly allowed Kristen to tackle the lodgings. Admittedly, if there were one other person in the group I trusted to arrange for our hotels, it was her. If we left it to Kiana, I would likely be sleeping on a cot on the floor of a hostel for college students.

Free reign over the historical sites was of course left to me, likely because no one else wanted to bother with the research that's required for the educational part of trips.

The obvious must-see that I already knew about was the famous landmark known as the Cliffs of Moher, and Kristen had agreed that two nights in Galway were a necessity to build into the itinerary.

Kilkenny Castle was another resounding favorite of the travel blogs I had read, noting it had been so well maintained that it currently looked nearly the same as it did a hundred years ago. But what about some of the ruins? Dunluce Castle in Antrim looked intriguing. Where was Antrim? I flipped tabs quickly to my Google maps.

Kristen and Marissa arrived at my place right on schedule the next day-a two o'clock pickup for an overnight flight that departed for Dublin at five in the evening. To an ordinary vacationer, this schedule might have seemed excessively cautious, but I had had too many travel disasters to risk any hiccups.

"Your glasses!" said Marissa. "I love when you wear your glasses."

My face flushed. I personally hated my glasses, but the idea of wearing contacts for an overnight flight was simply not realistic. I would likely spend the entire first day of the trip in my thick black frames before my sensitive eyes would be prepared to face the battle of daily contacts again.

"Thanks," I murmured as I got into the backseat of Kristen's BMW, and then I clarified. "For talking me into this trip. I still hate my glasses."

The rest of the travel evening was mayhem. Traffic in Tampa is generally disastrous, but particularly in the late afternoon. As we had already accounted for it, nobody truly panicked until we saw the lines at the airport. The Delta counter was slammed with complaining customers fumbling with their oversized checked bags and I raised my eyebrows at my friends in an "I told you so" sort of way, grateful for packing cubes and the myriad of other space-saving measures that allowed for carry-on luggage to be our only burden.

All three of our boarding passes were loaded on my phone and stamped with TSA Pre-Check as I had insisted Kristen and Marissa make emergency appointments for approval the moment I was told about the trip. I led the way, zooming straight past the regular line and into the much shorter one just beyond it.

"I forgot you're like this," said Marissa, panting behind me as she caught her breath.

Kristen's mysterious (but greatly appreciated) work perks granted all three of us access to the Delta Sky Club and I was thrilled to find it was located directly across from our gate so I could watch the flight screen like a hawk. About an hour later, the boarding process went smoothly, and I felt my airport anxiety subsiding. Before I knew it, we were in the air and I was closing my eyes for the night.

My dreams were riddled with the typical side effects of poor sleep quality that often accompanies a flight of any kind: trauma, fear, and the innate sense that I was in constant danger. Perhaps that wasn't *actually* a universal experience in the way I thought it was, but I had anxiety problems whether I was on a plane or not. In light of recent events in my life, my mind had certainly perfected its skill of creating terrifying nightmares.

At one point, I dreamt that I was being chased by a shark, his jaws snapping at me through the black waves as I swam as fast as I could. I was hindered by something that resembled clumsiness (despite my certainty that I was a good swimmer) and was paddling at an infuriatingly slow pace. Winded as though I had run a marathon, I at last broke through the surface where I found myself gasping for air but unable to find the shore. I swam and swam, but I couldn't get closer to the rocky beach that loomed in the distance. It was taunting me.

CHAPTER 3

THE COLLEGE ON COLLEGE GREEN

The cabin lights came on and Kristen let out a groan beside me.

"You okay?" asked Kristen, yawning. "You look like you've seen a ghost."

I yawned in reply. "I can never sleep on flights."

We opted for private transportation from the airport to our hotel. Traveling in our late twenties was certainly preferable to our early twenties, I thought, smirking as we zoomed past the hostels on the outskirts and toward the center of the city. Sometimes working a soul-sucking corporate job in America paid off.

I was instantly enamored with the cobblestone streets of Dublin. I had been to tons of European cities, but I had never seen anything like this. In lieu of the typical skyscrapers of London or the towering churches of Rome, Dublin had shorter, stout buildings that all seemed to be beckoning me indoors with their wafting chimneys and delightfully colored window frames. Each street we zoomed down seemed to weave us further away but somehow closer to our destination at the same time. I could not fathom how the driver knew where he was going.

"Lots of one-ways here," I mused as we took yet another sudden lurch to the left when I was certain we were going right.

At last we reached our hotel and I was pleased to see that Kristen had chosen marvelously. The Iveagh Garden, it was called, was a picturesque boutique hotel with a doorman that came rushing out to greet us. I stepped into the street and took my first deep breath of perfect autumn air, wondering how on earth I had ever thought summer would have been a better time to visit. Directly behind the doorman was another eager figure, this one with billowing brown curls and dark eyes that lit up as soon as she saw us.

"Kiana!" I shouted as my friend crashed into me. "This is-"

"Incredible, I know," she beamed at me.

We had spoken about the trip several times since she heard I had agreed, of course, but seeing her in person was entirely different. *Now* the trip was real. Unfortunately, I could not help but notice the slight flicker of surprise when she took in my appearance. I knew I must look gaunt-and perhaps even malnourished-since she last saw me a year ago. Embarrassed, I yawned widely.

"So tired," I said, pointing to my eyes. "Overnight flights are the worst."

"I know, but worth it," she said, embracing the other two who had emerged from the taxi, also yawning, behind me. "I'm so glad we did this!"

"Me too," I said, truly meaning it.

I walked arm and arm with my childhood best friend into the hotel and we all plopped onto one of the cushions in the bay window while Kristen ran to the check-in desk.

"How long have you been here?" I asked.

"Just about an hour before you," she replied. "Sorry I didn't wait for you at the airport, I-"

Kristen came bustling back over and interrupted.

"The room isn't ready, but we can freshen up in there," she said, pointing to the powder room beyond the elevators.

Accustomed to the inconveniences of an overnight flight, I had come prepared and did my best with a travel toothbrush, miniature hairbrush, and even a small can of dry shampoo. I was pleasantly surprised at how awake I felt, but I knew the afternoon would bring a severe crash.

Having packed our itinerary with as many activities as we could squeeze into each city, I knew we had a long day ahead of us and there was no time to waste. As our return flight was also out of Dublin, we would have an extra night in the capital at the end of our trip, but none of us could resist our first day being as full as possible. We headed back out into the street and in search of a nearby coffee shop to fuel the remainder of the morning, knowing it would be the first caffeine fix of many.

The search did not take long. The streets of Dublin were lined with adorable cafes and restaurants that were just starting to open their doors. The smell of warm, freshly baked goods seemed to draw us to a cozy spot that was perfect for catching up and recharging as it was lined with a wide selection of squishy velvet chairs.

I looked around at my friends, realizing it was the first time we had all been together since *that* day, and found it nearly impossible to imagine that anything terrible had ever passed between the four of us. It felt like a clean slate-a chance for me to reestablish myself in their lives, and them in mine. I chose to sit back and listen to them talk rather than contribute anything substantial of my own. I was content.

"Alright, what's first?" asked Kiana, checking her watch. "It's just about nine now which means things will start to open up."

"Ask the travel guide," said Kristen, pointing to me.

I laughed. "The only musts I have in Dublin are the library at Trinity College-"

"Of course," nodded Marissa seriously, who also shared my desire for educational enrichment while on vacation.

"And Temple Bar tonight because you know," I shrugged. "We have to."

"You forgot about the Guinness and Jameson factories!" exclaimed Kristen. "We have two tours booked today!"

The thought of mixing a dark stout and whiskey in the same afternoon made me doubtful of my energy levels by dinnertime, but I knew I had no choice. We had to see it all.

Marissa clearly shared my sentiment as she briefly shuddered over her lavender latte.

"What about your dad's friend? Did he get back to you?" she asked curiously.

I nodded. Professor Brennan had been most thrilled to hear that I was finally making a trip to Dublin. I planned to meet up with him and his family on our first day and potentially the last day as well.

"Yes. You guys can totally go on ahead if you don't want to hang around for that," I said apologetically. "But I really do have to say hello while we're here."

"I'd love to see Trinity," said Marissa. "We'll tag along."

Kristen seemed less than thrilled about this decision, but seeing as she was outnumbered, she said nothing. With plenty of time to spare, we indulged in a second round of coffees and then made our way on foot, lazily padding through the alleys toward the river.

I had always been excellent at figuring out the various public transportation systems in different cities, but there was no need in Dublin. The air was perfectly mild with not a cloud in the sky as we wound our way through the busy streets. At last we reached the square in the center of Trinity's campus, gasping in awe at the beautifully structured buildings that lined the grass.

"UCF looked nothing like this," said Marissa wistfully,

admiring the sweeping lawn leading to the four-hundred-and-some-years-old grand university.

It was true. The air of prestigious academia that surrounded us was intoxicating, and I had never felt such a deep sense of intellectual inferiority. Having been surrounded by higher education my entire life due to Raj's profession, I had always had the feeling that any school where he was posted was within my grasp-likely because they had been. While Miami was certainly nothing to scoff at, I was by no means an Ivy League contender. When my time for college selection had come, Raj himself was slightly disappointed I had chosen UCF rather than the U, but I knew his wallet was more than pleased. I had told everyone I got denied admission, which was believable considering Miami's acceptance rates. The truth was, I had been afraid to compete with others at or above my level. UCF had felt safe.

"Jasmine!" came a voice from behind us, and I whirled around to see the kind face of Liam Brennan, looking much older and wiser than he had the last time I saw him. It had to have been at least five years, now that I thought about it.

By his side was his wife, Bridget, looking equally as thrilled to see me, and I grinned broadly.

"And who's this?" I said excitedly, bending down to meet the gaze of the small boy who was hiding behind his mother.

He quickly buried his face in her sweater and Bridget rolled her eyes. I knew they had a son, but I couldn't recall his name. He was about four now, if my memory served correctly.

"This is wee Angus," said Bridget, nudging her son forward. "Can ya say hello to Miss Jasmine?" Her accent was much thicker than her husband's since Liam had spent a good deal of his life abroad, and I had always thought it sounded lovely.

"Hello Miss Jasmine," the boy said shyly, and all four of us squealed with glee at the sound of his tiny voice. He blushed furiously at first, but ultimately grinned in appreciation of our awe, sending us into another fit of giggles.

"He's a doll," I said, beaming. Bridget ruffled her son's hair appreciatively.

I introduced my friends to the Brennans one by one, and after pleasantries were exchanged, the professor offered to take us on a tour of the campus.

With our newfound companion, Angus, slowly warming up to us and beginning to show his personality, my friends were much more inclined to tag along. The little boy took an immediate liking to Marissa and reached for her with his free hand, which she gladly welcomed. As the oldest sibling of five, leading the way for those half her size was nothing new to her. I supposed that's where she had learned patience, the virtue that generally eluded an only child like myself.

My neck could hardly keep up as I spun my head around to capture all of the various statues, buildings, and other remnants of old world tradition and intellectual inquiry at Trinity. Although it had likely changed shape on countless occasions over the past two centuries, I found it surreal to think I was walking on one of the same stone paths that Oscar Wilde or Bram Stoker may have taken on their way to class. Ignoring what had transpired between them after their schooling, I liked to imagine them philosophizing as good friends on this campus, unaware of the great names they were destined to become.

"This way to the *books*," Professor Brennan said, shaking me from my daydream.

"Not agaaaain," moaned Angus, dragging his little feet as Marissa held his left hand and his mother clutched his right.

I looked down at him, unable to suppress a smile at the sight of a tiny Irish toddler pouting in a miniature Barbour waxed jacket. Being a child of a professor myself, I recalled the long afternoons of paper grading and the campuses that had felt like a prison. Of course, Trinity was a much more preferable setting than some of the dingy buildings *I* had been stuck in as a little one. Now, I would have given anything to spend one more afternoon with Raj in his office.

"Here we are," said Liam, opening the door to reveal the splendor of the most iconic portion of Trinity College-The Long Room.

I let out an audible gasp as the grand shelves containing nearly two-hundred thousand books peered back at me. Despite it being a center of academia, I was overcome with the same feeling of deep reverence one experiences upon entering a house of worship. It felt as if anything I said or did would be seen; the slightest sound being capable of disrupting the higher powers that had granted me access to such a miraculous place. Something about the preservation of centuries-old architecture and the abundance of knowledge that had passed in this room made me feel as though I were very small indeed.

"It's incredible, isn't it?" asked Liam in a low voice as he sidled next to me.

I was now standing face-to-face with the marble bust of Jonathon Swift and nodded slowly. As a group of tourists shuffled by, completely oblivious to the creator of Gulliver's Travels with whom I was now well acquainted, I surmised that being invited on a private tour led by a member of faculty was certainly preferable to the kind that required a ticket. I allowed the stillness of the moment to linger. The rich smell of leather seemed to echo the years of my childhood spent immersed in reading, and I could almost feel Raj standing next to us. It was one of those rare occasions in life that even as it was happening, I knew it was a time I would never forget.

The professor sighed.

"I was so excited to show this to Raj," he said, gesturing around him.

I knew he meant more than the bookshelves. He wanted Raj to see the career he had built-the life he had. He wanted my father to be proud of who his star student had become.

"I know," I said, smiling up at him.

"He inspired me so much," Liam continued, the shiny wood floors beneath his feet making the faintest sound as we crossed from one bay of books to the next.

I resisted my intrusive desire to slip under the ropes and examine the volumes at closer range. It was best to not get kicked out of the university on my first visit, I thought. It would probably ensure I never got a second invitation, at the very least.

"And we had some good times, your dad and I."

"Oh, I know," I replied.

Since it was fresh in my mind, I laughed about my most recently rehashed memory.

"I think about the day on the boat in Portugal all the time. One of my best memories," I said.

"Is that right?" he laughed, the lines of wisdom on his face wrinkling in amusement. "I would imagine most children would have found it traumatic to fall off a boat in a foreign country. But I suppose it *is* a good story to tell."

"It is," I said, and I turned my palm upward, revealing the opalescent white line that had marked my hand since that day. "And I have the battle scar to prove it when people doubt me."

The professor did a noticeable double-take as I extended my hand. He reached for it in a swift, urgent motion that seemed out of place given the tranquility of the room and it took me by surprise. I resisted the urge to flinch, not wanting to offend him.

"I always thought it was so strange, how this healed," he said, a significant hint of incredulity in his voice.

He peered at my hand not in the typical way of marked curiosity in which others observed it, but rather as if it were some sort of miraculously unbelievable anomaly to behold. I supposed in a way it was.

"How odd..." his voice trailed off as he frowned and brought his face closer to the mark, nearly touching his nose to my fingers.

"Yes," I said, wondering what was going on inside his head to provoke such intrigue. Before I had much time to contemplate the matter, I heard my name from across the room.

"Jazz!" came a whisper-shout from Marissa. "Come look at this."

I took the momentary distraction as an opportunity to politely pull my hand away, but the faint look of puzzlement lingered on Liam's face. He plainly wanted to examine it further, but he released it, nonetheless. I made my way over to Marissa quickly, hoping to gloss over his strange reaction by ignoring it.

While I was the reader of the group, Marissa was certainly the historian. Her nose was as close as it could get to the glass case that housed the 1916 Proclamation of the Irish Republic.

"One of the last remaining copies in the world," she said in awe. I joined her and nodded in appreciation, reading the words that marked the beginning of the Easter Rising:

"IN THE NAME OF GOD AND OF THE DEAD GENERATIONS FROM WHICH SHE RECEIVES HER OLD TRADITION OF NATIONHOOD, IRELAND, THROUGH US, SUMMONS HER CHILDREN TO HER FLAG AND STRIKES FOR HER FREEDOM."

The bored chatter of Bridget, Kristen, and Kiana buzzed behind us, growing ever so subtly in volume the longer we stood reading the old text. Liam swooped down to take Angus in his arms, the wee lad clearly also having tired of the temple of academics. I sensed the entire group was ready to go, and I was more than happy to oblige given the strange interaction that was still on my mind. I would have dropped it entirely had it not been for me catching the professor staring at my hand once more.

"To Irish nationalists, that was like the equivalent of an original copy of the Constitution," Marissa grumbled as we exited the grand building to the utmost relief of our other friends. "And no one cared!"

"Heathens," I remarked.

"Well, I hope you enjoy the rest of your time in Dublin," said Liam, his arm around Bridget while Angus clawed at his leg like a cat on a scratching post. "And then onto the Cliffs, Galway, and Cork, and Lord knows what other trouble you'll get into here."

He smiled jovially, all intrigue toward my scar melted away as he embraced me tightly in farewell. I wondered then if I had exaggerated his reaction in my mind.

"It was really great to see you," I said sincerely. "Thank you for the tour."

"Anytime," he beamed, hands on my shoulders and looking upon me like an uncle does his favorite niece. A goddaughter was about the same thing, I supposed. I thought I saw a tear beginning to form in the corner of his eye and I hoped I wouldn't do the same. "I can't wait to see what's next for you, Jazz."

"And be sure to give us a shout if you've a bit of time when you're back in Dublin next week," Bridget said, kissing me on the head in the same way as her husband. "No pressure if not, *a leanbh.*"

We made our departure, with Angus turning to wave to Marissa several times before eventually running on ahead of his parents as they all disappeared back into one of the buildings. I felt suddenly guilty that I had not carved out more time in my trip for my godfather. I tried to push the thought out of my head for now. I'd make sure to see them on the way back.

"Great people," Marissa said.

"Onto the next activity," said Kristen quickly.

I took one last look at the grand campus before the four centuries of knowledge disappeared into the background of the bustling city.

CHAPTER 4

GUINNESS VS. JAMESON

Kristen had now entered her timekeeper mode and was shuffling us along through the thickening crowd in George's Street Arcade as quickly as possible. I watched as the sights passed me by, hoping we would find time to explore the endless alleys and streets of the charming city.

"Let's go check out St. Stephen's Green," Kiana suggested. "It's right over here."

The park lingered within eyesight and while I wanted to take a detour, I knew Kristen would not allow it.

"We have exactly thirty minutes before our Guinness tour," she said, shutting down the suggestion with a tone of finality. "No time."

"Sorry, that took longer than I thought," I said, quickening my pace to match Kristen's.

While only a moment ago I had wished for more time with the Brennans, I now felt slightly guilty for having monopolized the morning for everyone else, particularly since the entire purpose of the trip was already largely for my benefit.

"Don't be," Kristen said, and I was happy to hear the sincerity in her voice. "It was great seeing you excited like that. I know you love books. And your dad would have wanted you to see the Brennans."

She spoke very matter-of-factly (as was her way) but I appreciated her saying it, nonetheless. She glanced sideways at me and we exchanged a quick smile. I took her by the arm as the others trotted behind us.

"So we start with beer before lunch, and then we go straight to the whiskey," said Kiana, catching up to us as Kristen scanned our tickets at the entrance of the museum. "You're an ambitious travel agent."

St. James's Gate had a massive black-barrel door that boasted the iconic Guinness logo. I briefly examined the details on the harp, never having given it a second thought despite seeing it in all the bars and restaurants throughout my lifetime.

I had very little time to examine the artistic detailing on the outside of the factory as I was swiftly yanked inside by the group leader. We roamed through the self-guided tour with Marissa now leading the way, as was customary for her in any kind of museum. Once inside and safely on schedule, Kristen fell to the back of the group

"It's actually very educational," Marissa said, reading about the processes of malting, milling, and mashing while polishing off her glasses. "So we're learning something here, too."

She wasn't entirely wrong. I found the museum to be extremely informative as I learned a good deal about the famous malty beer that I would never have otherwise chosen to drink were I not in its birthplace. We lingered in the first room of the tour for nearly twenty minutes because Marissa insisted on reading each placard with interest-aloud for the benefit of all. Kristen and Kiana were taking photos with the grass wall that donned another massive logo and harp, plainly ready to move onto the next floor as quickly as possible, because each level got us closer to the bar.

At long last, we reached the top floor of the museum where

the promise of a pour of our very own Guinness as well as a 360-degree view of Dublin was to be fulfilled. None of us particularly cared for the famous stout, but we drank it ceremoniously while we enjoyed the view, anyway.

After running around all morning, it felt nice to sit down. I grew sleepy in the sunny window, my mind wandering again to Professor Brennan's curious interest in my scar. I simultaneously strained my memory while turning my hand over in the sun, casting an unmistakable light across the room with the deep gash of silver. Hadn't he reacted strangely when he saw it the first time, as well? I couldn't remember.

"Jazz, that shit's blinding me," said Kiana, shielding her eyes from the rainbow sparkle that was refracting off of my hand in the same way a beam of sunlight does when glancing off of a diamond. Long accustomed to the anomaly of my palm, she hardly thought twice about it. I was overthinking it, too.

"My bad," I said quickly.

The dark beer certainly tasted fresher when being poured at its source, or so I thought at the time. Whether or not it was the jet lag or general dehydration of overseas flight, the Guinness also went straight to my head.

"I can't finish this," I said at last, noting I was becoming increasingly full on the thick malt. "Not if we're going to lunch next."

"Agreed," said Kiana, pushing hers to the side.

Kristen, on the other hand, shook her head in disappointment as she finished the last gulp of her own.

"Okay let's get going," she said, setting her glass down. "We have an hour and a half until Jameson."

She stood up quickly, dragging her jacket with her. I saw it before anyone else; the denim sleeve caught on the edge of her beer glass and it dangerously teetered at the edge of the table before toppling over. Despite my exhaustion, my reflexes were sharp and I reached out my left hand, snatching it out of the air as it fell.

"Good catch," Kristen acknowledged, her eyebrows raised.

We swept down the staircase rather than the elevator in a poor attempt to walk off the beers, but there were several more winding flights than I thought.

"Where's Marissa?" I said breathlessly as we reached the bottom, realizing she had disappeared.

Kiana shrugged. "Let's wait for her in the gift shop."

A few moments (and several browsed knick knacks that I did not need) later, Marissa came rushing back from the bathroom, her face flushed.

"Jazz, you left this on the table!" she said, handing me my crossbody bag.

"Oh, shit," I said, gratefully seizing it with one hand while feeling for where it should have been against my body with the other, wondering how I could have been so absent-minded.

"Some guy found it after we left," she continued. "He chased me down the stairs just now."

"Wow, that was lucky," I mumbled gratefully, checking that my passport was still in the inside pocket. All my money was still there, as well. It was unlike me to be careless, particularly when traveling.

We were blessed with a sunny afternoon that made our walk to the next destination a pleasurable one. We stopped for a quick bite to eat just on the other side of Mellows Bridge, but the sleepy haze of international travel had begun to descend on us all. I disappeared into a coffee shop around the corner and returned with two cappuccinos in hand.

"With an extra shot of espresso," I said, handing one to Kiana. I looked at Marissa and Kristen in amazement as they had declined my offer of caffeine. "Aren't you two exhausted?"

"Yes," said Kristen, yawning. "But saving myself for espresso martinis later."

We rounded the corner onto Bow Street and came upon the famous Jameson Distillery, looking exactly as I had expected it would. A stone building with modest outdoor seating on either side opened up to a cozy, high-ceiling room that smelled of rich woody notes.

My understanding of whiskey was limited to the correct amount of bourbon needed in an old fashioned as that had been Matt's cocktail of choice. Despite being told I was good at making them, I didn't particularly enjoy them myself. Still, I was looking forward to the tasting.

The title of "World's Leading Distillery Tour" was fairly earned by the conclusion of our nearly two hour guided experience, beginning with the intriguing history of the Jameson brand and ending with a tasting that included varieties of the spirit that no one in the group had been aware existed prior to our visit. Black Barrel had been my favorite of the four tasters, and I made a note to try and find it back home. We tipped our tour guide, and, each of us feeling significantly more appreciative toward the art of whiskey making than we had been before, decided to stay for a drink in the lobby bar before departing.

"Ooo look, we could have bottled our own," said Kristen as she scanned the back of the menu, seeing an offer for a custom Jameson bottling experience. "That would've been fun."

"We'd have to ship it home though," said Kiana. "Since Jasmine didn't let us bring checked bags."

I laughed. "You'll thank me when we're rushing through the airport next week."

The bartender brought our drinks and I raised my glass to my friends.

"Thanks for planning this," I said, feeling my cheeks flushing.

I was not entirely sure what I wanted to say, but I certainly wanted my friends to know that I was grateful for their thoughtful endeavor. Even if it weren't the case in reality, it was nice to temporarily pretend that everything was alright.

"And I'm sorry," I continued, my eyes now welling despite myself. "I'm sorry I've been distant. And for what I've put you through this past year."

"Jasmine-" began Marissa, reaching for my hand, but I waved her off. The others looked as though they wanted to speak up as well, but I knew I had to take ownership for how I had treated them while I was busy feeling sorry for myself. And I had to do it now.

"No I mean it," I said. "I just want you all to know how much I appreciate you."

"We're just glad you came," Kristen said, beaming with uncharacteristic warmth.

"Just like old times," said Kiana, tapping her glass to mine.

Marissa grinned widely. "Cheers to that."

Her gaze then flickered above my head.

"Oh my God, that's the guy who found your bag, Jazz!" she whisper-shouted to us, nodding at someone in the distance. "Do you think that he's coming over here-oh no."

"Sorry to interrupt," came a voice from behind me.

I turned around to see a group of laughing men watching from the other end of the bar as their friend-the designated sacrifice, no doubt-approached us.

The young man in front of me looked charming in a boyish, immature way, but he smiled with a confidence that made him seem much older.

"Hi," he said to Marissa who waved awkwardly. She used her left hand-a subtle gesture to show her engagement ring, maybe.

He didn't seem to notice, or perhaps he just didn't care, but his gaze landed on my bag.

"It's been returned to its rightful owner, then!" he said, pointing to it.

As he spoke, I heard a thick accent, though it was certainly not like any I had heard in Dublin for the past few hours.

"Oh, that was you! Thanks," I said sincerely.

"Just doing what I can to prevent tourist theft," he replied with a sarcastic sigh.

He then looked back at his friends and stifled a laugh. It reminded me of high school and I nearly rolled my eyes at the immaturity, but we were slightly amused.

"Is that all?" asked Kristen boldly, and Kiana snorted into her drink.

Again, he wasn't bothered. His attention now fully on Kristen, he broke into a wide grin.

"I saw there was a toast being held and I thought you might like to learn how the Irish say it," he said smartly.

"That'd be great, you know anyone who's Irish that could teach us?" Kristen said, her brow raising.

"Well, see, that's why I'm here," he said in mock grandeur, bowing so deeply that his sandy hair nearly touched the bar. "I'm James, by the way."

He extended his hand and she took it.

"Kristen," she said shortly, her golden hair catching the light in a way that made her seem all that more unattainable to the ruffian, I thought. "But you're not Irish. That's a British accent."

"I'm caught," he said, grinning without a hint of embarrassment in his face. "Americans are right detectives, it seems."

Kristen seemed to want to smirk, but I knew her smile was genuine. Was she *actually* flirting with him?

"Do you mind if I call them over?" he asked. He did not take his eyes off of Kristen as he gestured to his friends who were watching in anticipation, clearly expecting him to make a fool of himself.

"Taking all of the attention of four beautiful ladies while they stand there like dumb blokes would make me a bad mate, don't you think?"

I saw there were five or six of them at a quick glance, and I rolled my eyes internally, preparing for my friends to shoo them away. However, I was surprised to see that all three of them seemed indifferent and possibly even interested in the idea of adding a group of noisy Brits to our party. I supposed I didn't care one way or another, but was admittedly slightly annoyed that my heartfelt toast had fallen flat in the wake of our new distraction. Immaturity abounded on my end as well.

"Alright," shrugged Kristen, Marissa and Kiana agreeing.

As we were outnumbered by our new British friends, it was far easier to keep one large group conversation in play rather than attempt any side conversations-a dynamic for which the jet-lagged version of myself was grateful.

I discretely observed them each in turn and thought that although they were objectively a good-looking group, they weren't particularly interesting beyond their charm. Still, I couldn't help but glance at each of their hands, seeking anyone with a wedding ring for no reason other than mere curiosity for how old they were.

I thought of the dynamic within my own group of friends as I watched them turn on their own charms. Marissa was engaged to her boyfriend of nearly a decade, but always chose to politely, innocently flirt. Kristen was newly single, having broken it off with **Christian** over the summer. Kiana was far too busy with school and hadn't mentioned anyone of interest to me in a while. And… my heart sank. I supposed I was single, too. The familiar sting of longing for my old life hit me in the chest. I hated it.

"I'll be back," I murmured to Kiana, sliding off of my bar stool.

Though nothing had happened yet, I knew enough about over-exhaustion and alcohol consumption to know that tears were never far away. It had been a while since I cried in public, and I wanted to keep it that way.

"Bathroom?" Kiana asked, hopping down. "I'll come with you."

We slipped away relatively unnoticed, Kiana glancing back to look at the group once more before we disappeared around the corner.

"They're fun," said Kiana in the mirror next to me.

There was a hint of caution in her voice that irrationally irritated me, but I understood why it was there. My friends were naturally overly-sensitive in situations that they thought would remind me I was starting completely from scratch (by no choice of my own) in the world of dating and romance.

"Fun to hang with for now, anyway," she continued after my lack of reply.

"Agreed," I said, attempting the inflection of indifference. "For now."

Apparently the others thought differently about the duration of our time together, because upon our return, Kiana and I learned that Kristen and Marissa had committed to plans with the group that evening following our dinner.

"*Slawn-che*," James was saying, glass in hand. "Did I get that right, Seamus?"

"Close enough," responded another of the guys who had been in conversation with the bartender, away from us and seemingly uninterested. His head of dark red hair towered over the others as he straightened up from leaning on the bar, and I noticed his deep green eyes seemed to smile with his mouth. They also looked nice against the moss colored shirt he was wearing.

"*Sláinte* is how ye say 'cheers'," he said in what I thought was flawless Gaelic, turning back to his conversation with the man behind the bar, shaking his head in dismayed laughter. He did not turn back to us.

"See?" James said, gesturing to the one we now knew was called Seamus. "We need an Irish bloke to take us 'round Ireland or we'll look like a bunch of barmy idiots."

"We should get going," Marissa said, nudging Kristen and pointing at her watch. "It's a bit of a walk back to the hotel."

Kristen went to flag down the bartender, but James waved her off.

"No, no, I'll get these," he said, gesturing to our drinks. "Long as you promise we'll see you later?"

"Sure," said Kristen, a mischievous smile on her face.

"All of you!" he said, plainly trying to include the rest of us in a most chivalrous gesture that I *did* appreciate. I smiled and thanked him for the drink, saying polite goodbyes to the other guys as the four of us stepped out into the street. Seamus did not acknowledge our exit at all-a fact that strangely annoyed me.

Whether it was the sharp contrast to the inside of a whiskey-barreled room or the effects of the whiskey itself, the sun seemed significantly brighter as we made our way back to the hotel. Each of us yawned in the pools of light that peeked between the buildings, our pace slowing collectively like a herd of lost sheep. The weather had so far been on our side, but having prepared for much colder conditions, my shirt was nearly sticking to my skin with sweat. I longed for a deep drink of water and some shade as we traipsed across the river, squinting my eyes into slits.

"No naps," snapped Kristen as she saw Kiana's eyes fluttering. "That is how we fall prey to jet-lag, right Jasmine?"

I stifled another severe yawn but nodded in agreement. "No, she's right. We have to stay awake."

I rubbed my eyes as we entered the lobby of the hotel at last, grateful for the coffee bar that was situated conveniently next to the elevators.

Our bags having already been brought to the room, we were left to drag nothing but our feet down the hallway and into the suite. The room was spectacular, leaving me infinitely appreciative of Kristen's proficiency in accommodation seeking.

Though there were not too many incredibly picturesque views to be had in Dublin, the suite itself was fabulous enough without even peeking out the window. There was a vast, open living room with dark wood floors and velvet furniture that provided the utmost cozy atmosphere situated around the fireplace. On either side of the sitting room were two rooms, each with relatively large beds ("I thought Europe only had *twin* sized beds," Kristen observed appreciatively) and our own bathrooms to share in pairs of two.

"Mine!" shouted Marissa, shooting through the door frame and jumping on the bed to the left.

I followed Kiana into the other room where we claimed our own territories. Naturally the two best friends would be together. We always were.

"Closest to the door?" Kiana asked rhetorically, knowing my sleeping preference had not changed since Girl Scouts.

"Always," I said sleepily, tossing my backpack on the floor.

Kiana threw her things next to the other bed and shrugged. "In case of an intruder, I don't want to be the first to go, so that's fine with me."

"No naps!" I heard the familiar warning voice call from the other room, and we rushed to freshen up accordingly.

CHAPTER 5

DUBLINERS

*D*esiring as much authenticity as possible, we went to a pub that Professor Brennan had recommended where I had a warm comfort meal that consisted of a rich stew and a dense loaf of soda bread.

Initially, I expected to eat only enough to quell any of my friends' suspicions regarding my obviously unhealthy weight loss, but after a few bites I found myself enjoying it thoroughly and there was no need to pretend. The warm stew slid comfortably down my throat and I radiated coziness from the inside out.

"This has been the longest day of my entire life," I said, sinking back in my chair as I recalled in shock that we had only landed that morning.

"It's not over yet!" said Kristen. "So you better wake up."

"Alright, alright," I replied, taking a deep swig of my cider.

I noticed Marissa and Kristen side glance at one another as they observed my empty bowl in surprise, but chose to ignore it in my state of contentment as I felt truly satiated for the first time in as long as I could remember. I waited for the familiar feeling of regret that followed after eating too much, but it never came. In fact, the heavy bowl of soup and cider had left me feeling perfectly refreshed.

After dinner, we re-entered the now bustling street to begin the rest of our evening. Kristen led the way through the famous Temple Bar district in search of a live music joint where we were to meet up with James and the others. I vowed to do my best at socializing, but my brain was chugging along slowly with fatigue and I hoped we would not stay out long. The lights seemed too bright around me and I desperately longed for the comfort of my bed.

"There they are!" came the familiar voice from earlier in the day.

James was at the corner of the crowded bar, waving us over. Two of the others leapt off of the seats and chivalrously offered them to us. I gratefully took one of them, and Kiana the other. Before I had time to speak, a small glass of what looked suspiciously like more Jameson appeared in front of the four of us, and I tossed it back in hopes it would revitalize my mood.

Unfortunately, it only succeeded in burning my throat and traveling painfully into the pit of my stomach where it sat like a rock on fire. I looked around at the group to see Kristen, Marissa, and even Kiana greeting the guys like old friends, whereas I couldn't recall a single one of their names. Had I really been *that* absent during the conversations earlier?

"Are ye lookin' forward to tomorrow?" came a deep voice to my left that made me start.

"What?" I said distractedly, willing my brain to move faster.

"For Galway, an' the Cliffs," he said.

"Oh!" I said, peeling my eyes away from the chipped paint I had been examining on the bar.

I stifled a yawn as I looked up to see the same bright green eyes I had noticed earlier looking at me expectantly. He stood taller than the rest of his friends (and nearly everyone else in the bar, I noted), and his seemingly brown hair turned a rich mixture of auburn and redwood when it caught the light. I remembered that this one was Seamus.

I nodded politely. "Yes, I'm really excited! It's always been on my list."

"It's a tourist's favorite, but for good reason, so it is," he continued, setting his beer beside me.

He leaned over me to put a hand on the bar, and I couldn't help but notice that he smelled lovely. Not too pungent, but a rather nice, woody type of scent that reminded me of a crisp, fall day. I fought the urge to glance at his forearm that was now so close to my own; sleeves rolled to his elbows.

"I've just heard 'bout yer busy schedule, and I reckon yer mad for crammin' it all inta just a week," he said, breaking into a brilliant grin.

I began to feel my brain kickstarting itself out of necessity. It was one thing to linger quietly in the background of a group conversation, but to be in a one-on-one discussion while lethargic was plain rude. And (much to my irritation) I had the strong urge to make a good impression on this one. I cleared my throat.

"Well, I don't know if you've heard, but we get one to two vacation days per decade in America," I said sarcastically. "That's compared to what-the three months of holiday plus the entire summer you get in Europe?"

I emphasized the word *holiday* ironically, recalling my own jealousy at my European colleagues' extensive out-of-office messages that appeared like clockwork each year between May and September. Working for a foreign technology company had certainly shown me the disparities between the German and American versions of *"work-life-balance"*.

He was surprised by my response and his eyebrows raised in amusement. I felt a strange sense of satisfaction at his expression. Did he think I was witty? Did I care if he did?

"I meself haven't a lot of time for *holiday*," he said, matching my inflection with a smirk. "Much too busy growin' potatoes, pluckin' shamrocks, an' looking for pots of gold."

I laughed. Although I had already determined he was handsome enough, I decided he was also now *amusing* enough to engage with for the time being.

"So how did you end up as the tour guide for them?" I said, signaling to James and the others as another round of Jamesons were being handed out. I shrunk back slightly into my chair, hoping to escape their notice as the last one was still eating away at my insides.

"Well, as ye mentioned holidays, we all work together in London," he said, his freckles catching my attention in the dim light. They made him look good-natured, I thought. "Themuns never been to Ireland, so I thought I'd take them on a wee adventure."

"Where are you from?" I asked, charmed by his unique accent that seemed to fluctuate between the British intonation I heard from his friends and his native Irish roots. "Obviously Ireland, but where, exactly?"

I found myself suddenly more than mildly interested, partially due to his rich smile that extended to his eyes, but additionally the presence of genuine curiosity. Having lived abroad when I was young, I was always intrigued to hear of what childhood was like in other countries. My years in Portugal had made such a lasting impact on my own life, those memories still as vivid as the day they happened. To think that someone could live all of their formative years entirely differently from someone else across the world seemed profoundly fascinating. Perhaps not to others, but to me it was.

"Norn Iron," he said. It took me a beat to translate what he had said, but he clarified anyway. "Outside of Belfast."

Northern Ireland. Got it.

"Birthplace of the Titanic," I said instinctively.

He smiled again. Damn, it was a nice smile.

"That's right," he said. "Except-"

"I know, Cobh was where it actually left from," I said again, before I could stop myself. "Or Queenstown as it was called back then."

My voice trailed off at the end, hoping I hadn't sounded like a know-it-all. I had been called that once or twice in my youth and I shuddered to think that I had not kicked the habit as an adult.

"Ye know more of Irish history than I do," he said, raising his glass to me. "Maybe it's *you* that should be showin' them around."

I did know a good amount about Irish history as it was customary for me to study up on a country before I visited. Or maybe I *had* wondered about my mother more than I let on in my sessions with Marianne. I believe Raj had said she was from somewhere very far south, but I couldn't remember the name of the place anymore. I wish I did.

I laughed and then felt suddenly extremely aware of how I was sitting and the placement of my hands. Wanting very badly to say something to Seamus but not knowing what, I ordered a cider to pass the time. It still annoyed me that I cared, but I sincerely hoped he wouldn't leave in the meantime.

He didn't.

"I'm Seamus, by the way," he said suddenly, realizing that neither of us had introduced ourselves. Of course I had remembered his name from earlier, but it was nice to be formally acquainted.

He extended his hand to me. His muscular forearm exposed, I noticed a tattoo on his wrist, but couldn't quite make out what it was. I had an impulse to reach out and touch it, but resisted for obvious reasons.

"Jasmine," I replied warmly, allowing him to take my hand in his grasp. It was warm and sturdy, as I expected.

"That's a lovely name," he said, and he looked like he really meant it. I imagined there weren't too many Irish women named after the Himalayan shrub that ran rampant in the gardens of Florida homes. Or the Disney princess, either.

My cider appeared, foaming faintly at the top. I took a sip as I thought about what to say next; a painful reminder of how long it had been since I had intentionally flirted with someone. I was not necessarily insecure, but certainly out of practice.

However, it was clear that Seamus had no intention of letting the conversation end and it put me at ease to realize the feeling of intrigue was mutual.

"I heard yer all from Florida, is that right?" he asked, his expression mingled with curiosity and something else. Was it nervousness? I liked the thought that it might be.

"Yes," I replied. "Well, sort of…I've lived in Florida for some eight or so years now. I stayed there after college."

As soon as I said it, I found myself wondering how old he was. Earlier at the distillery, I had been sure that they all looked so much younger. But now that I was face-to-face with him, I noticed that his freckles added a touch of handsome maturity to his features rather than the boyish effect they usually had. There were faint lines on his forehead and around his eyes that were features of a man's face, not a boy's. No, he was certainly around my age. At least I hoped.

"Are yer parents there as well?" he asked.

I hesitated, dreading the awkward apology that would inevitably follow my next statement.

"No, actually they-they're both gone."

"Oh, I'm so sorry," he said, his eyes not leaving my own as he wrinkled his brow to match his frown. In fact, he had not yet broken eye contact with me at all. I found it odd that I did not look away as I always instinctively did during uncomfortable moments. But for some reason, I wasn't uncomfortable at all.

He cleared his throat. "My mam passed away when I was vurry young… so I understand," he finished.

I nodded appreciatively as we both silently decided nothing

more needed to be said on the topic for now. I wanted to reach out and touch his hand in a comforting manner, but again, I resisted. Why did I, someone who loathed physical contact with acquaintances and even with *friends*, constantly want to touch him?

"But my brother's outside of Galway," he said, changing the subject. "I'll catch up wi' him at some point durin' this trip."

He had leaned in slightly closer to me as the live music had grown louder.

I felt my cheeks getting warmer as Seamus ran a quick hand through his hair, sending a fresh wave of his fireplace scent my way. I nearly stamped my own foot for being ridiculous, but he smiled at me in a way that silently confirmed he was more than mildly intrigued by me as well. I couldn't have explained it to anyone-I just knew there was nothing I needed to be embarrassed about. I noted that I couldn't recall a single other time in my life where I had felt so nervous and so comfortable at the same time.

"So do ye-" he began, but was cut off by roaring laughter from our friends next to us, thus breaking the spell that had hung over the two of us.

I turned to my friends and saw that Kiana was nearly doubled over in laughter, Marissa covering her mouth in a fit of giggles, and Kristen had tears in her eyes. The guys were loving it, whatever joke they had told. I, on the other hand, had nearly forgotten they were there.

"How many more til he's pure banjaxed, ye think?" Seamus whispered to me as James took a subtle stumble dismounting his bar stool.

"I reckon he's steamin' within the hour," I said. Seamus roared with laughter at my poor attempt at his accent.

"That's class," he said, pointing at me. "I'm impressed."

"Next place," James called to Seamus, who reluctantly tore his gaze from mine. "Ready, *ye wee skitter*?"

"Aye, let's keep 'er lit," Seamus said, finishing his beer.

He nodded at me, indicating I should do the same. I clinked glasses with him and blushed at the sound of his *Norn Iron* accent once more. It seemed his friends were as amused by slang his terms as I was, because I heard James calling the rest of them *"a bunch of melters"* when they declined to finish their drinks.

All remnants of my exhaustion had faded and were swiftly replaced by a faint whisper of excitement and anticipation that was explainable if not infuriating. Perhaps I'd order something stronger at the next place, I thought, hopping down from my seat and rejoining the others who greeted me with mischievous smirks.

"The hottest one *would* be into you," whispered Kiana, punching me in the arm as she eyed Seamus over my shoulder. "You know he's the only one who's actually Irish."

I felt my cheeks go scarlet.

"Stop, and yes I know," I said, laughing and feeling extremely immature.

"And he's so *tall*," said Marissa, eyes wide with admiration. I lightly nudged her so she'd stop looking at him.

"The tall guys always like the shortest girls and it's so unfair," Kristen groaned exasperatedly.

She, as always, was either eye-level or towering over the majority of the group. Her model figure paired with her fierce personality generally intimidated most suitors, but James looked as though he could hardly be discouraged, even as he stood an entire head shorter than her. I admired him for that alone.

"But happy for you, though," Kristen said. "You'd make beautiful children. Dark hair like yours, light eyes like his. I can see it now."

Kiana and Marissa erupted into laughs at this, clearly relishing in my distress. The thought of any of the guys overhearing us was unbearable.

"Enough!" I whispered fiercely, but I laughed despite myself. "You are all beyond annoying."

Something about Seamus' warm, genuine smile made me certain that, however attractive and charming he was, he certainly was not fully aware of it. There was a definite unbothered characteristic in his demeanor that I could not quite identify, but I wanted to keep it that way. My friends' silence on the matter was indispensable for the sake of preserving his humility. At least in public.

The rest of the night was admittedly a blast. I finally got around to meeting the rest of the group and discovered their names to be Oliver, Jack, Benjamin, and of course (as they were British) there was a Harry. He was clearly the youngest of them all, shy around us at first, but hilarious and personable after a few drinks, nonetheless. I joked with all of them, but found myself repeatedly-though discreetly-seeking out Seamus in my peripheral. Each time I did so, I found him to be looking at me as well, eyes bright and a smile on his face that was directed solely at me.

We eventually made our way back to talking with one another, and I wondered if it were the dimmed lights, the volume of drinks, or his confident charisma that made him more appealing by the minute. The accent didn't hurt, either.

"I'd never seen anything like it," he said, talking excitedly about his trip he had taken to America last summer and of all things—the wonders of shopping for groceries at a bulk store.

"There's food in proportions for a family of elephants-" he said, and I almost spit out my drink. "Furniture, dog food, and jewelry all in one place. Who would be searchin' for all those yokes in one go?"

His laugh was contagious. It was the kind of laugh that went on longer than it should and made me feel like I was the only person in the world who could be this much fun to be around.

In the smoothest, most natural way, he placed his hand on my thigh as he leaned in toward me, bowing his head to hear me as I spoke over the noise. I felt that I had his undivided attention, which was something I had not wanted from anyone in quite some time.

He told me about his childhood and in turn asked about my own. By the middle of the evening I felt we had known one another for much longer than a few hours.

He had once been extremely close with his older brother, Aidan, but it sounded like the nine year age gap had caught up to them in adulthood-this trip would be the first time they'd seen one another in a while. They had spent their childhood in Northern Ireland doing the normal things that all kids do-playing sports and getting into moderate degrees of trouble.

His eyes flickered with something I couldn't read when we talked about his parents, and I gathered that his relationship with his father was not at all like the one I had had with mine.

"We were scared to death of da," he said with mild bitterness in his voice. "But Aidan bein' so much older than me, he protected me from some of the worse punishments he likely got as a wee one. The times had changed by then, too. Beatin' yer own son with a stick in the yard wasn't as accepted as it once had been."

He winced, and I could tell he had tried to make light of something that was likely much more traumatic in memory than he wanted to let on.

I tactfully avoided asking about his mother, having heard earlier that she was no longer alive. However, I felt as though the topic would have been just fine to discuss, given the level of comfort that now existed between us. I wondered if there would ever be an occasion to tell him about my own tragic family, but then reminded myself of the sobering reality that I was on a girl's trip in Ireland and we'd likely never see one another again.

Still, something about laughing with someone-perhaps it could have been anyone-was breathing life back into me. The heaviness that had weighed on my soul was still there, of course.

The wound still existed. But it began to feel as though the bandage had been torn away, replaced by a scar that-while it may never fully heal-would fade into the background as I continued to live the rest of my life as normally as possible. Flirting with a guy I met in an Irish pub was about as normal as it could get, after all.

"We have an early morning tomorrow," said Kiana at last, rising from her bar stool. This rendered loud protests from the guys, but everyone knew she was right. The itinerary had left no room for sleepy, late starts.

"You can live the rest of the night without us," said Kristen, patting James on the shoulder as he rolled his eyes at her. "Besides, we'll see you in Galway."

"Is that right?" I asked, turning to Seamus and attempting to conceal my excitement at the prospect of seeing him again.

"Aye," he nodded, doing nothing to hide his own. "We'll be there a few nights, and return to London at the end of next week."

It was then that I realized we had talked of so many other things-interests, friends, our upbringings-that I hardly knew anything about his regular life. I had nearly forgotten that he lived somewhere else at all. I didn't even know what he did for a living! It felt like we had spent the entire night together, but there had still not been enough time. He then put his hand on top of mine, taking me by surprise.

"We'd love to see ye again tomorrow night if ye'll have us," he said warmly, gesturing to his group of innocent-if not slightly obnoxious-companions with his free hand. Then he paused. "I mean-*I* would like to see *you* again if ye'll have *me*."

My stomach fluttered in an extremely adolescent way, but I welcomed the feeling. He didn't let go of my hand.

"Sure, I'll have you," I said, perhaps a bit stronger than I intended, but he hardly seemed to mind.

They escorted us back to our hotel and Seamus gave me a

particularly tight hug as he said goodbye. His solid arms and warm chest seemed to envelop me in a strangely familiar way, leaving me surprised by how nice it had felt.

* * *

"So what on earth did you two talk about?" asked Kristen excitedly as we crossed the threshold of the lobby.

I shrugged. "Just about Ireland, his trip to the US, nothing crazy."

The elevator arrived, and they continued to press me for more information about Seamus. I held back, not wanting to say too much about someone I had just met. Now that we were out of the dimness of the pub and back under the fluorescence of the hotel hallway, the magic seemed to be slipping away while my exhaustion returned.

"He was very nice," I said carefully, my diplomatic answer garnering a series of impatient sighs as we ascended to the top floor of the small hotel.

We entered the suite with the other two girls passing out immediately. As I was unable to sleep, I jumped in the shower while Kiana talked to me through the bathroom wall.

"He was clearly very into you," she said, plainly relying on the hope that her best friend would disclose more information now that we were alone.

"Mmhm," I said vaguely.

"His friends commented on it as well, saying he's usually the last one to talk to a woman all night," she said. "He's been single for about a year and apparently it wasn't very serious before that."

Her voice rushed out excitedly, confirming my suspicions that my interaction with Seamus had been much more of a topic of conversation amongst the others than they had initially let on.

"Oh?" I replied. Finding I was indeed curious about his past relationship, I shook my head under the hot water as if to wash away the foolishness. *Seriously, who cares?*

"Who knows, maybe you'll fall in love and never leave Ireland," Kiana said in a sing-song voice, flopping loudly onto the bed.

"Well he lives in London, first of all," I called from the bathroom, turning off the shower and towel-drying my hair. "And that's crazy. I just met him."

"Well, is it though?" Kiana called back to me in an altered tone as she began to seriously contemplate the logistics. "People move their lives around if it's for the right person all the time."

I paused, the comb in my hair unsteady as my hand trembled. It was very sudden-the familiar, sharp pain cutting like a knife and without warning. It felt as though Kiana's words had torn at the scabbed wound from earlier and a fresh stream of blood had begun to ooze from it once more. I know she hadn't meant to, but it hurt all the same.

I had *already* found the right person once. I didn't want to find another one. Had I brought the ring on the chain with me to Ireland, I would have clutched it to my chest until it made a dent.

CHAPTER 6

NOTICEABLE CHANGES

I awoke to the water running.

"You're showering already?" I groaned, pulling the sides of my pillow tightly over my ears.

"I was too tired last night and now I'm grossed out," replied Kiana from the bathroom as she sniffed her hair with disgust. "I dreamt of cigarettes last night."

I rolled over to take a whiff of my own; grateful for my borderline obsessive habit of always showering before getting into bed. My locks were surely a frizzy mess, but at least they were clean.

"If anyone cares, *I* was still sleeping, but not anymore," called Marissa loudly from the other room across the suite.

"How can you even hear me all the way over there?" shouted Kiana, shutting off the water at last.

"I'm up now, too," called Kristen in a fierce, but muffled tone that suggested her pillow was still over her face.

I hopped out of bed and crossed the threshold of the short but elegant living room, making my way into the other bedroom where two fluffy beds sat across from one other. I jumped onto Kristen's like a cat.

"It's just like college," I said, picking up one of the pillows and winding up for a swing. "Me waking you two lazy asses up." Kristen blocked the pillow with her arm and squealed, nearly rolling off the bed.

"I'm done," shouted Kiana from the other room, saving Kristen from another blow. "Bathroom's all yours."

"My turn," I said, scurrying away before Kristen could retaliate.

Kristen and Marissa dragged their feet across the living room and plopped down in the comfy armchairs on either side of the couch.

"I love watching the news in other countries," Kristen said, snatching the remote from Kiana.

Marissa nodded in agreement. "It *is* so important to know what's going on in the rest of the world. Not just in America."

Kristen looked at her incredulously.

"Sure," she said. "But I meant for the accents."

She turned the volume up on the news anchor as Kiana barked out a laugh and Marissa shook her head.

I entered the bathroom and flipped the switch back on. I yawned widely as I made my way to the sink, nearly toppling over as I slid across the slick tile that Kiana had carelessly dripped all over. Cursing my friend's messy habits, I threw an extra towel on the floor and mopped it back and forth as I stared out the window and into the streets of Dublin.

The River Liffey was not exactly impressive or beautiful, but watching the people cross its bridges from the bathroom window was interesting enough. I gently combed out my hair as I saw the sun peeking over the horizon. There were dozens of pubs and restaurants already opening the doors for an early crowd. I spotted one called "The Woollen Mills" that had plates of sausages and eggs being wheeled out to their outside patio. My stomach grumbled regrettably as I knew we would not have time for a full meal before hitting the road to Galway.

I went back to the sink and saw my contact case had been left open. I reached for the tiny lid labeled "R" and stopped. My contacts were still there, sitting in the solution. I frowned. Of course I had not put them in yet, but-

Rushing back to the window, I rubbed my eyes and sure enough, I saw the sign for The Woollen Mills, letters clear as day. I stupidly pressed a finger to my eyeball and was met with the stinging pain I should have expected considering I poked myself in my own eye, but there was no sign of any contact lens.

"What the hell?" I whispered to myself as I began to read all of the signs that lined the street: Litton Lane, Swift's Row... As someone who had needed glasses (and strong prescriptions at that) since the age of ten, I could not fathom how it was possible that I could suddenly see with such clarity.

Trying my eye once more, I confirmed that there was indeed nothing there. My irises now stared back at me in the mirror, surrounded by a ring of red irritation from my prodding. I dropped a few bursts of false tears to wet them and blinked wildly, waiting for my eyesight to disappear. But it didn't.

"Jazz, how long til you're ready?" called Kiana from the living room.

"Sorry, just another minute," I called back, tearing my gaze reluctantly from the window.

Everything else in the room seemed clearer as well, now that I was paying attention to it. Strange as it was, I was certainly not angry with my newfound eyesight. I would have rushed to tell the others, but the clock on the nightstand told me we were all running very late. There was no time to open the floodgates for Marissa who simply loved contemplating a medical mystery. I quickly got dressed, throwing on my rain boots and jeans with my favorite gray raincoat.

It was a chaotic twenty minutes that followed my strange discovery, but at last we made it to the lobby where a sleepy valet had pulled our car around. If Kristen were nervous about being the chauffeur driving on the opposite side of the road, she certainly didn't show it. She hopped in the driver's seat with authority and I joined her up front, resting my head on the cold window.

"Ooh, there's the Ireland weather I was expecting," acknowledged Marissa as she nestled in the backseat and rubbed her arms. This morning was significantly chillier than the last, and we had all thrown on extra layers before stuffing our bags in the trunk.

"Navigate for me?" Kristen asked and I nodded sleepily, pointing to my phone in my lap that showed the single road we were to stay on for the majority of the ride.

The road from Dublin to Galway was relatively straightforward and not at all exciting. I watched cows munching lazily on the greenery outside my window as we zoomed along in the gray of the early morning light. I had nearly forgotten about the anomaly of my eyesight when I started to count the cows as far away as I could see. I tried to turn it into a game to keep myself awake, but to no avail. I was grateful to be navigating rather than driving myself as I continuously nodded off and was awoken only by the sound of my maps app shouting directions.

"What was the rush again?" yawned Marissa from the backseat. "We're not even going to the Cliffs until tomorrow."

"Exploring the city," said Kristen. "Since we'll be gone all day tomorrow, I want to make sure we leave enough time to actually see Galway. We only have two days in Galway and then we head down to Limerick, remember?"

"Tight schedule," Kiana mumbled. I heard Marissa's "*hmmph*" of agreement as she laid her head back on the window.

The three hour drive felt particularly lengthy given the monotonous landscape. I had made little effort to find any historical sites between the two places, deciding to forego a stop in Athlone, the small city that marked the halfway point. Although I would have been interested to check it out for no reason other than it was another place to see, I doubted my friends would find a city with nothing but a tiny castle and a modest museum all that enthralling, particularly when the sun had barely risen. We passed the exit for the small town just as I was nodding off again.

My mind wandered sleepily to my conversation with Seamus from the evening prior, recalling his closeness to me as he had rested his hand behind me in conversation. There had been something so unique in the way he watched me as I spoke-as if there was nothing I could say that would not interest him. At least that was how it seemed last night. I hoped I had not imagined it. I certainly hadn't imagined the smell of his warm neck as he bent his head toward me in conversation, the alluring scent practically begging me to run my hands through his mahogany locks.

Almost as suddenly as the thoughts of Seamus had crept into my mind, they disappeared with a blow of guilt that hit me directly in the chest. The familiar heat of uncontrollable emotions rose in my throat and I shut my eyes tightly as I thought of Matt. Even from our first meeting, he had looked upon me with that same unwavering interest Seamus had-his large brown eyes twinkling with perpetual adoration any time I spoke. I recalled how *he* had not had the same effect on *me* initially, considering the whirlwind of a day I had already experienced before I met him.

"I'VE GOT IT, but thank you," I said, my irritation reaching its peak.

I had just deplaned from visiting my father while on his latest research trip in Dubrovnik, and the two layovers it took to get to Tampa were testing my patience to the highest degree. It was nearly eleven o'clock at night and my bag had naturally been one of the last to appear on the conveyor belt, further solidifying my reasoning for avoiding anything but a carry-on at all costs.

However, the trip had lasted nearly a month as it would be my last opportunity to take any real time off before I entered the terrifying world of true adulthood-getting my first corporate job that would occupy me from nine to five for the rest of my life. I sighed as the man who had so eagerly jumped to assist me plopped his suitcase at my side.

"No problem," he said, straightening and meeting my eyes.

I noticed he was very handsome; his dark hair looked far too neat for having just flown overseas. He must have come directly from the Atlanta layover. Too tired to care about my own appearance, I yawned widely and rubbed my eyes. I began to roll my suitcase away before his voice made me pause.

"That's probably on its last legs," he said, pointing to the wheels on my suitcase that had very clearly taken a beating on the cobblestone streets of Eastern Europe.

"I know," I sighed, looking sadly at the massive suitcase that I had bought specifically for this trip. "This is an accurate representation of how I feel after my day of travel."

He laughed briefly, revealing a crinkle in his nose that was endearing almost immediately. I thought he looked older than myself, but I couldn't say by how many years. Having just graduated from undergrad where everyone was at the same stage in life, I had a hard time telling how old anyone in the adult world actually was.

I glanced down at my phone to see that Kristen was still several miles away from picking me up and sighed. Not wanting to sit down after being confined to an economy seat on and off for the past eighteen hours or so, I opted to continue standing right where I was.

"Were you on the flight from Atlanta?" asked my new friend curiously, clearly wondering how a quick hour-and-a-half trip had worn me out to the state I was in.

I noticed he only briefly glanced at the belt to look for his bag before returning to watching my side profile. It made me self conscious-I've always hated my side profile. I turned to face him instead.

"Yes," I replied. "And London before that, and Dubrovnik before that."

His eyes widened in surprise and he nodded. "Okay, that explains it then."

"What, do I really look that awful?"

I had certainly caught him off guard with my bluntness.

"Oh, no, not at all," he stammered, fearing he had offended me. "I just meant-"

I laughed. "I know," I said quickly, meeting his eyes and surveying his attractive features more closely.

He had an excellent jawline that made him appear intelligent and refined, and a slight bump in his nose that, oddly enough, was incredibly appealing to me. He had a sophisticated, charming element to his looks that was like that of a movie star or news anchor. I wondered again how old he was.

"So what was in Atlanta?" I asked, not caring if I were being too nosy. After all, he had stuck around to chat with me for this long, and I was too sleepy to mind my manners.

"Quick trip to visit family," he said. "They were disappointed I didn't match anywhere in Georgia for my residency, so I try to get out to see them as much as possible."

Residency, I mused, counting the years of medical school in my head. So he was quite a bit older than me. Four or five, at the very least.

"What kind of medicine do you practice?" I asked, trying to sound older and more mature, suddenly extremely aware of my sorority backpack that rested atop my suitcase. It was surely time to retire the use of Greek letters in my daily wardrobe. I shifted the letters from view as subtly as I could.

"Pediatrics," he said.

I smiled for some reason at this, immediately picturing him calming a screaming child while giving it their booster shots. He certainly had the gentle demeanor to do so, from the few words we had exchanged.

"I'm Matt."

He reached to take my hand. I took it, despite all of my instincts regarding germs in an airport begging me not to do so. Besides, I expected a doctor to take these types of factors into consideration himself. His grasp was firm but gentle at the same time, and his long fingers had something artistic about them. Perhaps he would go on to become a surgeon, one day.

"Jasmine," I said, and felt a small rush of satisfaction as the surprise flickered in his eyes upon hearing my relatively unusual name. It always happened with strangers.

His bag then rolled off the conveyor belt, signaling the conclusion of Delta flight 5023's unloading.

"Are you waiting for someone...?" he asked me tentatively.

It was obvious that neither of us wanted the conversation to end so abruptly. Airports have that way of creating urgently romantic situations out of everyday encounters.

"Yes," I said. Knowing it was silly, I clarified the person's relationship to myself, anyway. "My friend Kristen should be here in a few."

This distinction was not lost on him. "I'll stay and wait with you if you'd like," he said, shifting on his feet ever so subtly, but his slight nervousness was apparent.

I wondered how a *doctor* could possibly be nervous around me-a college graduate with a ratty suitcase who looked like a complete mess.

"That's alright," I said, smiling. "She'll be here soon."

As soon as I said it, I regretted it. I hoped he didn't think I was dismissing him.

"Well-alright, Jasmine," he said, and I could not help but notice how rich the sound of my own name was in his voice. He turned to leave the terminal but immediately reconsidered. My heart leapt despite myself; I knew he had more to say and I hoped he had the courage to say it.

"I'm sorry if this is weird," he said, a nervous laughter on the tip of his tongue as he scratched his neck.

He paused, but I made no reply. *'Keep going,'* I thought to myself.

"But I'd like to see you again," he finished, his cheeks flushing with the general excitement and fear of making a bold request. I broke into a wide grin.

We did see each other again.

AT LAST WE began to see an increased number of traffic lights, signaling the city limits of Galway. I awoke from my blissful daydream, my fingers instinctively reaching for my eyes in case of any sign of absent-minded tears.

Kristen glanced at me sideways from behind the wheel; I quickly yawned and rubbed my eyes as a cover. It was an unnecessary measure as the recollection had surprisingly merely taken me down memory lane without the accompaniment of despair. I let the memory simmer quietly rather than choosing to dwell on it, the result being I felt generally peaceful. Marianne had told me that one day this would be possible. It felt too soon, but maybe I *was* healing.

If I had loved Dublin, I needed a new word for Galway. I was entirely infatuated with the general old world charm that hovered over the city and its brightly colored buildings. Its proximity to the sea seemed to add an extra layer of appeal to the town as it made everything seem more casual, light-hearted, and fun.

The valet took our car to an off-site parking location and we entered the snug lobby of the hotel. Our rooms were ready-this time we would be sleeping in pairs as there were no suites available that were large enough for our entire party at the quaint inn.

"It said *boutique hotel* online," grumbled Kristen as we lugged our suitcases up the carpeted stairs after discovering the absence of an elevator. "I guess that was code for shitty."

"It's fine," Marissa said sleepily, waving her hand in dismissal. "It looks very traditional, in fact."

I tended to agree with Kristen when it came to standards of accommodations. Matt and I (being the frequent travelers that we were) had often split up the tasks of itinerary-making and hotel-seeking with myself taking the latter. This being mainly because I knew to check for the non-obvious amenities in European hotels such as elevators and air conditioning. Matt had had his hotel booking privileges revoked when he reserved a rental house in the Smoky Mountains that had no driveway, leaving us to trudge up the vertical hill with all of our luggage for the week.

"At least they put our rooms across from each other," said Kiana as she fumbled with the lock that was an actual, real key rather than a card.

The gigantic artifact seemed to weigh five pounds at least, and I made a mental note to avoid the burden of carrying it around all day if I could get away with it. There was nowhere to put such a thing in my tiny travel purse.

"Let's meet downstairs in fifteen minutes?" asked Kristen, the only one who seemed wide awake in the group.

We all groaned but nodded in agreement. I cursed myself for having played such an integral role in the creation of a packed itinerary.

Kiana swung the door open across the hall and I felt my qualms about our hotel melt away in an instant.

It felt like I was stepping into the pages of a romanticized and upgraded version of Moby Dick. The dark wood furniture complimented the red walls and nautical decor, but the bathroom was fully updated with all of the modern amenities we could have needed. The window revealed a view of the busy street, bustling with tourists already beginning their day. Whether it was reality or the illusion created by the decor, the smell of the sea seemed to envelop me on all sides. I decided right then and there that Galway was a lovely place.

I flopped onto the bed, but Kiana immediately yanked me back up.

"No, we'll fall asleep," she said sternly, and then imitated Kristen. "*'No naps allowed'*, remember?"

"You're right," I said, yawning and feeling extreme deja vu from the day before. "I need to splash some water on my face."

Kiana nodded. "I'll put on some music."

I lazily brushed through my hair, blinking the cold sink water out of my eyes. I paused as I saw my reflection for the first time since that morning, remembering my strange gift of eyesight that I had nearly forgotten in the haze of my nap in the car. The peculiarity of it piqued my interest once more as I leaned in to examine my irises.

My eyes, in addition to their newfound functionality, also seemed strangely lighter in color; seemingly having paled from their usual dark brown to a near hazel with distinctive flecks of green. I leaned in closer, my nose brushing the glass. I had certainly heard of eyes slightly changing hues over time, but not a single person in my family had green eyes. Well, maybe my mother had. I had never asked Raj. I blinked several times over, wondering what had caused this sudden change.

"Kiana, come here," I called into the room.

My friend loped into the bathroom, rubbing the sleep out of her eyes and joining me in front of the mirror.

"Do my eyes look lighter to you?" I asked intently.

"Maybe," she yawned as she squinted. Then she stopped and genuinely considered the question with intrigue. She frowned. "Actually, maybe."

"Here, come in the natural light," I urged.

I took my friend by the shoulders and moved her into the beam of sunlight that poked through the clouds and into our window. Opening my eyes wide, I said, "Look closely."

Kiana examined me and her brow furrowed in confusion.

"They do look a little lighter," she said. "They're kind of…green?"

"How weird is that?" I said, returning to the mirror.

"Strange," said Kiana, but I could tell she was-understandably-too sleepy to take a genuine interest. It was certainly not as baffling to her as it was to me.

I had not long to contemplate whether to press the matter further as we were interrupted by a loud ringing of the phone in the room that made us both jump.

"I'll get it," she said.

Without exchanging a single word with the person on the other line, I heard Kiana drop the old-fashioned receiver loudly with a sigh.

"That was Kristen," she said, laughing ironically. "She seriously called from the lobby and said we're taking too long."

Once out in the street, I understood Kristen's eagerness. Despite Galway's digestible size, there was so much to see. The Latin Quarter held the majority of the tourist spots, but there was no shortage of alleys that promised hidden treasures. We spent the day wandering in and out of shops, enjoying the unexpected sunshine that seemed to have followed us from Dublin. It was noticeably colder, but not at all unpleasant.

"Rainy season, indeed," mused Kiana, looking up at the clear sky appreciatively.

"Yeah, I just hope this holds for tomorrow," I said tentatively, knowing my friends would be less than thrilled by the outdoor wonder of the Cliffs should they be enveloped in a rainy mist. If there were a single day on our trip that we desperately needed clear skies, it would be the day we ventured to the most iconic landmark in the country.

The morning flew by as we zigzagged through the streets, each of our individual tastes drawing the group into a variety of establishments ranging from leather goods to tourist traps, to cozy sweaters knitted from the finest Irish wool.

Although I had not particularly set out to do so, I found myself suddenly obsessed with the idea of buying some jewelry. I rarely wore anything besides earrings, but I supposed if I were to buy a new piece, it may as well be a memento from our trip. My hands had been bare for the past year, after all.

"I like this one," I said in one of the boutiques, eyeing a simple silver ring adorned with a twisting symbol brushed with a faint line of what looked like opal. It was tasteful.

The shopkeeper who had been helping me smiled, her eyes crinkling in the corners.

"That'll be The Triskelion. It represents the three realms of the physical world, spiritual world, and the afterlife."

She reached into the case and positioned it on the middle finger of my left hand.

"The afterlife," I repeated quietly.

"That's right," she replied. "The Triskelion's said to bring you good luck and happiness."

Thinking I could do with a bit of both, I agreed to the surprisingly expensive price and slipped it over my finger, satisfied with my purchase. The jewelry store *had* been a bit off the beaten path and the ring *was* supposedly real silver. A week or two with or without a green finger would confirm the truth, regardless. I felt its sturdy presence as I met the others who had been waiting across the street.

"I really like that," said Kiana, taking my hand. "It's unique. Unlike the shamrock and harp jewelry I've seen everywhere else."

"It matches your scar," said Kristen, laughing as she turned my palm to face upward. "Look!"

Indeed, she was right. The faint white line of moonstone or opal (I had forgotten to ask which it was, but considering the price, I assumed the latter) caught a ray of sun and reflected the light in the same, supernatural way that the line on my hand always seemed to glow. The subtle sheen was white in certain lights, but nearly blue or green in others.

"It's meant to be," I said, shrugging as I smiled.

We slowly started making our way back to the hotel when Kristen mentioned that James had reached out to her while I was in the shop.

"Are we okay hanging out with all of them again tonight?" she asked the group, but her eyes lingered on me a bit longer than Kiana or Marissa. I shrugged in response while the others murmured variations of "Sure," and "Sounds good to me."

Another quick turnaround at the hotel meant I had a little less than an hour to dry and style my hair, which I likely wouldn't have bothered with if it hadn't been for-

"I *knew* he would text you," Kiana said, the smugness in her voice noticeable even over the roaring shower. "Don't act like you're not excited."

I rolled my eyes but smiled as I ran the flat iron down my locks. Matt had always told me that my hair looked like a sheet of fine silk when I straightened it. I wondered if Seamus would think so, too.

"I guess," I said loftily, refusing to meet Kiana's gaze.

But admittedly, I *was* excited. After reminiscing on our conversation from the evening prior during the drive to Galway, he had been on my mind quite a bit throughout the day. I had saved his number in my phone as "Seamus" and made a note to catch his last name this time.

As I mindlessly stroked the brush through my last few sections of hair, I stopped suddenly, noticing that the ends of my strands disappeared below the extent of the mirror. Grasping a chunk of hair in my hand, I held it up to the light and frowned.

Perhaps it had been a long time since I had bothered to go through the trouble of straightening my entire head, but my hair suddenly seemed absurdly long. I swished it behind my back and turned, noticing that the ends were thick and healthy, despite not being able to recall the last time I had cut it. Moreover, I distinctly remembered thinking only days ago that it was thinning and dull, undoubtedly the result of neglecting my physical health for several months. How it had suddenly reversed course was beyond me, but I supposed I was grateful for it.

"Can I?" asked Kiana, emerging in her towel and reaching for my brush that sat on the counter. She paused at the sight of me in the mirror. "Your hair looks amazing, Jazz!"

"Thanks," I said, still running my fingers through it in disbelief.

"I never see you straighten it," she said as I made my way back into the bedroom. "It's gotten so long!"

I caught another glimpse of my mysteriously lengthy hair in the mirror on the back of the door, thinking that there was no logical explanation other than Ireland was really good for me.

CHAPTER 7

NEW POSSIBILITIES

"Ihope it's not *that* long of a walk," said Marissa. "We've got the Cliffs tomorrow."

After dinner, we had all been told by Kristen that the plan was to meet the guys at a path near the docks called The Long Walk, and adventure on from there.

Although I would have usually agreed with Marissa's sentiment, I had no idea if this would be my last chance to get to know Seamus or not, making me eager to spend as much time with him as possible. I was only mildly irritated at my own excitement for seeing someone I hardly knew.

Sure enough, we saw Seamus, James, Harry, Oliver, Jack, and Benjamin waiting for us while they were engaged in some sort of sophisticated game that involved throwing rocks as far out into the marina as they could.

"Boys," murmured Kiana as the group *ooh'd* and *ahh'd* following the loud splash Oliver's rock had made.

I was pleased to see that Seamus appeared just as excited as I felt. He did no job of hiding it, and I couldn't find a semblance of embarrassment in his face as he waved me over. He lit up as bright as the sun when he saw me, and I hoped my cheeks were not as red as they felt.

"Cailín álainn," he said quietly into my ear as he pulled me into a solid, warm hug.

I didn't know what it meant, of course, but it made my stomach flutter like a teenager. He clarified, anyway.

"Lovely girl," he said simply, brushing my arm gently as he pulled away.

Unsure of whether I preferred it in English or Gaelic because of how charming it sounded either way, I tried not to look surprised—as if I were addressed in this manner by vague acquaintances all the time. I thought I heard Kiana audibly gasp as she overheard his greeting and made a mental note to step on her foot later.

We spent some time on The Long Walk as the sun began to sink, discussing the events of the last twenty-four hours since we had seen one another. It seemed as though the men had a much more chaotic day, as their drive from Dublin to Galway involved a detour to an abbey that didn't exist. I enjoyed hearing from the others, though I still couldn't get their names quite right. They all looked the same to me, besides Seamus, of course.

"I should've listened to Seamus," said Oliver, who had obviously already enjoyed a drink or two before coming to meet us. "I dunno what I was on about, thinkin' I knew more'n the actual Irishman that's been our tour guide."

"So what did you all do?" asked Harry. "I hope you got on better than us, at least."

"We got here hours ago," I said. "We did some shopping, exploring."

"Get anything good?" asked James.

"Jazz got this cool ring," said Kiana. "Look."

They gathered round as I revealed my Celtic jewelry. Whether out of genuine interest or mere politeness, the men all complimented it most chivalrously, with Seamus holding onto my wrist to examine the tiny ring a bit longer than anyone else. The sun had nearly set, casting a shadow over his downward gaze.

"What's this?" he asked, turning my hand over to reveal the scar on my palm.

"I know, it matches," I said, comparing the mark to the opalescent streak on the ring. "The scar is from an accident when I was a kid-I fell off a boat in Portugal."

He raised his eyebrows. "When yer dad was teaching in Porto?"

I had mentioned Raj's profession only very briefly last night, and I was impressed that he remembered.

"Yes," I said.

"Must've been incredible, livin' somewhere across the world at that age," he said wistfully. "Ye probably have loads of memories such as that one."

"It *was* a great experience as a kid," I acknowledged, and then pointed to the scar. "Obviously aside from the injuries incurred."

"It's strange how this healed," Seamus said with fascination as he examined the mark.

Even in the dim light, the faint sheen of luminescence that exuded from my palm beamed in a nearly mystical way. His interest in it was certainly reminiscent of Liam Brennan's from days ago.

I shrugged. "I probably should have gotten stitches," I said, repeating what Matt had observed the first time he saw it. "But it stopped bleeding pretty quickly. It's looked like this ever since."

"Is that right?" Seamus said, laughing, his hands still glued to my own. His face lit up with good-natured humor and I hoped my palm was not sweaty.

He ran his finger along the scar, sending what I prayed was an undetectable shiver up my spine. My cheeks burned as the line on my hand seemed to glow even brighter at his touch, making me want to laugh, snatch it away, and clasp my hand on top of his all at the same time.

I was also extremely aware of my friends' eyes on my back and my embarrassment was nearly unbearable. Seamus looked up at last, his gaze locking with my own. I wondered, as we looked at one another, if he noticed the change in the color of my eyes that I had seen.

"Seamus!" called James from afar. I took my hand back and slowly shuffled over to Marissa whose jaw was hanging open like a cartoon character.

"Don't even start," I warned as my other two friends came to join us at the edge of the water, knowing grins plastered on their faces.

"Can I see that scar? Oh, how did I end up holding your hand? Oops," said Kristen mockingly, grabbing my hand, kissing it deeply and sending Marissa and Kiana into a fit of giggles.

"I can't let go of ye now, lovely girl," whispered Kiana in a terrible Irish accent that made Kristen howl with laughter.

"You are all insufferable," I said. I shook my head and tore my hand away. "They're going to hear you!"

I looked over toward Seamus and felt suddenly guilty for being moved by his touch at all. I reminded myself once more that I hardly knew him, and all of this was childish behavior. My feelings had become so unpredictable and uncontrollable over the past few days. I cursed them.

James called to us to suggest we head inside somewhere for a pint and I was grateful for the distraction.

"The Brits love to drink," observed Marissa, who was still clearly nursing her hangover from the evening before. I privately agreed with her aversion to more alcohol, but my annoyingly jittery stomach was nearly begging for a sip of anything.

Seeing that a dark cloud had begun to loom closer to where we stood, a pint indoors seemed like the best idea for the moment. I led the way, now thinking I wanted to put some distance between myself and Seamus in order to avoid an entire evening of teasing.

I ran my hand through my hair in slight distress and jumped at my own touch. I felt a distinct shooting pain from my palm that slowly began to radiate through my arm. It was as if I had been scraped by a sharpened icicle-running so cold that it almost felt hot. Turning my hand over, I saw my scar appeared to be throbbing as it emitted a bright white light from where the gash marked my skin forever. Just as soon as I noticed it, the feeling and appearance had both vanished.

Immediately excusing myself for the restroom once we got indoors, I ran my hand under cold water. Nothing. I then ran it under hot water. Also nothing.

I looked into the mirror and again noticed my strangely lightened eyes, now with distinct amounts of green littered throughout my irises. Surely my friends would have noticed it by now? My hair fell heavily far below my shoulders with not a trace of frizz despite the humidity that hung around me. I pushed a strand out of my eyes and felt continuing pulses of sharp, unpredictable pain in my hand.

"Are you alright?" came a voice from behind me. The door closed with a snap and I jumped.

I turned to see Kristen, whose eyes were narrowed in concern at me.

"What? Oh yeah, I'm fine," I said, fumbling to appear casual. "I just wanted to check my hair."

Kristen looked at me doubtfully. It had been a very uncharacteristic statement for me to make.

"Well, it looks fabulous," she said, shrugging and sliding next to me in the mirror as she applied her lip gloss and powder that she carried with her everywhere she went. She caught a glimpse of my reflection in the glass and her eyes widened in admiration.

"Are you not wearing any makeup right now?" she asked incredulously.

"No," I said absently, still staring into my own, eerie eyes. "I didn't have time."

"Your skin looks incredible," she said earnestly. "I mean, really, even in this terrible light… it's like glass."

I had to agree with my friend's observation, though I again had no explanation for it. I touched my forehead lightly and noticed there was a hint of brightness in my face that had certainly not been there in a while. My cheeks were plump with moisture and the dark circles that had been my permanent under eye accessory for the past year had all but disappeared entirely. But it was more than that. I seemed to look healthier, fuller… simply better.

"Thanks," I uttered at last, unsure of what else to say.

Kristen turned around and leaned against the countertop with her arms crossed and smiled.

"I really love seeing you like this. I'm so glad we did this trip."

I then did another quite uncharacteristic thing and pulled my friend into a crushing hug. Kristen seemed surprised by the gesture, but eventually succumbed to the embrace. While I wished I could say my aversion to displaying affection had improved from consistent therapy, the truth was that I was adamantly attempting to get another look at myself in the mirror behind her back. My strange physical changes were beyond the typical results of well-being and self-care. And I could not explain them, for I knew earnestly that I had engaged in neither of those behaviors.

I re-entered the pub with Kristen, and Seamus winked at me from across the room. I felt the same push and pull of my excitement from seeing him followed by my sudden guilt for it. Coupled with my strange discovery about my physical appearance, I found myself frozen in place. He may or may not have noticed my apprehension, but he came straight toward me anyway.

"Bout ye?" he asked.

"I'm fine," I lied.

It was not lost on him-he looked at me doubtfully. Was I

imagining some unspoken understanding that somehow already existed between us, or was I just *that* easy to read?

"Care for a wee dander?" he asked casually, motioning to the door. I nodded gratefully.

My friends, desperate to show that they had even an ounce of discreteness, chose not to acknowledge my departure underneath Seamus' guiding arm and out the door. I didn't know whether I had wanted the layer of privacy or not. Once I had it, I had no idea what to do with it. Nevertheless, Seamus had offered his solid arm, and I gladly took it as the chill of the early evening descended upon us.

I drank in the autumn air of coastal Ireland, appreciating the slight breeze that nipped at my face. I was relieved to find that we didn't need to immediately fill the silence in the way that one usually does when they're nervous. I simply enjoyed being in his presence.

"I'm proper clueless about what I should be sayin' to ye," Seamus said at last as we rounded a corner. I looked up at him in surprise; his voice was strained.

"What do you mean?" I asked, but as soon as I said it, I was more than halfway confident that I already knew.

There was the obvious fact that although we barely knew one another, there was a looming sadness regarding our upcoming departure.

He sighed and turned to me, coming to a stop. The streets still had plenty of people on them, but I felt there was a bubble of seclusion that had appeared, enveloping the two of us in our own private exchange as it had the night before. His rich, dark red hair blew gently in the wind, carrying his scent of spice to my nose. I had a strange impulse to reach for him the way one reaches for an old friend, but I suppressed it as he looked like he had more to say.

"I want to see ye again," he said softly.

I noticed for the first time since I had met him, he seemed

shy-perhaps even uncertain of himself. He cleared his throat and continued.

"But I dunno how to ask ye for that when we've such different lives. An' of course, ye barely know me."

He looked at me with a wholesome honesty that made my heart swell. I was about to speak, but he continued.

"D'ye feel the same way? Or is it just me?"

He laughed shakily, but his voice unmistakably finished in a tone that was nearly begging me to withhold any judgment. It was unnecessary-I had none to begin with.

I stopped myself from blurting out too eagerly and considered my next words carefully.

"Yes," I said at last. "I-I do feel the same. Though I can't explain why."

He looked down at me with a mixture of relief and understanding.

"Neither can I," he said. "But I s'pose that's what it should feel like, if yer lucky."

I nodded silently but my smile faded. Although I shared his sentiment to some extent, I could not agree entirely. With Matt I *had* been able to explain. There was no mystery at all. I could have written a novel describing the reasons I loved him and wanted to be with him forever. It felt concrete, certain, and everlasting.

With Seamus, I felt something more mystifying. It was as if we could only exist like this in a specific time and place. As someone who typically engaged in nothing but methodical, purposeful behavior, I found the mysterious pull between us to be unfamiliar and inexplicable. It was as if something beyond my own will was drawing me to him. It was certainly not within my usual limitations of a comfort zone, but I deeply wanted to pursue it.

He noticed my silence and reached forward to tilt my chin upward. His touch in such a tender place surprised me, sending a shock through my body as I strongly desired to pull him closer. But I hesitated.

"What is it?" he asked, his eyes swimming with genuine concern and intrigue.

I sighed. I shouldn't, but I *had* to.

"I want to tell you something," I said slowly as I turned on my heel and began to walk in the other direction. He joined me and kept pace, waiting for me to say more.

"But I don't really want to relive it again."

I didn't know why I wanted to suddenly tell him about Matt, but the impulse was gnawing at me.

We reached The Long Walk once more, this time riddled with other couples such as ourselves, out for a romantic stroll on the not-so-romantic docks. After a brief moment, however, the smell of stale fish and algae seemed to fade into insignificance as the brightness of the moon captured all of my focus. I loved when I could see the night sky clearly. It reminded me of my childhood; stargazing with Raj while he jotted down notes for his lectures. The moonlight shone on Seamus' face just long enough to show the handsome structure of his cheekbones and nose from his side profile before he turned to me and spoke first.

"I feel it's dishonest to not tell ye that I know about yer fiancé's passing," he said abruptly, and I looked up in mild astonishment. "At the same time as yer father."

"Oh," was all I could say. I looked at him inquisitively, feeling suddenly relieved that I would not be the one who had to say the words.

"Yer friend Kristen had mentioned to James that this trip was for the four of ye to get back together and…" his voice trailed off when he saw my face, sunken with sadness in the white light of the moon.

"Boys a dear," he said sincerely. "I'm sorry, Jasmine. He took me by the shoulders and forcing me to look at him. There was no hint of anything but kindness in his eyes. No ulterior motive, no judgment. I was sure of it.

"Yes, well," I said with a shrug. "That *was* what I was going to mention."

I mindlessly picked up a rock and chucked it into the marina, breaking from his grasp. It made a loud *'plunk,'* and I watched the water ripple around it. We were quiet for a bit, but it didn't feel unnatural.

"My mam went missing when I was a wee one," he said after a few moments. I knew she had died, of course, but I didn't know how. I waited for him to tell me more.

"I knew she n' my da didn't get on, but it hurt to think that she left Aidan and me like that."

He paused, looking out at the dark water.

Heaving a large sigh and shaking his head, he then said, "The peelers found her body washed up on the shore of Bangor Bay 'bout three weeks later."

My eyes went wide with bewilderment. I had certainly not expected that outcome.

"Seamus, I can't imagine…" my voice trailed off as I felt there was nothing I could say.

I refrained from telling him at that moment that I had never known *my* mother, thinking we had discussed enough tragedy for one night.

It also felt slightly dishonest to compare our situations. I couldn't grieve someone I never knew. To imagine what he had been through with the loss of his mother made me feel pathetic for ever thinking about mine at all.

He shook his head and waved in dismissal as if reading my thoughts. "I'm just wantin' to be as honest with ye as ye've been with me."

I smiled appreciatively.

"All that's to say that I'll gladly talk with ye about what's happened to ye if you'd like. Or I'll sit with ye here quietly if ye don't."

I nodded, still looking out at the water as I reached out to squeeze his hand affectionately; all shyness between us dissolved. He bowed his head as he smiled.

"I do want to talk about it, that's just the problem," I said quietly. "But I don't know if it should be with you."

He seemed to understand.

"It was so sudden," I then said, unable to stop myself. "To lose my whole world in one day."

The raw honesty of my own words lingered in the air. I chose to leave my explanation simply at that, deciding to keep the rest of my thoughts to myself for now-tucked away in the safest, most secluded parts of my heart. Out of habit, I closed my eyes to keep the tears at bay, but found they were not there. I was entirely calm as I felt Seamus' gaze upon my side profile. I uttered my final statement on the matter.

"It's been an incredibly painful year."

I sat down on the edge of the marina, not caring how filthy the ground was. I was tired.

He bent down to join me, his eyes twinkling even with the sun long gone.

"I know it's ridiculous to even suggest ye'd feel this way about me already," he began, sitting beside me. "But I'd be happy enough just being part of yer life, if it helps ease the hurt for ye."

I glanced at him briefly, his eyes wide with earnestness as well as something else that I could not describe. Maybe it was protec-tiveness? Whatever it was, it meant something more than the shallow pity I had grown so accustomed to receiving from others.

"You *have* eased it," I said, my voice barely more than a whisper as I admitted what I had been thinking for the past two days. "And I feel guilty for it." A tear fell down my cheek and I swiftly wiped it away.

"I can't allow *that*," he said, reaching for me tentatively.

I received him despite myself, and let him wrap his arms around me. It was as comfortable as I expected it to be.

"Ye deserve to find happiness," he said softly, the hum of his voice warming me as his lips brushed against my hair.

I barely knew him, and yet the depth of our sudden connection was undeniable. It was as if the universe had pulled me, kicking and screaming, from the gallows of my misery and into the bright world of the new possibilities I was experiencing now. They were not the possibilities I had ever envisioned for myself, but I wondered if those were the kind I should be happy to find. I had spent the past year wallowing in my predetermined fate without considering that I might have another one.

Seamus then slowly placed his hand on my cheek and pulled my chin up toward his own. There was no hesitation, but also no urgency. We simply met in the middle and he kissed me softly, our lips fitting as perfectly as I had known they would. He tasted faintly like whiskey, but in a fragrant, ornamental way that I didn't mind at all. I pressed more deeply as his free hand found its way beneath my thick mass of hair, his own locks now gently brushing my forehead.

I melted into his tall frame as he pulled me closer, kissing my neck and certainly not caring what any others around thought of us. Had I been anywhere other than a foreign country where I'd never see these people again, I might have been self-conscious.

"Ye are really lovely, ye know that?" he said, speaking directly into my ear as his accent rolled the relatively common words into a pleasant, musical sound that made me want to hear more.

He slipped a hand up the back of my shirt with familiarity, confident that no matter how little we knew one another, I'd welcome it. I encouraged him and felt the strength of his arms around my comparatively much smaller frame, picturing what it would be like if we were anywhere but near the smelly docks. My body temperature was rising and I was sure he could hear my heartbeat, it was pounding so loudly.

I tried to recall feeling this fiercely attracted to anyone besides Matt…but the sensation was different even from *that*, as much as I hated to admit it. What I had with Matt was nothing more than a memory now, whereas Seamus was happening in the present. It was the sheer element of possibility that I think excited me more than anything else.

Well, that and the fact he was extremely attractive and had an accent that made me swoon, I supposed.

Whether it was the buzzing of alcohol in my head or the strangely heightened feelings I suddenly had, I knew that I'd say yes if he asked me to go somewhere else. I felt his grip on the back of my hair and knew he wanted to.

Then I suddenly felt the surge of remorse that I recognized, though I had hoped I wouldn't feel her tonight. She was with me always, whispering to me that it was too soon. How could I have thought I'd ever be a suitable, loyal partner when I was so anxious to sleep with another man already? When my fiancé was barely in the grave? I wanted Seamus so badly, but I couldn't do it yet.

A small tear quivered at the edge of my eyelid as I battled with the wills of my primal desires and rational thoughts. Seamus must have sensed it, for he pressed his hand against the back of my neck tenderly one last time before he gently pulled away. Our eyes met for a moment before he placed my head back into his chest and wrapped his arms around me.

"What do we do now?" I asked quietly, speaking mostly to my own feet.

"I dunno," he said. "But I can't let it end."

"Me either."

Somehow I knew it would not. Though I did not know when or where, I felt in that moment that there was no doubt we would see one another again, even after our two days that overlapped in

Galway. We simply needed to, making me certain that the universe would make it happen in one way or another.

He grasped my hand—the one with my scar—and I felt a bolt of lightning shoot through me again. He didn't say anything, but I could have sworn he noticed it, too.

* * *

Some time later, we made our way back to the pub where we had left our friends, taking our time as neither of us was too keen for the night to be over. As we approached the doors of the dingy establishment, we hesitated with uncertainty, wondering if we had in fact left the gang at the other one next door. Both places were equally shabby, making it impossible to tell.

As if in answer to our silent question, the door flew open and out tumbled two drunken men who had clearly been booted from the bar for fighting. The one nearly knocked me over as he hit the ground hard, the security guard dusting off his hands and shaking his head in the doorway as he watched the man's flailing limbs attempt to find solid ground. I stood with my mouth open as Seamus caught me from behind. Just beyond the doorway were our friends, plainly watching in awe as they sat in the aftermath of the brawl indoors.

And then, as if nothing had happened at all, the one man picked up the other by his elbow and they strode off into the night, singing and joking like they were old friends.

"Typical Irish bar fight," Seamus shrugged, leading me back through the door.

CHAPTER 8

MOTHER NATURE'S WILL

*I*t was dark.

For some reason, I felt that the air was thicker than normal and I took deep, dragging breaths, as if I were inhaling and exhaling in slow motion.

He pressed me against the door with the force of his full body weight and told me to be quiet, his hand above my head. He was significantly taller than me, of course, so I didn't dare move. Unable to meet his gaze, I fixated on the tattoo on his forearm, again extremely curious as to what it was.

"Seamus—" I began in a whisper.

"I said houl yer whisht, woman!" he said severely, eyes darting around the room anxiously.

He looked more rugged than the version of him that I knew. A shadow of dark facial hair lined his jaw and his chocolate-amber waves were wildly unkempt. I was startled by his sudden ferocity in both words and appearance. Startled, but not afraid.

"They're looking for ye."

Before I could inquire further, he took my hand and started down the hall with the stealth of a jungle cat. There were books everywhere. But which library was this? I thought I recognized it, but not entirely. Was it Trinity College? Or were we back in Coral Gables at The U, the place where my father had spent so many years of his career? The shelves shape-shifted before my eyes, transitioning from the rich cherry of ancient academia to the stark white of luxurious American modernity.

"Where are we going?" I finally asked as we rounded yet another corner. I was unable to recall how I'd gotten here.

He turned to face me and brought me into the shadow near one of the tall windows. I resisted the urge to look outside of it, knowing whatever he had to say now was much more important than identifying the scenery around me.

"They're comin' fer ye," he repeated, the Norn Iron features of his accent even more prominent than usual. Maybe that happened when he was anxious. "I dunno why, but it's somethin' to do with yer family."

"Family," I repeated blankly. "But I don't have any family."

"Aye, but ye do," he said, his voice low with urgency. He grasped me tightly by the shoulders. "Jasmine, I need ye to listen to me. I'll follow ye, but I can't come with ye just yet."

"Why not?" was the question that left my mouth, but what I had wanted to say was, "*What are you talking about?*". For some reason, my brain didn't seem connected to my vocal cords.

"I will come find ye, I swear, but ye have to go now without me," he said earnestly, and he pulled me into him.

I kissed him deeply while he lifted me with ease in one arm, shoving the scrolls of parchment that were on the table behind us out of the way. They fell to the floor with a faint clatter that made us both jump, but we didn't stop. What were they? I wondered faintly. Maps?

He laid me backwards and kissed the base of my throat, his hands surprisingly warm as they slid up my shirt. He explored me in the dark and I yielded entirely, suddenly fearing that this would be the last time I would ever see him.

In fact, I somehow knew that something was about to change

that would drive us apart before we were ever together, but what was it? We were supposed to be hiding from someone, weren't we? I seemed to be experiencing short-term memory loss... nothing made sense from one moment to the next.

He quickly undid the top button and zipper of my jeans in one swift motion, dropping to his knees on the floor of the library. Whatever intensity his fear of being discovered had held, it was now clearly overcome by something else more powerful. He slid the denim down past my knees and brushed his thumb up my inner thigh, sending a visible shiver through my entire body.

"I want ye so badly," he said, the warmth of his breath tickling me gently as my anticipation became insurmountable. His hands were on my outer thighs, pulling me closer to him as I neared the edge of the table.

His tongue grazed me just above where I wanted him to go, and I begged him silently to just do it already.

He then paused and looked up at me from between my legs, green eyes swimming with angst and regret.

"Fuck," he muttered. "There's no time."

"But why?" I asked, my suspense now poisoned by confusion and disappointment.

"They're going to take ye."

"Where?"

He let out an exasperated sigh. "Into the sea."

I woke up sweating; fearful and confused by my inability to comprehend what my twisted subconscious had created. The consistent recurrence of dreams in which I was being hunted was growing old. I now almost longed for the nightmares where everyone I knew was dead, because it was closer to the reality I had already learned to live with when I was awake.

Worst of all, I was plagued with guilt that I had dreamt of a man going down on me that wasn't Matt.

* * *

THE CAR RIDE wrought a relentless inquisition from the others, but I had been expecting it given the duration of my moonlit walk with Seamus from the night before. However, I was surprised to find that the interrogation was led by Kiana of all people. Usually my ally in the matter of keeping things private that were supposed to remain private, I scowled at her in the rear view mirror of the rental car.

"Are you really not going to tell us anything?" she begged me exasperatedly.

"Seriously, we've given you your space but now we're dying for details," Marissa added with emphasis.

I had always been extremely discrete when it came to romantic interests, a habit that was undoubtedly rooted in having no mother to confide in when it came to amateur crushes of my formative years. Raj had not been severely over-protective, but rather painfully awkward and embarrassed when any topic of men crept into our conversations.

It was only when I was a grown adult and living on my own that I had disclosed any information regarding my private life to my father, and that of course had been when I was very certain of the man in question. Even then, my hands had broken into a violent sweat when I prepared to mention that I had been seeing someone consistently for almost five months. But my anxiety was nothing compared to my father's. Raj nearly dropped the phone upon hearing that his daughter's boyfriend was seven years older than herself.

"GOOD LORD, Jazz, what's a grown man interested in a young girl like you for anyway?" he exclaimed.

Even through the phone and several time zones away, I could

picture him pouring a glass of port in distress while rubbing his temples.

"Gee, thanks, dad," I replied flatly.

He sighed after a long pause.

"Honey, you are incredible, and I know that. But you're barely out of college!"

"And I'm a year older than I should be at this stage," I pointed out. "Because *you* insisted on holding me back a year."

He let out a defiant huff.

"Well, Portuguese and American schools don't exactly have identical curriculums," he murmured.

It had been upon our return from the Iberian Peninsula that Raj had made the decision to have me repeat the ninth grade. A brutally inconvenient year to live twice, I still found it impossible to remember the beginning of high school without over-whelming bitterness.

"I learned more over there than I ever did here," I shot back, recalling the years of visiting historical sites and museums on weekends. "So there-I'm older, *and* I'm more mature. You always said so."

"You're also excellent at engaging in behavior that ages your poor father," he said, but I heard the resignation in his voice. "Well, alright, what's this *Matt* like?"

No, my aversion to spilling the details of my private life was hardly unwarranted. Even with my girlfriends, I had always erred on the side of caution.

"Well you didn't go back to his room," said Kristen conclusively. "Harry told us that much."

"Jesus, Kristen, I met him two days ago," I said, feigning outrage as the small voice in my head reminded me of my fiery dream. I shifted in my seat and looked away from her.

Kiana laughed loudly while Marissa turned around from the front seat and spoke in earnest.

"But Jazz, we really just want to hear more because we're excited for you."

I caught a glimpse of Kristen and Kiana's identical troublesome grins. They were both well aware that Marissa's genuine good-naturedness was fully disarming. If *she* were the one to ask, I would feel guilty for not answering her.

I sighed in exasperation and told them an abbreviated version of my walk and talk with Seamus, loosely alluding to the fact that we had discussed some of the less pleasant parts of my recent past. I was grateful that my friends had enough tact not to press for more on *that* particular subject, though they shamelessly clung to my every other word.

"How was the kiss?" asked Kristen with a raised brow. "I feel like it was hot."

"It was," I said simply.

This statement was met with the raucous outburst that I had anticipated, but it made me blush furiously nonetheless. I laughed incredulously as my friends went on to gush about everything from Seamus' rich, dark red hair to his thick accent. I disagreed with none of it, remembering the roughness of his hands as they wove through my thick mane of hair, and I recalled his dominating nature in my dream. I wondered if that was actually how he was when he-

"So what happens next?" Kristen asked seriously. "I mean, are you guys going to like-date?"

I paused, coming back to reality.

"How can we? I live in Tampa and he lives in London, you know?" I said with slight dejectedness as I admitted the unlikelihood to myself.

Still, the connection had been there, and we had made a mutual agreement that we were going to pursue one another beyond the extent of this trip. I anticipated our final meeting tonight, and my vivid dream had admittedly intensified my desire to explore the depths of our chemistry while I still had the chance.

Kiana put her hand on my arm. "Remember what I said the other night? If it's the right person, you'll make it work."

The statement rang so much sweeter in my ears now that I had spent more time with him. I nodded silently as the others launched into a discussion on the logistics of moving overseas, but as the conversation progressed, I felt the hole of guilt gradually opening up within my chest, pestering me like a fly I could not swat away.

"Jazz I really think this could work," Kiana said encouragingly, reaching to touch my shoulder. I weakly smiled back at her, but quickly resumed staring out the window.

Unable to quiet my mind, I begged for them to change the subject and at last, Marissa obliged.

After what felt like an eternity, we began to see the faint outline of charming, pastel buildings that faced the sea. I looked out the window, hoping that the clouds looming over the Atlantic were much further off the coast than they appeared. Nevertheless, the lightly overcast sky seemed relatively unthreatening for the time being, and the view of the Cliffs would undoubtedly still be fabulous.

"We have arrived in the bustling city of *Doolin*," said Kristen, doing nothing to hide the sarcasm in her voice.

Tiny as it was, I spotted one or two small establishments where we were certain to grab lunch after our journey. My stomach rumbled with dissatisfaction as it digested the singular banana I had scarfed down in the hotel lobby that morning. There were several cars parked on the street that lined the low stone wall where we pulled up; a promising sign that the weather had not deterred any of the other tourists, either.

"How long of a walk did you say it was, Jazz?" asked Marissa, eyeing the misty road that led along the shoreline of cliffs.

"Not far," I said reassuringly. "I promise it will only take us half an hour…but it will be way better than just driving directly up to the visitor's center."

"Where would be the fun in that?" asked Kiana sarcastically.

I rolled my eyes as I knew the girls were less than thrilled at the prospect of a hike on the way to the Cliffs, but it was really more like a leisurely stroll. I had done some research on other ways to see the Cliffs aside from just driving up to them straight away, which in my opinion took away from the authenticity of it all. I preferred to imagine myself as a 16th century explorer, rummaging my way through the green pastures at the edge of a cliff that dropped off into nothingness, rather than an American tourist with an iPhone.

Kristen locked the car, and we started off on the rocky pathway. I was immediately taken by the incredible landscape that had occupied my daydreams for years. I held back nostalgic tears as it reminded me instantly of Portugal. Although the two countries' climates could not have been further from one another in likeness, the massive cliffs that dropped into the sea were nearly identical in their magnificence.

I wondered how the main viewpoint at the Cliffs could surpass what was already before my eyes. Even at the start of our path, the massive rocks were littered haphazardly among one another, creating a jagged maze of black and brown which kept the crashing waves at bay, demonstrating the pure might of Mother Nature. A permanent light mist hung above our heads, but the visibility of the water beyond was crystal clear. In lieu of Portugal's romantic aqua waters, these cliffs descended into tumultuous waves of black and gray, breathtaking in their own fearsome way.

There was plenty to see on land as well. Cows grazed lazily in the pastures and came right up to the fences to greet us, their pink tongues flopping lazily from side to side as they chewed at their endless supply of grass. Perhaps it was the briny air that surrounded us, but I was not bothered by the smell of their large piles of manure in the slightest. I greeted them each in turn with a gentle pat and smiled. I became suddenly aware that the cows belonged to someone, and I should probably refrain from taking it upon myself to pet them without asking permission. I withdrew my hand.

"Sorry, buddy," I muttered.

"Look at that building over there!" Marissa called.

To refer to it as a building was more than generous. It looked to be a severely dilapidated ruin that barely held its shape to the point where none of us could even determine what it had once been. Was it an old church? No, surely it was too small for that. The walls seemed to crumble before us and I suspected one large gust of wind would have finished it off. I made a mental note to research what it possibly could be upon our return to the hotel.

"Are we going the right way?" asked Kristen, her boot sinking into a deep pile of mud.

"I'm no navigator but it appears there is only *one* way," said Kiana sarcastically, gesturing toward the edge of the path that dropped into the ocean. "Unless you'd prefer to swim and meet us there?"

We all laughed, even Kristen, and continued at our leisurely pace. I looked nervously behind us as the dark cloud out at sea continued to hover menacingly in the distance. At least it wasn't getting closer, I thought with a sigh.

The salty air felt incredible on my skin. I closed my eyes and breathed deeply, feeling a wild urge to climb down the rocks and walk along the shore just to be closer to the waves. I only wished that Matt could have experienced it with me. I wistfully imagined my silent observations were being relayed to him, and it made me feel peaceful.

"I think we should be able to see the Cliffs just around the corner up there," said Kristen, who was growing impatient as she sloshed back and forth in the never ending puddles that lined the trail.

"Gray was probably not the best choice of color," Marissa said, pointing to Kristen's boots that had a thick layer of brown mud already caking over on the toes.

She groaned in regretful agreement as she trudged along, leaping over the intermittent pools. Her acrobatic dance around the inevitable floor of lava was much to my amusement as I followed comfortably in my own waterproof, black Chelseas.

At last, the first glimpse of the miraculous Cliffs of Moher was upon us. We were still at quite a distance, but we all agreed it was the optimal spot for photos.

"All the tourists will be up that way," I said as we snapped our perfectly undisturbed shots. I stood with my back to the water as a massive gust of wind blew my hair behind me in a dramatic sweep of pitch black.

"That turned out so well!" exclaimed Kristen from behind the phone. "You're going to love it."

We marched along the remainder of the trail, each of us silently agreeing to pick up our pace. My theory regarding the volume of tourists was proven to be correct instantly. There were no less than five tour buses of people crowding around the main cliff's edge behind the visitor's center, leaning over to take photos and pose with the breathtaking scenery around them. The waves crashed against the shore as if putting on a show for their audience, breaking apart the loose rocks that lined the bottom of the landmark.

"This is magical," breathed Marissa.

I peered over the edge and nodded. The entire place certainly had a mystical feel about it. I wondered if the water here ever calmed to a gentle breeze or if it existed in a permanent state of catastrophic destruction.

It was certainly getting colder by the minute. The dark cloud that had followed us along the shore now towered above our heads, threatening to explode with rain at any moment.

Marissa eyed the tour bus longingly and I bit my lip with guilt, well aware of the long wait we would have to endure indoors before it was pleasant enough to walk back. Luckily, it was still relatively early in the day.

"Can we head inside for a minute?" asked Kristen, shivering and eyeing the tourists through the window enviously.

As if on cue, a warning crack of thunder rang through the air and a misty rain followed, prompting the majority of the observers to sprint for cover indoors.

"You guys go ahead," I said. "I want to walk on a bit further if anyone wants to join."

I looked hopefully at all three of my friends as their eyes darted between one another under their now tightly pulled hoods.

"No thanks," said Marissa, rubbing her arms furiously. "I need a warm drink."

Kiana, whether it was out of guilt or genuine interest, agreed to stay outside with me.

"Only for another few minutes, though," she said as we sloshed along the path toward the edge. "As soon as it starts to pour, I'm outta here."

We journeyed in peaceful silence for a few moments, arriving quickly at what seemed to be the end of the path. Once there, we stopped and I looked out at the sea appreciatively. My mind had been so full of loud thoughts over the past few days, and I ironically found that the rough pull of the sea quieted them. There was nothing to do but enjoy what nature had afforded me to experience.

"James asked what our plans were tonight," Kiana said at last, kicking pebbles off the ledge. Her words shook me out of my tranquil state as I had almost forgotten my friend was there at all.

"What?" I asked absently.

She leaned in closer to me and ducked her head in a fruitless attempt to dodge the rain.

"James," Kiana repeated. "He said they have tickets to some boat cruise tonight and wanted to see if we would join. I'm sure Seamus already told you."

"Oh," I said absently. "Yeah."

Of course Seamus had mentioned something of the sort last night. It would be the last time I'd see him for a while, of course, but it oddly seemed trivial now as the scales of my emotions alternated once more. I stared out at the sea, suddenly feeling very far away from who I had been the last few days.

Noticing my misty gaze, Kiana spoke up once more. "Yeah, you know, they obviously had a great time with us again last night."

"Did James reach out to you?" I asked, only mildly interested. I never took my eyes off the waves.

"No, he texted Kristen," she said slowly.

I looked up, surprised, and spoke more sharply than I had intended. "So *you* three have already talked about it, then?"

Kiana shrugged innocently. "Not really, she just asked if I thought you would be okay with that."

"Why didn't she just ask me herself?" I grumbled. I kicked a loose rock off the cliffs, watching it tumble in slow motion until it disappeared into the blackness.

"She thought you might-I mean, we weren't sure how last night went since you didn't tell us until this morning," she said, stammering slightly. "And you barely told us anything, to be honest. You haven't seemed particularly excited to talk about him at all, actually..." Her voice trailed off.

"What do you mean you weren't sure how it went?" I snapped, startled by my own inclination to suddenly push buttons. "How did you *think* it would go?"

I pictured them all talking about me amongst themselves-as they likely had many times in the last year-and a sudden, hot surge of anger pulsed through me. They probably assumed I had started bawling my eyes out about Matt, scaring Seamus away.

Kiana stared at me, evidently confused by my demeanor.

"I didn't know, Jazz, that's what I'm saying," she said slowly. "I couldn't read you. The day before you seemed like you wanted nothing to do with them, so I wasn't sure how much had changed last night."

"I never said I wanted nothing to do with them," I muttered defensively, brushing the wet hair out of my eyes as the wind began to pick up.

"Well you didn't seem too thrilled they were going to be in Galway at the same time as us," said Kiana, her voice rising. "When they told us back in Dublin. Remember?"

Her tone was pointed. She was speaking in the same defensive manner that I had grown accustomed to after being friends with her for over a decade. It wasn't entirely unwarranted, but it irritated me, nonetheless.

"I just thought we were on a girls' trip, that's all," I said.

"We *are* on a girls trip!" Kiana exclaimed.

"Doesn't seem like it," I said, kicking another rock with more force. The childish tone of my own voice was impossible to ignore, but equally as impossible to subdue.

Kiana looked at me incredulously.

"What are you talking about? Come on, Jazz," she said, shaking her head.

The angry waves below seemed to encourage my behavior. I felt the uncontrollable, unpredictable nature of my self-control beginning to boil over the surface.

"I just didn't realize this entire trip would revolve around all of you being so desperate for a bunch of random guys!"

I knew I had gone too far, but I was too heated to care. The wind howled loudly, rising to match (or compete with) the volume of my own voice.

Kiana stood up straight and rocked back on her heels, clearly taken aback by my sudden outburst.

"Ouch," she said quietly.

I turned around, annoyed that my moment of peace had turned south so quickly. I felt guilty for lashing out at my friend, and I spoke my next words slowly in an attempt to soften them.

"Seamus is just-entertaining. You know I'm not actually interested in meeting anyone right now."

"Oh, we know," said Kiana with a faint eye roll that she instantly regretted when she saw my warning glare.

Her emphasis on *we* did nothing to quell my embarrassment-fueled fury, either. Any statement that solidified my friends' collective worry and, consequently, their pity toward me was a reminder I did not need.

The wind began to roar as I stepped toward her.

"I'm sorry, do you have a problem with the fact that I'm not ready for this yet?" I said coldly.

"Jazz, of course not," said Kiana over a crack of thunder. "But you're allowed to have fun! And Seamus seems like a great guy!"

"Matt is dead and I have nothing to remember him by except the ring he never even got to give to me himself," I spat. "And you think some random person I met at a bar in Ireland being a *'good guy'* is relevant to me right now?"

I felt like I was listening to another person speak in my voice. The words were too irrational to have been my own. It seemed like all of my emotional progress from last night (and the months prior) had been swept out to sea in the wake of what I knew was a pointless argument with my friend. But simply knowing I would regret my words later did not mean I had control over them now. The water blasted against the rocks, egging me on again.

"Do you really think Matt would want you to be like this?' Kiana shot back at me.

"It's like you're resigned to being miserable for the rest of your life and Jesus Christ, Jazz, you're not even thirty years old!"

The wind and rain both came to a momentary halt and I said nothing. Kiana took a deep breath and continued at a normal volume.

"Matt would be happy for you if you moved on in your life with someone who appreciated you! He-he would want this kind of a fresh start for you."

She was breathless as the two of us stood face-to-face, the space between us wider than the Atlantic.

"You do not have a clue what Matt would have wanted," I said with quiet severity that signaled the end of the conversation. "So just please *shut the fuck up*."

The words stung me as much as they did her. I shook my head dismissively and stared at the ground, unable to look at her.

"I-" Kiana began, and then she let out a sigh of resignation.

I heard her footsteps squishing in the muddy grass, trailing off as she headed back to the visitor center. I turned around to say something, but she had already disappeared inside.

Regretting my behavior but not ready to apologize, I continued to stubbornly walk along the cliffs alone. Nearly all of the tourists had retreated inside as the rain was turning to a significant storm, and the sky was darkening with each minute that passed. The clouds above seemed to shadow my every movement, suffocating me in the dark misery that I had created for myself.

Before I knew it, hot tears were rolling down my face. I let out an uncontrollable sob that I had been keeping at bay for weeks. I was shaking violently from the cold, wet air, but I knew even the warmth of the indoors would not bring me comfort.

"Why did you have to take everything from me?" I shouted over the cliff before I could stop myself.

I closed my eyes as the rain began to soak through to my feet and overwhelming anger bordering madness took over my thoughts. I was angry with my friends for discussing plans behind my back, but more angry with myself that *I* had been the one to create an environment where they felt they needed to do so. Angry that I had no family, but more angry that I could not seem to put the tragedy behind me. *Why* could I not grieve and move on with my life like everyone else learns to do?

A burst of white lightning accompanied by a thunderous boom made me jump. I momentarily lost my balance and tumbled backward onto the wet grass.

"Shit," I said as I felt the mud seeping through the seat of my pants.

I brushed it away as best I could, leaving my hands too filthy to wipe my tear-streaked eyes. Even my newfound miraculous eyesight was challenged by the mist that now surrounded me. Sobered and humbled by my moment of clumsiness, I rose to return to the visitor's center, defeated and (while not wholly eager to do so) prepared to apologize to Kiana.

But as soon as I stood, a strange glimmer in the water below caught my eye.

I squinted to examine the black waves, but the sparkle had vanished. Against my better judgment, I dropped to my hands and knees and peered over the edge.

'*It was the lightning,*' I thought to myself as I scanned the lapping waves.

But no-no it wasn't. The shimmer suddenly appeared again, like a slithering snake beneath the surface of the black water. Even without the illumination of the lightning, I could see an iridescent glow that shifted from white to green to silver before my eyes. I thought it could be an animal, but how would I be able to see that from up here? Only after seeing it flash across the water again did I realize that it was familiar.

Unable to stop myself, I extended my left hand toward the water. I was sure the glittering shape was something I could grasp, even from all the way up here...I simply had to. I didn't know what would happen if I didn't pursue it, but I thought faintly that I might die.

I remembered this feeling. I had felt this way about something in the water before. I knew it hadn't ended well, but it was no longer within my control to avoid it. It was calling me.

A roll of thunder echoed through the sky and shook the entire western shoreline of Ireland. I lost my feeble grip, slipping from the edge of the most treacherous cliffs in the Atlantic Ocean before my mind could process what was happening. I seemed to be watching myself from afar in slow motion-a helpless rag doll tumbling from the sturdy greenery above and into the depths of the savage sea below.

No scream escaped my lungs as I hit the water with a deafening thud. I immediately registered in my mind that the impact should have felt much harder than it did. And then my world went black.

CHAPTER 9

INVESTIGATION

"*I* can't believe she said that to you," Kristen said, sinking back in her chair.

Her mug of hot chocolate sat untouched, having gone from scalding hot to ice cold as she missed the window of drinkability entirely while listening to Kiana's recount of the argument outside. Only a few moments had passed since she had come bursting through the door of the visitor's center, hair as wet as her eyes that were full of tears.

"It was so unlike her," Kiana replied, shaking her head in dismay as she recovered her nerves. She had certainly had an argument here and there with Jasmine over the years, but nothing like this. "I've never seen her snap like that."

"Well, that's certainly more commonplace for her these days," Marissa said, pushing her glasses up her nose. She bit her lip before continuing. "Her temper has been very unpredictable."

The group fell silent as each of them dreaded the inevitably awkward atmosphere that would linger amongst them on their lengthy walk back to the car once Jasmine returned. Kiana was willing to accept the apology that she was sure would come, but the sting of her friend's words would remain.

The rain outside had subsided and been replaced with a cold fog that obstructed their view of the sea, prompting the tour guides to call it a day. Without a photo opportunity, there was hardly much else with which they could entertain their patrons. One by one, the tables began to clear as the buses outside the visitor center fired up their engines.

"Should I go get her?" asked Marissa, craning her neck to get a better look out of the window. It was fruitless; there was nothing to be seen but an ominous fog. "I'm surprised she hasn't come back yet."

"Yes, it's probably best if it's you that talks to her first," said Kristen. "She doesn't listen to us."

Marissa bundled up in her jacket, tucking her auburn hair beneath the collar as she disappeared into the mist outside.

Kiana watched her go with an absent stare, her mind far away as she began to feel the ebbs of regret eating away at her. Jasmine had been her best friend since childhood, and she should have been more understanding of what she had been going through. Having never lost so much as a pet guinea pig, Kiana was hardly one to understand a significant death in the family. The more she reflected upon how she had treated Jasmine over the past year, the worse she felt for her impatience.

"You guys," said Marissa urgently, bursting through the door with alarm painted across her face. "She's not out there!"

"What do you mean she's not out there?" Kristen asked cautiously as Kiana shot to her feet.

Marissa shook her head and threw her hands in the air.

"I mean, I walked all the way down to the end and back-both ways-and there's no one there."

The few remaining tourists in the building began to look up in curiosity as Marissa's voice had risen above normal conversational volume while cracking in fear.

"Maybe she went to the bathroom?" Kristen said doubtfully, and Marissa shook her head.

Kiana darted across the room and approached the two young men working at the front desk. She pulled her phone out of her pocket and showed them the picture of Jasmine that she had taken from their walk not even two hours ago.

"Has this woman walked through here?" she asked.

They both shook their heads.

"No, ma'am," said the one on the left, clearly alarmed by her concern. "Not that I know of."

Kristen and Marissa rushed to Kiana's side, Kristen pushing her way to the front and tossing her long hair back with authority. Kiana stepped aside, thinking it best that the most intimidating of the three of them continue the inquisition.

"Look again," Kristen demanded, pointing at the phone. "You swear you haven't seen her in or around this building?"

Her voice would have come across as accusatory to anyone who didn't know her, but Kiana knew it was her inflection of fear.

Evidently, they had caused somewhat of a disturbance as an older woman who looked more like a manager came striding over to them, her face crinkled in worry.

"Is everything alright over here?" she asked, looking between the three distraught women.

They explained that Jasmine had gone missing, and after relentlessly refusing to wait for her to turn up, the manager at last agreed to call the police. It took them far too long to arrive as far as any of the friends were concerned, and when they did, it was hardly reassuring.

"You left her out there alone after this argument, did ye, then?" asked the newly arrived Officer Kelly, his eyes narrowing suspiciously upon Kiana.

"Yes," she said, refusing to break eye contact. "What exactly are you suggesting?"

Of course she knew where his mind was headed-two women fighting at the edge of a cliff and one of them disappears. *Or was she pushed?* Kiana's stomach turned with revulsion at the thought.

Another tourist sitting nearby had been intently eavesdropping on the questioning and piped up as she heard this response.

"I saw zees girl you speak of outside by 'erself, walking long after zees one (she pointed to Kiana) 'ad come back eenside," the woman said in a thick French accent. Her husband nodded furiously in agreement, corroborating her story. The woman then tossed her hair over her shoulder in irritation for nothing other than her holiday having been interrupted.

"You should bee lookeeng for zees girl instead of accusing her friends an' wasting everyone's time."

Kiana nodded appreciatively, grateful for the stranger's nosiness in addition to the general intimidating demeanor of the French.

Apparently the second officer agreed with her that the next best step was to actually take action and search; he began to walk the perimeter of the building while radioing in for some kind of backup. Kiana looked to her friends to see that Marissa was trembling in fear and she reached her arm around her in comfort.

"It's alright," she said, watching Officer Kelly join his colleague outdoors. "We'll find her."

They waited for what felt like another hour and a detective entered the building this time. The tourists who remained looked up curiously, and Kiana felt a stab of annoyance at the spectacle this was becoming. The regret she felt now plagued her mind. She should have just turned back around, told Jasmine she was sorry, and brought her safely inside. What could have happened to her?

Detective Murphy then introduced himself to the group. Whether he was great at pretending or simply good at his job, he did not seem to share the suspicious sentiments of Officer Kelly. However, his assumptions were much worse.

"The security cameras caught nothing, unfortunately," he said bitterly, his mustache quivering. "Fog's too thick."

Kristen rolled her eyes. "Of course," she muttered.

Detective Murphy nodded in agreement. "Did your friend-Jasmine-do ye have any reason to believe she may have run away?"

The three friends looked at him blankly.

"Run away?" Kiana repeated, having heard this term only used in reference to stubborn, small children. How on earth could Jasmine, a twenty-eight year old woman, be classified as a "runaway"?

"Yes," the detective said, his eyes hard with the look of someone who had seen much stranger occurrences than a tourist who chose to disappear on vacation.

"I'm asking because the patrol in the water hasn't yet recovered a body. Which isn't entirely uncommon given the strength of these waves, mind ye."

A sharp chill ran through Kiana's spine at the callousness in which he mentioned the possibility of Jasmine's corpse. Having had no time to think of anything but finding her, the theory that she might be dead rang with painful sobriety in her ears. There was no possible way.

"How far could she really get on foot, though?" asked Marissa incredulously, her logical mind beginning to recover from shock. "I mean look at where we are."

Detective Murphy nodded in agreement once again.

"Correct," was all he said in a darkened tone that unsettled them all.

He sat in contemplation for a moment, watching the officers patrol up and down the shoreline in what they all now seemed to be deeming a useless effort. The sun had peeked through the clouds in the late afternoon, but another dark storm cloud hovered over the sea beyond, promising a secondary shower of rain.

"These waves are mighty powerful," he said at last, sighing. "We may not find a body for days."

Kiana flinched at his choice of words again. "Do-do you think she fell?"

"There aren't too many possibilities," the detective said carefully. He looked at the friends and, apparently deciding against sparing their feelings, finished his thought. "She either fell or jumped."

Kiana clapped her hand over her mouth in horror before she could stop herself, taken aback by his bluntness. Kristen and Marissa, however, exchanged a glance that lasted no more than a second, but it was not lost on the wily detective. He looked between them knowingly.

"Do ye have any reason to believe your friend may have committed suicide?" he asked sharply. His words pierced through Kiana's chest like a knife. She could hardly believe she was hearing such outlandish conclusions after such a short period of time.

"Of course not!" she blurted out, but Detective Murphy wasn't looking at her.

Instead, he had narrowed in on the other two. Marissa and Kristen shifted uncomfortably in place but did not respond. Their reaction (or lack of one) was enough for the detective, and he nodded curtly with understanding. Kiana felt entirely dismissed, but she had no strength to continue to argue.

"We'll continue the search," the detective said at last. "Do ye three have a hotel near here tonight?"

They shook their heads and Kristen explained that their car was in Doolin and they were spending the night in Galway.

"Not a problem," the detective said, and he arranged an escort to their car and promised to call them with any new developments.

Kiana, while relatively surprised they had been released,

noticed that Detective Murphy got their hotel information and confirmed they would be in Galway for at least another day. She supposed "going down to the station" was not a universal next step in every country's law enforcement handbook, and felt grateful for not being treated like a suspect. After all, the French tourists had stuck around long enough to repeat their statement to him.

* * *

"How the security cameras caught nothing is beyond me," Kristen said angrily from behind the wheel.

Detective Murphy had offered a full police escort back to their hotel, but she had insisted she was fine to drive them all. Watching her hands shake on the steering wheel as they shot through the dark, winding roads, Kiana wondered if that had been the wisest decision.

They were silent for most of the drive, no one daring to speak. The tension between the three of them was nearly unbearable as the detective's words regarding potential suicide burned in Kiana's ears.

"Why did we bring her here?" Marissa finally whispered, tears silently falling down her face from the front seat. "We should have known she wasn't ready. We rushed her...we-"

"She was going through so much more than we could have understood," said Kristen quietly, reaching her hand across to pat Marissa's shoulder as she buried her face in her hands. "We couldn't have helped her." Her voice faltered and she fell silent.

Kiana scoffed from the backseat angrily, unable to restrain herself. Kristen snapped her gaze to the rear view mirror.

"What is your issue?" she asked sharply.

"Stop that!" Kiana exclaimed as she caught her gaze. "Stop talking like this was on purpose! Jasmine did not jump off of that cliff! She would never do that."

Marissa and Kristen exchanged a look and Marissa turned around to take Kiana's hand, but she swiftly snatched it away.

"I know we don't think that she'd be capable of that," Marissa said slowly, her eyes red behind her glasses that were still streaked with poorly wiped raindrops.

"But Kiana, *you* haven't seen her the way we have for the last year." Her voice seemed to have a hint of defiance in it that took Kiana by surprise.

"Oh yeah? Exactly how much have *you* seen her?" Kiana shot back fiercely, anger boiling in her chest. "Because I'm pretty sure that you dragging her on this trip was the first time either of you had even checked on her in months."

How dare they accuse *her*, Jasmine's best friend since childhood, of not checking in on her? These two were just her superficial, surface-level friends from her stupid sorority and knew nothing about who Jasmine really was. Kiana's heart pounded with resiliency. No, *she* was the one who knew her. Kristen opened her mouth to shoot back what was undoubtedly an aggressive comeback, but Marissa silenced her.

"You're right," she said, surprising both of the other parties. "We haven't checked in as much as we should have. Let's just wait until we hear from Detective Murphy before we come to any conclusions ourselves."

Marissa spoke with finality and authority that was wildly out of character for her, but Kiana nodded in agreement.

Though she knew Jasmine better than anyone and refused to believe this could have been anything but a horrible accident, a tiny voice in Kiana's head told her she might be wrong. She had, after all, not been to visit her once during this extremely difficult year. All of their phone conversations now seemed like nothing more than pathetic attempts to clear her own conscience. She should have tried harder, searched for more depth in her friend's answers about how she was feeling. How could she have been so stupid to think that a *vacation* was all Jasmine needed?

They arrived back in Galway as the barely visible sun was setting. The front desk agent greeted the three of them warmly as they dragged their feet into the lobby, oblivious to the horrific day they had just endured. They made their way slowly through the small crowd of people huddled around the bar and went straight to the elevators, each one of them feeling far too drained and sick to eat. Sleep called to them as it was their only relief; a notion that Kiana realized-painfully-had likely been very familiar to Jasmine this past year as well.

Kristen's phone buzzed loudly, breaking their silence of nearly two hours.

"Oh, it's James," she said lifelessly, her voice barely a whisper.

Kiana's heart surged with pain, remembering the source of her argument with Jasmine.

"Who cares," she said exasperatedly, hoping Kristen had the sense not to suggest they see the guys again right now.

"No, I assure you I don't," Kristen said severely, tossing her phone in her jacket's pocket carelessly.

All three of them individually revisited in their minds the two evenings prior, the laughs and lighthearted fun now feeling worlds away. It was hard to imagine that twenty-four hours ago, Jasmine had been right there in the elevator with them, seemingly happier than she had been in a year...and now she was gone.

As much as Kiana wanted to believe her friend was still out there, waiting to be found, the hour of numbness had faded to sober realization. The Cliffs were at the end of the world. There was nowhere else she could be.

CHAPTER 10

INTRIGUE

Kiana was the first to wake, though she could hardly have said she slept. Her dreams were riddled with horrifying visions of death, loss, and falling from stomach-turning heights. The final terror of her subconscious that wrenched open her eyes was forgotten immediately upon waking, but the haunting aura hovered around her like a black cloud.

Making her way to the window, she avoided looking at the empty bed or Jasmine's open suitcase on the floor. The street outside was still, but the clock at her bedside showed it was nearly time for the world to awake. The sudden, desperate need to flee the room where her friend's ghost was lingering came over her and she swept out the door.

The elevator opened to the lobby where she was surprised to see several people had already gathered. The smell of fresh coffee wafted through the hallway and Kiana followed it to a cart where she helped herself to a large, steaming cup. An extra sugar cube, because why not.

A large velvet armchair that sat relatively secluded in the window seemed to beckon to her and she sat down at once, facing the large flatscreen that hung above the cozy fireplace. A commercial for fresh Irish butter ended and the screen cut to a scene that made her freeze.

Caution tape, the Cliffs of Moher, and a reporter in a snug jacket, her teeth chattering in the rain. She spoke in the strange way that all reporters do-with blunt inflection and emphasis in all the wrong places as her thick accent wove a terrifying tale to her viewers. Kiana listened intently, mesmerized by the factual rendition of her own nightmare.

"A terrible accident occurred here just yesterday," the reporter said, her brown eyes twinkling with emotion. "A group of four American tourists were visiting the Cliffs of Moher when one of them suddenly went missing. Suspected to have potentially fallen from the treacherous cliffs, Jasmine Atarga has not been seen since around two-thirty yesterday afternoon."

Footage from the night prior was next. Kiana and her friends hovered unseen in the distant background as of course they had declined to speak to anyone from the media. In fact, no one had really asked. She suspected Detective Murphy was to thank for that. Perhaps the Irish thought it in bad taste given the circumstances.

"As of now, we are actively looking for a missing person." Officer Kelly spoke into the microphone, his thick, auburn mustache drenched with rain-or sweat. "We have confirmation that she was left alone at the edge of one of the Cliffs, but her body has not been recovered at this time."

"Left alone?" probed the reporter, angling for a nugget of excitement that made Kiana ill.

The officer nodded. "She had gotten into an altercation with one of the other women in their group." Why on *earth* would he say that? Was it necessary to sensationalize absolutely *everything*?

The screen cut back to the reporter in real-time, the sky behind her still misty and foggy, but brighter with the morning sun peeking behind the clouds. Her lips were pursed in a serious way.

"Officer Kelly confirmed that the other woman is not a person of interest at this time. As of this morning, they have still not recovered a body and County Clare police are still actively searching for Jasmine Atarga. If anyone has any information..."

Kiana drowned out the voice as a picture of Jasmine, smiling and laughing came up on the screen. She stared for a moment at the photo she had taken herself before snatching the remote from the table and shutting the TV off entirely. A crack of thunder outside made her jump, and she looked out the window to see it was just as dreary in Galway today as it had been at the Cliffs yesterday.

She sat back in her chair, cupping her coffee in both hands in order to prevent them from shaking. Should she call Detective Murphy? He had promised to reach out to her if anything had changed, but that was more than twelve hours ago. Surely the lack of information on the news could not be the full extent of the truth...

As she gazed out at the street, Kiana saw a tall figure rushing down the sidewalk. His rich, dark red hair caught her eye as it was the singular splash of color amongst the myriad of grays that painted the sky and streets. She watched curiously as he approached the doors of the lobby where she sat, throwing them open while his hunter green raincoat dripped all over the pristine, white tile of the lobby.

"Can I help you sir?" came the voice of the front desk attendant, alarmed at the young man's sudden, disheveled appearance.

Despite his chaotic entrance, the man straightened up and stood with a look of utmost authority and confidence.

"Yes, I'm looking for-" he began.

Kiana jumped to her feet, nearly spilling her coffee.

"Seamus?" she asked, recognizing his voice.

He turned around and let out a sigh that indicated he was

relieved to see her. He waved in thanks to the front desk agent who smiled weakly as he watched the young man pad muddily across the tile and then onto the equally delicate carpet.

"What are you doing here?" Kiana asked.

"I came as soon as I-" he said. "We saw the news, boys a dear." He shook his head in dismay.

Kiana stared at him blankly for a brief moment. Then there was a slight quiver of her lip that was entirely uncontrollable, immediately followed by tears. They were not the aggressive, noisy tears, but rather the extremely tired tears that only come in the most unmanageable and overwhelming situations.

Unsure of what to do, Seamus did what any gentleman would do for a woman in distress. He went to prepare her a wee cup of tea.

He returned with the steaming mug, positioning the chair that sat across from Kiana so it faced the TV as he flicked through the channels for another news station. Kiana had no heart to tell him she did not wish to see anything else, but he seemed to have gotten the gist as he quickly reduced the volume to background noise. She waited for him to speak, having nothing to say herself.

"When Kristen messaged James last night of course we hadn't a clue why all of ye canceled," he said through his thick accent that had puzzled Kiana in the few days she had known him. British mingled with hints of his Irish roots, it seemed. "This morning we're all in the lobby and heard some blokes talking about a tourist who-" he stopped short, seemingly reconsidering his choice of words before continuing.

"I saw Jasmine's photo on the news an' I-they've been running the story over and over this morning," he cleared his throat. "Kristen had told James of yer hotel, so I came right away to… well, to see how yer all getting on." His words came out in a rush and ended abruptly.

"Thanks," said Kiana dejectedly. She sat in silence for a

moment, not knowing what to say. As much as she appreciated the sentiment of Seamus coming to check on them, there was nothing he or anyone else could do for them.

"Has anyone contacted ye this morning? With any updates?" he asked eagerly.

Kiana shook her head. "Not yet. I'm expecting a call from the officer we talked to last night, but it will just be a courtesy as we just heard they didn't find a body last night." She gestured to the news that was still running on a loop.

Again, there was a long pause as Kiana finished her cup of tea.

"I expect ye'll all be going home early, then," Seamus said after a while. He clearly had not thought through what the purpose of his visit would be, and was now feeling slightly awkward at Kiana's lack of attentiveness.

But at this statement, Kiana looked up in astonishment.

"Of course not," she snapped, a little more aggressively than she had intended. She met his gaze and saw there was sincere sadness there, and she felt a pang of sympathy for him.

"I'm not leaving until they find her," she continued softly.

"I think that's noble of ye," he said quietly, looking down at his folded hands. "So ye think she *is* missing, then?"

Of course what he had meant to say was, "*So you don't think she's dead?*"

"Yes," Kiana said. "I do."

"Jasmine had told me about Matt," Seamus said, his voice extremely low as he tread lightly. "We spent the greater part of that evening talking about it when we left all of ye."

Kiana was surprised. Though she had caught Kristen whispering to James about what she assumed was Jasmine's past, she had certainly never expected Jasmine herself to discuss it extensively with Seamus. She was a very private person, after all. Kiana bitterly recalled how they had relentlessly pestered her in the car. Another moment she wished she could take back.

"Jasmine did not kill herself," Kiana then said abruptly. She knew it was blunt, but she felt it needed to be said. "She was my best friend. I knew her better than anyone. She would never do that."

Seamus sat back in his chair and nodded in a way that was quite unlike the doubtful looks Marissa and Kristen had given her the night before. There was no sign of obligatory appeasement in his face and it was clear he felt the same. His next words he spoke quietly, but severely.

"I believe ye," he said reassuringly, placing his elbows on the table as he leaned in closer. "I didn't know her like ye did or even nearly-but I know she wouldn't have done that."

The manner of certainty with which he spoke took Kiana aback and she nodded gratefully, her spirits lifting. At least *someone* still seemed to have hope. She met his gaze but saw his eyes seemed very far away; as if he were not in the room with her at all.

"That's why I can't leave," she said in a delayed response. "I worry that without the pressure from us-from me, they'll give up the search."

Even as she spoke the words aloud, they sounded pathetic to her. What kind of power did she really have to pressure an entire foreign police department into continuing what they had already deemed a useless search?

They sat quietly and Kiana let out a sigh of frustration.

"She was doing so well," she said. "She seemed healthier even from the moment she got off the plane. She was eating again, laughing with us... it was like Ireland was bringing her back to life."

Seamus opened his mouth to speak, but Kiana cut him off. She wasn't done.

"Everything about her just seemed brighter," she said with finality. "I was so happy to have the old Jazz back."

Seamus smiled. "She did have a glow about her that would

stop a man's heart," he said, again surprising Kiana with the depth of his words. She couldn't help but smile back.

He stroked his chin thoughtfully in a way that made him look much older than he was. He appeared to be having some sort of internal debate, though Kiana could not guess what it was. She stared out the window, too exhausted to worry about the awkward silences that continued to fall between them.

"Was there anything unusual about her to ye these past few days?" Seamus asked suddenly, and Kiana shook her head.

"What do you mean?"

He leaned into his fist contemplatively.

"I thought there was somethin' different about her eyes when I saw her again here in Galway," he replied, shaking his head in dismay. "I dunno."

"Hm," Kiana said politely.

Perhaps this crush that Seamus had on her friend was more serious than she had thought. She studied him intently as his furrowed brow reflected the troubled nature of someone who would have known her friend *much* longer than he had. Then again, Jasmine *did* tend to have that effect on people. Before the accident, Jasmine had easily been the most charming of their group of friends; not only because she was beautiful, but because she carried the wittiest sense of humor that left nearly everyone who met her in awe. The result of being the daughter of a professor, no doubt.

Kiana sat up quickly, realizing she missed what Seamus had actually said. She snapped back to attention.

"Her eyes," she said, looking up sharply. "You said something about her *eyes* being different. What did you mean by that?"

Seamus nodded.

"They seemed like they had bits of green," he said, his own eyes misting over as he recalled the memory. "Which I noticed right away. I remembered thinking she had the deepest brown eyes the first night I met her."

"The mirror in the bathroom," Kiana muttered to herself. She looked up at Seamus. "She was asking me that morning if her eyes looked lighter to me."

She frowned in deep concentration, trying to remember if *green* had been the color she noticed.

"She also told me she didn't need her contacts anymore," Seamus continued. "She said that the fresh Irish air must have cured her eyesight. I remember talking about that for a bit."

At this statement, Kiana confidently shook her head.

"No, she's had terrible eyesight since the fourth or fifth grade. She always wore thick glasses growing up," she said with certainty. "She wore them on the plane here."

Seamus frowned. "She told me she hadn't worn her contacts in Galway at all."

It seemed minor, but Kiana couldn't help but feel perturbed by his statement. She had known Jasmine nearly their entire lives, and her friend had always had alarmingly high levels of prescriptions. She recalled a Girl Scout trip where Jasmine had forgotten her contacts and they had to turn around and drive two hours back to get them…no, it was not possible that she could walk ten *feet* without her glasses or contacts, let alone wander around Galway for multiple days. She strained her memory from their conversation in the bathroom. Had she mentioned her eyesight as well?

Kiana tucked her hair behind her ears in distress, attempting to find purpose in the conversation she was now having with Seamus. After all, what was the point of rehashing insignificant details during her friend's final days? She was about to voice this opinion to him, when he looked up at her.

"That scar on her palm," he said, suddenly, absently rubbing his own hand. "It's a bit strange, innit? Seems to glow in a certain light."

"Oh, yeah, it looks that way sometimes," Kiana said distractedly. She didn't want to be rude, but she was beginning to wonder if he always spoke in erratic patterns or if he had a point he was going to make. "She probably should've gotten stitches."

He said nothing but seemed to fall back into a deep reverie in which Kiana was more than obliged to leave him undisturbed.

She reluctantly turned her eyes back toward the television. No updates. The picture of Jasmine came up on the screen once more, Kiana flinching as she saw the face of her best friend looking down at her. Her glowing smile blanketed by her signature wild black hair was the picture of happiness; she looked so excited to be alive in that photo. Was it possible she hadn't been? Seamus looked down into his hands.

"Pause it," Kiana demanded suddenly, her eyes glued to the screen.

Seamus obliged and she moved swiftly to the TV, standing on her tip-toes for a better view.

"Her hair had gotten longer," she said slowly, tracing the outline of Jasmine's mane that was blowing in the wind. "I didn't realize how much."

But her statement, she knew, was more than a casual observation. Kiana quickly scrolled through her phone to find a photo from their first day in Dublin.

At last she found a clear shot from the Guinness Storehouse in which Jasmine's hair was falling down just past her shoulders, looking somewhat stringy and dull. She held it up to the TV in comparison, frowning.

It was unmistakable. Despite being taken only two days apart, Jasmine's hair was nearly three inches longer in the photo on the news and shiny as glass even against the grayscale of the rough sea behind them. Kiana had certainly noticed something of the sort at the time, but she had chalked it up to Jasmine's curling it one night and straightening it the next. Now looking at the photos, the true contrast was shocking.

"Do you see that?" she said, handing Seamus her phone as he

looked between the two stills of the woman he barely knew. "Look how much longer it is there."

To anyone with *eyes* it would have been obvious, but to her best friend as well as a man who had run his hands through it just days ago, the changes in Jasmine's hair was even more apparent.

As they stared at the two photos, more anomalies began to present themselves. The subject of the photo had easily detectable differences in her eyes, skin, and hair between the two shots. In Dublin, she looked sunken, tired, and frankly… malnourished. But the photos from the Cliff showed a much different woman; one with bright eyes and the plump skin of a happy and healthy person. The contrast was beyond anything she could rationalize occurring in just three days' time.

"What does this mean?" Kiana whispered, talking more to herself than Seamus.

To her surprise, he stood and joined her, crossing his arms across his chest. She wondered for a moment if he had been waiting for her to come to some sort of conclusion on her own, because he seemed to already have one.

"I've got somethin' in mind, but ye'll think I'm mad," he said.

Kiana turned to him and saw nothing but sincerity in his eyes. As Jasmine's best friend, she had seen a lot of boys swoon over her throughout the years, but the only one whom she had ever trusted to care for her best friend's soul had been Matt. She looked at Seamus now, wondering if he could have done the same. The fact he was standing next to her in the lobby as the only other person who believed that Jasmine was alive…she thought she would call him anything in the world but mad.

CHAPTER 11

LEGENDS & LIMERICK

"There's nothing else we can do," said Kristen desperately during what she hoped would be their final breakfast in Galway. She softened at seeing Kiana's face, riddled with sadness and worry, and bit her lip before continuing.

"Look I know we're all scared but-the police will keep looking and-and *when* they find her, we'll get a call." Kristen's carefully chosen words were spoken lightly-Kiana knew she did not believe it was a matter of *"when"*, but rather an extremely doubtful *"if."*

The morning following the incident had been somber, with Marissa and Kristen all but claiming certainty of Jasmine's suicide in their demeanor if not explicitly in their words. Kiana had insisted the two of them go on the remainder of the trip without her, but whether it was lingering hope or deep guilt that kept them there, they had remained with her in Galway as well-at least for one additional day.

Kiana, on the other hand, remained hopeful for a reason that she had not yet disclosed to the others. Whether she ever would or not remained to be seen. The reason being it was an absolutely outlandish theory that she wasn't sure she believed herself. She recalled her conversation with Seamus that had concluded not even an hour ago, leaving her deeply lost in contemplative and unimaginable thought.

"Selkies are an old subject of Irish and Scottish folklore," Seamus had said, avoiding Kiana's eyes as he undoubtedly had assumed she would cringe in disbelief.

"In the traditional myths, they're seals who can transform into people. In their human forms, they're known to be charming, seductive, all of that…" His voice trailed off as he gauged Kiana's expression. She grasped her teacup more tightly, but nevertheless encouraged him to continue.

"One of the old famous stories tells of a fisherman trapping a selkie in her human form by hiding her seal skin on land, thus forcin' her to wed him."

Kiana screwed her face up in disgust.

"Okay," she said at last, setting her cup down and shaking her head. "And what does this have to do with Jasmine?"

Seamus looked at her cautiously, but seeing as Kiana had promised not to call him mad, he went on.

"The old myths are the only ones ye can read about, of course as they've been passed down for generations," he explained and then proceeded to lower his voice. "But my brother, Aidan, he's a fisherman ye see. The fisherman on the west coast, they're always telling tales… he's told me for years they're superstitious folk."

"Okay," Kiana said slowly, attempting to see the direction he was headed.

Seamus sighed. "And there's been some sightings, he says, in recent times, of people resemblin' something like selkies," he said. "Beautiful people-both men and women-with long hair, bright eyes, swimmin' about much too far at sea for it to be standard. Just when they're spotted, their tails propel them back into the waves. No one can get near enough to see what they are or if they're even real."

Kiana stared at him, expressionless.

"So you're talking about mermaids?" she said flatly.

He sighed and rubbed his nose.

"Sorry, keep going," Kiana said quickly.

Seamus hadn't struck her as abnormal in any way up until now, and there was evidently something very special between her best friend and the man in front of her. She wanted to hear what he was thinking. She owed Jasmine that much.

Perhaps comforted by nothing other than the sheer fact Kiana had not excused herself from the table, Seamus continued.

"Of course all of its deemed rubbish talk amongst seamen, getting battered in the pubs in the port cities," he said, waving his hand. "But what if it's not?"

"So you think Jasmine is a selkie?" Kiana asked, failing to see the connection Seamus had clearly drawn between the mythical legends and her friend's disappearance. "Why?"

"The changes in her eyesight, her hair," Seamus began. "That's how it starts, I think."

Kiana mulled over the possibility, wondering vaguely if mythological theory was a common topic of conversation between the brothers, but Seamus spoke before she could ask.

"An' her *scar*," he said with finality. "That's the color of a selkie's tail, I'd bet my right hand on it."

An awkward pause followed, and Kiana felt the tiniest glimmer of hope fluttering in her chest. She had no inclination as to how her friend could have befallen a mysterious Irish curse of the sea, but Seamus seemed more than mildly convinced it was possible.

The only fact that made the theory worth pursuing, in Kiana's mind, was knowing that should this have been Jasmine's fate, it meant her friend was *alive*. And that was all that mattered. Kiana had an endless list of questions burning in her mind, but she knew Seamus would not have the answers.

"You said Aidan's seen selkies," said Kiana. "Can we speak with him?"

Seamus nodded and a small grin began to form in the corner of his mouth.

"Yeah, it was a welcome reunion after years of hardly speaking to one another," he said. "Givin' him a ring this morning to ask about *selkies*."

Kiana smirked. So he *had* already pursued his theory.

"Do you love her?" she then said abruptly, not knowing what had possessed her to ask.

His deep green eyes never broke contact with her own.

"If I get the chance to, I certainly will."

THEIR CONVERSATION HAD ENDED with the sudden arrival of Marissa and Kristen in the lobby, their eyes full of redness that indicated a mixture of crying and lack of sleep. They made their way over to Kiana at a snail's pace, eyeing the coffee and tea cart that was now devoid of either caffeinated beverage.

"Oh! *You're* here," said Kristen, doing nothing to hide her surprise as she saw Seamus sitting across from Kiana.

"Just wanted to stop by an' offer my condolences," said Seamus, his eyes twinkling with sincerity. "We all saw the news this morning."

"That was very kind of you," said Marissa sweetly. "We're still waiting on updates from the police."

"Ah, I expect ye'll hear somethin' soon," said Seamus kindly. He then excused himself, shooting Kiana a knowing look to which she nodded subtly in response.

* * *

SEAMUS FOLLOWED THROUGH. Sure enough, Kiana received a message from him less than an hour later that made her heart jump with an emotion that lay somewhere between fear and excitement.

> Aidan's willing to discuss. Can you get to
> Swigg's at eleven?

Unfamiliar with any establishments that fell outside of the main tourist stretch, Kiana glanced down at the map on her phone and traced the path to what she was imagining to be a dingy pub. It was certainly walking distance, but there would be a few alleyways to navigate on the way.

While physically getting there would hardly be a challenge, she was much more concerned with the means by which she could quietly slip away from her friends. Luckily, Kristen seemed to have her own plan in mind that perfectly lended hand to Kiana's own. She glanced sideways at Marissa before speaking up over the breakfast table.

"So we were thinking, since we still have the rental car and we've seen pretty much all of Galway," she began tentatively. "What if we checked out Kylemore Abbey today? It's about an hour away. I think we should still-I mean, while we're here..." Her voice trailed off.

It was clear to Kiana that the two of them had already discussed whether or not sightseeing was insensitive given the circumstances, with their main concern being Kiana's opinion on the matter since she *was* objectively Jasmine's best friend. Whether she thought it to be in poor taste or not, Kiana saw her opportunity and she took it.

"I-I'm really not up for it you guys," she said slowly. It wasn't *entirely* a lie after all.

She saw Marissa's face fall and quickly added, "But you both should totally go. I'm really fine staying here by myself."

She tried to look as convincing as possible, flashing her

attempt at a somber smile that likely turned out to be more of a grimace.

"Are you sure?" asked Kristen, and Kiana wondered for a moment how she truly *would* feel about it had she not had her ulterior motives for getting rid of them.

"Definitely," she replied.

Seeing they were not convinced, she added, "It's not like us sitting here sulking will bring back answers any sooner. I would go with you, I'm just really exhausted."

At last she convinced them to go on without her. Kiana waved goodbye to her friends around eleven and encouraged them to check out a few more abbeys on the way back. She pushed aside her guilt, praying that her white lie was worth it.

'*Take your time,*' she thought to herself as she watched them go.

Kiana set out not long after them, entering the bustling street with a sense of foreboding. As much as she had felt convinced earlier in the morning, the simplicity of seeing ordinary people living ordinary lives all around her seemed to emphasize the absurdity of what she was doing.

She kept her head down and focused on the directions on her phone, afraid that the window to the world of normalcy would encourage her to turn around. While she walked, she attempted to piece together coherent questions for Seamus' brother, but each time her mind turned up blank. How did one adult ask another if they thought their friend could have transformed into a mythical being from Irish folklore?

Kiana found the pub and was not surprised to find it already open and well in the swing of regular business for the day. She made her way inside, feeling instantly out of place in an establishment that clearly catered to fishermen-well-just *men* in general. That being said, she found it difficult to object to her position when getting a drink was as easy as breathing. Her existence alone seemed to stir some interest and the bartender waved her away when she tried to pay for her cider.

"Jus bring sum o' yer pretty friends next time," he said, winking and sliding her the glass.

Drinking so early in the morning made her shudder, but she needed her mind as open as possible for the conversation that was ahead. She took a few sips and felt her nerves subside.

Though she had hoped Seamus would arrive first, Kiana had no trouble identifying Aidan when he came through the door. He looked startlingly similar to his brother, but about a decade older and with lighter, nearly flaming red hair in contrast to his brother's darker chestnut waves. The lines on his face had been hardened no doubt by the nature of his work and lack of sunscreen, but these features seemed to emphasize his ruggedly handsome appearance. Good looks ran in the family, she supposed. Kiana shifted in her seat slightly, unsure of whether or not to call across the bar to him.

Apparently *she* was easily identifiable as well, because Aidan walked right up to her, rendering her hesitation unnecessary. His mouth curled into what she thought might be a smile, but it vanished as quickly as it had appeared. He sat across from her as a beer was brought directly to him by the bartender. He handed the man some coins and it was clear to her that he was a regular.

"Hi," said Kiana tentatively. Not knowing how to begin their conversation, she added, "Thanks for coming."

He nodded. "Seamus should be along in a moment."

Sure enough, Seamus' tall frame came through the door and he sat in the third and final stool at the tiny high top table. He smiled at Kiana briefly before clapping hands with his brother in what she thought was an oddly stiff handshake for siblings to exchange.

"I see the two of ye have been acquainted then," Seamus said, gesturing to them. He shook his head as the bartender silently asked him what he'd take. Kiana observed him closely; she thought he looked nervous.

"Only just," she said, waiting for him to take the lead.

"What's the craic, brother?" asked Aidan in a voice that was not unkind but not wholly warm, either. Was it smugness?

"Well," Kiana began, and Aidan seemed surprised at her being the first to speak rather than his little brother.

"Seamus tells me you've been hearing some selkie stories-in your-your line of work."

She finished the sentence lamely, deciding it was best to jump right to the matter rather than dance around it.

Seamus nodded and continued for them while Aidan's expression was blank and unreadable. "We want to know more about what's been said in the ports, about the selkie sightings."

"Catch yerself on," said Aidan, shaking his head with amused dismissal and Kiana's heart sank.

She noticed his beer was empty and eyed the bartender who understood. He swiftly brought another to which Aidan gulped gratefully.

"It's probably nonsense, sure," said Kiana with emphasis. "But you yourself have seen one, haven't you?"

Aidan glanced at Seamus and something that could have been embarrassment flashed across his face. Again, it was gone in an instant. "Well-ye can never be sure, can ye now?"

"No," said Seamus slowly. "But yer not the only one. There have been stories, haven't there?" His expression was strained; he ran a distressed hand through his hair.

Aidan glanced between the two of them as it became clear that both Kiana and his younger brother would not be satisfied with dismissal. After all, he *had* agreed to meet them and the nature of the meeting was certainly no secret.

"Yea," Aidan said. "There's talk of the *seal people* lurkin' 'round these parts and in the waters. In the old tales, they remove their seal skin to-"

"To become humans and then put the seal skin back on when they go back to the ocean, I know," Kiana said impatiently, having done a quick Google search following her conversation with Seamus. "But I'm more interested in what you've heard *recently.*"

Aidan raised an eyebrow at her but did not seem irritated by her interruption. He set his already half empty glass on the table and leaned forward.

"I've been hearing that women and men alike have lately been drawn to the sea to resume their selkie forms, though they may never have known they had the selkie blood to begin with," he said mysteriously, his voice low. "And the reason we keep seein' them off the shores of Galway is because there's a colony out there…tryin' to catch a glimpse of their old lives."

"Have there been disappearances?" asked Seamus. "To coincide with these sightings, I mean."

At this, Aidan shrugged.

"A few, I think," he said. "No one important enough for everyone to go on worrying about, though."

Kiana studied him, unconvinced by his apathetic attitude. She noticed he spoke like an educated man, despite the way he portrayed himself. Curiosity for the dynamic that existed between the two brothers began to eat at her, but Seamus interjected and brought her focus back to the matter at hand.

"Is there some sort of mark they have?" Seamus asked. "A selkie when they're in their human form, that is."

Aidan eyed his brother with interest.

"Now where would ye be hearin' of somethin' like that?" He spoke carefully; it made Kiana suspicious.

Seamus looked at Kiana. "D'ye have a picture of Jasmine's hand?"

Kiana pulled out her phone and scrolled furiously back in her albums, finally locating a picture from the dreadful day last year where Jasmine's scar was visible. Of course the picture had been taken before they had all found out what had happened, and the back of Jasmine's hand was resting gently on the table as Kristen was bent on one knee in a mock proposal beside her.

Even in the small aspect ratio of the frame, the uniqueness of the mark was apparent. Kiana slid the phone across the table to Aidan who eyed it with intrigue. He frowned and zoomed in and out several times while Kiana and Seamus took turns glancing at him and one another. Aidan did not speak.

"In person ye can see it glow even more," said Seamus at last. "When I went to hold her hand, it-"

"Ye touched it?" Aidan asked sharply, his eyes darting away from the small phone and locking in on his brother's gaze. In an instant, Kiana could see he was afraid and smirked with satisfaction as he had given himself away. Clearly he took more stock in the old legends than he had initially let on. She raised an eyebrow, and Seamus immediately capitalized on the opportunity.

"I did," said Seamus without a flicker of fear in his own demeanor. "Why shouldn't I have?"

Aidan rolled his eyes slightly at the irony in Seamus' voice but he was unmistakably disturbed.

"That there looks like the mark of a selkie if I've ever seen one," he said to Kiana, sliding the phone back toward her as he seemed to recall a memory. "That's how their scales are, anyway-silver and green, matching their lamplight eyes...made to look like treasure at the bottom of the sea. They use it to entice their prey."

"Their prey," Kiana repeated, the disbelief in her voice more than apparent.

Seamus spoke next, voicing what Kiana had nearly forgotten to mention. "But she got this mark as a child-when she was living in Portugal," he said. "It was a wound that healed like this."

Aidan wrinkled his brow in confusion. "Ye mean to say she wasn't born with that mark?"

"No," Kiana said definitively.

Aidan ran a hand through his own hair in the same distressed manner as his brother, though his fingernails were dirty and ruddy in comparison. He looked at Kiana with what appeared to be a mixture of empathy and regret, an expression she was surprised to see on his stoic face.

"I dunno, in that case. I'm sorry to tell ye, as ye seem like a nice girl concerned about yer friend," he said. "But if ye do believe yer friend's got the selkie curse, there isn't much ye can do."

He took another swig of his drink and Kiana wanted badly to slap it out of his hand.

"You don't think she can change back?" she asked severely. "You said they can shed their seal skin and become human again."

"The legends only talk of selkies who are born that way," he said. "I don't know what would be the case for someone like this. That mark looks like one of them came after her, dunnit?"

"Does it?" Kiana asked, looking at the photo again. Was the true nature of her scar that Jasmine been *attacked* by one of these creatures in the past?

Aidan shook his head. "I don't know," he said. His voice trailed off as he absently stared past both Kiana and Seamus.

"No," said Kiana with more conviction than she felt. "She can change back." Admittedly, her hope was fading significantly, but she felt that a state of delusion was preferable to the pit of sadness that awaited her acceptance of reality.

Aidan looked up at her.

"Well, I s'pose it's possible, but how would we find out? Are ye planning on takin' a dive off the Cliffs to find her an' ask her yerself?"

"Aidan," Seamus said exasperatedly, putting his head in his hands. "Come on."

"No, it's alright," Kiana said. She looked at Aidan and saw his version of pity lingering behind his eyes, despite his rough appearance.

"I wondered if Seamus had told you who she was-if you'd seen the news already."

"Yes," Aidan said. "I recognize her face. It was all over the news, and I'm sorry to hear of it."

Kiana nodded and they sat in silence for some time as she thought of what to say. She looked at Seamus and was reassured to see that he appeared more contemplative than defeated. His brow was furrowed, deep in thought.

"Is there anyone else we might talk to?" Seamus asked tentatively, and Kiana was grateful *he* had been the one to ask it. "I understand ye haven't much interest in the matter, even if ye believed in it."

Aidan's eyes flashed with something Kiana could not read. Was he irritated that his brother had deemed him useless? Or did he know more than he was letting on?

"Yeah," the older brother replied. "I can point ye both in the right direction. Ye'll want to talk with someone called Mrs. Byrne. I can get send ye her way."

Seamus and Kiana both stared back blankly at him while Aidan waited for what was clearly some sort of expression of gratitude.

"Thank you," Kiana interjected and flashed her brightest smile, making the man go red. She purposefully batted her eyelashes for extra reassurance. Whether or not she imagined it, she thought she saw Seamus smirk knowingly from the corner of her eye.

In any event, Aidan continued.

"Well Mrs. Byrne'll know all the secrets of Irish lore-what's true and what's not," he said. "But ye be careful, now. There are people who go to her with…unsavory requests. Dark magic n' things like that."

Kiana, who had no experience with witchcraft beyond reading the lighthearted kind in fairytales, felt a definite shiver run down her spine despite her rational mind telling her she was being ridiculous.

The possibilities surrounding Jasmine's disappearance

seemed to grow more plentiful by the moment as she sat across from someone who seemed to live in an entirely different reality than herself. She wondered if Seamus felt the same.

"This girl must be something special," said Aidan, this time with a grin of amusement on his face. "For the two of ye to go around seekin' answers in Irish folktales."

"She is," both Kiana and Seamus said at the same time. Kiana glanced sideways at Seamus' profile to find his cheeks slightly flushed. They sat in silence for a few moments before Kiana had an abrupt thought.

"What's your last name?" she asked the brothers collectively.

"McCarthy," they said together.

Jasmine McCarthy,' Kiana thought, despite herself. Jasmine had never said much about wanting to change her last name or not when she was preparing for her engagement to Matt, but it sounded nice, anyway.

* * *

"So this Mrs. Byrne," said Kiana as she stepped out of the dark pub and into the sunlight with Seamus. "She's what-some kind of occultist? How does Aidan even *know* her?"

She had hardly had the time to wonder why someone like Aidan would be acquainted with a modern day witch while in the dingy pub, but now in the sunlight it seemed like the first question she should have asked.

"I dunno," said Seamus, letting out a sigh. He bit his lip and frowned as he watched the clouds roll across the gray sky above them. He turned to her and rubbed his face in distress. "I understand if ye don't want to come."

"I do!" exclaimed Kiana, and she meant it. She wanted to leave no stone unturned in the search for her friend, but the logistics were admittedly complicated.

They had left Aidan, who seemed none too keen to leave the

rundown watering hole as he gave them his final piece of advice. He told them about Mrs. Byrne, an old woman who lived in Cashel and told folktales to tourists and villagers alike. Supposedly she had made quite a business out of it, and gathered relatively large crowds. She was easy to find, but not necessarily so easy to get by herself. Should they be fortunate enough to score a conversation with her, she would-*allegedly*-know much more about the modern day selkie than anyone else in Ireland.

And so Kiana was left with the daunting task of trying to convince her friends to change their itinerary in order to spend an afternoon in Cashel without arousing suspicion. The thought of telling them where she had been and what she was planning to do made her shudder. Seamus plainly felt the same way as Kiana could nearly see the goosebumps of embarrassment rising in real time as he committed to humoring such a wild plan.

"It *is* somewhat near Limerick," Kiana said as she examined the map on her phone in search of the tiny village. "I can make it work. And if I can't, I'll tell them to go on the rest of the trip without me."

Seamus stopped as they rounded the corner near Eyre Square.

"I wouldn't blame ye if ye thought it was time to let this go," he said. "But for some reason, I can't."

"I know you wouldn't," said Kiana, smiling as kindly as she could. "But neither can I."

She made her way back to the hotel where she had plenty of time to concoct her plan as the other two would not be back for some hours. She ultimately decided the best course of action was to suggest they visit the famous Rock of Cashel and Hore Abbey in the late afternoon and stay overnight there instead of Limerick.

"The hotel *is* refundable," Kiana said to the others upon their return.

Another trick they all had learned from Jasmine-always book a refundable rate in case of an emergency. Kiana likely never would have predicted that the emergency in question would be a midnight meeting with a witch, but still.

"Is there enough to do there, in Cashel?" asked Marissa doubtfully. "It's kind of more like a stop along the way, isn't it?"

"Well, by the time we see both landmarks, do we really want to backtrack toward Limerick?" Kiana said lightly. "Besides, Cashel is right along the same highway that will take us down to Cork...which is where we're headed next, anyway."

Both mildly alarmed and impressed by her own ability to lie, Kiana fell anxiously silent while the other deliberated.

"I guess it makes sense," said Kristen, shrugging carelessly. "We'll need to get up early tomorrow in order to have enough time in Limerick, in that case. I suppose we can plan to leave for Cashel after lunch."

"Perfect," said Kiana, searching for signs of suspicion in Kristen's face. She thought she saw a shadow of something, but could not decipher it.

"But-do you think we're...allowed?" asked Marissa tentatively.

"To leave?" said Kristen, raising her eyebrows. "Why wouldn't we be?"

Kiana knew what she meant. There had been radio silence from the police department since their return, which was unfortunately a bad sign as far as potential leads on Jasmine's whereabouts. It also meant, however, that Kiana could assume none of them were being further pursued as persons of interest. Her stomach turned again at the thought, recalling the cold officer's suspicious eyes on her as if she could have possibly wanted to hurt her best friend.

They turned in early that evening, with Kiana laying awake until the early hours of the morning with anxiety. Her dishonesty was eating away at her, but she knew it was the only way she could continue to seek the answers she needed. Whether or not she would believe anything that this strange Mrs. Byrne had to say to her was another matter entirely. But for Jasmine's sake, she needed to try. If she determined it was nonsense, then she could at least return home knowing she did everything she could.

"Off we go," yawned Kristen as they piled into the rental car for yet another early morning.

Kiana had rolled Jasmine's suitcase out with her in silence as no one quite knew what to do with it just yet. The ghostly passenger lingered in the spare backseat, haunting the thoughts of everyone in the car. No one spoke of Jasmine, having all silently agreed that nothing productive would come from their speculation. As far as Marissa and Kristen knew, all they could do was wait.

"Maybe we should have sent her bag back…?" asked Marissa faintly from the backseat, to which no one replied other than a subtle shrug and shaking of their heads.

The sun was not up yet and Marissa and Kristen immediately dozed off during the hour and a half ride to Limerick. Kiana, on the other hand, remained wired. She had offered to drive, thinking it best she keep her mind as occupied as possible.

The plan with Seamus was simple-he would go straight to Cashel to seek out Mrs. Byrne, staying in one of the small inns so long as it was not the same one as Kiana and the others. How he intended to depart from *his* group of friends, Kiana was uncertain, but she found her own mind far too busy with scheming to help concoct one for him as well.

"I wasn't sure what to say to them," said Kristen quietly, breaking the silence that had engulfed them for nearly thirty minutes.

"What? Who?" Kiana replied.

"James and the others," said Kristen. Kiana straightened up, feeling eerily as though Kristen had been reading her thoughts.

"Oh, I know," she said distractedly. "What *did* you end up saying?"

Kristen shrugged and let out a deep sigh. "After we saw Seamus yesterday morning, James sent me a text saying he was thinking of us and asked if there was anything he could do. Of course, there's not."

Kiana nodded silently.

"It was nice of Seamus to come by," Kristen continued. "Jasmine must have really left an impression on him."

"Hmm? Yeah, she did," said Kiana distractedly. Was she hinting at something else? Or was Kiana just paranoid?

Kristen glanced at her sideways.

"I think *she* really liked *him*, too."

* * *

KIANA'S GUILT for misleading the group vanished almost instantly upon their arrival in Limerick. As it turned out, no one seemed all too enthralled with the city. Perhaps it was because they had already experienced the gorgeous scenery of the western coastline as well as the bustling activity of Dublin, but the generally subdued aura that now surrounded the group made everything about the inland city seem gray. They spent the majority of the morning wandering around with coffees, yawning lazily as they laid out their itinerary for the day.

"There's a castle here, right?" asked Marissa sleepily as she trailed behind the other two.

"There's always a castle," Kristen said flatly.

She was right. King John's castle stood just next to the Thomond Bridge that connected the two sides of the city across the River Shannon. It was a relatively small fortress, but impressive when one considered it had been originally built in the 1200s.

"1210?" read Kristen on a sign at the entrance incredulously. "How do they even know that? Like who was keeping track?"

It was obvious that the prosperity that followed the building of the castle became the reason for its significance in history. As the watchtower for both a now wealthy trading hub and port city, Kiana was mildly interested to learn that the castle eventu-ally housed its own mint at the direction of King John himself. It had remained relatively intact and undamaged until the Siege of Limerick in the mid 1600s.

"Maybe I'm missing something, but it doesn't seem like much interesting went on here until at least the mid 1600s," said Marissa as she read of the Protestant conquest of Ireland as it pertained to the surrender of Catholic Jacobites in Limerick.

"Interesting for us. Probably not for them," said Kristen, pointing to a particularly bloody sketch of a fallen soldier floating down the River Shannon.

After they had learned a sufficient amount of Limerick history, they made their way to the St. Mary's Cathedral, where a large and ominous graveyard greeted them in the hazy mist.

"I hope I get one like that," said Kristen, pointing to one of the numerous, towering gravestones that stood as tall as herself. "I'll bet that was someone important."

And it likely was a Cardinal or Bishop of some sort, but Kristen immediately fell silent upon seeing the look on Kiana's face. A chilling thought had crossed all of their minds-would a stone like this soon be adorned with Jasmine's name?

"Sorry," Kristen said quickly. "That was-"

"It's fine," said Kiana, waving her hand in dismissal. "Let's go inside?"

Kiana had never been wholly religious, but something about stepping into an eight-hundred-year old place of worship brings out the reverence in just about anyone. An immediate hush washed over them as they respectfully made the sign of the cross and stood off to the side so as not to disturb any of those deep in prayer. Kiana was mesmerized by the beautiful stained glass that filled the gothic archways with rainbow scenery of the Virgin Mary cradling her baby Jesus.

"Shall we-say a prayer for Jasmine, you think?" asked Kristen tentatively. Marissa and Kiana nodded solemnly and they all closed their eyes, taking each other's hands.

The three of them stood quietly in the back of the church, each having their own unique experience with the elusive phenomenon called faith. Kiana felt a fresh wave of guilt for her dishonesty with her friends, but it quickly melted away to make room for reflection.

Up until now, she had repeatedly told herself that Jasmine was okay, though a doubtful voice in her head had reminded her of the more likely reality that she was not. But in the peaceful quiet of the church, surrounded by so many other symbols of uncertain belief, she found herself (almost) believing it could be true.

"Ready?" asked Kristen, wiping a loose tear from her cheek. Kiana had never seen her cry, and she guessed Marissa hadn't, either.

CHAPTER 12

THE WITCH OF CASHEL

Their moods now thoroughly subdued, no one was particularly disappointed to be leaving Limerick in the afternoon. The tranquility of a quiet village like Cashel seemed all the more appealing as the emotions from the past two days caught up with them.

"I'll drive?" offered Kristen. Kiana sensed she had the same desire to quiet her mind with the distraction of being behind the wheel and nodded.

They passed through more farmland, and Kiana could see clearly how the beautiful country had earned its name The Emerald Isle. Even in the cloudy mist of September, there was a definitive, lush glow to the rolling green hills that sandwiched the highway. The sun was peeking through the clouds, casting small pools of light onto the lazy cows munching in the fields. The drive was not long, and they soon found themselves facing yet another graveyard outside of a looming stone ruin.

"They all start to look the same, don't they?" said Marissa dully as they wandered the grounds of the limestone outcrop.

The Rock of Cashel towered above them, casting a late afternoon shadow upon the side of the steep hill. Despite it possessing the most impressive collection of medieval buildings in the country, including the site where St. Patrick himself converted the King of Munster to Christianity in the fifth century, not one of the three were wholly interested in sightseeing.

Kiana watched as the sun began to set over Hore Abbey in the distance. Beautifully impressive by day, she feared what it might look like at night. Not much longer, now, she thought to herself.

"I'm exhausted," said Marissa. "Can we go get something to eat?"

Upon hearing that even the historian of the group had no appetite for further exploration of the landmark, Kristen sighed with relief.

"Yes, let's go," she said. "I'm starving."

Of course Kiana was the furthest thing from hungry as her stomach was busy squirming with thoughts of her plan later in the evening. She would need to sneak out undetected to meet Seamus, get information out of Mrs. Byrne, and decide whether or not she believed it all before sunrise.

After a quick bite to eat, they settled into the cozy lobby of the inn and kept to themselves for a while while the fire crackled in the background. Marissa buried her nose in a book she found on the table-it looked to be quite a lengthy volume detailing Cashel history, and Kiana wondered aloud how a village so small could have enough to fill its pages.

Kristen sat on her phone, the mist of boredom clouding her eyes as she likely was beginning to regret their decision to come. The sun sank behind the hills and the evening passed slowly, with Kiana repeatedly yawning and indicating she wanted to make it an early night. Luckily, it seemed the other two felt the same.

"There's not much to do here, anyway," said Kristen, sipping the house red wine of the inn while making a face of mild disgust.

"At least we're seeing the beauty of the countryside," said

Marissa optimistically. "It's so much cleaner away from the cities."

Just as she spoke, a fresh burst of cigarette smoke wafted through the cracked window beside them. Kristen laughed sardonically.

"Well, *tomorrow* will be fun," Marissa continued. "I'm looking forward to Cork."

She suddenly sat up and brushed her hair from her face.

"Sorry," she said, staring into her lap. "That was really insensitive."

Kristen sighed and Kiana reached her arm across the table to hold Marissa's hand.

"It's not," she said. "The police haven't given us any updates. Jasmine would expect us to finish this trip. What would she have us do otherwise? Go home early to do what? Sit around and be six hours behind any potential news we might hear of her?"

Marissa nodded, wiping a tear from her cheek. Kristen looked at Kiana curiously.

"I agree," she said, her brow furrowed. "I'm happy to hear you say that."

Kiana nodded, avoiding her gaze. Kristen's words spoke one sentiment while her eyes told another. She was suspicious of Kiana's sudden change of heart, and she should be. The truth was Kiana felt exactly the same as she had the day Jasmine had disappeared. She pressed on for the sake of finding her, not because she thought her dead friend would have wanted them to go on without her.

Saving her from needing to respond to Kristen, the door swung open and Kiana's jaw nearly dropped as she watched the very person whom she sought walk into the lobby of the tiny inn. Had the old woman's strange dress not given her away, the loud welcoming of the innkeeper reassured her that she indeed looked upon-

"Mrs. Byrne!" said the woman behind the desk. "Are ye here to tell some tales?"

The old woman nodded, revealing crooked teeth that lined a mischievous grin. "For anyone who will hear them."

The small bed and breakfast had only a few guests aside from the girls gathered in the lobby. As there was very little else of interest going on, they all turned their heads to the newcomer in curiosity.

The old woman removed her long, black cloak to reveal a subsequent black dress that hung about her in a most unflattering way that made her look more like a witch than ever. She quietly floated to a place in front of the fire while the ten or so people in the lobby moved instinctively toward her. Kiana glanced at her friends who shrugged in apathetic indifference and turned their attention toward the woman as well.

"Has anyone heard the tale of the isle of Hy-Brasail?" she asked.

Her question was clearly rhetorical as there were several welcome murmurs from the crowd. Kiana, Marissa, and Kristen (unsurprisingly) seemed to be the only three who were unfamiliar.

Mrs. Byrne cleared her throat and began to recite a poem. Despite her elderly appearance, her words were spoken with the liveliness of a young woman. They were full of vibrance and melody that made it almost sound like a song:

> *"On the ocean that hollows the rocks where ye dwell,*
> *A shadowy land has appeared, as they tell;*
> *Men thought it a region of sunshine and rest,*
> *And they called it Hy-Brasail, the isle of the blest.*
> *From year unto year on the ocean's blue rim,*
> *The beautiful spectre showed lovely and dim;*
> *The golden clouds curtained the deep where it lay.*

And it looked like an Eden, away, far away!"

Here the old woman's eyes grew cloudy with mystery and she leaned in closer to the crowd that was now paying rapt attention in one way or another. Some of the onlookers closed their eyes in the relaxed contentment of one hearing a familiar lullaby or tale from their childhood.

A peasant who heard of the wonderful tale,
In the breeze of the Orient loosened his sail;
From Ara, the holy, he turned to the west,
For though Ara was holy, Hy-Brasail was blest.
He heard not the voices that called from the shore-
He heard not the rising wind's menacing roar;
Home, kindred, and safety, he left on that day.
And he sped to Hy-Brasail, away far away!

Morn rose on the deep, and that shadowy isle,
O'er the faint rim of distance, reflected its smile:
Noon burned on the wave, and that shadowy shore
Seemed lovelily distance, and faint as before;
Lone evening came down on the wanderer's track,
And to Ara again he looked timidly back;

Oh! Far on the verge of the ocean it lay.
Yet the isle of the blest was away, far away!

Rash dreamer, return! O, ye winds of the main,
Bear him back to his own peaceful Ara again.
Rash fool! For a vision of fanciful bliss,
To barter thy calm life of labour and peace.

> *The warning of reason was spoken in vain;*
> *He never revisited Ara again!*
> *Night fell on the deep, amidst tempest and spray,*
> *And he died on the waters, away, far away!"*

SHE FINISHED the final line with a grandiose bow and the small crowd broke into a polite applause at a volume that was appropriate for the intimate setting. Mrs. Byrne took a sip of her brandy that had been set at her side by the innkeeper during her tale and looked upon her spectators appreciatively before clearing her throat in preparation for her next story.

"How about a more frightening tale this time?" she said in a low voice. "Perhaps we're familiar with The Pooka?"

Kristen snorted next to Kiana and whispered, "It can't be that scary with that name," she said. Kiana grinned and stifled her own laughter.

Mrs. Byrne continued to tell her tales for the next hour or so, highlighting the folktale mysteries of Ireland that seemed to grow darker as she carried on. From banshees to ghosts to sinister fairies who drowned young men, Kiana was growing more uneasy by the moment as she became acquainted with the folklore of a country much older than the one that she was from.

The stories that had been passed down for generations seemed to come alive by the fireside and she felt the same familiar feeling of possibility that she had experienced during her meeting with Aidan in the pub. If there were a place where such things could exist, it would certainly be a country as mysterious as Ireland.

Kristen and Marissa's attention spans had reached their limit and they began to nod off to sleep. Kiana, however, kept her ears open for any mention of selkies as Mrs. Byrne pressed on. She heard the word "merrow" in a story of a mysterious sea creature that resembled both a man and fish who tricked a companion into joining him under the sea for a whiskey by placing a special hat on his head… but the *selkie* was never mentioned at all. She sank back in her chair with disappointment.

"Are you sure you don't want to stay in our room?" asked Marissa as the three of them trudged up the stairs a few moments later. "The couch pulls out…I don't want you to feel lonely."

"I'm fine," said Kiana. She had insisted she get her own room, which was hardly suspicious considering the inn had plenty of vacancies and the size of the queen bed would hardly fit all three of them. "I snore like an elephant anyway. Jasmine always hated sharing a room with me."

"See you in the morning then," Kristen said, yawning as she closed the door behind them. Kiana entered the room across the hall, making sure there was an audible "snap" as it clicked into the frame.

She immediately sent a message to Seamus letting him know she would be ready in twenty minutes, wanting to be certain the others were asleep before she slipped outside.

Kiana looked out the window of the small inn and saw Seamus' figure in the shadows of the streetlight. She changed into black pants and a black sweatshirt, feeling like she was back in high school, preparing to sneak out for a party. A party would be a much preferred destination than a haunted abbey at night to meet a witch, she thought to herself with bitter amusement.

She opened the door silently and crept down the staircase, hopping over the one that creaked at the bottom like a cat. The lobby was now entirely empty and devoid of all light save the tiny lamp glowing at the door, seemingly guiding the way for the lonely endeavor ahead.

"Bout ye," said Seamus as she approached him in the street. His face was strained with what could have been anxiousness, but his eyes were resolute. "Ready?"

Kiana nodded, shivering in the chill of the September air. She quickly told Seamus that she had already seen the woman in the lobby and he inquired immediately if she spoke of selkies in her stories.

"No," Kiana said, sensing his disappointment as it matched her own. "That one didn't come up."

"That's alright," he said distractedly. "At least ye'll know what she looks like."

They crept across the silent street, with Kiana turning around every few moments, feeling the eerie sensation they were being followed. It was not a long walk, but somewhat hilly and convoluted. She saved herself from tripping more than once-the darkness made even the slightest dip in the gravel pathway treacherous.

Their first sight of Hore Abbey was nothing too sinister as the black sky blanketed the majority of it from far away. They approached it from the side rather than the front as they cut across the expanse of the grassy field, Kiana's boots crunching too loudly in the grass.

As the building came into full view, the crumbling walls towered over her in a decayed opulence that was both impressive and terrifying to behold. Kiana felt she was stepping back in time; into a ruined version of Dracula's halls where she would be taken prisoner. The aura of a haunted graveyard began to descend upon her, sending a shiver up her spine.

"Ye doin' okay?" said Seamus over his shoulder as he was several steps ahead of her. Kiana scrambled to keep pace with him.

"How will we find her...?" she asked, uncertain as to how far the ruins stretched. She felt her confidence in Mrs. Byrne's appearance waning as the once solid halls of the abandoned abbey began to swallow them in dilapidated silence. "Are we sure she'll even be here?"

Seamus shrugged. "That's what Aidan said. And I suspect she may find us first," he said. His voice was low, but not quite a whisper as he scanned the archways for any sign of movement.

Crunch.

Kiana whirled around as she heard the sound of footsteps that were not their own coming from behind her. Their curiosity had drawn them further into the maze of the ruins than Kiana had realized, and she suddenly felt trapped as the archways seemed to close in on them.

"I recognize ye," said a quiet voice from the shadows.

Kiana knew it instantly to be the same one that had told stories at the inn not two hours ago, but it was followed by the distinct sound of a *man's* voice whispering words that were too muffled for her to decipher. Apparently Seamus heard this as well and he moved instinctively toward the sound, protectively stepping in front of Kiana.

"We're here to ask ye some questions," he said in a steady voice. "Are ye willin' to talk to us?"

Suddenly the witch was upon them. She held a burning torch and her crooked teeth were arranged in a strange, humorless smile. Small a figure as she was, she carried herself with an air of authority that made Kiana cringe as she came far too close. But Seamus stepped closer to her rather than backing away. The shadowy figure of the witch's companion lingered in the background. She could not see his face, but Kiana could tell he was a tall, lanky man.

"I'm Seamus, and this is Kiana," he continued. "We've heard yer the one to seek should we have questions about folk legends."

Kiana noticed the hesitation in his voice, but it was not to be mistaken with fear. He did not appear to be deterred by the woman's accomplice, and it was clear he was not leaving without answers.

"That depends," the old woman said, the shadows dancing across her face in the torchlight. Her eyes now narrowed in a sly, haunted way that made Kiana want to turn around and sprint in the opposite direction. "What kind of legends are ye speaking of?"

"Selkies," Seamus said. "Ye'll know about the Irish mermaids?"

Mrs. Byrne seemed intrigued by his statement, but her reaction was nothing compared to her mysterious companion that stood behind her. As if shaken from a dream, the man started and immediately emerged from the shadows. Kiana gasped as she met his eyes.

"What are you doing here?" she exclaimed in surprise.

Of course Kiana had conjured absolutely no guesses as to who the mysterious man could be, but if she had formed a prediction, it certainly would not have been this. She found herself face-to-face with the professor from Trinity College that she had met only days ago. Liam Brennan seemed just as astonished as she was, clearing his glasses on his shirt as if to confirm what he was seeing.

Seamus glanced sideways at Kiana. "Ye know this man?" he asked cautiously.

"Yes!" Kiana said. "He-he's a Professor at Trinity College!" She fumbled over her words. What was he *doing* here?

"One of Jasmine's friends, am I correct?" the professor asked, his tone uncertain but not at all unfriendly. He stepped further into the light and Kiana was surprised to see his kind, objectively handsome face looked much older and tired than she remembered.

"Kiana," she said. She thought of offering her hand, but refrained.

"I'm amazed you're here," he said quietly. "Amazed, but I suppose I shouldn't be surprised that Jasmine has such intelligent friends."

"How d'ye know Jasmine?" Seamus asked suspiciously. The professor sighed, extending his hand which Seamus took cautiously.

"Her father was one of my closest friends and mentors," he

said. "When I heard the news about her, I couldn't help but wonder…"

Kiana felt a stab of guilt at having not called the professor to tell him about Jasmine's disappearance, but then again, how were they to have known how to contact him? She imagined him and his wife and their darling child, turning on the news that morning…her stomach turned.

"Couldn't help but wonder what?" Seamus asked sharply, the accusatory tone he had assumed still prominent in his voice. Kiana wanted to put him at ease, but was admittedly slightly intimidated by the ferocity she now saw in his demeanor.

The professor looked at Seamus intently. "Well, the same thing I presume the two of you were wondering about," he snapped. "After all, that's why we're all here, isn't it? To ask Mrs. Byrne about the legends of the selkies and modern day sightings?"

Mrs. Byrne cleared her throat, causing Kiana to jump. She had nearly forgotten the witch was there. "Not the most commonly discussed in Ireland that one," the old woman whispered.

"That's right," said Seamus, his eyes steely as they fixed momentarily on the professor before returning to the witch. "What is it that ye know?"

"Everything," the witch said carelessly.

Seamus, apparently unable to suppress his frustration, let out a loud scoff. While Kiana empathized with his impatience, she knew it wouldn't be productive with a woman like this.

"Alright, alright," Professor Brennan said, rubbing the bridge of his nose in exasperation. "Please, Maeve, tell them what you started to tell me. We all have the same goal here."

Kiana was taken aback to hear that an academic like Professor Brennan was on a first name basis with someone like Mrs. Byrne, but thought it unimportant for the moment. Questions for later, she supposed.

Mrs. Byrne cleared her throat, signaling that the theatrics

were about to begin. Professor Brennan looked at Kiana and Seamus with a reassuring nod, and they all stood quietly with the same rapt attention the woman had commanded back at the inn.

"Well first ye'll be needing to hear the tale of Thady O'Dowd, Chieftain of the O'Dowd clan," she said. "As I was just beginning to tell yer friend here." She motioned to the professor.

"Thady O'Dowd, Chieftain of the O'Dowd clan, was walking on the seashore and spotted a beautiful mermaid wearing a cloak which shimmered like the silver scales of a fish," she said in her same mesmerizing voice that was simply made for folklore. "Without her cloak she would remain human and unable to return to the sea...so Thady stole her cloak and asked her to marry him."

Seamus made a subtle "mmhm" sound in his throat that indicated he was relatively familiar with this tale. Kiana wondered what it would be like to grow up as a child in Ireland, hearing bedtime stories such as this.

The old woman went on. "The mermaid knew the man would not return the cloak to her and so she chose to relinquish it. They lived happily for many years and she bore him seven children. One day, his eldest child saw the father hiding the cloak and told the mother where it was. While he was away at battle, the woman took the cloak and her children and went to Scurmore."

Then followed a long pause. Just as Kiana was about to inquire if that was the conclusion of the story, the witch spoke once more in dark tones of mystery and intrigue.

"Her children tried to stop her returning to the sea, but its call was so strong she could not resist. She turned six of the seven into stone and brought the youngest off with her."

Kiana thought an ending where a mother turned her own children into stone was a bit harsh for a bedtime story; she felt momentarily appreciative that the sounds of her own childhood included tranquil lullabies and various renditions of "Three Little Pigs".

"The call of the sea was so strong," Seamus repeated the witch's words quietly. Kiana recognized the words as an echo of what Aidan had said in the pub just yesterday.

"That's right," Mrs. Byrne said, rocking back on her heels, satisfied that she had entertained her audience. "The call of the sea is too strong for a selkie to resist. Her physical body will come alive as if for the first time the moment she feels it."

Kiana thought about Jasmine's changes; her hair, skin, eyesight… could it have been the *call of the sea* turning her into her healthiest, strongest version of herself in preparation for her transformation?

Professor Brennan stepped forward, commanding the attention of all three.

"I was telling Mrs. Byrne about what had happened to Jasmine as a child," he said. "In Portugal."

"The scar," Seamus said instantly, turning to the witch. "That is the mark of a selkie, is it not?" His suspicions toward the professor momentarily forgotten for the sake of discovery, he looked at her intently.

The witch nodded and broke into her signature crooked grin.

"It is," she said cautiously. "It means she is not of original selkie blood, but she surely has it in her now, from what he describes is on her hand." She gestured toward Professor Brennan.

"So this is really possible," Kiana said breathlessly, turning from Seamus to Professor Brennan whose stone-faced looks were identical in the dim light. The night air seemed to stand still. None of them dared to speak.

"It is," the woman said at last, shaking her head. "And I'm sorry to tell ye, she's been cursed. There will be no bringing her back to ye if she has the mark."

For the first time since their meeting, she had something that resembled empathy in her eyes.

"What do ye mean?" Seamus asked, his voice shaky, but refusing to crack. Kiana's feet went cold.

The woman opened her mouth to speak, but Kiana cut her off in desperation.

"Thady O'Dowd had only trapped his selkie bride by stealing her tail while on land," she said quickly. "Jasmine should have her choice still in the sea, shouldn't she?"

Although the words she spoke seemed to be logically consistent with the story she had been told, a tiny voice in her head said there was more to it than that.

"I mean she's been called to the sea as a half-breed. An Amalgam, they're called," said Mrs. Byrne. "Not quite a selkie...but trapped within the mercy of Mother Nature as she sees fit. They cannot return to the land like the others."

Kiana and Seamus both froze, unable (or unwilling) to understand what she had said.

Professor Brennan cleared his throat. "So this particular-curse, (he shuddered at the word, his intellectual mind evidently challenged by the ambiguity of folklore) has taken away her ability to change forms at will?"

"That's right," the witch said quietly, her expression unreadable.

"But there must be-" Kiana began, tears welling in her eyes.

"Child! Do ye not hear me?" Mrs. Byrne snapped, her eyes flashing with sudden impatience. "Am I not the one ye sought for answers?"

Kiana fell silent. Seamus closed his eyes while the professor let out a heavy sigh.

"But *you*," Mrs. Byrne suddenly turned to Seamus, reaching for his hand and examining it closely as she pronounced the word in slow motion. "*You.*"

Kiana straightened in alarm at her sudden movement, but Seamus looked too tired to pull it away. He did not take his eyes off of the witch, but he did not reply, either. The same steely look returned to his face as he waited for what she had to say.

"Ye care for the lass?" the woman asked him.

Without missing a beat, Seamus nodded solemnly. "I do," he said.

Of course Kiana knew that her friend had a peculiarly strong connection with him, but she was again taken aback by the manner in which Seamus spoke of her; like someone who had spent years rather than days with Jasmine. Mrs. Byrne ran her long fingernail down Seamus' palm, deeply examining it while Kiana shuddered on his behalf.

"Well, ye may have yer chance to be with yer woman just yet," she said at last, patting Seamus on the wrist.

"How's that?" he asked, no hint of anything but curiosity in his voice. The professor stepped closer to examine Seamus' hand and Kiana joined him, but they saw nothing there. They looked up at the witch in confusion.

"She cannot return," the witch said, folding Seamus' hand on top of his palm. "But it may very well be *ye* that goes to *her.*"

The old woman paused, whether for dramatic effect or an internal debate of whether or not to reveal more information, Kiana did not know. At last, she snapped her gaze from Seamus' hand and instead rested her eyes on his face.

"Ye've lain with the woman, have ye?"

Kiana looked away in embarrassment. Professor Brennan subtly shifted on his feet uncomfortably as well, plainly not wanting to know the intimate details of his goddaughter's romantic life.

Of course Jasmine had *said* nothing beyond a kiss had been shared between the two of them, but Kiana knew her friend better than to assume everything would have been disclosed in front of Kristen and Marissa. Additionally, Jasmine's private moments were surely not any business of hers after having been such a distant friend for the past year. But still... she would have hoped her best friend felt comfortable enough to tell her if there had been something more. They used to share all of their secrets.

But to everyone's surprise, Seamus shook his head. "No."

The witch wrinkled her brow and examined him once more. She ran her hands down his full arm and looked into his eyes.

"Then it seems ye've the selkie blood in *you*, lad," she said simply, releasing him from her grasp at last.

"What do you mean?" Kiana asked incredulously.

Mrs. Byrne shrugged.

"The descendants of selkies are sometimes called to the sea in childhood as the others are," said the witch. "And sometimes they're not. Sometimes it takes the touch of another selkie to remind ye where ye come from."

"But I don't have the mark of a selkie," said Seamus blankly, staring at his own hand. "I'd have a scar like Jasmine, wouldn't I?"

"None of ye listen, do ye?" the witch exclaimed with ferocity. "Ye wouldn't have a mark should ye be a selkie descendent. The scars are of those who are *chosen* to become one, not born one."

"But I'm not a descendent of selkies," Seamus said flatly.

"And ye happen to *know* that?" the witch asked mysteriously. "There's never been a parent or grandparent in yer life that's had mystery about them?"

Kiana was surprised to see that Seamus froze in what looked like contemplative understanding. Even in the dark of the night, she could see his eyes misted over in thought; as if he were trying to recall a memory. She caught a glimpse of the professor in the corner of her eye to find he was studying Seamus as well.

"My mother went missing," Seamus said quietly, shaking his head. "But her body was found. She washed up on the shore." He looked up at the witch, the doubt on his face apparent in the lamplight.

But the witch rocked backward on her heels, nodding in satisfaction. "The selkies will transform back to humans just as they take their last breath."

Her eyes glossed over as she uttered what sounded like a chilling incantation:

"Their bodies are found on the shore, united with the land once more."

Seamus and the professor remained silent, but Kiana could not hold her tongue any longer. While Mrs. Byrne had undoubtedly drawn her conclusions about Seamus and Jasmine's mysterious connections to the selkies of Ireland, Kiana was more interested in next steps. The witch had an aversion to concrete answers, but Kiana knew she needed to ask her question or else their entire mission in Cashel had been a waste of time.

"What do *we* need to do to find *her*?" she asked. "Nevermind if she can't come back to us!"

Her voice cracked with uncertainty, but something about it seemed to bring Seamus back to the present. He snapped his gaze up to meet the witch's stare.

"That's where ye have a challenge," said the woman, dismissing Kiana's tone in favor of preserving the aura of mystery. "For the selkies stay well hidden away...they're not likely to show themselves anywhere where ye can see them."

Kiana recalled Aidan's statement about the selkies being sighted as they tried to catch a glimpse of their old lives, but refrained from voicing it as Seamus seemed prepared to speak.

"Where are they?" he asked coldly. "Ye must know."

His gaze challenged her; daring her to deny that she knew more than she was letting on.

The witch surveyed him with interest.

"Hy-Brasil of course," she said at last. "Where all the selkies of the Aran Islands live."

Seamus scoffed in exasperation, but Professor Brennan started at the statement.

"The phantom island?" he exclaimed with intrigue. "You don't mean to say it's real?"

"I thought ye were an academic of sorts," the witch said coldly. "Surely ye must have come across it once or twice in yer studies."

Kiana recalled the poem recited by the fireside of the inn only hours ago. Mrs. Byrne had of course mentioned *the Isle of Hy-Brasail* (as she had pronounced it then). The impending despair of failure began to close in on her as she recalled the subject of the story. An island that no one could find. Great.

She was surprised to see the professor seemed to be taking this theory seriously and even seemed to be working through possible plans in his head as he stood in contemplative silence.

"But I warn ye," Mrs. Byrne continued, her finger wagging in the air as she turned back toward Seamus. "Her *body's* bound to change soon."

The significance of her emphasis was not lost on Kiana, but Seamus' impatience had returned.

"We know that," he said shortly. "She's a selkie now."

"No, ye don't know what I mean," said the witch, waving him in dismissal. She leaned in closer and spoke her next words with relish. "I mean yer lass will lose her desire for ye as she's becoming a different species. The passion ye may have shared as humans will fade as she accepts what she's become."

Seamus' face was white and still as stone, but he did not speak.

"Seamus," said Kiana seriously as she reached for his arm. The way Mrs. Byrne seemed to be taunting Seamus had made her highly suspicious, and she had had enough. She suddenly felt desperate to return to the sanctuary of the inn. How could this foolish old bat possibly believe all of this ridiculous folklore to be true?

No. It could not be so. If Kiana had to guess, Mrs. Byrne had seen an opportunity to take advantage of a man down on his luck and play with his emotions, for.... for God knows what reason. Kiana decided then and there that the conversation was over.

"Right," Seamus said slowly, not responding to Kiana's grip on his arm. "We'll have to find her then, I suppose."

"Ye will never have her as ye stand on two legs," said the witch, shaking her head.

Kiana started forward.

"Thank you for your help. We'll be leaving now."

She spoke with authority and pulled Seamus from his daze. The professor evidently shared some of Kiana's reluctance and murmured a weak goodbye to the woman as well. The three of them took off through the grassy field and started toward the village together, no one daring to speak until they were well out of earshot of Mrs. Byrne. Kiana glanced behind her, but the woman seemed to have vanished into the darkness.

Once back in the dimly lit street, Seamus turned on the professor.

"Do ye believe her?" he asked. "I mean, ye're a *Professor*."

He emphasized the word *professor* with a bit of unflattering doubt that was not lost on Liam Brennan, but the academic plainly thought it not worth arguing over.

"I have heard the same tales of Hy-Brasil as you, I'm sure," he said slowly. "Though I had never imagined that it would be some sort of habitat of the selkies."

"So you believe in all of this?" Kiana interjected, raising a doubtful brow. She found it absurd that someone who not only *taught* higher education, but at one of the world's most renowned, prestigious universities, would have thought any of this remotely possible.

Professor Brennan rocked back on his heels and let out a low sigh.

"I learned long ago that legends and folklore of a place such as Ireland are not to be taken lightly," he said. "Jasmine's father would have agreed with me on that."

Seamus, seemingly less doubtful than Kiana, pressed him further. "And ye think ye'd know where to find this place?"

"A mysterious phantom island that men have sought for centuries?" the professor said with a hollow laugh. "Certainly not. But I *do* have some theories."

Kiana looked between the two men in dismay. While Seamus and Professor Brennan seemed to think there was truth in Mrs. Byrne's words, she could not have felt less convinced following their moonlit meeting. The mysterious aura that surrounded the old woman had now disappeared in the lamplight of the village, and her confidence in finding her friend alive gone with it.

"We're grasping at straws because we're desperate," Kiana said quietly, dropping her hands to her sides. "We don't want to believe what's most likely because we can't let her go."

Her words hung stagnant in the chilly night air. None of them spoke, but Seamus' eyes fell downcast. The professor's expression once again melted into stoic obscurity.

"I'm really sorry," said Kiana as tears welled in her eyes, speaking mainly to Seamus as her heart hurt for him the most.

"I need to go home. And I think you should, too. I know there was something special between you two, but she… Seamus, she's gone." She looked up at him, praying that he would see reason.

Seamus looked at her sadly, green eyes clouded over.

"I know," he said. "But I can't stop looking. I dunno why. I just can't."

Kiana nodded, having expected him to say something of the sort. She wondered just how long he would continue to chase the wild possibilities of legends, but she knew this was where they would need to part ways. After all, Ireland was *his* home, not hers. She pulled him in for a hug and held his shoulders for a moment longer.

"I won't forget that you did this," she said tearfully, looking up at him.

"And I'd do it again."

Unsure of how to handle her departure from the professor,

she merely shook his hand and he returned a similarly friendly smile.

"Jazz is lucky to have a friend like you," the man said.

His speaking in the present tense was not lost on her, but she thought it best to leave the two of them to discuss their theories alone for as long as they may. It was her time to leave.

Kiana dragged her feet up the stairs of the inn, walking away from any faint hope she had for Jasmine's life. She wanted to believe it all, she really did. But her flight out of Dublin and back home was in four days, and she knew she needed to be on it. As there were only a couple of hours of darkness left, she did not bother to try and sleep. Instead, she mindlessly scrolled through dozens of pictures of herself and Jasmine while tears rolled silently down her face.

The scar on her friend's hand had been so insignificant throughout her life. It was hardly noticeable in any of their photos. To think it could be a symbol of some strange bloodline to which she was destined seemed less and less believable each time she caught a glimpse of it.

THE MORNING CAME, as it always does. Kiana packed up her things quickly and made her way downstairs, plopping into one of the cozy armchairs by the window. She was already on her second cup of coffee when Kristen and Marissa made it downstairs.

"You're up early," Kristen said. Then, noticing both Kiana and Jasmine's bags on the floor, she mused, "And you're ready to go."

"I am," Kiana sighed deeply.

"Well," Marissa said uneasily. "You should know... we-we got a call this morning. I think they got our numbers wrong and Detective Murphy must have thought it was yours-"

"The point," Kiana said through teeth that were gritted not in irritation with Marissa's stalling, but rather with her own nerves. She braced herself for the worst.

"They found her clothes and her phone on the shore near Doolin," Kristen said bluntly. "And they've declared it a suicide."

Kiana closed her eyes and buried her head in her hands. The myths and legends that seemed *almost* possible over the past few days vanished instantly as the truth slapped her across the face with crippling sobriety.

She had wanted to hold onto the tiniest bit of hope she had in her heart despite her resignation at the abbey. Strange as it was, she felt closer to Jasmine now than she ever had, because only *she* would have related to this feeling of loss.

PART II

OCEAN DWELLER

CHAPTER 13

UNDERWATER

It was warm.

Warm, but not hot. It felt as though the sheets had been pulled up to my chin on a cold winter night, or like I was sitting exactly the correct distance from a roaring fireplace, toasting in the haze that hovers above head just before falling peacefully asleep. I would have been perfectly comfortable if it weren't for the certain sensation that something was wrong. But what was it? I tried to remember.

I believed I *had* fallen into a deep sleep… but then I recalled the ice cold wind sweeping me off of the cliff in a powerful gust that sent me tumbling into the water.

That's right. I had narrowly avoided the sharp, jagged rock as I grasped desperately for anything that could soften the impact. I had hit the water and I never resurfaced. But I had no memory of gasping for air or even any form of struggle beyond the sharp pain I had briefly felt in my lower body. After that, everything had gone dark. I was now certain of nothing other than the fact that I had to be dead…right?

Lying on an unknown soft surface, I felt that my movements were soft and agile; like I was painting with my fingertips. My nails ran through something slippery and rich, and as the grains tumbled slowly between my fingers, I came to the realization that it was sand. Soft, wet sand that seemed to move in slow motion. It was not what I had expected, but it didn't bother me in the slightest. Despite the unfamiliarity that surrounded me, my mind was strangely at ease.

I breathed evenly, allowing the sweetest air I had ever smelled to fill my nose and linger on my tongue. It was so rich that it almost tasted like salt. I sensed a faint breeze on my neck and reached for it, pausing in surprise. I felt the three tiniest slits on either side, moving in succinct rhythm with my breath as if carrying out my heartbeat's own will. I had gills.

But a small voice in my head began to shake me from my dreamlike state. It seemed to be the awakening of my instincts as a human being, telling me it was time to move.

'Time to wake up,' said the voice inside my head.

'I can't,' said another, more pessimistic voice.

But suddenly, I could. I gently rolled over, but it only made me *more* comfortable. It was like I was being enveloped by a gentle blanket, made just for me. No, I was fine right where I was.

Whoosh.

What was that?

I attempted to wiggle my toes and suddenly found that my mind had no recollection of how to do so. In fact, I felt a strange sensation of fluidity in my entire lower body as if my legs had become one and the bones had been removed.

The sound of gentle, hushed voices came from the same place where I had heard the noise and I froze.

"Should we-"

"No! Are ye daft?"

I shifted my weight to one side, finding that my eyes were now shut in fear rather than exhaustion. I opened them as narrowly as slits, but there was no one there. It looked like there was nothing but sand and floating particles of... I couldn't tell what, exactly. I sat up slowly, opening my eyes more widely.

There was nothing but sand and rock for miles behind me, but directly in my line of sight was the distinct outline of the sinister, jagged cliffs from which I had just fallen; I was sure of it. I had not drifted far and that was good news, but how was I ever going to attract the attention of a rescue crew from the crashing waves ahead?

I paused with chilling realization. I didn't *need* to be rescued. I took another deep breath of water, my heart racing.

"Hello?" I called out into the water. I was definitely being watched.

A response finally came. "Are ye a friend?"

I whirled around, my body seeming to drag beneath me, but I still saw no one. The realization of why I could not feel my legs hit me in the gut before I even dared to turn my look down. In some deep recess of my mind, I already knew.

Where my legs should have been-and *were* only moments ago-was a long, scaled, and brightly iridescent fish tail, exactly the same color as the mysterious scar that had marked my hand since I was eleven years old.

"I am," I replied to the bodiless voice.

"What are ye doing all the way out here?"

This time, the voice revealed itself.

In the silky water now ahead of me, there stood-no, *bobbed* above the ocean floor-a man and a woman. Except they were hardly man or woman at all considering the lower half of their bodies took a drastic departure from the typical human anatomy. The two of them had tails that matched my own, with bright scales of metallic luminosity that while resembling a fish's, were immediately identifiable as something much more mystical.

Their faces, while containing the traditional features of eyes, nose, and ears, were distinctively supernatural as well. Their eyes seemed to reflect the light of the moon, moving sharply like an animal's as they observed me closely. The woman's hair was so blonde that it was nearly white, with streaks of the same sheen of her scales scattered throughout the massive blanket of strands. The man was darker in features and had his brown hair pulled back into a long plait at the base of his neck. They both wore expressions of shock and concern on their beautiful faces.

"The shallows are far too dangerous," the man said cautiously, inching toward me so as not to frighten me. I appreciated the thought, but my sense of fear had gone numb and was replaced by amazement. "And this area is much too populated to alight for land."

"I wasn't-" I said tentatively. After failing to produce a reasonable explanation for my sheer existence in my own mind, I certainly had no answer for the inquisition of the two mer-people in front of me.

I noticed with sudden self-consciousness that my clothes had disappeared entirely, while the woman in front of me had on a beautifully beaded brasier that consisted of two white seashells for modesty. So the movies had gotten *that* part correctly, I guess. I crossed my arms in embarrassment and uttered the safest answer I could surmise.

"I'm lost."

"Come with us," said the woman quickly.

She looked somewhat worried, but her eyes were unmistakably kind. I followed her willingly but slowly; my tail flapping awkwardly behind me as I clumsily dragged my body through the water. My struggle was not lost on my new companions, and understanding seemed to dawn over them both. The woman reached for my hand and I took it appreciatively, having no choice but to trust her. The man watched more warily, glancing behind me and toward the rocks from which I had come.

"Has anyone seen ye?" he said in what felt like a mildly accusatory tone. I was taken aback, wondering how he thought it possible anyone could see through the mist that hung over the entire western coast of Ireland this time of year, let alone into the depths of the black water below the Cliffs of Moher.

"No," I said, narrowing my eyes. "I fell from the Cliffs."

My words seemed to stun him, giving me a minor sense of satisfaction that evaporated almost instantly. The woman nodded as if in confirmation of her own assumptions and spoke to me very quickly and severely.

"We will discuss that, but not here," she said, her lamplight eyes flashing in the depths. I wondered if that's what my own looked like.

Without another word, she whipped around and shot through the water in the opposite direction of the rocks, dragging me behind her. The man brought up the rear, alternating flanking us on either side in protective wariness. I felt a flicker of fear rooted in something other than the obvious terror that comes with being somewhat kidnapped by strangers. What else was out there that they were so worried about?

"Where are we going?" I asked tentatively.

"Not yet," the woman answered curtly. I sensed she was concerned for all of our collective safety and made a mental note to ask what *her* business had been in these parts if they were so dangerous.

We went on for some time, with me turning around only once to see that the signs of land had long disappeared. The speed at which the woman swam was like lightning, and I tested my own tail to find it was equally as powerful, if not yet fully within my control.

In addition to the prolonged distance, the water was also growing deeper. The sand below us slanted downward sharply, and my eyes continually adjusted to my darkening surroundings. Even as my fear subsided, I was not all that interested in the ocean floor. The landscape at the bottom of the Atlantic near Galway was rather monotonous and gray, I thought.

My eyes narrowed in on the next major obstacle I saw as if I were wearing magnifying glasses, leading me to understand the reason for my improvement in sight from the past few days. I was surprised to find that we were approaching a massive network of beautiful coral. Directly ahead of me was a large fan of pink with a porcelain-like skeleton, waving gently in the muted waves of the deep ocean. The vibrant color seemed so oddly out of place for Ireland, and I wondered what it could be.

"Almost there," the woman said in a reassuring voice.

Despite being nothing more than a co-pilot, I felt exhausted as my new lower body worked furiously to stay afloat. The tail felt heavy and slightly awkward as I forced it to mirror the movement of the two next to me; up and down in quick, flapping waves that seemed to flit like a bird's wings rather than a fish's tail.

The coral grew thicker and nearly methodical in the way it was positioned-I thought it looked like the entrance to a garden outside of some grand estate. The signs of deep sea life were teeming all around me with a variety of animals and plants I knew in addition to those I had never seen. Sea fans, sponges, worms, starfish, crustaceans and a variety of fish species were buzzing through the reef and I was reminded of Raj. He would have been able to name them all.

The sand began to slant upward once more, but the woman took a sharp turn away from what I assumed was the nearing shore, diving downward into a thick mass of coral and rock. In the distance, I saw the flash of iridescent tails flitting about and gasped with realization that there were others. I was coming upon some sort of colony.

"Here," the woman said kindly, slowing to a casual bob near a massive fluffy orange anemone.

Were clownfish indigenous to this part of the Atlantic? Surely their houses weren't this large? It looked as though it could fit four to five people inside. A combination of rising sea temperatures and depths that had not yet been discovered, I supposed. The woman flashed through the dancing stalks and urged me to follow. I hesitated, having seen Finding Nemo once or twice in my childhood.

"It won't sting ye, dear," the woman assured me, noticing my apprehension. "Not even if yer out of practice."

She smiled at this final remark and I would have laughed had the circumstances been different. However, I trusted the mermaid in front of me knew better than I did and I followed her through the silky fronds.

There was certainly a sense of security inside the cozy plant that I had not felt in the open waters, as if I had now disappeared through a barrier that made me invisible to the rest of the planet. The woman dug in the corner of one of the fronds, silently tossing another one of her brasiers to me which I fastened around my body quickly and appreciatively. As I dressed, I gulped at the thought of my friends (if they had noticed my disappearance yet) finding my clothes washed up somewhere on the rocks.

The man joined us inside and I waited, not daring to speak. Besides, there was hardly much for me to say. I knew nothing of my whereabouts or how I had become what I was.

"I am Sorcha," said the woman, pronouncing her Gaelic name in a beautiful sound that I could never have replicated. She gestured to the man who was trailing the perimeter with a watchful gaze on both myself and the outside of their hiding place. "And this is Lachlan. What's yer name?"

"Jasmine."

"Ye say ye fell off the Cliffs," Lachlan stated, his voice softer but still full of caution. "Do ye mean to say ye intended to landwalk permanently?"

I looked between them, confused at the verbiage he used to describe the only method of movement I had ever known. But Sorcha seemed to understand, swimming toward me slowly with her face twisted into a soft smile charged with a mixture of empathy and worry.

"I do not think ye have yet been in yer sea form, until now, have ye, child?" she asked me kindly.

To be called 'child' was something that took me by surprise, but I admittedly felt at ease hearing such a term of endearment come from an unfamiliar face. I shook my head in silent confirmation.

"It is uncommon for such a late age," Sorcha said, the corners of her mouth turned down in a frown of contemplation as she surveyed me closely.

"What is not common?" I asked tentatively. And then, as if thinking of something for the first time, Sorcha looked up at me with intrigue.

"Where were ye raised? Yer not Irish or Scottish."

"America," I said lamely, and then reasoning that mermaids of all creatures would likely be familiar with a *coastal* state if any at all, I added, "Florida, specifically."

"But ye are not a child of Ne Hwas," the woman said, looking me up and down in a curious manner. Not knowing what she meant, I said nothing.

"Ye have lived there all of yer life?" Lachlan asked me.

I began to nod in confirmation but stopped. "Well, I spent a few years in Portugal," I murmured. "When I was a child." I doubted it was important, but I felt that anything aside from complete honesty would do me no favors in this strange new company.

The two then exchanged a look whose meaning I could not decipher.

"Have ye any markings?" the woman asked. This time, her eyes began to mist over with an emotion that I could not read. Was it fear?

I held out my left hand and turned my palm upward to reveal the straight line of silver that seemed more vibrant than ever under the rolling waves. If anything on my body were to be classified as a "marking," it was certainly this. And if its appearance had been mysterious on land, it was undoubtedly magical underwater. My two new companions exchanged glances loaded with revelation and something like pity.

"My child," said Sorcha. "I am sorry to say that ye have been cursed."

To this, I had no response. The cut on my hand continued to glow, the colors seemingly melting from one to another; from hues of pink to purple to green, like a streak of opal on my skin.

"Yer similar to us," Sorcha continued, swimming away in thought. She paused and whirled around to make eye contact with me. "But not exactly."

"And what are you?" I asked shakily, already knowing the answer. I attempted to soften my tone by adding. "Sorry-what are *we?*"

They glanced at one another, evidently debating how to phrase the fantastic reality to me. "Are ye familiar with Irish or Scottish folklore?"

I dug deep within the recesses of my mind, attempting to recall any semblance of a memory regarding Irish folktales. I had always been drawn to gothic horrors rather than fantasy or fairy tales when it came to the realm of classic literature. Fairies and leprechauns seemed to fuzzily come to the forefront of my thoughts, but I could not recall anything involving mermaids off the coast of Ireland. At last I shook my head in defeat.

Sorcha settled onto the soft surface of the anemone, her tail trailing lazily off to the side as it brushed the fronds without fear of pain. She invited me to sit beside her and I reluctantly obliged.

"*Selkies*, or *Silkies*," Sorcha began. "Are sometimes referred to in Irish and Scottish folklore as the seal people, although in reality we appear in a form that looks like the traditional mermaid with which ye are most familiar."

Right, I thought, observing that Sorcha much more closely resembled Ariel than a seal.

"There are also merrows, a very close cousin of ours," she continued.

Lachlan let out a scoff. "I wouldn't be too proud to be related to them," he grumbled. Sorcha ignored him.

"We can choose to exist in either our sea form or walk on land," Sorcha said. "The old tales tell of us removing our seal skins once out of the water and putting them back on when we wish to return." She smiled mischievously. "I wouldn't say that's exactly how it works, but it's something like that."

My jaw hung open in disbelief. "So we can choose to be a human or a mermaid?" I corrected myself. "A *Selkie*."

Hope began to stir in my heart-perhaps I was not lost to this life forever. I thought of the worry that was undoubtedly plaguing my friends back on the surface. Kiana, Marissa, Kristen... what on earth could they be thinking at this moment regarding my whereabouts? Had they even noticed I was missing? How much time had passed?

Lastly, another, almost stronger emotion tore at me from deep within in a way that surprised me even more than my physical state had. What about *Seamus*? All I wanted to do was tell all of them that I was alive. Not necessarily *safe*, but alive.

Sorcha bit her lip. "Well-"

"*We* can," Lachlan said. The distinction was not lost on me and I snapped my gaze up to meet his. "But I am afraid ye have the curse of an Amalgam, and ye will remain like this forever."

"What's an Amalgam?" I asked, my voice slightly louder and more wobbly than I had intended. Of course in the literal sense, I was well aware that the word meant a hybrid or synthesis of some kind, but to be called one on the heels of discovering the word *selkie* for the first time, I didn't like the sound of it at all.

"An Amalgam," Sorcha explained gently. "Is someone who is not of the original selkie blood, but has been cursed with it later in their life. Someone who has been marked by another selkie."

She pointed down at my scar. "That is the mark of an Amalgam's curse. It will only call ye to the sea in which ye were cursed should ye ever return."

"The sea in which I was cursed?" I repeated quietly as I dissected what she had said.

The mark on my hand had been donned upon me in the Atlantic Ocean of course, but I had lived in Florida for many years of my life. I had been in the Atlantic Ocean countless times and never experienced what I had now. Not until this trip to Ireland had I even felt any of the signs that I now knew were signs of me being *called to the sea.*

I voiced this to Sorcha, but it was Lachlan who responded.

"The selkies do not map the seas the way the humans do," he explained patiently. "To call The Atlantic one ocean would be to call the Earth one nation."

I didn't know how to reply to this. I looked at Sorcha for further explanation.

"But ye *have* been in one of our shared waters once before," said Sorcha. "Is Portugal where you received this mark?"

It seemed to be a rhetorical question; she already knew. And Portugal being much closer to Ireland than Florida, I began to understand.

"Yes," I said in nearly a whisper, examining my hand more thoroughly than I ever had before.

I recalled my memory from the day in Porto, the searing pain that ripped the skin from my hand and the miraculous speed at which it had healed. The flash of bright light that had drawn me to the water in the first place, and the strange human-like hand that had reached for me in the blackness of the sea...

I then told them the story, watching their faces change from concern to wonder to pity. Sorcha sighed as she gently reached for my hand.

"I'm sorry this has happened to ye," she said sincerely.

"But why?" I said, speaking more to myself than my companions.

I thought back to my years in Portugal and cursed my young self for my curiosity that one night. Why had this happened to me? I ran my hands over my tail, watching as my scar began to glow to match the scales.

"That I cannot say," said Sorcha sadly and with the sincerity of someone who truly understood. "Ye may never know who marked ye or why."

"I have to go back and find my friends," I said suddenly, my mind snapping back to the present. What had happened in the past could not be changed. "I need to tell them I'm alright."

"No, child," said Lachlan, his eyes flashing with fear and warning severity. "Ye can never go back to the shallows again."

"Why not?" I asked sharply. "What would happen if I did?"

Sorcha sighed and looked at Lachlan. "She must know the truth for her own safety."

He agreed and began to explain.

"In the shallows, yer throat will burn like ye've swallowed fire, and yer tail will become paralyzed," he said simply. "Ye will be left to die, unable to breathe the air for longer than the span of fifteen minutes."

"Perhaps even less time than that," he continued, knowing I had been calculating in my mind. "There is no way to know for certain. The only time we ever venture to the shallows near the human mainland is when we plan to take our land-walker form."

"And *that* we have not done at the Cliffs in a long time," said Sorcha sadly. "It is far too populated for it to be safe anymore. We would be too easily seen."

"So do you ever take your-*land-walker*-form?" I asked tentatively, and then quickly added, "I know that I can't, but what about you? Surely you miss it?"

I thought that distracting them in their own affairs would

give me time to think. Admittedly, the task of returning to land to communicate with my friends was daunting and likely impossible. Even if I could get to the surface unscathed, what if I were seen by someone else? I certainly knew enough folktales to be wise to the fact that the mysterious creatures of legends didn't ever want to be found out for their truth. *Besides,* I thought as my heart sank, *what would be the use if I couldn't return to my human form?*

"Yes, we do take our land-walker form," said Lachlan. "But it is in a place where the shallows cannot hurt us and the humans cannot find us."

He broke into a grin which Sorcha returned.

"We are in those shallows right now," Sorcha said to me. "And ye will be safe in the waters here. Let me show ye where the selkies of the Aran Islands live."

CHAPTER 14

THE PHANTOM ISLAND

I took off with Sorcha, Lachlan following closely behind. I instinctively knew that it was not far to the surface; we had already approached the sloping shore before we entered the anemone. I turned to see my sparkling tail flickering in the now visible sunlight and I felt my eyesight shift with the ease of a plane's landing gear.

"Up we go," said Sorcha brightly.

I broke through the thickness of the water and into the gentle lapping of the waves above where I was greeted with air that smelled unfamiliar to me now. It was tinged with something that I did not quite like, though I could not identify what it was. It was as if everything below had been fresh, and now I was faced with the staleness of the ordinary air I used to breathe.

"Feels differently now, doesn't it?" she asked me.

"Very."

I bobbed effortlessly above the waves, discovering that we were overlooking the shore of a beautifully luscious island unlike anything I had ever seen. Everything looked wildly different to me; sharper, richer, and more *alive*. I blinked as I confirmed that there seemed to be a slightly green tint to all I saw, but in a wonderfully appealing way. The clearness of the day seemed intensified, as if someone had placed a lens in front of my face and turned the sharpness filter as high as it would go.

"Ye need not hold yer breath," Lachlan said to me with a look of amusement on his face. I hadn't even realized I had subconsciously been afraid to take a deep breath, and I let out a laughter of surprise.

"Still getting used to this," I murmured as I choked on the dry air.

As I spoke, I was surprised to hear my own voice was slightly altered. While my voice beneath the sea sounded exactly as I had remembered it, it now seemed almost musical as the notes of my laughter danced across the waves. I laughed again to repeat the strange phenomenon. Sorcha noticed me and smiled broadly.

"Another one of our natural tricks to lure prey into our midst," she said mysteriously, her voice ringing like a bell. "Prey, meaning the land-walkers."

I looked at her, startled. We didn't *eat* them, did we?

"Ye sound like a Merrow," said Lachlan good-humoredly, and I laughed weakly, clearly having missed the joke.

I looked around to find there were several selkies lazing both in the shallows near the shore as well as walking upon it in their human forms. I watched them in disbelief; trying to understand how I could have lived in ignorance of this world my entire life.

Those who walked on the shore certainly *looked* like humans at first, but it was obvious that they were something else entirely. They moved with an impeccable grace that looked like dancing upon the sand, and their features seemed brighter, fresher, and more alive than a regular person's.

I gasped as I watched one of the female selkies alight from the water. She rose slowly as her tail melted away seamlessly and was replaced by graceful legs enveloped in a cascading skirt of what looked like fine green silk. As if it were as common an occurrence as stepping out of a shower, the woman proceeded on land to join her friends who were waving at her in the distance.

"As ye can see, the legends of us 'removing our seal skins' are not entirely accurate," Sorcha said, bobbing next to me. "They are not an external garment, but rather a part of us. They cannot be stolen from us."

I tried to imagine one of the beautifully elite creatures in front of me hiding their seal skin on land as if it were a cape; it seemed impossibly silly that anyone could believe such a thing.

"And you said I won't be able to-" I began.

Sorcha shook her head sadly. "No, my child."

Then, her face brightened with optimism that I did not quite feel, but nevertheless appreciated. "But there are many of us who choose not to. Ye will find yerself a home here."

She gestured to the many selkies swimming playfully near the shore, plainly not interested in land at all. I flinched, knowing I would never be as content as they were. Were selkies *born* knowing what they were?

"Where *is* 'here' exactly?" I then asked, realizing I had no clue as to how far I had traveled. The island I looked upon certainly did not seem to share the same biosphere as Ireland with its wildly colored plants and volcanic terrain. There was a myste-rious mist that seemed to surround the landmass like a protective barrier, thick with white clouds that despite their fluffiness, generously allowed the sunshine to peek through.

"This is Hy-Brasil," came a voice from behind me that made me jump, even in the waves. I whipped my wet hair over my shoulder to see who had spoken.

I found myself face to face with another selkie, much closer to my own age than my two companions. He had a boyish face that was good-natured; with rosy cheeks and eyes that smiled along with his mouth. But what really caused me pause was the resem-blance he bore to Sorcha. I knew immediately they were related.

"This is my son," said Sorcha, placing an arm around the young man and beaming. "Fintan, this is Jasmine."

Fintan's shoulder-length fair hair bounced in the waves and the similarities between himself and his mother was made even more uncanny in their mannerisms and expressions. Their smiles were nearly identical with a soft curve on the right side of their mouths that instantly gave them both the appearance of a friend.

I noticed that the young man's face shared no trace of Lachlan's own harsh features. Wondering if he was indeed Lachlan's son as well, (and in fact how mermaid reproduction was even possible) I caught myself once again rudely staring.

"Nice to meet you," I said simply, offering my hand. As though he thought it amusing, he glanced at his mother with a raised eyebrow before taking it and donning an obnoxiously long kiss upon it.

"That's how the land-walkers greet, innit?" he asked as he flashed a bright smile.

I laughed. "Not exactly. You're supposed to shake it."

He seemed confused by this and I recalled Sorcha saying she had not "land-walked" in a long time. I wondered just how many years she had been alive. Was the lifespan of a selkie significantly longer than a human's? Could Fintan, who looked no older than myself, possibly be from a time when men still greeted women with a kiss upon the hand? Questions I supposed I would be able to ask in time, should I truly be damned here for the rest of my life.

"Jasmine was asking about Hy-Brasil," said Sorcha as she began to lead us in a swim along the perimeter of the island. I followed eagerly as I wanted to see more of the mysterious place. Now having heard the name more than once, I knew it sounded familiar.

"Ahh of course, the home of the Aran Island selkies," said Fintan, looking upon the land wistfully.

"And hopefully the home where ye'll *stay*," Lachlan said, nudging him playfully.

Sorcha looked at me and explained. "Fintan is engaged to a lovely selkie who lives in the North. I'm hoping that once they're married, they'll choose to settle here with us."

I nodded, noting that if nothing else, the family dynamics of selkies seemed similar to those of land-walkers, at least.

"I will!" Fintan said with certainty before turning back to me. "As I was saying, Hy-Brasil is-"

"I know about Hy-Brasil," I said abruptly, at once recalling where I had heard of it. I dug deeply to unearth a memory from a few years ago.

I had been home from school for the holidays at my father's new house in South Florida during his time at the University of Miami in Coral Gables. Liam (by then already a Professor in Ireland, though not yet posted at Trinity) and Bridget Brennan had come to stay for Thanksgiving. Their attempt to celebrate in the most American fashion possible resulted in a slightly burned turkey, causing everyone to opt for Bridget's Irish stew instead.

It was a rare chilly night in Fort Lauderdale, and after dinner we had all taken to the squishy chairs on the screened in patio that overlooked the golf course out back. Stuffed to the brim, I had been nodding off while Professor Brennan and Raj's discussion had faded from stories of holiday traditions to dry, academic topics, before finally settling on the mysteries of the Atlantic. Raj's romanticism of marine life had only intensified during his time at Miami, and it was almost impossible to imagine him having been an astronomer at one time at all.

"THE GREATEST NAUTICAL enigma lies just off the coast of Ireland," Professor Brennan said mysteriously. "But you surely aren't interested in that." He waved in playful dismissiveness as he took another sip of whiskey.

"Here we go again," Bridget whispered with an eye roll, nudging me and thus awakening me from my post-Thanksgiving stupor. "He loves this one."

"Enlighten me," said Raj, grinning with anticipation.

Professor Brennan straightened up in preparation for optimal story-telling.

"Hy-Brasil, also known as the supernatural island, is a mysterious island that appears only once every seven years for a single day off the western coast of Ireland. It's been shown on maps of the Atlantic Ocean for centuries, dating back to as early as the fourteenth century," he said. "But it could never be found by the same person twice, as it was never in the exact same location. Many expeditions were launched to try and find it, but to no avail. It remains a mystery of the seas, shrouded in a magical gray mist that none can permeate..."

He paused for dramatic effect, but the crowd (consisting of Bridget and myself) merely yawned.

"I'm actually familiar with this, now that you mention it," Raj then said thoughtfully. "In Porto, I referenced quite a few nautical charts in relation to astrological events. I remember a small island separated by what I believe was called the 'brasil river'."

Professor Brennan nodded satisfactorily as he took another sip of whiskey.

"That map will be the work of Portuguese cartographer João Teixeira Albernaz in the 1600s. Hy-Brasil appeared on maps of the seas all the way up until the nineteenth century."

"How on earth do you know that?" Raj said, laughing incredulously and looking at Bridget who shrugged in dismay.

"He can remember something like that, but somehow forgets our anniversary nearly every year," she whispered to me again. I stifled a laugh.

"Hey, that was one time," Liam said, winking at his wife. "And I was actually a day early. I think that's preferable to the alternative."

"So where's the mystery?" I asked sleepily, struggling to keep my eyes open. "About Hy-Brasil."

"Well the mystery is that it disappears and now it's merely a legend," said the professor, grateful for my intrigue, even if it were out of mere politeness. "But I think it's real."

He finished his thought with a slow and dramatic nodding of his head.

Raj laughed but I recognized the twinkle in his eye that appeared whenever presented with an academic challenge.

"Surely historians only continued to place it on the map after seeing so many others before them do so," he said. And then, satisfied that he had presented the logical answer, he took to the side of legend for argument's sake. "But it is curious that there were so many documented sightings."

"Well, I suppose we'll never really know," sighed Professor Brennan. "I'll add it to my bucket list of destinations."

"An island that's visible for a single day every seven years and it moves around from place to place?" Raj mused, shaking his head. "Your odds aren't looking great."

I FELT my eyes widen as I looked upon the legendary island, wondering just how many folktales had truth to them after all. I laughed incredulously, my heart aching that I couldn't share this revelation with the two people who would have wanted to hear it most.

"Yes, it *is* real," Sorcha said, reading my thoughts, though she could never have possibly understood the emotional depth that accompanied them. "The humans can't seem to keep track of it, but we always know where it is."

"So it *doesn't* move from place to place?" I asked curiously.

"Oh, I didn't say that," Sorcha replied mysteriously, and I eyed the mist that surrounded the island once more with newfound curiosity. It would certainly not be easy to find, whether it moved or not, and there was undoubtedly magic in this place.

"Come for a swim with me?" asked Fintan, grinning as he observed my wonder. "I don't ever land-walk, personally. It's not for me. A bit overrated."

He waved at the shore dismissively, whether to make me feel better or in sincerity, I did not know, but I appreciated the gesture nonetheless. I looked back toward Sorcha and Lachlan who nodded encouragingly. They plainly wanted me to enjoy myself, regardless of their own motives to ensure I never sought the shores of Galway again. I shrugged, thinking if nothing else, a swim around the island would give me a better understanding of where I was in relation to the Emerald Isle.

"See you later," I said to Sorcha and Lachlan.

I followed Fintan and we paddled lazily across the surface. I found it felt more like gliding than swimming as I skimmed the water effortlessly, my tail propelling me at a leisurely speed while I basked in the bright sunlight that poked through the clouds.

I did not have long to wonder where we were headed as Fintan rounded a particularly steep cliff that looked eerily similar to the one from which I had fallen only a day prior. However, this one boasted a much more welcoming inlet with calm, lapping waves. There was a small shoreline along the black rocks where the water moved soundlessly, and where the sand ended, an impressive entrance to a cave rose from the sea and seemingly straight into the heavens above.

"It's quieter over here," said Fintan. "This is where a lot of the Amalgams congregate."

I looked up at him, startled. How had he known what I was? Had he silently communicated with his mother? Or had he seen my scar?

As if he had read my mind, he pointed to my hand as I was tucking my hair behind my ear.

"I've seen nastier marks than that one," he said. "That one actually looks kind of cool."

I smiled, appreciating his kindness as we paddled further into the inlet.

"This way!" he said brightly, and I began to feel as though I were being dragged on a leash but an excitable puppy as he gestured for me to follow him toward the cave.

I was met with a more subdued, tranquil type of retreat where there were several selkies lying lazily on the rocks in the shadows of the cave. I watched them closely to see some of them were braiding each other's hair while others played some sort of game that involved tossing shells at the walls; their tails flapping in the shallows. As an outsider, it seemed to me like an extremely monotonous existence. But I tried to put on a polite face of mild interest, at least.

Another selkie, perhaps a few years older than ourselves, waved Fintan over to join him on the rock where he was lounging in the sun and beading some sort of necklace of shells. He dropped his art project carelessly back into the sea and made room for us, embracing Fintan in a half-hug from his position out of the water. He then noticed me and I felt strangely insecure as he eyed me intently.

"Cearbhall, this is Jasmine," said Fintan excitedly. "She's an Amalgam too!"

"Oh?" the man said, eyeing me with interest.

"Apparently I am," I said, laughing nervously. "I just found out I-well, what I am."

The words seemed to come out too fast, and I felt foolish for my embarrassment. Why did I care what any of them thought of me? After all, I had no intention of staying. Despite what Sorcha said, I knew in my heart that I would find a way to reverse the curse that had been laid upon me.

Cearbhall seemed not to hear me; he was far more interested in my physical features than anything I had to say. He looked upon me not with a typical man's leer, but rather with a deep reverence coupled with a hint of an almost hunger-adjacent fascination. I could not tell which I would have preferred.

"You're stunning, aren't you?" he asked as his dark eyes continued to survey me.

The longer he looked at me, the more I thought he resembled a sea creature rather than a human. It made me uneasy, but Fintan's friendship with him made me think I was being too harsh.

"Thank you," I responded politely. I almost said *"you too,"* but thought better of it.

"Well, I want to hear all about it," Cearbhall said. Noticing my blank stare, he laughed. "About your first impression of this." He gestured broadly to suggest he meant not only Hy-Brasil, but my general existence as a selkie.

I was caught by surprise, having hardly formed an opinion of my life at all beyond the fact that I was planning to find a way out of it. The past twenty-four hours or so had been a whirlwind of fear, change, and uncertainty, leaving no room for any thoughts of preference.

I felt a stab of agony as I imagined Seamus' face when he heard the news of my disappearance and I prayed he would somehow know that I was alive. Though I could not explain how it was possible, I knew he longed for me more than anyone. I also missed him deeply. My dreams crept to the surface of my thoughts, but I shook them away.

As I could see Cearbhall waited for an answer, I forced myself to focus only on the superficial positives-the parts of my new life that would be understandably thrilling and keep everyone's expectations at bay.

"Well, I love how fast I am," I said slowly, feigning my best excited smile. "And I can't say I mind the hair growth, either." I flipped my hair in a light-hearted manner that caused a chuckle to escape from both of them.

"And how did you discover you were chosen?" Cearbhall pressed.

I looked between him and Fintan in confusion. I thought I saw a flicker of something like discomfort on Fintan's face before he seemed to busy himself with examining a particularly unremarkable pebble.

"I don't know if I'd say I was *chosen,*" I said with emphasis. "But I've had this scar since I was a child."

Cearbhall laughed dismissively and took my hand with more force than I would have liked as he examined the iridescent scar.

"Well of course you were chosen," he said, not taking his eyes off of my hand.

He ran a finger along my scar in fascination. I felt a shiver run down my spine that was entirely different from the one that I had felt when Seamus had done the same only a few days prior. Back then, I had tingled with excitement and the desire for closeness with him. Now, I had to will every muscle in my body to keep from flinching.

Fintan seemed to notice my discomfort and he cleared his throat.

"She's had quite the day, I think," he said loudly. "Care to see more of the island?"

I nodded at him appreciatively. He suggested the two of them show me around and I was grateful to be mindlessly ushered to and fro, greeting the others who lounged in the cave. No one else we met seemed particularly interested in me beyond a polite hello; I supposed amongst the selkies I was relatively ordinary.

"A lot of us have figured out why we were chosen," Cearbhall said to me quietly as Fintan was called away by another group of selkies further inside the cave. I wished he wouldn't go, but I felt it would look childish to ask him to stay with me like he was my babysitter. He was younger than me, after all. I continued to watch him, but felt Cearbhall's gaze on my side profile.

"Have you?" I asked politely, suppressing a yawn.

The dark, damp atmosphere of the cave was beginning to wear on me along with the longevity of my day. It occurred to me that the sun still appeared high in the sky, and I wondered if Hy-Brasil experienced the same twenty-four hour day that the rest of the world did. If I *did* try to escape back to my old life, would I emerge from this dream-like island's orbit and find myself in the blackness of the sea at night? I shuddered to think of what that would look like.

Cearbhall then resumed his stance of casually authoritative apathy, leaning against a rock in the darker confines of the cave while he tossed shells against the rocky wall. I reluctantly joined him, feeling it would be rude to flutter away. Not wanting to remove myself fully from the water, I sat on a rock next to him, half-submerged. He didn't seem to mind; in fact, he seemed to enjoy his position of looking down upon me, as if I were a subject of his own, private court.

"The existence of selkies is merely a biological phenomenon… but the creation of *Amalgams*, well. It's purposeful," he said to me with an air of superiority that was impossible to miss.

"Purposeful," I repeated, only mildly interested. I kept Fintan in my peripherals, prepared to leave as soon as he was ready. For the time being, I would humor Cearbhall, as I had nothing better to do. "In what way?"

He threw his head back with exaggerated conceit; he clearly meant to draw his theatrics out as long as possible. Patience being a virtue that had always eluded me, I found his demeanor extremely irritating.

"Amalgams are a specialty among the breed of sea folk," he continued. "There are merrows, selkies, or *silkies* as they're sometimes called-depending on whether you ask the Scots or the Irish-but they all consider themselves to be cursed. Because *they* don't know any better."

The distinction was not lost on me, and I watched as his eyes flickered to Fintan.

"Well, we *are* cursed," I said, recalling Sorcha's words. "*Especially* the Amalgams. We can't even take our land-walker form. At least the other selkies can choose what they want to be."

I looked down at my tail resentfully. It *was* objectively beautiful, but certainly not a body part I wanted to be stuck with forever.

Cearbhall raised a doubtful eyebrow.

"Of course that's what *they* told you," he said, smirking and cocking his head toward Fintan who was now doubled over in laughter; unaware of the conversation happening just a few yards from him.

"But my dear, there are a great number of *powers* that we have that the traditional selkie does not."

"Like what?" I asked quickly.

My once feigned interest was becoming sincere, despite myself. Did he know more about Amalgams than Sorcha? *Was* there a way for us to transform back into humans? I knew enough about men like him to know that this type of information would come at a price, and I shifted uneasily as I thought about how to ask.

"I can certainly show you," he said slowly, sensing what was on my mind.

He gestured to Fintan who was slowly approaching us once more as his conversation with his friends had come to an end. "But not around them. We'll need to be with our own kind."

The way he said *them* created an instant barrier between myself and my only companions I had trusted thus far, and I didn't like it. I looked at Fintan, willing myself to not see him or his family any differently. After all, I knew instinctively that Sorcha and Lachlan had been trying to keep me safe, and I couldn't help but feel that whatever Cearbhall knew about our *powers* was sinister.

"I can show you how to go back," he then said simply, his

words coming out in a rush as Fintan approached. "That's what you want, isn't it?"

"Yes," I whispered back with the same level of severity, feeling guilty for a reason I couldn't explain. "Please."

He leaned in closer and said something that surprised me and infuriated me all at once. "Only if you promise it's not for a man. That would be a terrible waste."

"Of course not," I snapped, thinking of my friends.

But as soon as the words left my lips, I wondered if they were true. Kiana, Marissa, and Kristen had their own lives filled with purpose and direction. Their own families, dreams, and futures. But I had no family. I had no one. The only person I had was Seamus, and to say I *had* him at all was quite a stretch.

I allowed no semblance of my thoughts to creep into my expression, and I believed Cearbhall was nearly convinced.

"Remember, selkies are born. Amalgams are chosen," he said.

Fintan then appeared. "Sorry about that, got caught up with some old friends!" he said excitedly.

Then, noticing the atmosphere he had just entered, his smile wavered for a moment. "Everything alright?"

"Yes!" I said brightly. "All good."

Cearbhall nodded with a smirk, but Fintan looked between us and shrugged. "Ready to go?" he asked me.

"Great to meet you, Jasmine," Cearbhall said. "Come back and see me anytime."

With that, he held out his hand to shake mine and the iridescent scar that ran down his forearm lit up like a sparkler in the faint sunlight that streamed into the cave. Although I had known to expect it, I was still in awe laying eyes on the first scar I had ever seen that was similar to mine.

The journey back to the other side of the island was relaxed and quiet. I was deep in thought and in no mood for chit chat with Fintan. My companion did not seem to mind as he lazily flitted on his back across the surface, enjoying the blissful sunshine of his life that began and ended within the confines of the mystical island.

I longed for his carelessness, but my mind was far too crowded with what Cearbhall had just said on top of all of my emotions I had been too busy to acknowledge since being called to the sea. The further we swam from the cave of Amalgams, the louder my thoughts of my old life became. I knew I needed to go back and see Cearbhall again when I was alone. I blinked away the tears in my eyes as I focused on the only possibility that kept me sane-he could show me how to go back.

CHAPTER 15

SELKIE SIGHT

I tried to remain still. I willed myself to fall back asleep. Sleeping had been a strange experience in my new body as I learned it was easier done suspended freely rather than lying flat on a surface. The consistent bobbing of the waves would have been relaxing under normal circumstances (such as on a water bed or a gentle train ride) but to be engulfed by it was moderately suffocating as it was a raw reminder of where I was.

I was continuously learning new phenomena about the lower half of my body, which kept me distracted enough from the loudness of my mind while I planned my escape. For one thing, I found there was no need to use the bathroom-ever. I simply did not need to. Surely there was enough waste in the ocean without my own contributions, I supposed.

The next marvel to behold was my agility and coordination. I was effortlessly graceful and quick, my tail propelling me through the thick, temperamental water with ease. My body temperature remained regulated at all times, and I felt content knowing I would never again feel too hot or too cold. Having already discovered my keen and adjustable eyesight, I could see through the murky Atlantic as if it were a fishbowl of filtered spring water.

While all of these attributes were impressively designed to make me a resident of the sea, I was most intrigued by my physical appearance. The initial shock of seeing my reflection had worn off but I remained moderately mesmerized by the uniqueness of my face. My eyes continuously shifted their level of brightness and color depending on the depths in which I swam, alternating between near white opalescence and electric green. The traces of my brown eyes I had had as a human were still there, but hidden like flecks of sand among the rich new irises.

Sorcha and Lachlan kept a watchful if not protective eye on me at all times, making my plan of escape extremely challenging.

I was simply not ready for it, either. I had not yet returned to see Cearbhall to learn how I could walk again, and I was equally not confident that returning to the Cliffs would do me any good. My friends would be long gone by now, and I had no idea how I would explain my sudden reappearance to anyone.

"I didn't mean to wake ye," came Sorcha's soft voice from beyond the coral where I had been resting. I turned and my eyes flicked open, but I smiled softly.

"I was already up," I said.

"Good," she said. "Will ye come for a swim with me?"

Having nothing better to do, I agreed. I shook my tail and hair (similarly to a dog, I thought) as I quickly learned we always did upon waking, and flitted to her side.

"I told ye how we map the seas differently," she began, and pointed toward a direction that I somehow knew was south.

"As ye know, Hy-Brasil sits near the Aran Islands-or at least it has for the past seven years or so. That's where we are now. But south of here there is another large colony of selkies just near the Blasket Islands. We are friendly with them."

I knew the general geography of Ireland, but I had trouble placing the group of islands she mentioned.

"Is that near Dingle?" I asked.

Sorcha nodded, impressed. "Very good."

"And beyond that, there is a vast expanse of the Celtic Sea where some free roaming selkies pass every now and then," she said. "But most of us choose to stay relatively close to the shore. Within a day's trip, at least."

"Why's that?" I asked curiously. "I thought you didn't land-walk aside from Hy-Brasil?"

"Ah, that's just us," she said. "Others choose to live differently."

I nodded, sensing she did not wish to elaborate. I withheld my questions regarding the dangers of the shallows for the time being. I wondered now if that warning had just been something they'd voiced to me for fear that I'd be seen.

"Beyond the Celtic Sea, there is a region called Galicia," she explained.

I cut her off without meaning to. "The Celtic region of Northern Spain," I said quickly.

She raised an impressed eyebrow at me once more, unbothered by my abruptness.

"That's right," she said. "And I believe the selkie who marked ye may have come from there."

I closed my eyes, trying to picture a map of the Iberian Peninsula. I traced the flow of the Rio Duoro in my mind… it originated in Spain, but it ultimately wove through Northern Portugal and dumped right out into-

"Porto," I said aloud. "Sorcha, do selkies live in rivers as well?"

"They certainly can," she said. "And *ye* certainly know yer geography."

I smiled, remembering the times I spent in my father's various offices around the world and the seemingly useless knowledge of geography I had garnered from the one artifact that every university professor's office would have without fail-a globe.

· · ·

"CAN WE PLEEEEASE LEAVE?" I begged.

My father had been pouring over the papers he was grading for nearly an hour, and I was exhausted. He had promised me we would be leaving no later than four o'clock. I checked the watch on his left wrist.

"Five!" I exclaimed impatiently. "I want to go see the Christmas lights!"

Raj smirked as he looked up from his papers. "Well, they look better once the sun is down, you know. In the dark."

Defeated, I flopped onto the leather armchair near the door that was rock solid and horribly uncomfortable. The University of Miami was easily one of the more picturesque campuses I had seen from the outside, but the faculty offices were nothing special. This one was particularly sparse, with a single tiny window that opened to a courtyard that was now nearly pitch black; the cruelty of daylight savings having descended upon us. I tapped my fingers impatiently on the crisp leather. In the silence of the room, I'm sure the sound was extremely irritating.

"Five more minutes," my father said, refusing to look up from his work. "You know how the end of term is, Jazz."

"Alright," I said at last, turning to the only source of entertainment I could find-the lonely, scratched globe that sat on the oak table next to me. I had always thought it strange that there was a globe in every office my father inhabited. It seemed there was a surplus of small, spinning replicas of our planet that higher academia had collectively agreed to litter about their campuses like loose leaf paper.

I spun the globe as fast as I could and closed my eyes, dropping a finger wherever it may land. (It usually ended up being a body of water, of course). This time it had been somewhere northwest of France. The Celtic Sea.

I traced my finger down the sea and ended up in Northern Spain.

"A Coruna," I said, attempting to pronounce the Spanish port city.

The butchering of the word caused my father to look up in surprise.

"I would have expected better pronunciation from you-haven't you been studying for Portugal?"

"Portuguese, yes," I said stubbornly. "Not Spanish."

He wagged a disapproving finger at me.

"Ah, but they are very similar," he said. "You'd be wise to try and learn both, Jazz. Being bilingual is the mark of a highly intelligent person. Being trilingual is even better."

"I'll try, dad," I said, rolling my eyes.

I spent the next half an hour quietly pronouncing the names of the Spanish cities and eventually made my way to Portugal, following the Rio Duoro the entire way.

I HADN'T KNOWN it at the time, but I would be back in that very office at the University of Miami nearly a decade later, tracing the very same globe with a deep scar on my hand. My father had returned to The U in his mid-career crisis to pursue a new position in the marine biology department. Although Raj had quite an impressive resume behind him by then, he still chose to return to the same modest office where he had gotten his start. It held a special place for him, and for me as well.

"IS THERE a way for me to know?" I asked, shaking myself from my reverie.

"To know who marked ye?" Sorcha said, shaking her head in dismay. "Would that really bring ye peace, my child?"

"No," I said quickly. "But I might be able to find out why."

At this statement, Sorcha wrinkled her brow in confusion. I

thought I saw a flash of something like worry come across her face, but it was gone in an instant.

"Why I was-" I began to clarify, but a voice of instinct within me warned me to stop. I had meant to ask why I was *chosen,* but I felt a strange sense that that choice of wording would not be perceived favorably.

It had not slipped past Sorcha unnoticed, and she surveyed me closely before speaking.

"There are Amalgams that believe they are of a higher status because they have been *selected* for this life," she said bluntly, speaking with an intonation that emphasized the absurdity of the idea. Her eyes had no hint of judgment toward myself in them, but I felt embarrassed nonetheless.

"But they are misguided," she continued. "Ask yerself-who would choose this life? A curse which damns you to living an elongated life, damned to outlive everyone you've ever known or loved?"

Her voice fell along with her eyes as she broke contact with my own. My question regarding how long selkies could live now partially answered, I felt a pang of sorrow for her, having never previously considered that she could have possibly loved someone other than Lachlan. But of course she had had a life before this. I wanted to ask just *how* long our elongated lifespans were, but I had another more pressing question.

As if reading my intrusive mind, she divulged more. "I was very young when I first knew. The curse had skipped my mother's generation, and my grandmother was long gone by the time the signs began to appear. I was not prepared." She looked up at me, her eyes severe but not unkind.

"I'm sorry," I said quietly.

She shook her head dismissively, her soft demeanor returning. "Think nothing of it. It is a story for another time."

I understood what it was to be dismissed, and I obliged,

feeling I had already overstepped personal boundaries with someone I hardly knew.

"Are ye hungry?" she asked, plainly eager to change the subject.

My stomach had roared with hunger overnight despite my vehement verbal insistence that I had no appetite since my arrival. The reason I had refused any food from the sea thus far was I feared what it might be. I had an affinity for raw fish, certainly, having spent a good amount of my life living in Florida. But usually sashimi-grade tuna that was neatly prepared by a sushi chef was my delicacy of choice. The fish around me seemed far too...alive.

I had already discovered that I would need to eat less as a selkie; considering two days without food would have nearly killed me as a human. But still, I was reaching my limit and would need sustenance soon.

"Come with me," Sorcha said, disappearing through the fronds. As always, I braced myself for searing pain from the temperamental plant, but was met with nothing beyond a gentle tickle.

Sorcha then reached for a massive chunk of seaweed and tore off a large leaf (if that was the proper term for seaweed increments). She popped it into her mouth and offered me the rest.

"Um-" I began, attempting to form a polite way to decline.

"This is all we eat," she said, raising an eyebrow. "At least ye have *me* to tell ye that. I had to figure it out on my own. Imagine that kind of hunger."

I smiled weakly as she laughed at her own past miseries. I remembered Raj's advice any time I was forced to try something that was questionable by my (what I believed to be reasonable) standards.

. . .

"No one likes a picky eater," he said as I wrinkled my nose at the menacing tentacles on the plate. "This is a Portuguese favorite. You better get used to it."

I looked doubtfully at the steaming Polvo à Lagareiro, wondering whose idea it was to leave the octopus looking so alive. I picked around the mollusk and opted for another of the soft potatoes.

"Hey!" Raj exclaimed. "No hogging the potatoes. Close your eyes and take a bite, already. It's getting cold."

"Fine," I said at last.

Not for the first time, I was surprised to find that my father was right. The garlic sauce overpowered what would have been a questionable texture and the taste was irresistible. I took another, willing bite of the octopus and decided that the people of Portugal knew better than I did when it came to seafood.

"Told you," Raj said, grinning at the look of astonishment on my face.

I ate Polvo à Lagareiro several days a week for the rest of the time I lived there, and it was the first dish Matt ever cooked for us.

Following the same method, I shut my eyes and took a small bite of the seaweed that felt slippery as an eel in my hand. Something like instinct within my new anatomy took over, and I immediately took another, more generous bite. I hated to admit that it was surprisingly delicious. Texture notwithstanding, the taste of the wild seaweed was rich and dense, immediately flooding my aching insides with a warm feeling of long-awaited satiation.

"Pretty good," I said with my mouth full.

Good enough to eat for the rest of my life? Perhaps not. But I supposed in time my body would become accustomed to it. Like a dog who lives their whole life on kibble. I frowned at the thought.

"Ye know Dillisk is extremely nutrient-dense," Sorcha said, a satisfied smile on her face. "*Humans* in Ireland eat it all the time, too."

"Yeah, after it's dried," I said as the rubbery snack slithered down my throat. I ignored the sensation as best I could.

"Ye feel better, though, don't ye?" Sorcha inquired as she watched me tear another piece from the ocean floor hastily.

"Actually, yes," I said, realizing it was doing more than quelling my hunger.

The real impact of the sea-vegetable was instantaneous. I could nearly feel the nutrients seeping from my stomach lining and into my blood system and then my very bones. I flicked my tail, noticing my control over it seemed more connected to my mind; as if I were gaining the feeling back in my fingers after coming in from the cold. My hearing was strangely more acute-I could sense the rustle of the seaweed against the water as they swayed back and forth in front of me. The last of the physical phenomena was the glow from my tail and my scar. They were instantly brighter-like a guiding lamp in the dark. I admired the strange scrape on my hand with more interest than I had in years.

Sorcha shrugged. "I thought so."

My stomach now full and senses revitalized, my clarity of thinking came rushing back to me like a crashing wave. I needed time to craft my plan of escape, but I knew that Cearbhall would be the one who had the answers on how I could do it. I sensed that Sorcha thought poorly of the Amalgams and likely wanted me to avoid their influence; so I would need to slip away undetected.

The tiniest voice of doubt whispered to me that if Sorcha had a poor opinion of the Amalgams, it was likely warranted, but I silenced it immediately. I could not accept that this was how I would be forever.

Out of nowhere, I felt a sudden, sharp pain in my head that seemed like it would crush my skull. I shut my eyes and had I been standing, I surely would have collapsed. I reached for Sorcha's arm and I felt her clasp my own, but her cries of concern were inaudible; nothing more than a faint echo as I began to feel the weight of the water force itself down upon me. Was it possible for a selkie to drown?

I felt like I had fainted, but dim shadows began to form behind my eyelids as the pain slowly dissipated. I experienced the awareness that comes with being awake, but my mind was enveloped by the easy sensation of dreaming. The outline of a man appeared, and I automatically recoiled in fear that it was another of my painful nightmares featuring Matt or Raj.

But it was Seamus. I looked at him inquisitively, but he did not see me. He was looking intently at some sort of large, antiquated looking book and I squinted to see what it was. Apparently my acute eyesight did not transfer to my dream, because I had trouble making sense of anything written within the pages. It was oddly illegible; as if written in a language I did not know. As I struggled to understand, another shadowy figure came into the scene and it became clear that Seamus was conversing with him. My mouth fell open as I realized who it was.

Professor Liam Brennan, my dad's old friend, sat across from Seamus while they were engaged in what appeared to be a passionate conversation regarding whatever was written in the book.

I desperately wished I could hear them. I tried to speak, but it was obvious that they couldn't hear me, either. I reached my hand out and placed it on top of Seamus' own. He leapt to his feet and pulled his hand close to him, whirling around as if in search of something. In search of me.

. . .

"Jasmine?"

I awoke on the ocean floor-Lachlan, Fintan, and Sorcha all hovering above me with looks of deep concern. I gasped and let the rich seawater fill my lungs with life; coming to my senses.

"Are ye alright?" Lachlan asked, shaking my shoulders. He pressed his fingers to my gills, apparently in search of my vitals.

"I-I think so," I stammered, looking at Sorcha. "What happened?"

"Yer whole body began to seize, and yer eyes shut," she said, her eyes frightful. "And then suddenly ye went limp. I called for help and-"

"I think I fainted," I said quietly, and one look between the three of them told me that *"fainting"* was not something that happened to selkies.

"Lets go for a swim," said Sorcha kindly. "If yer up for it?"

Too shaken to argue, I followed her without comment. I felt the others' stares boring into my back and I was glad to get away from them. We set out at a leisurely pace, her eyeing me as if I would collapse again on the spot. It felt like the old days; my every move being watched with caution as if I were as fragile as a glass vase.

It looked like we were heading toward the shore when Sorcha took a sudden left turn. There was a large boulder that ascended through to the surface directly in front of us; she motioned for me to follow and we both popped our heads out above the waves. My face was flushed with embarrassment as I emerged.

Sorcha then heaved herself up on top of the rock with ease and I joined her, despite my lack of confidence in my upper body strength. I was surprised that it was easier than I expected, and I plopped beside her. The view in front of us was of Hy-Brasil, but it looked distant and toy-like from the rock. I watched the tiny specks that I knew to be selkies wandering freely onshore and lazily playing in the water as the sun remained high in the sky.

Behind us was the thin layer of cloudy mist that separated us from the rest of the world.

"Who is Seamus?" she said suddenly, catching me off guard.

"I-well-" I stammered. "How did you...?"

She looked at me apologetically.

"I don't mean to intrude," she said. "But ye called his name out during yer fit."

"Oh," I said, feeling my cheeks ignite as brightly as a cherry tomato. "Well, he was someone that I had met, just before this happened." I gestured to my tail vaguely.

She looked at me curiously but I said nothing more.

"He was yer lover," she stated, more than asked.

I laughed nervously, feeling extremely vulnerable and awkward. "Well-not in that sense, but maybe we would have been if..." I allowed my voice to trail off and she nodded in understanding.

"If ye would have remained human, ye would have been with him," she concluded.

"Yes," I said.

We sat in silence for a long time and I found it odd (among countless other things that had occurred) that the man we were speaking of was Seamus rather than Matt. While my late fiancé still remained in my thoughts, so much had changed in the past few days that I felt a sudden, significant detachment from the person I had been when I had loved Matt.

In turn, I felt that I had finally been able to let him go. It was sad, in a way, but I felt at peace with it, as if a part of me was lying down at last for a long overdue rest. I supposed it was because I believed in an afterlife of some kind, and I felt that he must know where I was now. The dead were always all-knowing, I thought.

"I know it won't mean much to ye just now," Sorcha said, bringing my awareness back to the present. "But in time, ye will heal."

"Oh, I know," I said, feeling I was well-versed in the art of mourning. She, of course, did not catch the depth of my statement, and continued.

"It's a biological change," she said matter-of-factly. "Becoming one of us. And in time, there's no part of ye that will ever want to be with a land-walker romantically. They're a different species from us, ye see?"

I was dumbfounded once more by her ability to make statements about delicate subjects in such an obtuse manner, but I *did* understand.

"Oh," was all I could say.

"So while ye mourn for him now, it won't last forever," she said. "It can't."

"No, it can't," I said quietly, knowing all too well that the mourning would inevitably fade, biological changes or not.

BUT THAT NIGHT, I dreamt of us together again.

I was in a cabin with a roaring fireplace, but of course I did not recognize it. Seamus was by the door, peering out the window as if watching for someone. Another dream where I was being pursued. I had tired of it.

"What is it now?" I asked.

He turned to me, running a hand through his hair in distress. I caught the fall scent that I craved and I approached him slowly.

"Nothing," he promised, rubbing my shoulders. "It'll all be okay."

I looked up at him, confused. "*What* will be okay?"

He stared at me blankly, as if I should have known instinctively what he was talking about. "I'll find ye, of course," he said simply.

"How?" I asked. "How on earth could you ever find me here?"

"I won't stop looking," he said, as if it were the most obvious thing in the world.

We then sat side by side by the hearth and he leaned into me, taking my chin in his hand as he placed his other arm behind my head. I felt the familiar feeling of rising anticipation I had experienced in the library, praying this time we'd see it through. His arms cradled me like I was a fragile bird as he spoke to me.

"I'm so close to finding ye, I just need more time," he whispered into my hair. "Can ye just stay put for me?"

Again, my brain was disconnected from my thoughts because I was unable to tell him that I was trying to find *him*. I couldn't speak at all.

He pressed me all the way to the floor and kissed me gently, running his finger down my chest until he reached my stomach. I shuddered noticeably and he grinned.

"I can't live without ye," he said into my hair.

This time, I was in a dress and it was much simpler. He reached below and gently pressed his hand between my thighs, spreading my legs apart as I closed my eyes in preparation. I ran my fingers through his thick, chestnut hair.

"Can ye wait for me?" he asked, voice quiet but severe.

"No."

I woke up equally as disappointed as I had been before.

CHAPTER 16

MOTHER OF THE SEA

I was certain that mentioning I was going to meet with the other Amalgams on the opposite side of the island the next day would not be looked upon favorably by Sorcha and Lachlan. Fintan had alluded to it previously, but my conversation with his mother solidified that she did not think highly of those who believed becoming a selkie was anything other than a curse.

For that reason, I slipped away undetected in what I could assume were the early hours of the morning based on the light that trickled in from beyond the misty barrier of Hy-Brasil.

Surprised by my own navigational recollection, I broke the surface just outside of the cave where I knew the Amalgams congregated. Looking in from this new perspective, (without Fintan yapping at my side like an excitable dog) I sensed the isolationism that the hybrid species of selkie had built around their domain.

The sun was shining, of course, but the cave's entrance looked more ominous than I remembered it from the day before. The lack of shoreline and the statement it made to the other selkies seemed more significant as well-if you wanted to become a land-walker, you'd better not do it here.

"Welcome back," called a voice to my left, and I turned to see the exact person I was looking for.

Cearbhall flitted gracefully to me and embraced me in a hug—the familiarity taking me by surprise. Knowing what I needed from him, I welcomed it.

"I heard you coming," he said, pointing vaguely in the direction from which I had emerged from the water.

I opened my mouth to question him but he dismissed it as unimportant. "It comes over time, you'll see."

He then took my hand and began to guide me toward the entrance of the cave. I had hoped to meet with him privately, but it was clear upon our arrival that that would not be a possibility.

The cave was just as full as it had been the day before, but this time with a subdued atmosphere that was starkly different from the playful energy I assumed it always had. Loud, raucous laughter had been replaced by anxious whispers, and while very few people took notice of me, all eyes seemed to be on Cearbhall.

"This way," he said, leading me further into the cave.

I noticed that the crowd seemed to loosely follow the general direction in which we were headed. It felt eerily like a funeral procession and I looked around uneasily as the circle of light from the cave's entrance grew smaller in the distance behind me.

My eyesight naturally adjusted to the darkness as the water deepened and the cave's walls heightened, revealing a massive lake directly ahead. Even with my supernatural abilities of sight, visibility was limited. I felt certain it would have been pitch black to a human. I uneasily thought of myself as Bilbo Baggins, blindly stumbling in the cave while a lurking Smeagol tried to trick me with his riddles.

I had kept the others in my peripheral vision and noticed that a handful of Amalgams were now congregating near the outer edges of the pool. I tried to shake the feeling of entrapment as they seemed to surround me, whether it was intentional or not.

Cearbhall must have sensed my apprehension and he placed a comforting hand on my shoulder.

"Don't worry, they're not interested in you," he said. I wondered if what he implied was, 'they're here for *me*,' but I did not have time to inquire further as someone else was swimming toward us.

"Hello there," said the newcomer.

I watched as the woman emerged from the water, leading with her eerie lamplight eyes that glowed in the dark. I knew I must get used to it, considering mine must look the same. She was extremely beautiful, with a mass of curly brown hair and plump red lips that were curved into a welcoming smile.

There was but one imperfection on her face that would have stopped anyone in their tracks-human or selkie-and I tried my best not to stare.

She had a violent scar that looked like three claws had dragged down the entirety of her face and taken deep chunks of her flesh with them. Had it not been for the telltale iridescence, I would have surely thought it was the result of being mauled by a bear. She was an Amalgam, alright.

"Who's this?" she said, her eyes surveying me closely.

"*This* is Jasmine," he said.

"I see," said the woman, smile growing wider. "You have decided to come."

I got the sense they had discussed me ahead of time, though I couldn't imagine why. I nodded and smiled weakly. Despite her objectively kind demeanor, she deeply intimidated me.

"Forgive me, where are my manners?" the woman said. "My name is Camila."

As soon as she said her name aloud, I registered that something about her was different (aside from the gash across her face, of course) from all of the other selkies I had met. She had a very different accent from everyone else in that it was not Irish at all. In fact, having grown up in South Florida, it was one with which I was very familiar.

"You're not Irish…?" I began, but I hesitated, not wanting to come across as rude. After all, I still didn't know the lifespan of selkies. She could have lived *a lot* of places by now.

She noticed my apprehension and immediately put me at ease. "Cuban," she said. "You're American?"

"Yes," I replied. "Florida."

"Ah I spent some time in Florida," she said, smiling wistfully as one does when they recount lost memories.

Suddenly, as if she had just realized something for the first time, she looked at me with deep interest.

"Cearbhall tells me you have only just changed," she said. "But you were marked as a child?"

The term they used-*'marked"*-sounded much more glamorous than what had actually happened, I thought bitterly as I recalled seething in pain on the deck of a shitty boat in Porto. Knowing how they both viewed being marked as being *chosen*, I kept my response brief.

"Years ago," I said. "I was a kid."

Camila frowned as if something did not make sense to her, and I wondered if something *else* was wrong with me. Aside from being a selkie, and a hybrid version, at that. She then seized my hand in the same way Cearbhall had, and I again fought the intense urge to rip it away.

"This is really beautiful," she murmured. "Not all Amalgams are marked in such an inconspicuous way, as you can see." She pointed to her own face.

I had no response to this, but I was given the momentary distraction that excused me from replying as Cearbhall had started to swim away.

"Wait, Cearbhall!" I called, but Camila had not let go of my hand.

"Just wait," she said. "We're about to get started."

"Oh," was all I could say, having no idea what she was talking about, but feeling it was the wrong time to ask.

I followed as she swam closer to the center of the large lake where at least two dozen others were gathered, waiting anxiously for something. The general atmosphere was one of excitement, and I tried to eavesdrop on conversations happening around me.

"Just another minute," Camila said at my side, eyes fixated on the center of the lake.

The water then began to swirl, starting off like a slow churning of butter and then gathering intense speed. The selkies all started to whoop with joy and I tried to find the same level of enthusiasm buried beneath my apprehension. I looked toward the way I had come in, wondering if I could find my back out on my own.

"Now," said Camila, grasping my hand firmly.

Before I had time to think, she took me with her on a sloping dive, shooting like a bullet straight into the depths of the lake. I watched out of the corner of my eye as the other selkies did the same; a mysterious green glow bouncing off all of our tails and casting a shimmering light that looked like a thousand mirrors.

We reached the ocean floor more quickly than I expected, and my eyes changed gears again. It was dim, but visibility was there. I looked around the makeshift room to find that the cave had opened up wider at the bottom than the lake had appeared on the surface, while everyone was gathered closely around a massive statue of white stone.

The towering figure of a mermaid, wearing a crown and holding a spear in one hand and a fish in the other, looked down upon us all with cold, black eyes. Her exposed breasts were adorned with a thick chain that held a rich emerald amulet, leaving no question as to the wealth and royalty of whomever she was.

I wondered if we were supposed to engage in some sort of cult-like prayer and being skeptical of nearly all religions, (including but not limited to mermaid worship) I immediately wished I had sped for the exit when I had the chance. I glanced above my head, but I couldn't see the surface. I was trapped.

I suddenly choked and let out a stream of bubbles. Out of habit, I had been holding my breath. Camila roared with laughter.

"It takes getting used to," she said, gesturing to the water around us. "I don't think I'll ever get used to it, actually."

"How long-" I began, and again paused. Was it rude to ask? I would need to learn the proper social etiquette for asking which day it was that my fellow Amalgams were scratched by a mark that damned them to the sea for the rest of their lives.

She smiled warmly and leaned closer to me.

"Almost two decades. I was even younger than you are now when it happened. I still can't believe it sometimes."

Her voice trailed off as a flicker of something like longing and sadness crept into her eyes. I hoped to break the silence with a more cheerful subject, but was spared the theatrics given the reappearance of Cearbhall, telling me we were about to begin.

He cleared his throat and emerged from the crowd to hover dramatically in front of the grand statue.

"Thank you all for coming," he said. "I'm pleased to say we've made progress with our numbers. Last month you all met Camila."

He paused and there were several murmurs of approval from the others. I glanced sideways at Camila and wondered where she had just come from. It didn't sound like Cuba was her most recent home. I'd ask when I felt more comfortable with her.

"And today we're joined by Jasmine," Cearbhall continued, his and at least two dozen other pairs of shiny eyes turning toward me.

I felt immediately exposed and fought the urge to cower behind Camila as everyone surveyed me curiously. I hoped no one would be *that* interested in me, as it was clear that everyone else felt they belonged here and I certainly did not.

Above the surface and even in the confines of the anemone beneath Hy-Brasil, I had felt relatively safe despite feeling out of place. In this part of the ocean, however-submerged in an ominous cave with an eerie green light suffocating me on all sides-I felt wildly uncomfortable.

"Hello," I said awkwardly.

Smiles were returned, but having dozens of pairs of neon eyes focused on me was hardly welcoming. I tried not to stare as I caught glimpses of each of their scars. Fintan was right-most of them were nasty sights. I also wondered vaguely why Cearbhall bothered introducing me-it wasn't as if I were staying. I thought considering our conversation from the day before, he would have known that my desire to leave was why I returned.

Cearbhall, now having gotten niceties out of the way, turned back to the crowd to begin whatever business it was that we were going to discuss. I waited anxiously.

"I'll start with the good news," he said, flashing a white smile at the crowd. "We have successfully traced the stone of the North Sea and it is waiting in the possession of our brothers and sisters in Belfast."

At this news, there was an eruption of applause and excited whispers. I, however, winced at the mention of Belfast, recalling Seamus had told me that was where he grew up. I felt a lump in my throat forming as I remembered thinking that I might go there with him someday. That I might see what his childhood had been like. Of course the idea of that was now impossible.

As I registered the first part of his statement that had garnered excitement, I waited in anticipation, hoping to pick up more information regarding the importance of this stone through context clues.

"The bad news, as you already know," Cearbhall continued. "Is that several stones are still lost to the seas, and we have very little clue as to where they might be."

This was met with murmurs of concern from the crowd.

"Nevertheless, we have hope!" he said loudly. "Thank you again to Camila for her retrieval of the Stone of the Antilles. This brings our count to three, assuming all goes well in Belfast."

Everyone clapped heartily while smiling in Camila's direction. I looked at her with newfound curiosity, understanding nothing other than the great importance the stone must hold. I saw why she had been so easily accepted into this strange clan.

Cearbhall touched the stone around the statue's neck lightly. Despite its outward appearance as an ordinary piece of jewelry, it seemed to have a borderline hypnotizing effect on everyone, including myself. I thought I even heard a faint heartbeat coming from the gem, but I couldn't be sure. I desperately wanted to touch it.

"And now to adorn our Mother with the Stone of the Antilles," he said, and a reverent hush fell over the crowd.

He then gently placed another amulet over the statue's neck- this one being bright blue in color. I recognized it as a much more vibrant and mystical version of what appeared to be larimar. As a young girl, Raj had gotten me a bracelet made of the stone that could only be found in the Caribbean on one of his research trips to the Dominican Republic.

Cearbhall allowed the moment of silence to linger before he spoke again. "Does anyone have news to share?"

The silence that followed seemed to be expected as Cearbhall merely shook his head in mild disappointment.

"I thought not," he sighed. "Is there any other business that needs to be discussed?"

A selkie next to me spoke up, her short red hair fluttering in the waves as she bobbed anxiously.

"Are we certain the selkies of Belfast will surrender the Stone of the North Sea to us?"

Cearbhall curved his mouth into what he likely thought was a smile, but to me it looked more like a grimace.

"By the Law of First Discovery, we are the rightful keepers of the stones," he said carefully. I noted his avoidance.

"Are the selkies of the Arans aware of this new discovery?" asked someone else, a younger man from the left side of the crowd who had clearly been emboldened by the other selkie who had spoken up.

"No," said Cearbhall carefully, his gaze flickering toward Camila. "The selkies of the Arans requested long ago that we leave them out of this business. And so we shall."

Apparently his cryptic answer was satisfactory enough for the others (or else they decided not to challenge it) because no one pressed him any further. I now gathered that the divide between the Amalgams and the selkies was much deeper than I thought. Why did the others not seek these stones in the way we did?

We, I thought bitterly, catching myself. *I'm not one of them!*

Cearbhall cleared his throat once more. "If that's all, let's conclude with the prayer to Derceto."

Thoroughly feeling as though I had unknowingly entered a cult, I looked around uneasily as everyone closed their eyes and held hands with one another. All of the Amalgams seemed to bob in sync, their tails gently tapping the ocean floor in a strange rhythm that would have made me sleepy had I not been so uncomfortable. I listened carefully to the words:

> *We all originate from the Goddess*
> *and to Her we shall return.*
> *Atargatis, Mermaid Goddess,*
> *Mother of the Moon, Fertility, and the Seas.*
> *Your waters pulse through my veins,*
> *I give you all of me.*

Despite the haunting quality of the words themselves, I found the poem to be lullaby-like in nature; almost as if they had been recited to me in a dream long ago.

The meeting adjourned and I left it feeling more confused than I had been before it began. All I gathered was that there was some collection of stones, and the Amalgams were trying to find them. The same thought I had had earlier rang in my head once more-why had Cearbhall included me in this meeting at all? Camila must have noticed my disposition because she took me aside while the others mingled and ultimately dispersed.

"You're probably very confused," she said, brow raised.

"Yes," I said, clearing my throat. "What-"

"I'll explain," Camila said, and motioned for me to join her back on the surface.

We waited for the mysterious green glow around us to dissipate, apparently signaling our release from the meeting. As soon as it did, we shot above the surface and into the dark cave. She then took my hand and led me back out into the light, where I was grateful to see signs of the sun shining on Hy-Brasil once more. Outside of the dungeon-like cave, I felt less afraid. Now I was curious.

"Jasmine, how much do you know about being a mermaid?" she asked casually, ripping a piece of seaweed from the floor of the cave as she heaved herself up onto a rock. "Or a *selkie* as we're called in these parts."

"Nothing," I said truthfully, watching as her large, white teeth tore at the snack in a strangely ferocious manner that made her look much more like an animal than a human. "Only that Amalgams-those of us who were marked-cannot change back into humans at will like the others can."

Camila shrugged, seemingly finding this handicap to be entirely insignificant.

"I meant more in terms of our purpose," she said. "As an Amalgam, you know at least that you have been *chosen,* I assume?"

"Well," I said, and then choosing my words carefully, I continued, "Cearbhall told me that, yes."

"Well, at least we're clear on that," she said, and I couldn't help feeling as though it were a warning. As though Cearbhall's word shouldn't be the only reason I thought it to be the case.

She tossed her long hair to the side and looked at me more intently.

"I'm sure you know there are mermaids all over the world," she said. I nodded, though of course I had certainly *not* known that.

"We're called something different wherever we roam, and we look slightly different, but it's the same general idea. Fish tails, half human."

"Right," I replied, picking up a piece of seaweed to prevent my fidgeting.

She smiled.

"Well, the original mermaid goddess whom we worship is called Atargatis. Sometimes called Derceto, depending on who you ask and what part of the world you're in."

I recalled both the prayer and the mermaid statue, understanding now who she was. Her black eyes, frozen as they were, made me shudder.

Additionally, I *had* actually heard of Atargatis. After all, my father was an educational professional and mythology somehow always finds its way into academics at some point or another. But before I could dig deeper into my memory, Camila continued to explain.

"Atargatis was the Assyrian goddess of fertility, the moon, and the waters. She left behind several precious, extremely powerful stones that have within them the power to control more than you can imagine," she said, her eyes growing bright with excitement. "The very soul of the ocean lies in the balance of her gems and those who hold them."

"Oh," was all I could say.

Understanding that most who worship a god or religion of any kind generally expect others to respect it in the same manner as themselves, I attempted my best face of reverence. I began to see the source of Cearbhall's confidence in our powers as Amalgams-it must come from the stones.

"So far we have discovered-or rather, *re-discovered*-only three," Camila went on.

"I brought the stone of the Antilles to Cearbhall, the blue one you just saw" she said. "And as you heard, the stone of the North Sea has been discovered as well."

"And the third?" I asked, my curiosity getting the better of me. "The green one?"

She seemed pleased by it. "The third and final we have is the Stone of Manza. Cearbhall himself went to find that one, which is why he's our clan leader."

"Manza Bay?" I asked, my geographical mind of a professor's daughter once more at work as I pictured a map of the world.

"That's right," she said.

I could not fathom how a selkie from Ireland could have possibly traveled all the way to East Africa and back, but my vague knowledge of the region made me fairly confident that the stone was a tsavorite-an incredibly rare garnet that was green rather than red. Found only in the bushlands lining the border between Kenya and Tanzania, I wondered how it had ended up in the sea. I only recalled this tidbit of knowledge because of Raj's admiration at the discovery of a 238 carat tsavorite in Northern Tanzania a few years prior. But I supposed Atargatis would have found something like it centuries ago.

"How many of these stones are there?" I wondered aloud.

Camila shrugged.

"No one *truly* knows. We've guessed that there lies a stone hidden in each of the seas. So far they have all been found by Amalgams like us. Not regular selkies."

"I thought Cearbhall said that the regular selkies didn't want to be involved?" I asked.

"Or they *can't*," Camila said with a smirk. "Wouldn't you tell everyone it was against your *ideals* rather than admit you're limited in your abilities?"

'*No,*' I thought to myself, but I nodded for the sake of urging her to continue.

"And that's just it" she said, poking me in the chest. "We're the chosen ones, as I've said."

"Chosen by whom?" I asked before I could stop myself.

"By Atargatis herself, of course," she said. "*She* was a human. The mother to the great Assyrian queen, Semiramis. Only after accidentally causing the death of her mortal lover was she transformed into the goddess we know. Distraught with her mistake, she jumped into the water and assumed the form of a fish. But the gods could not allow her to relinquish all of her beauty…thus demanding her to take the form of a woman above the waist with a fish's tail."

Admittedly, I failed to see the connection between the ancient Assyrian mermaid goddess and being a selkie in the seas of Ireland. Camila seemed to anticipate this, and she had an explanation at the ready.

"For thousands of years, mermaids from around the world have attempted to track down these precious, lost gems. But no one aside from us-Amalgams-has ever had success. It is our calling."

"Why do the others-the regular selkies-say it's against their ideals?" I asked, attempting to sound casual.

Camila's face flashed with something that could have been disdain, but it was gone in an instant and replaced by an apathetic shrug.

"They *claim* to believe none of us-Amalgam, selkies, or any species of mermaid for that matter-should hold the stones in our possession at all. They think Atargatis hid them from us on purpose, afraid of their misuse." She paused and I opened my mouth to speak, but she cut me off.

"Atargatis has called upon *us* to rediscover them, you see? It's our duty."

I was grateful for Cearbhall's sudden appearance following her statement; I was certain my face revealed how irksome I found all of this to be. What I still did not understand, despite everything she had explained, was what exact power these stones were capable of. To say *"the very soul of the ocean"* was hardly descriptive enough to see why they were so important.

"Jasmine, how are you?" Cearbhall said as he emerged from the water and joined us on the rock. "I apologize for not having time to explain ahead of our meeting, but your arrival was admittedly not entirely expected. I *hoped* you would return, but one can never be certain."

"I was just telling Jasmine everything she needs to know," said Camila.

Cearbhall smiled excitedly. "Excellent," he said. "So you'll be accompanying us in retrieving the stone of the North Sea?"

I looked between the two of them incredulously.

"You can't be serious?" I asked.

"Jasmine, surely you understand what an honor it would be to be in the presence of a newly discovered stone?" Camila said in a strangely high-pitched voice. "After everything I've just told you?"

"Well-" I began, but Cearbhall cut me off.

"Of course she does," he said silkily, taking a strand of my hair in his hand. "You said you wanted to go back to your old life, didn't you?"

"Yes," I said slowly.

But at what cost? I was becoming increasingly certain that *I* did not want to find these stones. If they *had* been hidden by Atargatis, I thought they should stay that way.

"Well, we'll need the stones for that kind of magic," he said conclusively. "Let's get going."

My selfish desire for my legs, my life, and my potential lover made the tiny devil on my shoulder whisper that *I* wouldn't be using the powers for evil if I found the stones. So it was okay.

Another thought then occurred to me-one that had nothing to do with ideals and everything to do with practicality. I hardly understood how to use my tail or breathe underwater properly...I would certainly be a hindrance on such a far journey. I voiced this opinion to them and Cearbhall merely laughed and brushed me off.

"It's not far," he promised.

"Yes it is!" I said before I could stop myself.

Little as I knew about the life of a mermaid, I was certainly well-versed in geography. I knew that to swim from where I was-several miles off the *Western* coast of Ireland-all the way to the northeastern coast of Northern Ireland was quite a journey; even at our astonishing speeds. We'd have to swim all the way around the entire island!

"Oh, I forgot to tell her about the Green Windows," said Camila as she noticed Cearbhall's confused expression following my outburst. "Sorry."

"What's that?" I said, my irritation beginning to rise as the mysteries that surrounded me seemed to know no bounds.

"The Green Windows are a series of portals, for lack of a better term, that allow us to travel quickly from one sea to another," Cearbhall explained. "They're not very well hidden, mind you. But the humans can't seem to explain them. And they're dangerous for them, of course. You, yourself have probably come across one or two in your life."

I said nothing, my mind racing with thoughts of inexplicable happenings in the oceans. I could name at least five off the top of my head. Could *that* be the explanation for phenomenons such underwater crop circles, the Milky Sea of the Indian Ocean...

even the death pools in Egypt's Red Sea, an oceanic mystery that had been unveiled by *my own father* during his time at the University of Miami?

"So will you come? We'll need to mingle for a bit, make nice and such."

I startled myself back to the present. "Um-" I began.

"We can't just show up, take their gem, and leave, you understand?" said Camila, winking at me.

It seemed, no matter how friendly they appeared to be, that I had no real choice in the matter. How on earth I was to explain to Sorcha where I was going was something I would need to figure out, but more importantly, I needed to know why they wanted me to come along so badly. I knew it couldn't be for my own interests, alone.

"Why me?"

They exchanged a glance that had I not been more alert, I would have missed entirely. I had no idea what it meant, but it made me uneasy.

"I know how scary this new life can be," Cearbhall said, extending a hand toward me. I reluctantly took it. "But I think once you see the powers we're capable of, you'll start to enjoy it."

"Okay," I said slowly. "I'll just need to tell Sorcha and Lachlan."

I felt like a child saying it aloud, but the truth was, they *had* taken me in. And it would certainly be considered rude, if nothing else, to leave without telling them where I had gone.

"Already taken care of," said Cearbhall quickly. "Fintan will pass along the message."

"Fintan?" I asked. "Is he here?"

"He was," Cearbhall replied, failing to meet my eyes. "We best get going."

"What-now?" I asked, my eyes darting between the two of them.

Cearbhall nodded. "We're already a bit behind schedule."

Camila took me rather forcefully by the hand and we

followed Cearbhall out of the cave. He took off at an astonishing speed and I had no time to think. I matched their pace, feeling more like a prisoner than ever. I was terrified, but I had no choice but to go with them. Additionally, I was determined to figure out why my presence was necessary. Perhaps a part of me *did* believe that I was chosen to be an Amalgam.

I knew enough about these waters by now to see that while we were quickly speeding away from the cave, we were headed toward the misty divide that separated the supernatural island of Hy-Brasil from the rest of the world. We broke through the barrier underwater and my vision instantly adjusted to match the murky, eerie waters of the North Atlantic. I turned around for a final glimpse at the magical landmass, but it was gone.

I was alone in the middle of the ocean, my heart sinking as I realized I was being held hostage by two people whom I should have known immediately were certainly not my friends.

CHAPTER 17

FOLKLORIC ACADEMIA

"Can ye read it again?"

Seamus sat slumped in his chair across the discolored wooden desk from Professor Brennan, rubbing his eyes in distress. The steaming pot of black tea was not enough to keep him going much longer, and he wondered what exactly it was that the staff at Trinity College had against a strong cup of coffee.

It had been less than twenty four hours since Seamus and the professor (who insisted Seamus call him Liam, but it somehow still felt impolite) had left Mrs. Byrne in Cashel and parted ways with Kiana. The two of them had decided to go on searching for answers, but Kiana had, understandably, not been convinced. Furthermore, she had called Seamus first thing in the morning to relay the news that Jasmine's death had been ruled a suicide. Not that it changed anything to him. He knew it wasn't.

The inherent awkwardness that would have existed between himself and the professor given the absurdity of their common goal had been dispelled immediately for the sake of one thing-they needed to do research, and they needed to do it quickly.

Luckily for Seamus, the professor not only had access to the largest collection of books in the entire country given his post at Trinity College, but he also happened to have a personal fascination with folklore and legends of Ireland, Scotland, and Britain; meaning he knew immediately from which shelves to pull the lengthy volumes.

The first step was dissecting what a selkie truly was, and whether all of it (or any of it) aligned with what they knew about Jasmine's fate so far. As much as Mrs. Byrne had convinced them in the dark courtyard to believe in fairytales, they needed to believe it in the light of day as well. Then they could move forward with seeking Hy-Brasil, a daunting task that neither of them was too keen to rush into without as much evidence as possible regarding its whereabouts.

The professor reached for the small book on the edge of the table and fixed his glasses before reading a passage.

"In contrast to merfolk of most cultures, these kind creatures don't typically seek to hurt human beings. Fishermen consider them bonny luck and seeing a selkie is a sign of a successful catch. Most selkies only walk on land for short periods of time and create close, personal relationships with only one human at a time, if at all. Often that person-even if romantically involved with a selkie-does not recognize their partner's true identity."

"So selkies are dead on?" Seamus said brightly, his hope rising.

In his state of severe exhaustion, he had begun to envision Jasmine transforming into an evil monster of the seas, hunting her prey with demonic eyes and sharp teeth that tore through human flesh like tissue paper. She would still be beautiful, of course-as the mermaid stories *all* seemed to say-but terrifying.

His mind then focused on the second part of the passage. *"Often that person-even if romantically involved with a selkie-does not recognize their partner's true identity."* Was there any possibility that Jasmine knew what she was? And that she was hiding it from everyone?

No, of course not. That would be absurd. Seamus then eyed the professor who had his entire (somewhat large) nose shoved into the tiny, turquoise book titled *"Mermaids: The Lore"*. He sighed. *All* of it was absurd.

"This also says that the Welsh legends suggest they were born as humans, but soon after birth decide to live their lives in the sea," the professor said. "Something they can't really avoid, from the sound of it."

"Called to the sea, so it is," Seamus said. He then repeated the sentiments of both Mrs. Byrne and his brother.

"Bein' called to the sea is what happens when a selkie begins to transform. Their body starts to change and… they eventually can't help it."

Of course he had already explained the role his brother played in sharing his own perspectives on the mystical creatures of the sea, and to his surprise, the professor did not dismiss it as fishermen's lore, but seemed to view it as another reputable source of information.

"Being unable to avoid it *does* seem consistent with what's happened…" he mumbled beneath his breath, flipping through the pages of the tiny book.

Seamus nodded, still privately bewildered that a Trinity College Professor would take stock in the words of someone like Mrs. Byrne. However, when he had inquired about the nature of their relationship, Professor Brennan had merely said she had assisted in a few research projects of his in the past. Seamus wondered what kind of bibliographical reference he had cited on *that* particular project. Something like, *'Live conversation, Expert in Folklore and Witchcraft, 2023,'* he suspected.

"But Mrs. Byrne said that Jasmine can't change back," Seamus said, anticipating the professor's gaze as he repeated this statement for the tenth time since the evening prior.

"Correct," the professor said patiently, setting down his glasses. "She will not have the pelt that she hides on land such as the other selkies do."

"Seal people," Seamus said aloud, for no particular reason other than to exercise any muscle that could keep him awake. "And there's no mention of Amalgams in any of these books?"

"I'm afraid not," said the professor. "Unfortunately, that's the part of the puzzle we'll have to solve ourselves."

Noticing Seamus' exhaustion, Liam sighed, determining it was time to conclude this part of the discussion.

"We'll just have to operate under the assumption that Amalgams are a fairly new phenomenon. We can determine with relative certainty that this was indeed Jasmine's fate."

Seamus sat up in his chair and nodded. He had privately already been convinced of this back in the ruins of the Abbey, but he agreed to allow the professor to check all of his academic boxes. And then with a sinking feeling, something else came to mind.

"Professor," he said. "What are we to do if-*when*-we find her?"

His words were met with a very still silence as the professor had plainly not thought of this detail yet, either. So keen on proving their theories about *what* and *where* Jasmine was, the part of releasing her from this strange curse was another matter entirely.

"Well," Liam said with a sigh and a deep sip of his black tea. "I suppose that's where your own heritage comes in handy."

Seamus remembered the witch's hand on his own and the certainty with which she spoke that he, too, was a selkie. But an "original" one, for lack of a better term-one that had been *born* into the legend rather than cursed by it after the fact. For a moment, he had believed her, especially when she had been able to (unknowingly) explain his mother's mysterious death.

But it couldn't be. He had been in the sea many times as a child, and nothing even remotely similar to Jasmine's physical changes had ever happened to him. He voiced this to the professor who merely shrugged.

"I haven't a clue how it actually works, my boy," he said. "But I'd expect if the selkies of the Arans live on Hy-Brasil, it'll be *you* that's able to find it. I think the answers on what to do next will reveal themselves after that."

"I dunno," Seamus said, shaking his head in dismay at the professor's outlook. "All we can do is try, I s'pose."

"That's right," said the professor, slapping him on the shoulder genially. "Now, we're best off learning everything we can here before we set out. Onto the geographic search."

He clapped his hands together in a sign of action and began to rustle through a pile of large parchments on his desk. Seamus leaned forward as the professor pulled out an incredibly old looking map from the stack. Just as he was about to inquire after its origins, his eyes landed on the scribble at the bottom of the page.

'Chart from La Navigation l'Inde Orientale, 1609, on which the two islands of Brasil and Brandon are marked'

He saw that their own country, listed as 'Irlandt' was positioned just northeast of "Brasil". The other names 'Madera' and 'Sivilia' were listed nearby enough to help him wrap his head around the supposed location of this mysterious island.

"Back then, they were certain that the island existed. Scholars received grants to seek it out, Edmond Ludlow even escaped England on a boat set to sail to Hy-Brasil," Liam said with an explorer's excitement. Noticing Seamus' blank expression, he clarified, "He was an English parliamentarian that was involved in the execution of Charles I."

"Right," said Seamus, nodding slowly. "Must've missed the history chapter on that mucker."

"Anyway," the professor continued, flipping through what looked like at least ten maps that included the island, spanning from the early 17th century to the late 1800s. "These are just the maps. There are texts referencing the island as far back as the 11th century."

"It's always to the West, it seems," said Seamus, flipping through the pages and seeing the name spelled differently here and there, but the strange island indeed continuously reappeared.

"Maeve said near the Arans, yes," the professor replied absent-mindedly as he scanned the lines of latitude and longitude for consistency.

"What's this 'bout *visible once every seven years?*'" asked Seamus.

The professor frowned and nodded.

"That's what the tales usually say," he said. "We'll have to chance our luck that you'll be able to see it year round."

Seamus looked uneasily at the professor's side profile, feeling that the academic had much more confidence in the question of selkie blood running within his own veins than he did. He had never been much of a seafarer in general, much less one who could track down an island that had no trace since the 16th century.

"I think it's here," the professor said, drawing what looked to be an extremely general, large circle around a patch of water west of the Aran islands. "Yes, it's a rather large area, but it's the best estimate I can make. Let me just try one more thing…"

The professor disappeared from the room with promise to return shortly and Seamus sat back down across the desk, watching the clock on the wall. It was nearly two in the morning. Before whatever it was they were about to do next, he knew he needed a good night of rest.

Admittedly, he was afraid to sleep at this stage in his wild investigation, thinking the sobriety following a full night of sleep would shake his willingness to believe in the myths he had come to accept over the past two days.

But he had to. Despite hardly knowing her, he felt a deep, inexplicable connection to Jasmine and it seemed curiously even more prominent in her absence. Could she really be swimming around the mysterious isle of Hy-Brasil? What if she was actually *happy* there? He tried to picture it.

Seamus had, of course, heard the phantom island referenced in folk songs once or twice in his childhood, though he had been no more than mildly interested in the meaning behind it. To think it was actually a real place was a notion that had never crossed his mind. He felt his eyes drooping as he perused the pages of another folklore book in front of him, nodding off at some point reading the lyrics to *The Great Selkie o' Suleskerry*, his mind singing the words:

> *I am a man upon the land;*
> *I am a selchie on the sea,*
> *and when I'm far frae ev'ry strand,*
> *my dwelling is in Sule Skerry...*

His eyes were nearly closed when his elbow slid out from under his supported chin, startling him awake. Seamus swept a hand over his eyes and yawned widely, observing the professor's office as he willed himself back to consciousness.

Books, more books... a globe... every Professor seemed to have a wee globe in their office, which he thought was rather redundant considering the amount of maps that were in the room. What exactly did the professor teach, anyway? History? Geography? He felt it was simply too late to ask now. As his mind and eyes wandered around the room, he scanned for anything that might rouse his interest and keep him focused. Suddenly, he saw something that did.

He stood and made his way across the room to a glass case that held a rich amulet of greenish-yellow stone that hung on a golden chain. Had it not looked as though it belonged in a museum, Seamus would have been certain he had seen it before. But where?

"Alright," the professor said, announcing his return.

He carried with him two transparent sheets of plastic that had on them modern maps of the world impressed upon them. He plainly meant to trace the old maps documenting Hy-Brasil over onto his modern nautical chart. "Now-"

"Sorry, Professor," Seamus interrupted, still staring at the glass case. "What's this wee stone?"

"Ahhh, yes, the amulet," Liam said proudly, setting the maps down on the desk. "I found that beauty during a dive in the Mediterranean."

Seamus looked up, amused. "Ye dive?"

"That's right," laughed Liam. "I know I don't look like it, but I'm an adventurer, my friend. Want to see it up close?"

He reached into the glass case and removed the ancient artifact, ignoring the urgency of the matter at present as one often does when asked about their hobbies.

"It's Libyan sea glass, but with flecks of something else in it...see?"

The professor leaned in closer next to Seamus and pulled out a magnifying glass. Deep within the lightly colored stone there were indeed specks of a beautiful silver shade that looked like opal or moonstone, but with an almost mystical iridescence. Now he was certain it was something he had seen before.

"When did ye say this was from?" Seamus asked, slowly putting pieces together in his mind. "The year ye found it."

Liam rocked back on his heels and thought hard. "Hmm... must have been in the late nineties."

Seamus looked over it carefully and felt certain he recognized it, but refrained from touching it due to the innate sense he had that it was to be revered. "My mam had somethin' just like this."

"Is that right?" Liam asked, intrigued. "With the-"

Seamus nodded. "Yes, with the flecks in it as well," he said quickly, turning his focus from the amulet and back to The professor. "They never found it with her body when she died."

The professor looked aghast and then slightly apologetic. "Well-I'd certainly not want to have accidentally taken-"

"No, no," Seamus said, plainly understanding what he meant by it. "She was found off the coast here; there's no way it's hers. This is from the Mediterranean ye said?"

"Yes," said Liam, sighing as he recalled the memory. "I spent a summer in Cyprus. Bloody awful temperatures at that time of year, but some of the most beautiful diving I've ever seen."

Seamus nodded and suddenly wanted nothing more than to change the subject.

"What's that ye've got there?" he said, drawing the attention back to the present.

"Ah, yes," said the professor, putting his thick frames back on as he laid the maps out.

He traced with intricate skill over the blank part of the Atlantic and manufactured what he believed to be the general location of Hy-Brasil. He tilted the desk lamp to position it directly atop the sea. Seeing it transposed on a modern day nautical chart, Seamus let out a low whistle.

"Certainly looks like it could be real, doesn't it?" Liam asked.

Seamus nodded in dismay and stood back, his arms folded across his chest. He studied it more closely, spreading his hands across the map. Suddenly, he felt the distinct feeling of a cold, sharp grip on his hand and yanked it from the paper and into his chest.

"You alright?" the professor asked.

"Yes," Seamus said, rubbing his hand. "Hands fallin' asleep just like I am, I think." But he looked around the room for a sign of-well, he didn't know what he was looking for. A ghost, maybe, he thought as he shook his head.

The professor tapped his chin. "We're going to need a boat."

At this, Seamus glanced up and grinned broadly. "Pure luck my brother's a fisherman, then."

CHAPTER 18

CLOSING OF THE DOOR

With her hair black as night and her lips red as the apple from Eden, she was hauntingly beautiful. He wanted nothing more than to reach out and touch her. Not only to verify that she was indeed real, but to feel the curve of her waist sinking into his as he took her.

But he was also afraid.

She smiled at him sweetly, beckoning him to join her with her eyes slanted seductively in the darkness. While he was a relatively strong swimmer, she was better. Her tail whipped through the waves with ease and he chased her…but he was far behind.

"I'm waiting for you," her voice seemed to whisper in his ear. He whirled around but saw no one. She had disappeared back into the black water, undoubtedly slithering just below his feet like a wily serpent.

"Jasmine?" he called over the waves.

There was a whisper of something else, but it was too quiet for him to hear. She then laughed and it produced the sweetest sound he had ever heard-like the opening of an antique music box.

"Here," she said.

And suddenly she was upon him, wrapping her arms around him from behind. They were cold and slimy-her grasp made him shiver.

"Come," she said. It wasn't a request.

She towed him to the nearby shore, thrusting him upon the sand with more force than he had anticipated. He sat up, startled, as she looked at him from just above the waves, onyx hair falling over her shoulders and cascading around her like a witch's cape. She looked to be rising from the very moon that was positioned atop the sea behind her. She was terrifying.

"Don't you want me?" she asked, her eyes then softening to the chocolate brown he remembered.

She looked hurt and he regretted his apprehension. Of course he wanted her. How could she possibly think otherwise? Now he desperately longed to comfort her. Why had he been so harsh? He reached out his hand.

"Yes, cailín álainn," he answered.

She approached him slowly, her silvery skin glowing in the moonlight as she dragged her body through the sand, long fingernails silently clawing her way up the shore. Her tail flicked behind her like it had a mind of its own, casting a shower of iridescent sparks onto his legs. She *looked* like Jasmine, though something was undoubtedly different.

But he didn't care. He had wanted her for too long. Chills rippled through his body as she lowered herself on top of him.

Whatever the differences were between this Jasmine and the one he knew, they slowly began to fade as she kissed him. She was suddenly warm again-he caught her familiar scent of fresh flowers exuding from her wrist as her fingers brushed his face tenderly. Where her tail should have been, he felt her legs once more. They straddled him in a tight grasp as she brought her lips to his ear.

"I've missed you," she said quietly, her hand reaching for his belt. "Have you missed me?"

"Every day," he said, his expectancy unbearable as he ran his hands down her body.

He wanted to flip her over and forcibly have her the way he had imagined doing countless times, but he couldn't move. He was suddenly powerless in her grasp.

She descended slowly down his stomach, each kiss seeming to tighten her hold on his entire being. She looked up at him playfully one more time before dropping her head in focus, and he watched in awe. He grasped her hair in his hands and closed his eyes as her mouth opened for him.

"*Fuck*," he whispered.

And then she stopped. Her hands returned to the icicles he had felt moments ago as her gaze snapped back to him with the sharp reflexes of a predator. Her brown eyes had vanished and were replaced by a violent, nearly neon green. She curled her red lips into a grin that revealed a row of bright white teeth, pointed like daggers.

THE OTHER DREAMS THAT PLAGUED SEAMUS' poor night of sleep were hardly any better, though he remembered the details of them less vividly. Scenes of his mother and father arguing in their house in Belfast, to other evil sea demons dragging him into the ocean were just a few among the vague images he could recall. The overwhelming feeling of being half-asleep and half-awake never left him as he (even in his dreams) could no longer tell fiction from reality.

After having been awake for over twenty four hours and several of them being spent driving from Cashel to Dublin and then back to Galway, he had neglected to inform his friends (still in Galway) of his whereabouts. They certainly thought he'd gone rogue, but of course they would think him daft if he told them the truth. Instead he opted for an extremely believable lie.

"I don't feel like going back to work yet, lads," he said with a yawn.

He was sitting in the lobby of the hotel back in Galway, arms stretched over his head in an attempt to appear relaxed. With no luggage in sight, it was clear that he seriously meant to stay.

"Think I'll stay with Aidan for a few days."

The others looked at him dubiously, knowing the relationship between the two brothers of significant age gap was far from close.

Seamus had crept back into the hotel the afternoon previously, pretending to be asleep when discovered by the others. James did not question him upon his own return to the room during normal hours, but Seamus knew the inquisition would inevitably come. He could hardly blame them, considering he had disappeared for nearly two days with no communication beyond the vague "with my brother" every few hours.

Meanwhile, Liam was to meet both Seamus and Aidan the following morning after scouring the Trinity library one last time to gather the final bits of research he thought they might need.

James shifted uneasily in his chair and glanced sideways at Harry and the others who merely shrugged with moderate concern.

"Er-listen, Seamus," James said at last. "I know you fancied her, but you best be letting it go now."

Seamus' eyes flickered for a moment, but he would not give himself away. After all, how could they possibly know that during his mysterious absence, he had been anywhere but a few blocks away with Aidan? Surely meeting a witch in the middle of the night and studying selkie legends at Trinity College all for the sake of rescuing a woman he hardly knew wouldn't have been their *first* guess.

"What d'ye mean by that?" Seamus asked tentatively. The others quietly dissipated around the lobby, plainly attempting to busy themselves and leave the two best friends to sort it out in privacy.

"Well," James said, setting down his coffee and rubbing his nose in distress. "I know you've got to be holdin' out some kinda hope that she's still out there. But... she committed suicide, lad. The girl *was* troubled; her friends even admitted so."

The words made him wince, but Seamus did his best to keep a straight face as his friend looked upon him with uncharacteristic pity.

"I know," Seamus said slowly. "I just-I need to spend some time with my brother right now."

James slapped him on the shoulder and eventually broke into a grin.

"I didn't realize you'd fallen that hard in just a day, brother," he said. "You're a pitiful bloke. You really are."

"Anymore of this and there'll be less of it," Seamus said, hitting him back. "Not as bad as ye are, jumping all around her friend like a fucking yorkie."

James let out a sigh. "You know I fancy the tall ones."

He then slapped the table with his hands, apparently satisfied with the explanation he had been given. Even if he hadn't been, best friends have a way of silently communicating when the subject needs to be put to rest.

"Well, alright mate, I'll try and keep your job for you when I go back, but no promises."

"Thanks," Seamus said and he rose to shake his hand.

He felt a twinge of guilt, lying to his best friend, but it couldn't be helped. The truth was not an option. James grabbed his luggage and the others said their goodbyes, heading for the exit of the hotel where their van awaited to take them to the airport.

"Don't stay too long," he called back, and Seamus waved as he watched him go. He couldn't help but feel the departure of his London friends was significant-as if he were letting the last door of return to his normal life close with a snap.

* * *

"ANOTHER REUNION SO SOON," said Aidan, looking exactly the same as Seamus had seen him only days ago, nestled into his favorite corner at the dusty pub. "I don't see ye for three years and now ye won't leave me alone, eh?"

"Appreciate ye helping me out," Seamus said shortly, watching for Professor Brennan over his brother's shoulder.

He resented the smug look on his older brother's face that was all too familiar to him from childhood. To think that he would be sitting here, a thirty year old man, still leaning on his older brother for help-despite being objectively more independent than him in every way-was extremely irritating.

It was not that their relationship was *poor* necessarily-they had always gotten along as far as he could remember. Aidan had also stood up for him a fair amount of times when their father was deep in the drink, and Seamus had certainly not forgotten that.

But there were times that they simply could not see eye to eye and it had nearly broken them apart forever. Seamus recalled their mother's passing and how strongly the two of them had disagreed on it. Now knowing what he knew, (or what Mrs. Byrne thought she knew) he recalled the memory with particular bitterness.

"SHE'D NEVER LEAVE US," a ten year old Seamus wailed. He was simply inconsolable, and Aidan's patience was waning. He heard their father's steps growing louder downstairs and his cursing under his breath growing more severe.

"Da will hear ye," Aidan said desperately. "Just leave it, Seamus."

"NO!" the younger brother screamed. "Mam wouldn't have left us!"

"Yes, she would, now stop yer gurning," Aidan said, this time his voice slightly cracking in fear.

If their father heard them, there would be hell to pay. Another beating he'd have to take for Seamus' sake, no doubt.

"I know more about this than ye do. She's left us, and she's never coming back."

Their father's steps stopped suddenly, and Aidan put his hand over his brother's mouth to silence him. He felt Seamus' quaking dissipate to slow, quiet sobs, and he let go. He looked at him pitifully.

"I'm sorry," he said. "I know it's not what ye want to hear."

"What do ye mean?" Seamus asked, rubbing his eyes. "What d'ye mean ye know more about this than I do?"

His older brother looked at him exasperatedly, plainly irritated that he had said something he shouldn't have.

"I'll tell ye when yer older," Aidan said with a sigh. "Now go to sleep."

Seamus had racked his brain for days trying to recall the memory, and now that he had it, it all made sense. Mrs. Byrne had connected it all for him when she told the story of the eldest son, watching the father hide his selkie wife's pelt. He had purposely told Professor Brennan to arrive fifteen minutes later than himself, knowing he needed to pull these answers from his brother while they were alone.

"Where did mam go?" Seamus said bluntly, catching his

brother off guard, just as he had hoped he would. "When she left us. Ye said ye knew more than I did."

For the first time in as long as he could remember, Seamus saw his brother speechless.

"I-" Aidan began, but Seamus cut him off.

"There's no *time*, Aidan," he said desperately. "Ye've got to tell me what ye know. She was one of them, wasn't she?"

Aidan sat back in his chair and rubbed his eyes. "I didn't think Mrs. Byrne would quite lead ye to *that*," he grumbled. "I thought ye were more interested in the girl than our dead mam."

"I am!" Seamus said angrily, stopping himself from slamming his fists on the table. He leaned in closer. "But I'm part of this now, too! Don't ye see? *I'm* one of them."

Aidan looked up at him sharply, eyes swimming with contemplation.

"Catch yerself on," he said, but Seamus heard the uncertainty in his voice.

"It's true," Seamus said seriously. "I dunno how, but I know it now."

He sighed and quieted himself, noticing others in the pub had begun to turn around with curious stares. Truthfully, he still wasn't convinced he was a selkie, but he knew nothing else would get his brother to talk.

"*His eldest child saw the father hiding the cloak-*" Seamus began, quoting Mrs. Byrne's story.

"...and told the mother where it was. While he was away at battle, the woman took the cloak and her children and went to Scurmore," Aidan finished the verse and stared across the table at his brother. Understanding engulfed them in a wave of silence.

"So it's true?" Seamus said quietly.

"That mam had a selkie pelt that da hid from her?" Aidan barked incredulously. "Of course not, ye buck eejit."

"I feckin' know that," said Seamus, his patience waning. "But the rest of it. The eldest son. Ye knew, didn't ye?"

"I did," Aidan said, all pretenses dropped at last as he admitted defeat. "And so the legend goes-the eldest son, should there be one, almost always knows."

"And da?" asked Seamus. "Did he know?"

"Of course," he said. "That's why he didn't bother lookin' for her."

"How'd she die?" Seamus continued, not knowing when his brother's willingness to talk would run out. "She couldn't have drowned."

"*That* I don't know, hand on heart," Aidan said. "But I know there are others… not just selkies, ye see? Other merfolk 'round the world. I suspect they can't *all* be good."

"Right," said Seamus, at least believing his brother was telling the truth now, despite what he had hidden in the past. There'd be no use in lying to him now. He moved onto his next concern; one that had not occurred to him until just now. "Are ye…?"

"No," Aidan said with certainty. "I'm on the water every day, I'd know."

"Why, though?" Seamus asked. "Why wouldn't ye be one also?"

Aidan shrugged.

"I dunno," he said. "It might be because I discovered the secret too young. Got my *powers* taken away as a punishment from the selkie gods."

He was being sarcastic, but Seamus had no time to be offended by his callousness.

"Well, I've got a friend I'd like ye to meet," he said to Aidan as Liam Brennan stepped into the pub, perfectly on time and looking entirely out of place in his Barbour jacket and shoes that were far too shiny for a place covered in so much dust.

Aidan turned around and surveyed the professor before turning back to his brother.

"Who's this feckin' melter?"

"A Professor from Trinity College," Seamus said in a warning tone. "So ye might want to wind yer neck in."

"Alright," said Aidan, clearly amused. "Interesting company ye keep these days."

Professor Brennan joined them at the table. He went to set his briefcase down on the floor but immediately thought better of it upon seeing the thick layer of grime that blanketed the pub; opting to set it in his lap instead.

"Professor, this is my brother, Aidan," Seamus said, gesturing across the table.

Being the gentleman he was, Professor Brennan extended his hand which Aidan took, his grubby fingers a stark contrast to the professor's artistic, clean hand.

"Call me Liam, please," he said with a warm smile. "I thank you in advance for your help. Seamus has told me you know quite a bit more than we can read in books and maps about the selkies."

"I s'pose," said Aidan, shifting uncomfortably in his seat.

He was plainly much less confident in the presence of an academic than he was in front of his baby brother. Seamus attempted to subdue the smirk of amusement that was slowly creeping across his face.

The professor then reached into his bag and pulled out the transposed map he had created in his office the day prior. He pointed to where his hypothesized Hy-Brasil was located and looked up at Aidan questioningly. Seamus watched as his brother leaned over the map and surveyed it closely.

"You've heard of Hy-Brasil I assume?" he asked in a professional manner, as if he were discussing nothing less common than the existence of a grocery store.

"Of course," said Aidan. "The phantom island." His eyes gave nothing away, but Seamus knew he was curious.

"Well, this is where we think the selkies reside," said the professor in the same matter-of-fact tone. "Have you heard that?"

Aidan shook his head in dismay.

"I can't say I have," he said. "Mrs. Byrne was on about that?" He looked toward his brother for confirmation.

"Yes," said Seamus. "I forgot to mention that the professor- *Liam*-knows her as well."

"I never would've thought-" began Aidan, looking between the two of them and laughing. After noticing he was alone in this behavior, he abruptly stopped and cleared his throat.

"Well, I've been out that way countless times," he said, shaking his head. "I'd have seen a great big island by now, wouldn't I? Ye've got it drawn larger than Inis Mór here."

Seamus looked tentatively between the two of them and sighed. He hated how ridiculous it sounded, but he knew he would have to say it.

"I think given my *connection* to the selkies, I might be able to see it," he said. "I mean I might be able to find Hy-Brasil, even if the two of ye can't."

The distinct usage of "the two of you" was not lost on Aidan, and he looked up in surprise, clearly having not anticipated they would ask for his actual participation in the matter.

"And we need a navigator," said Liam bluntly. "As neither of us are equipped to captain a boat."

Aidan looked as though he might say something smart, but he stopped himself. Seamus met eyes with his brother and searched for the older sibling he had trusted and leaned on for most of his childhood. Would he choose to be that brother to him once more, or would he crawl back into his shell and turn away from him as he had for the past decade? There was a silent exchange between them and Seamus thought he saw a trace of his brother's protective instinct that he had once known.

"Is she worth it, Seamus?" Aidan asked, his voice surprisingly soft.

Seamus nodded. "Yeah, I reckon she is."

"Well, I can't say I'm an expert but I s'pose we have to try,"

Aidan said. His eyes wrinkled at the corners in a smile that was reminiscent of the brothers' shared childhood, and Seamus slapped him on the shoulder gratefully.

"Yer dead on sometimes," he said sincerely.

Liam then straightened up in his chair, evidently reinvigorated (or slightly encouraged at the very least) by the heartwarming exchange between siblings.

"Well then, we best make our preparations," he said, clapping his hands together.

"When can we go?" Seamus asked anxiously.

Aidan looked between the two of them and shrugged. "First thing in the morning, I'd say."

CHAPTER 19

HY-BRASIL FOUND

Seamus had not much to pack, seeing as he had already crammed the majority of his belongings into his hand luggage for his original trip. Having expected to stay no more than a week, he was running low on clean clothing, but the stale garments would regrettably have to suffice considering there was no time for laundering.

He had no notion as to what sort of boat his brother had procured for them, but he imagined it would likely be lacking in the way of proper amenities. Just as he was about to dash back out the door, he brushed his teeth one last time for good measure.

He met Liam at the docks and looked across the marina to see tourists strolling lazily up and down The Long Walk, the place where he had been standing with Jasmine only a few days ago.

If only he could go back in time; he would grab her by the shoulders and demand she go anywhere but to the Cliffs of Moher. He would force the damn woman to stay by his side where he could keep her safe, taking her as far away from the water as possible.

To think that he had her within his grasp only days ago and

now she was in the quickly disappearing unknown waters of the Atlantic made his stomach turn with regret. From the moment he saw that scar on her hand, he knew something about her was unique. If only he had understood back then.

"Ready?" The professor asked, pushing his glasses up his nose as Seamus approached.

Once again, Seamus thought he looked entirely out of place with his neat khakis and dress shirt on the grimy docks. He eyed Liam's backpack and saw it was stuffed to the brim with books and other references that they had already been over dozens of times.

"I am," said Seamus, and then he heaved a great sigh. He had been dreading this moment. "But I don't think ye should come along, man."

Liam stared at him blankly, his shoulders sagging in disappointment. "What are you talking about? The research, the preparation, I-"

"I know," said Seamus. "But ye've shown me everything there is to know. There is more that we *can't* know, anyway. I swear to ye-my brother and I have got it from here."

"You can't be serious!" Liam exclaimed incredulously. He looked out at the sea wistfully but Seamus remained firm.

"I am," he said with authority. "Ye've got a family, Liam. Bridget, and Angus. They need ye."

The professor looked surprised at the specificity of their names, but of course Kiana had told Seamus all about Liam and his family after their initial encounter in Cashel. Jasmine had mentioned the boy to him in passing as well. Knowing how it was to grow up without a parent, Seamus wouldn't wish it upon anyone. He wondered incredulously how the professor ever could have thought it wise to take such a risk, and knew he was doing him a favor by convincing him to stay.

"Well-" Liam began, but Seamus cut him off.

"And we dunno what's goin' to happen out there," he finished.

"I know yer optimistic but… there's a real possibility that we might not come back."

He met the professor's eyes with a steely look that left no room for argument. After all, the professor was a sensible man.

Liam hung his head and slowly began to nod.

"You're absolutely right," he said. The embarrassment of the foolish decision he had been about to make cast a dark shadow across his face. He recognized the danger that lay ahead and it was true; he could not afford to take the same risks that a young man could.

"I'm grateful for yer help," said Seamus earnestly. "But it's me that has to go after her."

"And I know you will," Liam said, slapping Seamus on the shoulder. "But then take this."

Liam reached into his pocket and removed the amulet that Seamus had been admiring in his office back in Dublin. He dangled the precious gem on its chain with one hand, and raised Seamus' palm to meet it with the other. Before Seamus could object, the stone touched his hand and immediately sent a sharp pulse through him that nearly caused him to lose his balance and tumble off the dock.

He recognized the feeling instantly as the same sensation he had felt when the professor had left him in his office-like a cold hand was tightly gripping his own. Seamus did not fear or recoil from the touch this time, now feeling as though the firm grasp was one of reassurance; urging him to confidently continue with his task. They both stared at one another in shock.

"I wondered," breathed the professor in amazement.

He placed the stone in Seamus' hand and let go this time. It rested lightly and began to pulse like a deep, rich heartbeat-one, two, three more times, glowing with the same magical iridescence that had haunted both of their dreams for days. And suddenly, it stopped.

"What-?" Seamus asked.

"I don't know," the professor said, his eyes scanning the gem for a sign of further activity. He looked up sharply and spoke quickly. "I brought it with me back to Galway on impulse. I noticed that the strange flecks of light looked like Jasmine's scar and I wondered if it might have something to do with all of this. I realized that while you had examined it, you never *touched* it. I didn't know what to expect, and I don't know what it means. But when you mentioned your mother..."

"It must be hers," Seamus said incredulously. "But how?"

He recalled Liam saying he had found it diving in the Mediterranean, oceans away from where his mother's body had been found. It seemed impossible, and yet once again he found himself more than halfway convinced.

"I suspect there are many mysteries that will reveal themselves on this journey of yours," said Liam slowly. "I can't say what the significance of this is, but keep it close to you. I have a feeling you'll need it."

"I will," said Seamus, hanging the chain around his neck where he thought it safest for the time being. He patted it underneath his shirt and shook the professor's hand. "Thank ye."

"Bring her back, alright?" Liam said. "I am her godfather, after all."

The Port of Galway had both commercial and leisure vessels lined up and though he knew his brother typically worked aboard the latter, Seamus was confident in Aidan's ability to steer any type of ship. He looked tentatively up and down the rows of boats and at last saw his brother's tall, rough figure heaving a cooler onto a surprisingly well kept sailing cruiser. A head and two cabins aboard, at least, he thought as he examined the length of the boat.

"Ye finally done faffin' about?" Aidan called to him from the deck.

Seamus hadn't thought much about how long their journey would take, but a trip to the Aran Islands was hardly an hour. He hoped (rather optimistically) that Hy-Brasil wouldn't be far beyond that, but was mentally prepared for a lengthy search. And what exactly he was supposed to do when (and if) they got there at all was another matter entirely. He tried to shake the creeping feelings of doubt from his mind.

"And what daft eejit lent ye this?" Seamus asked, laughing as he tossed his bag over and stepped onto the deck of the boat where Aidan was (rather pointlessly, he thought) swabbing the deck with a filthy looking mop.

"Lifted it, of course," said Aidan. He looked serious for a moment and then broke out into a wide grin. "Nah, of course ye wouldn't know since ye haven't been over to see my place in some six years." He stretched his arms wide in presentation, beaming at the vessel.

"*This* is where ye live?" asked Seamus incredulously.

Little as he knew about seafaring, he had somewhat of an idea regarding how much a boat like the one he was standing on would have cost. He did the math in his head and found it nearly impossible that his brother could have afforded such luxury on a fisherman's salary. But then again, Aidan *had* always been involved in other side businesses as well. Some of them less savory than others, if he recalled correctly.

"I'm but a single lad with no children," Aidan said, hand over his heart as if reading his brother's mind. "Not throwing away my savings into rents for a grand flat in *London* like yerself." He did his best British accent and Seamus couldn't help but laugh.

"Come see the best part," Aidan then said, slapping his brother on the shoulder. He led him to the stern and sat down. "Take a look on the other side here."

Seamus nearly turned his head upside down to read the navy blue cursive letters that spelled the boat's name across the back.

"Saoirse," he said with a smile. "After mum."

"She'll be keeping an eye on us like always," Aidan said.

He had a glint of warmth in his eyes that Seamus rarely saw, and appreciated it when he did. A fresh wave of guilt for his distance from his brother both physically and emotionally over the past few years hit him in the chest; there was so much about Aidan's lifestyle that he simply did not know. Him living full time on a boat was just one of many details he had never cared to ask about in the past six or so years. He watched as Aidan ran around the boat and jumped to attention as soon as orders were called to him. Feeling extremely awkward and out of place, Seamus felt mildly embarrassed at his lack of knowledge regarding seafaring.

"Last few checks and we're off..." Aidan muttered, lifting up seat cushions and throwing what looked like randomly placed ropes all around the deck. He scurried back and forth, fussing with levers and buttons that Seamus was painfully aware made no sense to him should he need to take over steering in the event of a disaster. "Check under that yoke for the life vests, will ye?"

Seamus lifted up a seat cushion as directed and found there were two, though one looked rather weatherworn and likely a size or two too small for either of the fully grown, tall men aboard.

"Er-" he said, holding it up doubtfully.

Aidan shrugged. "Well, hopefully ye won't be needing one since yer a selkie."

Seamus laughed weakly, struggling to find his sense of humor as he imagined (not for the first time) what it would be like when-and *if*-his selkie blood called him to the sea once they were near the mysterious island. Would he be warned? Or would he suddenly find himself flailing about the deck with a fish's tail, gasping for water?

"At's us nai," Aidan said with a satisfied sigh, rubbing his hands together.

* * *

IT WAS THE OFF SEASON, meaning there were fewer ferries running throughout the day on the usual route from Galway to Inis Mór. Seamus watched enviously as the afternoon ferry sped quickly away from the port, feeling his confidence in their own vessel slip away. The wind was certainly manageable for now, but the sky looked significantly darker to the west. Aidan being a professional or not, it was clear that it was not optimal weather for sailing.

"It's Baltic out here," his brother said, pulling his hood over his head. "Ye got enough layers on there, Londoner?"

"Freezing down to me kex, but I'm grand," Seamus replied.

He *was* beginning to notice the return of Ireland's typical weather for this time of year, thinking longingly of his winter clothes he had left back home in England. When initially setting out for his trip with his friends, he hadn't planned to stay this long, nor had he planned a voyage out to sea to be on the itinerary.

The sea was rocky. Despite Aidan's doubts in his brother's strength of stomach, (on which he commented several times, recalling it from their childhood) Seamus' sea legs had so far held up surprisingly well. They were upon Inis Mór within the hour and watched as the passengers from the ferry-that had only narrowly beaten them-disembarked onto the grassy cliffs in the distance.

"Take yer last look at civilization!" called Aidan from the helm.

His laughter echoed loudly across the waves. Of course his brother was much more comfortable out on the open water, having embarked on long-distance sailing trips many times in the past. Seamus, on the other hand, felt much more fear for the unknown. But he knew he needed to be brave considering what was at stake. He waved back to Aidan dismissively.

As they passed the Arans at a leisurely pace, there was a lull in the wind that slowed them down, but also gave Seamus time to think. From what he and the professor had read, they guessed that there would be a layer of misty fog that surrounded the mysterious island-a barrier that was apparently impenetrable by most human sight. He wished that there had been any evidence of a sighting beyond those of centuries long past, but he imagined the infatuation with Hy-Brasil had faded over time and no one had tried that hard in recent times.

He and Aidan had, of course, not spoken of it just yet, but the looming truth that Seamus may never return with his brother hung in the air between them. He looked back at Aidan and decided to join him at the helm.

"Ye gonna boke?" Aidan asked with a crooked grin as Seamus sidled beside him.

"I'm fine, ye melter," he mumbled, steadying himself as best he could.

A long silence followed as the brothers looked out at the sea, watching the dark sky in the distance. Suddenly feeling as if the looming clouds had now put a timer on their final moments together, Seamus blurted out what he knew needed to be said.

"I'm sorry I didn't visit," he said quietly. "For all those years."

Aidan looked down at his feet and then straight ahead, not meeting his younger brother's eyes.

"Well, ye had yer own life to live, Seamus," he replied simply. "I don't blame ye for it."

Seamus turned to him, studying his brother's side profile. They shared the same strong jaw, but Aidan's nose was softer and sloped more gracefully, like their mother's had. He also needed a shave, badly, but the resemblance between them was more uncanny than ever in adulthood.

"I hated ye for a while," Seamus said, the harshness of his own words stinging like the cold air that now whipped at their faces. Aidan didn't respond-his expression remained stoic in his signature manner of avoidance.

"Because of mam," Seamus continued. "Later on, as I got

older…I was sure that she left us because of ye."

He heaved a sigh, feeling the guilt of past decades press down upon him as he admitted the truth. Despite the age gap between them, Seamus had always known that Aidan had been no easy child to raise. Constantly in trouble at school for one thing or another, and increasingly more severe problems as he got older… Aidan had been the subject of countless disagreements between their parents. Seamus remembered listening to their mother's tears, brought on by their father's rage at her incompetence in raising children. He had tried to get in the middle of it more than once, resulting in being dragged by the scruff of his neck out of the house.

"Ye buck eejit, what d'ye think yer doing, getting in da's way while he's in the drink?" Aidan screamed at him in the backyard. "Ye'll end up with a broken neck one of these days!"

"It's yer fault they're fighting," Seamus shot back, tears streaming down his face. "Stop gettin' inta trouble and he won't get mad at her!"

"Anythin' will set the man off, don't ye see?" Aidan said. "He's not right in the head, Seamus."

Seamus wiped his tears with his shirt as he heard his mom's wails from inside the house.

"I just want it to stop," he wailed.

"Now that I know everything, I see that she left because she had to." Seamus said. "The sea, ye know."

Aidan sighed.

"I still could've made it easier on her," he said, his eyes swimming with regret. "And I should've been harder. I should've knocked the bastard flat whenever he raised a hand to her."

He looked out at the sea, spitting his words with bitterness that Seamus felt.

"Ye were only a wee lad as well, Aidan," he said. "Ye can't blame yerself."

"She needn't go through what she had with da in the final years of her life," Aidan said.

There was a long silence that followed, and Seamus felt another question burning in his mind. He needed to ask.

"How did ye find out?" he said. "What she was?"

"I saw her," Aidan said quietly. "I watched her go into the waves a few times before I understood. The call of the sea had started to take over...and by then, she was in so much pain she could hardly walk when she transformed back."

"It hurts them?" Seamus asked with horror. "To turn back?"

The stories he had read over the past few days made it seem as if it were a simple matter of putting on a cloak and taking it off. Knowing that Jasmine, who had been marked, could not ever turn back, he hadn't thought extensively about the possibility of it causing physical turmoil at all.

Aidan looked as though he would be sick. "No," he said seriously. "*That* was da's doing."

Seamus froze. *That fucking bastard.*

"Did she-did she know ye saw her?"

Aidan closed his eyes and Seamus thought he saw a single tear fall down his cheek before he cleared his throat.

"I told her to go," he said, his voice cracking ever so slightly. Had Seamus not known him the way he did, it may have even escaped his notice. "I told her to leave and never come back."

Seamus nodded. "Well, I understand if ye saw her with da and-"

"No!" Aidan said loudly. "Ye misunderstand me, brother. She never would've left us with da, knowin' the kind of man he was. But I told her I hated her, when I found out what she was. I said she was a sea demon, damning our family to an ancient curse of the devil."

There was no doubt of the tears on his face this time.

"It was the only way I could get her to go. To be free of that bastard forever."

Seamus hesitated for a moment, but ultimately reached out and pulled Aidan into a fierce embrace. They stood there silently for a long time, the wind whipping at the backs of the two brothers, the eldest cradled in the arms of the younger.

"Ye did what ye had to do, Aidan," Seamus said with certainty. "Mam knows that now."

The wind howled, and Seamus imagined he could hear her talking to them over the waves, telling them both it was alright.

* * *

THEY FINALLY PASSED alongside the smoother of the two coasts of Inis Mór, the deep inlet of Kilmurvey Beach full of tourists bundled up in their raincoats. Seamus looked to the west and saw that the ominous clouds he had spotted earlier as a distant threat were now upon them. He pulled his hood tightly over his head in preparation for the opening of the sky.

"What d'ye make of that?" he asked, noticing Aidan had not reacted.

"Nothing' but a minor inconvenience, mucker," Aidan said in response, slapping his brother on the shoulder. But his eyes betrayed his tone as his confident smile flickered momentarily. He was nervous.

And for good reason. The clouds above them continued to churn and droplets of rain followed; lightly at first before ultimately slashing into their line of sight with alarming force. What began as a gentle sprinkle quickly turned into a blanketing sheet of rain. Seamus could hardly see the bow, let alone into the water ahead. His brother's knuckles were white as he attempted to steer.

"Ye alright?" he called over the wind.

Aidan did not reply verbally but nodded his head curtly, refusing to take his eyes off the waves ahead.

Seamus squinted into the sheet of white rain for any sign of a landmass, but it was impossible to tell. There was a loud rumble of thunder that made them both jump, and Aidan grasped his brother by the shoulder to prevent him from slipping on the deck.

"Easy does it," he said, seemingly speaking more to himself than Seamus.

A streak of white lightning shot across the sky, followed by another thunderous boom that shook the entire boat. The black waves on either side of them began to spill over onto the deck, and Seamus looked at his brother in alarm.

"If ye could see somethin' any time now, that would be grand!" Aidan shouted sarcastically over the pounding rain. "Otherwise we'll need to turn back, dock at Inis Mór and try again tomorrow. This is mental."

"Alright, I'm going up there!" Seamus called and he made his way slowly toward the bow, wary of the fragility of his balance as the water sloshed around him on all sides. He knew the wise thing to do was immediately turn around, but they were so close… or were they?

Another flash of lightning blanketed the sky and Seamus paused. The moment of brightness in the dark illuminated something that he had not seen last time.

Again, he thought, desperate for visibility once more, despite knowing the danger that lightning would thrust upon them.

The sky answered his ask and revealed a natural phenomena that struck Seamus dumb. There was a distinct outline of a landmass just beyond a thin veil of…what was that? It looked like a calm, tranquil layer of fog was just ahead of them. The storm would end there, he was sure of it. If only they could reach it…

The reverberation in Seamus' chest began again; this time prompted by no thunder. He pressed his hand to the stone that was hot against his skin, and felt it beat as if in symphony with the waves that were crashing upon their boat from all sides.

"It's here!" he called to Aidan.

"I don't see anythin'," Aidan shouted back. "Which way am I going?"

"Just ahead!" Seamus called.

The stone was white hot and the bright yellow light was glowing through his shirt. He turned around to show it to his brother whose eyes widened in shock.

"He can see it," he whispered, but Seamus didn't hear.

Another bolt of lightning made him inhale sharply, but the thunder did not follow.

All of the sudden, there was complete and utter silence.

Seamus turned to look at Aidan again and instantly knew that the sudden loss of sound had fallen on his ears alone. His brother looked to him desperately for any sign of what to do.

"It'll be alright," he said into the quiet void. "Just one more minute."

The stillness of the veil was nearly upon them now; Seamus could *see* the individual flecks of rain coming to a halt as they crossed the barrier. He knew the water that roared around them would immediately return to calmness if they passed beyond it. Yes, in fact, it looked like there was *sunlight* on the other side. And more importantly, there was *land*. A towering volcanic island was appearing in the mist, its shores opening in welcome to the newcomers.

Seamus turned to motion for his brother to continue where they were headed, but stopped dead as he noticed the terror in Aidan's eyes, realization dawning upon him.

Aidan couldn't see the island, the sunlight, or the barrier. Of course he couldn't. Seamus knew instinctively that his brother would need to turn around immediately. To pass through the mist would kill him-he was certain of it. And he himself would only have a narrow window-seconds, maybe-in which he could communicate this message. The sound turned all the way up in his ears once more, and the waves roared with urgency, telling him this was his only chance.

"Aidan, ye need to turn around!" Seamus shouted, sprinting wildly back to him. "I've got to jump!"

"Are. Ye. Fuckin'. Daft?!" screeched his brother over the howling wind. "Ye can't!"

"I can," Seamus said, pounding the stone against his chest. "I know I can, I swear! I see it! I see Hy-Brasil!"

Aidan's eyes widened in amazement.

"Ye can?" he shouted in disbelief.

"Yes!" Seamus yelled. "It'll be alright, but ye've got to turn back now!" He locked eyes with his brother and silently pleaded for him to listen. *Listen to me; the way I never listened to you.*

"I can't leave ye!" Aidan yelled.

"Yes ye can," Seamus said desperately, watching with horror as the veil grew closer and closer. Their time was up.

Aidan nodded bravely and freed one hand from the sails to grasp his brother tightly on the shoulder.

"Ye come back to me, alright, lamb?"

Seamus, caught off guard by his brother's use of his childhood nickname, staggered backwards and nodded his head.

He made his way back across the deck and to the bow where he meant to dive out as far as he could. The mist was still there, beckoning him toward the shores of the volcanic island. The stone glowed hot as fire beneath his shirt as it thumped violently; all other sound around him ceased one last time.

He closed his eyes in preparation, but a sudden lurch of the boat seemed to hit him in the gut. Seamus felt the hands of Poseidon himself pick him off the deck and thrust him into the water like a rag doll.

CHAPTER 20

THE GREEN WINDOW TO BELFAST

POLL NA BPÉIST, INIS MÓR

"We'll need to be careful here," Cearbhall said as we slowed to a gentle paddle and emerged on the surface.

Now well outside the boundaries of Hy-Brasil, I was reminded of the temperamental climate typical to Ireland during this time of year as the clouds above threatened to open up at any moment.

Based on the position of the rising sun in the real world, I surmised that we had traveled overnight. But Inis Mór was not that far from Hy-Brasil if I recalled correctly... how long had I been underwater in the cave? I shuddered as I realized I had no concept of time and prayed that somehow Sorcha would know where I had gone. Would Fintan, innocent and naive as he was, know that I had been taken against my will? Would they even care? After all, who was I to them besides a stranger?

"Yes," agreed Camila, eyeing the shore ahead. "This particular

Green Window has become rather *commercialized,* unlike the others that are more discreet."

I was surprised to find that I knew immediately where we were. I recognized the anomaly from my extensive research of Ireland leading up to my trip. The days making spreadsheets and itineraries on my laptop seemed like a lifetime ago, but the famous landmark of Poll na bPéist, otherwise known as "The Wormhole," was as fresh in my memory as if I had Googled it yesterday.

The spectacular, naturally shaped rectangular pool sat at the base of the cliffs in front of us; the water incessantly bubbling in a manner that (now) seemed so obviously magical in nature.

To my knowledge, there was really no scientific explanation for the activity in the water nor for the perfectly shaped rock itself, and its name suggested it may be home to a Gaelic reptilian sea monster. It certainly looked like it could be. From what I had read, the water at high tide would spill over and fill the hole from above, but at low tide (as it was now) the source of the rushing water was an underground cave.

Suddenly, I gasped with realization, causing the others to turn toward me in surprise.

"The shallows!" I exclaimed with terror, pointing to the shoreline. "We-we can't be here!"

Camila and Cearbhall looked at one another and immediately burst out in fits of laughter. I was very aware that their cackling sounded much less like the singing of bells I had experienced when listening to my own voice for the first time on the surface since my change, and more like the scratching of nails against a chalkboard. Riddled with conceit, they looked at me like I was an absolutely *"daft eejit".*

"You didn't really believe that, did you?" taunted Camila. "Besides, we have fifteen minutes according to the others, right? Let's wait another ten and see what happens."

Cearbhall roared with laughter. I was irritated with them, of course, but my fear was stronger.

"Are you sure that's not true?" I asked tentatively. "We *can* go into the shallows?"

"Without suffocating and feeling like a thousand knives are tearing our tails apart?" Camila said with an eye roll as she quoted Sorcha's exact words she had said to me. "Yes. I thought you were smart, Jasmine."

I shot her a dark look but said nothing further. Cearbhall, despite his equally arrogant nature, at least offered me an explanation.

"That's what all the old legends say," he said. "And of course none of the superstitious selkies of the Arans would dare put the fifteen minute marker to the test. Even though the Belfast selkies have been living in the shallows for centuries…they think it's some sort of charm Oisin has placed upon their castle that makes them immune to the danger."

He shook his head in amused dismay while Camila snickered.

I opened my mouth to say something but thought better of it. I hardly thought Sorcha a fool-if she had a reason to fear the shallows, so did I. Nevertheless, I couldn't ignore the fact that the shallows in which we were currently floating had so far caused me no pain.

"Ready?" asked Cearbhall as he looked back toward me.

He and Camila both had their hands placed on the rock in front of us and plainly meant to dive straight into the mysterious pool. I looked longingly toward the east, knowing that I was closer to the Cliffs than I had been since the day I fell. If only I could get away and make a desperate attempt to call for some-one-anyone. I tried my best to count the days in my head and felt certain that whether it had been two, three, or even four-my friends would be long gone by now. But what about Seamus? Was he looking for me? Had my dream been real?

Again, I realized I had no choice as Camila and Cearbhall

sandwiched me-neither of them would let me go first or last out of fear I would attempt to escape. I looked nervously into the pool at the sinister, bubbling water and tried my best not to envision a sea serpent lurking below the surface.

Cearbhall plunged forward, heaving his entire body over the rocky edge and disappeared into the pool with a flash of iridescent green that sparkled in the morning sunlight. I gulped and looked at Camila who urged me forward. Her artificial smile of encouragement hardly made me feel confident but I followed dutifully, using all of my upper body strength to pull my (extremely heavy) tail over the low wall of rectangular rock. I felt it scrape gently as I slid clumsily headfirst into the cauldron of the sea.

I hit the water with a thud and my first thought was that it was extremely hot. My very scalp seemed to sear and I dared not open my eyes for fear of blinding myself. I had no time to wonder whether or not I was supposed to swim; the current simply pulled me under and I was whirling around entirely at the mercy of the ocean's temper.

After a moment, the water began to cool and I felt brave enough to open my eyes. I was able to regain my balance, but I continued to blindly trust in the current as it rushed me through a tunnel of wild colors and light. Above all other hues, I noticed there were consistent flashes of green, thus explaining the name of these strange portals.

Looking out at the bright plants, fish, and other wildlife that were flying past me, I felt I was indeed sitting in front of a window to the depths of the ocean. I forgot (for mere *seconds*) where I was and why I had been so afraid. It was beautiful.

"Jasmine!" I heard a voice call to me from up ahead.

The current was slowing ever so slightly and I wondered if the exit from this strange oceanic tunnel would not be as obvious as I had assumed. I looked around in search of where to go, fear returning as I thought for the first time about the alternative.

What if I missed the exit to Belfast? Where in the world would I end up?

"Here," said Camila from behind me, and I felt a gentle tug on my tail.

I slowly rolled in the direction she pulled me, and the world came to a stop as I tumbled out of the beautiful passage and into the dark, frigid waters of Northern Ireland.

"Welcome to Belfast," said Cearbhall with a grin.

"Eh, well, the Copeland Islands, actually," said Camila, squinting as she observed the landmass to which we were closest. "The windows try to stay slightly off the mainland, you see."

Right, I thought irritably. *Away from the shallows.*

The sky was visible through the dark water thanks to my ever-changing eyesight, and I could see that it was more or less the same gloomy weather we had left back near Inis Mór as a loud crack of thunder reverberated through the water.

I looked around me as discreetly as I could, attempting to find a telltale sign of the Green Window here, should I be able to escape and take the same passage back to The Wormhole. But there was nothing. No bubbling pool, no rectangular cutout in a mysterious rock. There was emptiness, and I recalled Cearbhall mentioning that most of the Windows were well hidden. My heart sank as I wondered if I would ever be able to find them on my own.

"They usually prefer to meet away from where they live. Way out in Bangor," said Cearbhall. "But this time Oisin has invited us to the *castle.*"

"Oooh so we're *distinguished* guests," Camila said with a smirk.

A sharp pain of recognition shot through my chest at the mention of Bangor.

"They found her body washed up on the shore of Bangor Bay."

Seamus had said that to me on the night we told one another everything. My stomach lurched, thinking that I would be meeting for some covert stone dealing in the same place where his mother's dead body had been discovered. I thought again of my dream, (if it had been a dream) wondering if this strange communication between us could work both ways. Could he see me in the way that I could see him? What would he possibly think if he knew where I was?

"Please, if you can hear me, I'm in Belfast," I thought to myself, feeling foolishly desperate for my attempt at telepathy, but hoping like an idiot all the same. After all, there had been a number of things I had previously thought impossible that had occurred to me, why not this as well?

"Let's go," Camila said, nudging me forward.

Her voice was colder, and I sensed immediately that all pretenses were dropped now that they had me in Belfast. We all knew I was being held prisoner, but I had surmised no theory as to *why*, aside from the possibility that the stones were dangerous and they meant to use me as a vessel to transport it. I gulped at the prospect, and also cursed myself for being so unlucky. Why had they chosen *me?*

We took off quickly and I eavesdropped on their conversation. Despite their attitude toward the man that we were on our way to see, I sensed there was an underlying element of respectful fear that they felt toward him. He was called Oisin as I had heard earlier, and he sounded like an older ruler of selkies-definitely not an Amalgam like us. He had a stone that they wanted, and they were prepared to make some sort of bargain for it.

Camila and Cearbhall then spoke in low tones during this part of the conversation, purposefully allowing me to swim ahead and out of earshot. I gathered that the plan was to stay the night and return in the morning, so I held out hope that I would be able to slip away after nightfall. The Copelands were not far from the bay, and I prayed I would be able to find the Green Window if I returned to the exact same spot. Looking at the monotony of the gray water around me, I didn't feel too confident I could.

"Not as many ferries this way as back in Galway," Cearbhall said, speaking to me for the first time in a while. "Isle of Man ferries only go a couple times per week. Off season, even less."

I nodded and feigned only moderate interest. I didn't care for the niceties any longer, and neither did they. I just wanted to get this over with and plan my escape back to Hy-Brasil. I would return to Sorcha and Lachlan, explaining everything that had happened, and then…

And then what? *They* had actively campaigned against my return to my old life, and that was the ultimate goal, wasn't it? Was I really any better off with Sorcha and Lachlan than Camila and Cearbhall?

I tried not to focus on the long term plan, and I welcomed the distraction that came. I had nearly forgotten that we were headed toward a castle when we reached the other side of what I assumed was the main bay where Belfast was situated. The city in the distance looked far less charming than Dublin, but I imagined the surrounding land was just as beautiful as the cliffs that seemed to line the entire country.

"Here we are," said Camila.

Carrickfergus Castle, the home of the Belfast selkies, was a small fortress that sat perched against the sea and looked entirely out of place and borderline cartoonish in contrast to the modernity of the city in the heart of the bay to its left. I was surprised by how well the medieval structure had been kept and before I could ask, Cearbhall told me it had been built in the 1100s.

"A bit before my time," he said with a wink, and I wondered, not for the first time, just how old he was and how long selkies actually lived.

Knowing how the majority of castles-turned-tourist attraction throughout the old world were structured, (museum, gift shop, etc.) I wondered where we could possibly be meeting that would be number one, underwater, and number two, secret to the tourists that were likely teeming in the castle's walls above. I looked doubtfully at gates below the murky water as we slid back beneath the surface.

Cearbhall took a sharp dive and Camila motioned for me to follow. I took off through the water like a rocket, swimming in Cearbhall's wake as he twisted and turned toward the shore. I was surprised by the effortlessness with which I now swam, feeling for the first time like I had full control over my tail and its navigation of the demands of the water.

Before long, there came into view the unmistakable entrance to an underwater cave. I could feel there was magic brewing within; the same strange glow of green that had enveloped me in the cave back on Hy-Brasil was beginning to descend upon me now as my eyes readjusted to the new depths.

"This way," said Cearbhall in a quiet voice, leading us through an extremely complex maze filled with passages of an entirely underwater version of the castle above. Or torture chambers, I thought grimly.

The halls flashed past us as Cearbhall clearly knew his way around the labyrinth of the castle's sunken dungeons. I hardly had time to marvel at the intricacy of the architecture that lie just beneath the surface of the known castle, but I did find time to wonder how on earth it could remain hidden.

At last we appeared in a vast room lined with grand marble columns that were certainly ancient, but just as well-preserved as the castle above sea level. Even if I had not been a selkie myself, I would have instinctively known that people who were almost human must have lived here, given its layout.

There were mirrors all around, reflecting the glimmer from my tail and eyes in a way that illuminated the depths to a daylight's brightness. The chamber seemed to expand with some sort of magical property as we entered, and I reminded myself that it was not at all out of the realm of possibilities for it to have done so.

"Welcome, Cearbhall," came a voice from the darkness.

I whirled around to find a strange figure seated upon a dilapidated, old medieval throne that was painted with the same color of all of our scales, glowing in the dark with the mystical power that connected us all.

The man then emerged from the shadows and out of habit, I searched for his markings. I found none. He had an old, wise face that reminded me of someone that I could not think of at the moment, and he surveyed the three of us with interest. I knew he had to be Oisin.

"How I so look forward to the visits from the royals of Hy-Brasil," the old man said with a good-natured smile, despite his hint of sarcasm.

Cearbhall seemed irritated by this, but he hid it well. Had I not grown accustomed to his mannerisms during my imprisonment, I would have never noticed the flicker of annoyance that flashed across his face.

"And who is this?" the man said with interest, his gaze turning toward me.

He emerged from the shadows to reveal deep lines across his face and flowing white hair that made him look as ancient as the surrounding room.

"Jasmine," I said, not wanting Cearbhall or Camila to speak for me.

"I am Oisin," he said, smiling at me kindly. He did not extend a hand, and I wondered if I was supposed to bow. Frozen with indecision, I attempted a weak smile and an awkward wave of acknowledgement that I sensed (based on his responding grin) he found amusing.

Although I had no reason for it, I felt that a strange sense of understanding existed between myself and the man in front of me, as if he instinctively knew I was different from Cearbhall and Camila. I hoped it was not merely in my imagination.

"Jasmine," the old man repeated. "A lovely name. And you are from the Americas, I presume?"

"That's right," I said with a slight stutter.

While he had recognized *my* accent, I had been wondering about his. The thick, *Norn Iron* accent I had expected (having heard hints of it in Seamus' voice) was sprinkled with sophistication and charm of the old world. Wherever in the world he was from, he was certainly not from *this* time. I thought I heard the same intonation in Cearbhall's voice as well, now that I thought about it. I wondered how long the two had known one another.

"I am sorry you have fallen prey to this curse," Oisin said unabashedly, securing my opinion of him.

He had true selkie blood within his veins and knew-somehow, despite the scar he had surely already noticed on my hand-that I had not *wanted* to be one. I smiled triumphantly, wondering if my powers of telepathy were possible after all.

"Oisin, we musn't make assumptions about new friends," said Cearbhall with mild impatience in his voice. "Now. If we may get on with our business?"

"In time, Cearbhall," the old man said, not taking his eyes off of me. "Will you not stay for a feast?"

My stomach seemed to growl loudly in answer and it was not lost on the old man. He winked at me in a genial way that made me smile.

"Jasmine would love something other than the Dillisk of Galway, I'm sure?"

I looked up eagerly, my heart practically leaping with joy at the prospect of eating something other than seaweed. My feelings of fear and plans of escape momentarily forgotten, my hunger had returned with a raging force. Having been told that Dillisk was my only option, I had failed to ask if that was only the case within the confines of Hy-Brasil. With one choice of food on the menu and an evil league of Amalgams that had kidnapped me, the sunny isle was hardly the selkie's paradise I had once believed it to be, I thought bitterly. Perhaps Belfast would have a wider variety of satiating foods.

"Jasmine, I think you will find good company in my great, great-ah forgive me I forget how many generations-granddaughter, Aisling," Oisin said.

He then called for the young woman in question with a low whistle that I thought was beautifully musical. I wondered how far the sound traveled, and felt more like an animal than ever as I realized I could *feel* the sound in addition to hearing it.

Within seconds, a beautiful girl no more than a few years younger than myself suddenly appeared, her red hair flowing behind her like a sheet of citrine that illuminated the abyss of the dungeon. Even beneath the layer of lamplight that all of us had in our irises, I could tell she had brown eyes that wrinkled in the corners in a smile that instantly told me she was kind-the same feeling I had had about Sorcha when I first met her. There was something about the young girl that was oddly familiar as well, but I could not place it.

"Hello," she said kindly. "Will ye come with me?"

She extended her hand and I took it willingly, not caring where she would lead me so long as it was far away from Cearbhall and Camila. I wondered if I could find my way out of the labyrinth of caves on my own, or if I could confide in Aisling. I would have to wait and see.

"Take Jasmine to your chamber and see that she has everything she needs, hmm?" said Oisin as he watched his great great granddaughter begin to take me away. "Cearbhall and Camila, we can discuss our business in due time, but for now I think we might chat about the goings on in Hy-Brasil..."

I glanced out of the corner of my eye to see the anxious faces of Cearbhall and Camila, watching me warily as I slipped from their grasp. I knew nothing of the hierarchy of selkies, but I certainly knew when one person outranked another. Whoever he was, Oisin was clearly superior to Cearbhall...and he knew it. I smirked gratefully as I swam away; distantly hearing Oisin begin to rattle on about unimportant nonsense. I wondered what his end goal was in wasting their time and was simultaneously glad I had been spared from it.

Aisling was fast. She led me speedily through the tunnels, her tail flickering swiftly and gracefully in a manner that made it clear she had been a selkie for most, if not all of her life. There were no markings on her of any kind (that I could see) and every time I tried to make eye contact with her, she bashfully looked away. I wondered if I would ever get the chance to ask her-or any selkie for that matter-how it was when they first transformed. Had they known it was coming? Or was everyone surprised like me?

We darted through a narrow pair of columns in the sunken dungeon, emerging into a vast room that looked exactly as I would have envisioned a mermaid's bedroom had I ever thought I'd see one in my lifetime. It was a rounded space with algae-covered stones large enough to sit upon and very few possessions that I could identify as anything from the world I was familiar with aside from a lone, long mirror that stood in one of the archways. There were collections of shells and knick knacks scattered about here and there that made me smile with irony. A teenager's mess was the same below as it was up above, apparently.

"Can I get ye something?" Aisling asked timidly.

My mouth hung open dumbly as I had begun to voice a request, but quickly realized that I had no idea what a selkie would need, having only munched on seaweed in my new physical state.

"Um, whatever you're having," I said lamely.

Understanding seemed to dawn on her and she nodded with a smile, disappearing behind one of the dark arches while I bobbed awkwardly in her living room.

She returned within moments, carrying a tray that made me hopeful. But when I looked more closely, I realized with disappointment that it was simply covered in a wider array of seaweed varieties. I politely took a strand and began to chew, once again surprised by the deliciousness of the simple snack and how it instantly revitalized me from the inside out. The Belfast seaweed was undoubtedly better, I thought, noticing the rich flavor in comparison to the relatively salty taste of the Aran Islands' delicacy. Aisling noticed the change that came over me and smiled warmly.

"Ye've only recently changed, I assume?" she asked, and then looked suddenly scandalized. "My apologies-that was a bit out of order to ask."

"No, not at all!" I said with my mouth full. I swallowed quickly. "I am. Just a few days ago, actually." And then, wanting to fill the silence, I finished quietly, "I had no idea what I was."

I had taken note that she thought it was rude to ask, which confirmed my suspicions of my own behavior during my encounter with Camila. In hindsight, I hardly cared at all if I had been rude to her considering she ended up kidnapping me. But I certainly didn't want to give Aisling the impression that I was offended.

Her eyes grew wide in awe initially and then slowly faded into the look of pity with which I was so familiar from both my land and sea existence. I looked away, not wanting to experience it all over again.

"Ye didn't want to be one of us," she said quietly, attempting to meet my gaze. I reluctantly made eye contact with her. "Yer not like the other Amalgams."

"No," I said.

Whether it was the seaweed's replenishment of my nerves or the general longing for a friend, I sighed and decided to confide in her further. "It-it was an accident. I've had this scar all my life, and I never thought anything of it until I fell."

I showed her my palm and she pressed her own hand into mine. It sparked faintly for a moment, and then fizzled out to its normal iridescent glow.

"Fell?" she asked gently.

I began to explain, but for some reason found myself starting way back at the beginning. I knew that I was oversharing, but I found it impossible to stop. There was something about Aisling that told my instincts she wouldn't mind it. I confided in her about Matt and Raj's deaths, my strange physical changes that began back in Dublin-even my fight with Kiana at the Cliffs. I told her about everything besides Seamus, wanting to keep that tiny bit of my history private.

"I want to go home," I said as my story came to an end. "But I know I can't. There's nothing really left for me back home, anyway." I finished with a hollow laugh that I had hoped would break the tension, but it seemed to only sadden her further.

"I'm so sorry," she said, and I knew she meant it.

"It's alright," I said with a deep sigh. I then became aware of my poor conversation skills in that I had talked incessantly for nearly ten minutes and inquired nothing after the person across from me. "Um. What-what about you?"

She waved a hand in the dismissive way that a modest person does when they know their story will only make you feel worse about your own, but at my urging, she *did* tell me.

"My mam was a selkie. When my da passed, she told me everything, and she said it was time for us to go back to the sea," she said with a shrug. "I went with her one day off the coast, and we came here to live with Oisin. He is my great, great-several generations-*great* granddad. That was all there was to it."

"And your mother is..." I said tentatively, recalling that the catacombs through which we had come seemed quite empty and I was almost certain no one else lived here besides the young girl and her grandfather.

Aisling smiled, understanding my hesitation. "My mam's still alive," she said. "I had a big family here once, but now it's just us and Oisin."

"Oh," was all I could think to say. I had so many more questions, but I felt it was rude to press a stranger any further. The way she mentioned having a large family at one time sounded as though there was an element of loss in her past, and knowing what that felt like, I was fairly certain she would share if she wanted to.

"Would ye like to rest for a bit?" she asked kindly, and I was surprised to find that I did. With my immediate fears somewhat quelled now that it was clear Cearbhall had a healthy fear of (or at least respect for) Oisin, I knew I would be safe for the time being. Aisling's presence made me sure of that.

"Yes, but-" I began somewhat timidly.

I did not know how much I should tell her. Did she sense that I was being held here against my will? Could I tell her?

"No one will enter," she said firmly. "I'll be just out there if ye need me."

She floated away gracefully, disappearing through one of the arches and into the shadows of the castle's labyrinth of tunnels.

There was a large mirror directly across from me; it was lined in ornate silver leaves that reminded me faintly of forest fairies. The reflection of myself, curled up on a large rock and surrounded by small trees of coral, still seemed unbelievable to me, even as I had grown accustomed to how my new body felt.

I watched as my hair bounced softly in the subtle waves; a curtain of onyx that had grown even more since I had changed. I avoided opening my eyes fully for fear of catching a glimpse of the eerie lamplight irises that still disconcerted me. I felt like I was still living in a dream-one where I occupied the body of a sea monster, and I'd wake up tomorrow back in my condo in Tampa.

I noticed the empty place beside me on the rock and pictured for a moment that Seamus was with me. Despite being as far away from him as I could possibly be, I had the strangest sensation that I could feel him. My logical, rational mind told me it was ridiculous to fixate on someone I hardly knew, but there was something deeper-like an instinct-that told me it wasn't in my imagination. There was a reason we were connected, even if I didn't see it yet. In my mind, I whispered to him that I was safe, but that I did not know for how long.

I began to nod off to sleep, and allowed myself to fall softly onto the rock, resting my head for no reason other than it reminded me of how I used to do it. I prayed I would awake looking out at the sparkling waves from my window rather than being trapped beneath them.

I was once again swallowed by a terrifying dream. But this time, I was certain it was a vision.

Ominous clouds blanketed the sky, and a sheet of white rain severely limited my visibility. The wind howled loudly and I was reminded sorely of the day that I had fallen from the Cliffs. Although I could not tell exactly what kind of vessel it was, I was certainly on a boat as I felt the familiar rocking back and forth of the waves beneath me. Memories of Porto fresh in my mind, I was none too keen to be near the bow.

I could not see Seamus, but I sensed that I was near him. I then heard his voice, and even muffled as it was, I could tell that my vantage point in the dream was through his eyes. Unlike last time, I was prepared to pay close attention to what was happening around me, because this one felt as if it was happening in real time.

"I have to jump!" he said.

I looked out at the tumultuous sea and wished I could slap him across the face. Surely he wasn't serious about diving into these waters?

Violent waves crashed all around me (or him, depending on how I thought about it) and there were calls coming from the helm of the boat. I whirled around to see to whom Seamus was calling; I knew instantly I was looking into the eyes of his older brother.

Of course he had told me about Aidan, but even if he hadn't, the resemblance was uncanny. Although the age gap that I knew existed between them seemed much wider in reality, they had the same handsome jawline and deep green eyes. I felt as if I were seeing Seamus in the future (should his future be riddled with cigarette usage and harsh sunlight). They were staring at one another intently, and I saw that Aidan was as distraught as I was upon hearing his brother's plan.

Seamus yelled something again, but I couldn't hear it. His words sounded as if they were desperately attempting to penetrate a brick wall, and I felt increasingly frustrated by the lack of clarity in my own vision. If only there were a way for me to harness this power; to control it. I would not only be able to hear what was happening, but I could speak to him as well.

Nevertheless, I held onto the singular ounce of hope that while I could not communicate with him, I certainly felt him. I felt his heart beating rapidly with what I would have thought was fear, had I not known it was anticipation for what he was about to do. He had called out that he would jump, and I knew he would. He was not afraid, because he knew he would be safe. I thought I knew it, too. But I couldn't be sure.

He turned back toward the bow that faced west, and I went with him. There was a thin veil of sky that seemed to separate what was happening to us now and where we were going. We were in the midst of chaos, but just beyond the veil was complete and utter stillness.

I couldn't see it, but I knew. It was Hy-Brasil.

<h1 style="text-align:center">CHAPTER 21</h1>

URGENT ALLIANCES

BENEATH CARRICKFERGUS CASTLE, BELFAST

"Jasmine! Jasmine!"

A loud voice punctured the bubble of my vision and I was suddenly torn from Seamus' world and thrust back into my own. I was irritated at the interruption, but not in the way I had been during my last, more sensual dream. This time, I was frustrated to be deprived of the chance to see more rather than feel more.

What had happened next? If only I could have watched Seamus cross the barrier between our world and Hy-Brasil, I would know he was safe. My eyes darted around the room to find the culprit responsible for ending my sight, but I softened when I saw the kind eyes of Aisling looking down upon me with deep concern.

"Aisling," I said, shaking my head and sitting up. "Yes, I'm fine."

She looked unconvinced.

I replayed the vision in my head, terrified that I would forget it in the way everyone forgets their dreams once they're awakened. But even as I recalled the details as carefully as I could, I felt triumphant in the fact that I had been right. Seamus *was* looking for me. And if he had already made it to Hy-Brasil... he was close to finding me.

"Ye started shaking and convulsing, and I—I didn't know what to do," Aisling said, waving her hand in front of my face to shake me from my daze. "Are ye sure yer alright?"

I didn't know why, but I suddenly felt extremely vulnerable as I came back to the present. Despite my exultation at confirming Seamus was looking for me, I sobered almost instantly with the realization that where I was now was extremely far from Hy-Brasil. What use was it if he had discovered the mysterious island now that I had been taken so far away from it against my will? And the only people who knew me were unaware of where I had gone? I found myself falling into hopelessness once again as I thought of Sorcha, unable to explain my disappearance.

Realizing Aisling was staring at me expectantly, I cleared my throat.

"I'm fine," I said. Even to me, my voice sounded as far away as my thoughts. I met her gaze and prepared myself for an answer I didn't want to hear. "Did I-did I say anything else?"

Aisling looked around with uncertainty.

"Seamus," she said quietly, not wanting to embarrass me. "Ye were callin' for someone named Seamus."

I groaned briefly, but sensed that she was not the type to make one feel mortified for such things. Or anything, really. She was kind.

"Is that yer man, I assume?" she asked shyly.

"Yes," I said quietly. "But..."

I looked at the girl in front of me and again could not surmise why I trusted her so innately when I barely knew her. I thought I had nothing to lose by asking the question, having already embarrassed myself enough in front of her.

"Aisling," I said slowly. "Have you-have you heard of selkies having powers?"

"Powers?" she repeated slowly. "What kind of powers are ye talking about?"

No, not from the stones, I thought.

"Like visions," I said. Noticing the confusion on her face, I continued. "This happened the other day, as well. I dreamt something but… but I feel like it actually happened. Like it was real."

She surprised me by suddenly rising and beginning to circle the rock where I still sat. Young as she was, she had the look of someone with a great sense of wisdom for her age; maybe it was because of her deep, brown eyes that held contact so sincerely, or her general sense of intuition that I felt she had. Her red hair trailed behind her like silk and it seemed as though she were thinking hard about something.

"This man, is he one of us?" she asked at last, tapping her chin thoughtfully. "A selkie, I mean."

"No," I said quietly.

Although I could never wish the curse that had befallen me upon him, I selfishly wanted him with me more than anything.

"And yer certain he's a human, then?" she asked.

I stared at her blankly. "Yes," I said at last.

Aisling frowned at this and sat beside me, taking my hand. I winced at her touch; not because I didn't welcome it, but because my scar once again seemed to ignite in a strange way. I thought she noticed, but she did not acknowledge it. I wondered if all selkies interacted in this way with Amalgams.

"I've heard of connections between selkies that are destined to be together being strong enough to see into one another's fates now and then," she said. "But it's not the case with the land-walkers, I'm afraid."

I hung my head and nodded. "I guess it's just my subconscious hoping."

Even as I said it, I tried my best not to believe it. The dream had felt so real... I could almost feel his heartbeat now as I reimagined it. He had been there, looking for me. Or did I just wish he was? Because I knew I had no one else that would?

"It's alright, Jasmine," Aisling said, my name sounding adorably funny in her Irish accent and I couldn't help but smile. "Soon ye'll find ye don't want him anymore."

"Oh?" I asked, caught off guard. I was taken aback by her bluntness and my face must have shown it, because she rushed to clarify.

"What I mean is, yer changing, ye know? And eventually those changes will wipe away yer old desires from yer old life," she said. "Ye won't remember what it's like to be with a land-walker anymore than I can remember what it was like to have been one meself when I was a wee one."

I felt that comfortable as I was with Aisling, now was not the time to disclose to her that I had not actually ever "been with" Seamus in the sense that I knew she meant. I smiled weakly, knowing she only meant to help, but of course it had made it worse. Additionally, I had already heard this warning from Sorcha once before. I did not know what to say, so I said nothing.

"If yer rested enough now, we can go back to Oisin. He'd like to see ye," she said.

I followed her willingly, hoping that when I arrived in Oisin's presence, Camila and Cearbhall would be elsewhere. I wondered if Aisling had communicated her suspicions about me being held prisoner to her great grandfather. Would he even care if she did?

As we made our way through the maze of countless tunnels that lined the ocean floor below the historic castle, a thought occurred to me.

"Aisling, is it really just you, your mother, and your-Oisin-that live here?" I asked, opting to not recite the numerous generations she had. "This place is massive."

I caught a glimpse of the rooms that lie beyond the passages, and it seemed there were countless others just like the one Aisling had shown me into. Despite my lack of knowledge regarding selkie habitats, I thought there could have been space for at least a dozen other merpeople in the grand palace.

"It's just us," she said with a smirk. "The selkie blood skipped several generations until my mam and my aunt. My aunt had no wee ones of her own and she waited here for her sister until I was old enough to walk. Or swim, I suppose is the right term." She smiled.

"And where are they now?" I asked carefully, attempting not to pry.

The smile flickered and faded from her face, causing me instant regret for my intrusiveness.

"Mam is away in Belfast just now. She still land-walks some-times, to learn about what's going on up there," she said quietly. "Oisin encourages it, but it's best if ye don't mention it to yer friends you brought, if ye don't mind."

She spoke kindly, but I knew the request was firm. Of course I had no reason to question why her mother chose to land-walk when so few others did. As far as I was concerned, Aisling's fami-ly's business was their own.

"They're not my friends, you know," I then replied quickly, the fear that had left me for the past few hours returning with a vengeance.

The thought of meeting with Oisin and being thrust back into Camila and Cearbhall's grasp immediately afterward made me shudder, and I wondered if this would be my last chance to ask for Aisling's alliance. My urgency was not lost on her, and she turned to face me.

"Have they done ye any harm?" she asked quickly, her eyes sharp.

"No," I said tentatively. "But-I mean, they kidnapped me to come here."

"I wondered," she said pensively. "But why?"

I grabbed her by the shoulders and halted, taking even myself by surprise.

"I don't know, Aisling!" I said severely. "I don't know why they needed me here!"

She stared at me intently, her eyes misted over with deep thought.

"Jasmine, I cannot let ye go back with them," she said urgently. Neither of us moved. "I knew ye weren't wicked like I've been told the Hy-Brasil Amalgams are-I could tell that instantly. But why they have brought ye here as a prisoner, I cannot say. It's disturbing, at the very least..."

"It has something to do with the stone they came for," I said. "Cearbhall mentioned it in a meeting we had back on Hy-Brasil and right after, he told me I had to come with them."

She looked up at me, something like distrust lingering behind her eyes. It made me uneasy.

"What do ye know about the stones?" she asked. "What have they told ye?"

I looked at her blankly.

"Nothing," I said honestly. "All I know is they have some sort of powers and the Hy-Brasil Amalgams are trying to find them... supposedly your great grandfather has one. That's why we're here."

She surveyed me carefully, though not wholly suspiciously.

"Ye cannot change back, I'm sure ye know this of the Amalgams," she said severely. "Some have tried and it-it doesn't end well."

"I know, I've heard," I said dully. "But-"

"Let me guess," she said. "Cearbhall's told ye there's a way if ye have the stones."

"Well, yes," I stammered, watching her brow raise slowly and feeling more foolish the higher it went.

"Oh, yeah, he'd say something like that, being one of the Hy-Brasils," she said with the air of superstition in her voice. "And there might be, for all we know." She shrugged.

"Aisling, if there's a way to do it with the stones, I have to know how!" I said anxiously, ignoring the disappointment on her face.

"Jasmine, ye don't want to be seeking those stones. No one should have them."

Of course knowing the nature of her kind demeanor, I had assumed this would be where she aligned in terms of pursuing the stones versus not. But a small part of me had hoped that the powers of the stones could be used for *good* in addition to the evil I was already certain for which they could be manipulated. Transforming myself back into my original, human form, would surely not be considered evil...

"Atargatis herself wanted them hidden forever," Aisling said fiercely. "She knew the dangers! Ye cannot believe what the Amalgams tell ye about it being their *destiny*."

"But what if-"

"Jasmine, I know these things!" Aisling cut me off, her voice full of urgency that I found impossible to question. "My aunt nearly killed herself trying to find these stones around the world and now she's just as lost as they are!"

"What?" I said, my eyes widening. I wondered if her omission of family history was more cryptic than I had initially imagined. "Aisling, what do you mean?"

"I mean this deal that Oisin has worked out with Cearbhall and Camila-he's doing this in exchange for information about his own great granddaughter's whereabouts-me very own Aunt," she said.

Of course I already had extremely negative opinions of the two Amalgams who had brought me to Belfast against my will, so learning that they were essentially holding another live person for ransom shouldn't have surprised me, but it did.

Aisling surveyed me intently once more and sighed deeply. I knew-even before she said it-that she was deciding whether or not to tell me extremely sensitive information.

"But he's giving them a *fake.*"

I saw the regret at confiding in me washing over her, and I instantly jumped to reassure her.

"Your secret is safe with me," I said earnestly, grabbing her hand. "I promise. I want nothing to do with this. I just want to go home."

She trembled slightly, the remnants of her demure personality coming to the surface. Knowing we both had reason to despise Cearbhall and Camila, I felt suddenly obligated to help her in some way. I pushed my selfish motivation for the stones aside as I pressed her for more information.

"So the Amalgams-Cearbhall and Camila, that is-have captured your mother's sister? Your aunt?"

"Yes," she whispered, pulling me into a tunnel to our left. "They have been holding her prisoner under the threat of harming her family. Her land-walker family."

I hadn't expected her to say that. "She has a family on land?"

She nodded furiously. "She did, she did. But not for many years now." She took a deep, steady breath, and I sensed that she was using all of her restraint to hold back tears for the sake of getting the words out. I knew the feeling.

"The Amalgams threatened to kill her family on land unless she helped them find the stones. They already knew that Oisin had one because *she* had found it. But it was an accident. She never meant to find it. It came to her!"

"Came to her?" I asked blankly. "What do you mean?"

Aisling looked up at me through a curtain of hair and dark lashes in a way that would have been almost haunting had she not looked so innocent with youth.

"The stones will always find their way back to their rightful owner," she said. "They say…my mam and Oisin, I mean, that my aunt was the master of the gems."

"Master of the gems?" I asked with a doubtful look in my eyes that Aisling did not seem to notice.

"Yes," she said. "They say my aunt birthed the Heir of Atargatis herself. But she was born a *human*."

CHAPTER 22

TRUTHS REVEALED

To this, I had no response.

Perhaps it was my lack of understanding (or believing in, for that matter) everything that had to do with the mysterious goddess of the mermaids that the Amalgams adamantly worshiped and the other selkies seemed to fear, but I had enough common sense to know that Aisling and all the others thought this information to be highly significant. Lineage aside, it was clear that Aisling's aunt somehow knew where the stones were and was therefore an extremely valuable prisoner.

We had turned down a dark hallway and I wondered how much longer it would be until Oisin (or worse, Cearbhall and Camila) would come looking for us. I still had more to say to Aisling.

"I want to help you," I said to her sincerely, forgetting my own worries in the wake of this new information I'd learned. "What can I do?"

"It's *me* that wants to help ye," she said earnestly. "If I can prevent Cearbhall and Camila from taking any other prisoner, it's a victory on our side. Though I still can't say why it is that they've put *ye* through this."

I shrugged. "If the stones are dangerous, I suppose they want someone else aside from themselves to handle their transport," I said.

"I s'pose it must be so," she said, but her mind was at work. I knew she thought there was more to it, but I had told her everything.

The tiny glimmer of hope I had held onto regarding transforming back into a human had disappeared as we concluded our conversation. Intentions pure or malicious, it was clear that using the stones for my own personal gain was too dangerous to be possible, even if I could track them all down. My purpose now extinguished, I committed in my own mind to doing whatever I could to help track down Aisling's aunt as soon as I was free myself. It was all I could do.

"We need to get going," she said suddenly, shaking me back to the present.

Now aware of his planned ruse, I found myself in fear for the old man's safety and hastily followed as we returned to the main passages. Oisin, formidable as he was, was certainly too old to conquer should it come to a physical battle between him, Camila, and Cearbhall. I hoped it wouldn't amount to that.

We entered the hall quietly where Cearbhall, Camila, and Oisin were deep in conversation, negotiating for the stone. Despite my fear for what was to unfold, I couldn't help but smirk as I knew the truth of the yellow gem that hung around Oisin's neck. Cearbhall eyed it hungrily. Aisling motioned for me to bob off to the side underneath a shadowy arch, but I saw Camila's gaze flicker to me as I entered. Tensions seemed high, and I wondered how long they had been in discussion.

"Cearbhall, I beg you to end this nonsense," the old man said with tired eyes. "I am tired. I would give all of the stones in the world to know of Aine's whereabouts."

My heart skipped a beat. I knew that name. But *where* had I heard it?

"We are after the same goal, Oisin," said Cearbhall in a silky manner that made me roll my eyes. "And as I've told you, *we* do not have Aine with us."

"Enough," Oisin said, and I saw the exhaustion of a grandfather who had spent at least a decade searching for his granddaughter creeping into every line in his face. If he had once been a great leader of any kind, he was too tired to carry on now. I suddenly wondered how selkies died. I hoped I wouldn't find out today.

"I have told you. The stone is yours," he said, removing it from his neck. "If you just tell me how I can find her." His eyes flashed briefly to Aisling whose expression was stony.

"Last we heard she was off the coast of Cyprus," said Cearbhall lazily.

Oisin scoffed, his demeanor now visibly mounting to anger.

"Do not stand in my house and insult me! I know she's in the Mediterranean," he said severely, making me jump. "In *which* of Atargatis's pools is she imprisoned? You tell me now, or the gem stays here." His words boomed through the hall with authority.

Cearbhall glanced at Camila who nodded.

"Let me see the stone," she said calmly, her expression unreadable.

Apparently confident in the quality of the replica, Oisin showed no outward hesitation in handing it over. I resisted the urge to glance at Aisling, terrified of giving anything away.

Camila twisted it around in her fingers, eyeing it in the same hungry manner as her accomplice had done. And then, to both mine and Aisling's surprise, she called me over to join her.

"Jasmine, why don't you come take a look at this?" she said, her voice riddled with a hint of something that I could not identify, but I feared it. "Tell me what you think."

Dumbfounded, I looked back at Aisling whose face was as blank as mine. I glanced at Oisin as if asking for permission, but his expression was unreadable as well. If he were afraid for any reason, he certainly didn't show it. I hesitantly drifted across the room and floated next to Camila, awaiting my instructions.

"What do you think?" she repeated, her mouth curling into a smirk at the corners.

"It-it's beautiful," I said lamely, refusing to meet her gaze. Instead, I looked up at Oisin. "Like Libyan sea glass." I mustered every fiber of my being to avoid shaking in fear.

"Is that all?" she asked with a sickeningly false sweetness, staring at my side profile. I had no doubt in my mind now that she knew it was fake. But *how?*

"Yes," I said slowly. Feeling I had a handle on my expression, I turned to her. "Why are you asking me?"

"Enough of this!" Oisin boomed.

While he plainly tried to appear as nothing more than outwardly frustrated at their stalling, I recognized fear in his eyes. I hoped Cearbhall and Camila were less observant than I. The old man quickly snatched the stone from Camila's grasp with force that surprised me, but she merely sighed and floated backward, making no attempt to take it back.

"Jasmine, why don't you tell Oisin about how you came to us?" she then said, speaking as slowly as if we had all the time in the world. My unease was nearly unbearable by now. What was she *doing?*

I looked at the old man, praying that he could read the pleading in my eyes. *They're not my friends, they're not my friends,* I repeated in my head over and over again, hoping he might hear my thoughts. Why I continuously attempted telepathy in times of distress, I could not say.

"I-I fell off the Cliffs of Moher," I said, stammering. "And then I transformed." I looked at Cearbhall, but his smirk merely matched Camila's.

"Jasmine, there's more to it than that," Camila responded, speaking as casually as if we were old friends. "Tell him about how you were marked in Portugal."

"Well I-" and then I stopped.

I slowly turned to face her, an icy chill running down my spine.

"What's wrong?" she asked sweetly, reaching for a lock of my hair. I swatted her hand away immediately and her eyes flashed with anger.

"I never told you about Portugal," I said.

I looked at Cearbhall and thought hard. But no, I had never told him, either. I had told Sorcha and Lachlan, but they would never have crossed paths with the malevolent woman beside me. If I knew anything for certain, it's that Sorcha had been right in warning her son against colluding with the Amalgams. She knew better, and I should have, too.

"How would you know that?" I said into the silence.

A flicker of fear ran across Camila's face which she instantly remedied with an evil smile that revealed her dagger-like teeth. I backed away from her slowly and Oisin looked between Aisling and myself in confusion that bordered something else…was it fear? I couldn't understand it.

Cearbhall used the momentary distraction to his advantage and flashed across the room, swiping the stone from the old man's neck in one swift motion. He thrust the yellow gem forcibly into my hand and I froze.

"Nothing!" Cearbhall screeched, watching as the piece of round glass sat dormant in my palm.

He and Camila wore matching looks of fury as they plainly had expected something to happen at my touch. I stood completely still, absolutely dumbfounded as I looked down at the stone.

"How dare you attempt to give us a fake, Oisin!" Camila said fiercely.

"What-" I began desperately, and looked to Aisling who had her hands clapped over her mouth in shock. Oisin's eyes were wide.

"You cannot mean to say-" the old man began.

"Yes," said Camila, satisfaction mingled with frustration painted across her horrifically scarred face as she pointed to me with one sharp fingernail.

"*She* is the Heir of Atargatis."

As soon as I heard the words, all movement in the room came to a halt. It took everything within me not to let out a scoff. There was no way that Camila could have thought such a thing possible. I was certain she had mistaken me with someone else.

"No I'm not," I said. "This-this is an accident. I was never meant to be a selkie, let alone a mermaid at all."

I met eyes with Aisling, silently pleading for reassurance, but was surprised to find that she was looking at me with deep curiosity; her face immediately told me that she actually believed what Camila had said could be true.

"Of course you were meant for this life," Cearbhall said in a haunting whisper. "I knew it the moment I saw you."

Camila laughed cruelly at this.

"You wouldn't have known if I hadn't told you," she said smartly. "There's nothing extraordinary about her."

She looked me up and down with disdain and I hardly cared that she called me ordinary. I *was*.

"What happened to me was an accident," I said firmly, shaking my head. "You're wrong."

"None of this was by accident, you fool!" Camila shouted, startling everyone in the room, even Oisin. She flashed to my side, eyes bright like a wild animal's, and whispered in my ear with demonic cruelty that made my blood boil.

"Neither was Raj's death," she said, her tongue nearly touching my ear as she seemed to relish in saying the words. "I suppose Matt's was, though. Rotten luck he happened to be out on the water with your daddy that day."

The room began to spin. I was frozen in shock, unable to think and seeing nothing but red. The way she so carelessly threw around the names of my dead father and my would-have-been husband spiraled me into a rage over which I had no control-I wanted desperately to strangle her. But my arms wouldn't move. I almost felt the water beginning to boil beneath me as it matched the will of my fury.

"What are you-" I began, but I couldn't speak. There was nothing to say. Could my father's death really have been orchestrated by this woman in front of me; someone I didn't even know existed until days ago? And why? Because of *me* being some sort of descendent of the most ancient mermaid in the world? None of it seemed real, and yet-

"Now, Oisin... tell us. Where's the real stone?" Camila said, turning to face him.

"You will never have it as long as I live," Oisin said, his voice defiant and terrifying.

I saw the ghost of the great selkie leader he once must have been emerge; his eyes turned red with rage and he towered over Cearbhall and Camila with unmistakable authority.

Aisling was suddenly at my side and had a death grip on my arm before I could resist.

"Jasmine, we must go now," she said urgently.

Oisin swept in front of me and reached seamlessly for a sword that hung on a shield on the wall, dragging it down through the water with ease as if he were slicing it through the open air. His movement was swift as a man's who was decades younger. It missed Cearbhall narrowly, but I had the strangest sense that Oisin had avoided it on purpose. His eyes seemed far away; as if he were deeply focused on something else.

"*Jasmine,*" Aisling said fiercely, dragging me away from the scene. I watched as Camila lunged forward to claw at Oisin's face and I yelped.

"We have to help!" I exclaimed. "Your grandfather cannot-"

"Yes, he can," Aisling hissed.

"Don't let her get away!" screeched Cearbhall to Camila as he watched Aisling attempt to drag me from the chamber, but she shook her head and yelled back to him.

"The stone is more important!" she hissed. "We'll deal with her later!"

There was a deep, low rumble that erupted through the hall. It seemed to originate from the very heart of the sea and even brought Aisling-who had been tugging at my arm incessantly-to a halt. Oisin's eyes had gone blank with a cloudy mist and he raised his palms to the sky.

"The Ollphéist is coming," Aisling whispered.

There was a mist of green fog that began to rise from the floor of the sunken castle as well as from the arches beyond, bringing with it a terrible stillness that pierced my heart with fear. I knew the creature of which she spoke, but nothing could have prepared me to see it in the flesh.

From the depths of the arches behind Oisin suddenly burst an enormous, formidable serpent that looked as though it had come straight from the pits of Hell; its blue and gold scales igniting the room in a blinding flash of light. It let out a singular, demonic screech as its moonstone eyes sought the cause of its disturbance.

"It won't hurt ye," Aisling whispered, reading my thoughts. "Ye are the Mother of the Sea's blood."

The creature indeed saw me; and sure enough, its gaze passed directly over me without interest. It instead locked its eyes upon Cearbhall and Camila, raising its long tail and preparing to strike.

"Go find the stone!" Camila yelled to Cearbhall who had frozen in fear.

They both cried out, narrowly dodging the beast's blow as it brought its tail down between them with a crushing force. Oisin seemed to be whispering commands to the creature, but his face was visibly strained beyond his murky eyes. I knew that even after unleashing this deadly weapon, something was wrong.

"Come, now," Aisling said vehemently. "We *must*, Jasmine!"

I took one final look at the scene of terror, wondering how

Cearbhall and Camila could possibly overcome the ancient serpent of the Irish seas. But even as I watched, I saw Oisin stagger; as if directing the beast was subsequently draining his own powers. He would die in this endeavor, I felt almost sure of it.

Cearbhall darted down one of the passages at Camila's orders and I desperately wanted to go after him-to do anything to prevent him from finding the real stone. But I couldn't. The serpent had blocked my way, and even if it hadn't, Aisling made it clear that my escape was more important than the preservation of the gem.

Camila yelled in anguish as she lunged for the sword that Oisin had let fall limp in the wake of us controlling the mighty Ollphéist, and that was the last I saw of the petrifying scene.

Aisling and I flew down one of the tunnels that (if my sense of direction were correct) seemed to lead back out to the bay.

"What-" I asked breathlessly.

"Manannán mac Lir himself gave Oisin the gift of control over the Ollphéist of Strangford Lough," she said, anticipating my question. "But he's too old now...I'm afraid-" she stopped abruptly, and I knew she had seen Oisin's struggle in the same way I had.

My head spun, unable to grasp the ever-multiplying quantity of impossibilities that now riddled my reality. The notion that the God of the Irish Seas had gifted Aisling's great-great-great-grandfather the power to control one of the ancient sea demons known to haunt the lakes and rivers of Ireland... I shook my head, thinking the question of this myth would simply have to wait. Time was of the essence.

"There's another Green Window," she said quickly. "One that they don't know about."

I flitted my tail as strongly as I could, my body evidently understanding that there was no time for attempts at graceful strides. I felt like a salmon swimming upstream as we dodged through the incredibly intricate maze, the current seeming to try and force me back into the danger. Aisling did not let go of me.

"I'm afraid this one won't take ye back to Hy-Brasil," she said, biting her lip as we burst through the castle's walls and entered the bay. My eyes adjusted accordingly, but I could see that it was pitch black above us, signaling the middle of the night. "This one in Bangor Bay is tricky-I-I've only done it once."

The fear in Aisling's eyes worried me. "How is this one different from the others?" I asked tentatively. "I've only been through The Wormhole."

She didn't respond directly to my question. "I'll take ye there, but we must hurry," she said. And then, looking skyward with fear, she muttered, "Pray that the Window is open-it's not always. If it closes while yer in it..." she stopped short, noticing the horror in my face.

We darted through the water like lightning and it was apparent Aisling was an exceptional navigator. I hardly noticed the anchors from the boats overhead and, more than once, she grabbed my arm to prevent me from slicing myself in half with one of the iron chains. I fought the urge to turn around and check behind me; there was no time to worry about whether or not I was being pursued.

"It should be here," she said, slowing suddenly and looking around in all directions. I watched nervously, wishing I could be more useful. She didn't look confident.

"What does it look like?" I asked hopefully.

"It's more what it *feels* like," she replied quietly, and she closed her eyes.

I mirrored her, not knowing what I was supposed to feel. To come to a complete halt on the heels of utter chaos felt nearly impossible, but I did my best to quiet my mind.

Raj, Matt, I thought painfully. *How could this be?*

And then suddenly, I felt it. I knew the Window was there. There was a distinct push and pull of a current that was nearly identical to the sensation I had felt back in the Wormhole at Inis Mór. The difference this time was that I could sense a circular motion, as if it were a-

"Whirlpool," I said aloud, pointing directly west.

Sure enough, there was what appeared to be an underwater tornado straight ahead of us, less than twenty feet away. Aisling turned to look at me and was visibly impressed, even in the heat of our hurry.

"Well done," she said with a note of awe in her voice. "Ye really *are* the Heir of Atargatis."

"No," I said, keeping my eye on the whirlpool for fear it would slip away. I knew there wasn't much time, but I had to put this to rest.

"Aisling, I can't be. I was scratched by a selkie during a freak boating accident in Portugal when I was just a child. Both of my parents are dead, and I'm nobody."

Nevertheless, I recalled what Camila had said about Raj's death and my stomach turned again.

Nothing is an accident.

"Jasmine, we don't have a lot of time," she said, gripping my shoulders tightly. "Let me ask ye this. Do ye know who yer mother is?"

"No," I said quickly. "She left me when I was just a child. She abandoned me and my father. He never found her again, Aisling."

"But she was Irish, wasn't she? Did ye know that at least?" Aisling said anxiously. The whirlpool in front of us started to roar loudly, and our hair began to whip violently around our faces. I pushed it out of my eyes.

"She was Irish," I said slowly. "But-"

"And was her name Aine, do ye know?"

I shook my head. "I don't-" And then I paused, recalling a story told to me by my father long ago.

· · ·

"THEN I'LL CALL you Annie, since I can't pronounce your name either,"
Raj said.

"AISLING…IT MIGHT HAVE BEEN," I said, hardly believing the words myself.

Her eyes were wide. "Jasmine, if yer the heir to Atargatis, ye are my cousin," she said urgently over the roar of the water. "You are my aunt's daughter and yer the only one who can save her!"

"How?" I asked desperately.

The whirlpool started to glow green and I knew that the Window was telling me this was my only chance. It would surely close if I didn't go now, and who knew how long it would be before it opened again?

"I'll come to meet ye," she said, putting aside the mystery of my heritage for the sake of acknowledging the pool's warning. "But first I have to go back to Oisin. Wait for me on the other side and whatever ye do-*stay hidden.* Word will have traveled already that her Heir has returned to our waters."

"Where will this one take me?" I called as she began to back away. I was overcome with fear as I recalled the horrific sensation of the Window's current from The Wormhole. And if I were alone, how would I know where the exit was?

"The Skellig Islands!" she called, her voice muffled as the pool began to separate us. "I'm sorry, it's the best I can do! Ye must get far away from here!"

I allowed myself to be dragged into the center of the violent current, understanding at once why the humans had dubbed them "Dead pools." I was at the mercy of the ocean once more.

"Stay hidden!" she called. "I'm coming right behind ye, I promise!"

I closed my eyes as I placed my faith in Atargatis, the goddess of the sea, or perhaps as I should think of her now, my very distant relative.

CHAPTER 23

CHASING TAIL

HY-BRASIL

Seamus was choking, gasping, and sputtering all at once. Had his heart not been pounding, he would have surely thought himself dead. But he was much too aware of his surroundings for that to be possible. He slowly opened his eyes and he saw pure darkness, but it lasted less than a split second. He felt the strangest sensation that his eyes were actively peeling back one layer to reveal another, clearer lens that was able to handle the depths of the ocean into which he knew he had descended. He looked around him in awe while he sat on the ocean floor.

Sat actually wasn't the right word. Rather, he was floating just above the sand that lined the bottom of the ocean and directly in front of him was a miraculous tail of bright, iridescent silver that alternated between shades of green and blue as he moved it back and forth. There was absolutely no mistaking the mysterious, distinct hue that he had only ever seen once before; the first and only time he had held Jasmine's hand. He laughed incredulously for a moment before clutching the jewel that hung around his neck as tightly as he could, ensuring it was still there. He breathed a sigh of relief and a stream of bubbles shot from his mouth.

He felt his chest rise and fall and noticed that his shirt had nearly torn in two at the mercy of the waves. He went to rip it from himself completely before pausing. The stone would be exposed if he did so, and for whatever reason-instinct or common sense-he knew that something so precious should remain concealed.

In the distance he could make out a faint outline of a land-mass that he had no reason to believe was anything other than Hy-Brasil. He awkwardly clambered to what resembled a standing position while his tail floated below him in the water. Having always been an excellent swimmer thanks to the time Aidan had tossed him headfirst into Lough Naegh at the age of eight years old, Seamus instinctively moved with a fair bit more of grace than an average new selkie would have and made his way as quickly as he could to the island. No time to marvel at his physical state. Jasmine was waiting.

His plan upon arrival was hardly sophisticated, but he had no real choice aside from asking around for Jasmine. Surely if she had fallen from the Cliffs, she would have ended up here by now. After all, Mrs. Byrne had seemed entirely certain of Hy-Brasil and there couldn't be many unknown selkie settlements off the Western coast of Ireland, could there?

He began to see signs of life popping up all around him as the landmass came clearer into view. The seaweed rose higher and higher and he saw strangely large anemones (far too large for a clownfish) begin to sprinkle the ocean floor. He thought he heard a whisper and whirled around, but no one was there. He continued at a slower pace, looking in all directions while attempting to maintain a consistent pace and depth in the water.

The ocean floor began to slope upward, signaling his

approach to the shore. Even if he had seen no selkies below, surely they would be wandering about on the island. After all, they could remove their seal skins and turn back into humans, he reminded himself. He tentatively slithered out of the water, popping his head up to the surface.

If he had harbored any doubts regarding the grandness of Hy-Brasil, they were gone now. The isle was just as beautiful as he had imagined, possibly even surpassing his expectations. The sunlight streamed through a cloudless sky that was entirely different from the threatening storm he had left only moments ago. Seamus laughed with delight as he saw the beauty of the greenery; looking like a volcanic version of Ireland with the saturation turned all the way up in celebration of the brightest colors that Mother Nature had to offer.

And the selkies were there, alright. There were dozens of them playing in the shallows, their tails flicking upward and lazing in the sun. He watched in amazement as a man rose out of the water and simply grew legs, his seal skin shedding and transforming before his eyes into a dark green garment that resembled a kilt but was seemingly made of leaves. He hoped it would be just as easy for himself.

A group of women passed on his right and whispered something to one another before erupting into a fit of giggles. Seamus self-consciously looked down at his chest, realizing he must look ridiculous being the only selkie wearing a shirt. Still, his aversion to exposing the stone was significantly louder than his insecurity or caring what others thought. He was here for one woman and one woman only.

"Hi," he said, approaching a group of men that looked around his age that were talking in the shallows, throwing what looked like a coconut back and forth. They eyed him suspiciously; it was plain that everyone here knew one another for the most part. Seamus already felt the stares of the others in the distance boring into his back. "I'm lookin' for a woman named Jasmine. Do ye know her?"

"Can't say I do," one of them replied unhelpfully. Seamus sighed and looked at the others who all shook their heads.

He went about this for a while, paddling awkwardly along the shore and praying that he might find her, beautiful and happy, lounging on a rock. Something in his chest told him that wouldn't be the case, but he held out hope nonetheless.

"I'll be your Jasmine," said one blonde selkie with a bright smile for Seamus. "What's your name?"

"Ah, thanks, no thanks," Seamus said, attempting politeness but irritated by the lack of leads he was getting. She scowled at him as he swam away.

"Please just let her be safe," he thought to himself.

He then came to a quieter part of the island where there was hardly a shoreline; just cliffs. They looked oddly like the Cliffs of Moher but far less menacing, and he winced as he imagined Jasmine plunging from that height and the terror she must have felt. He had to keep going.

He swam a while without seeing anyone, and at last happened upon a large cave that had several selkies swimming in and out. He caught a glimpse of one woman leaving the cave and he was instantly drawn to stare at her arm- she had a mark just like Jasmine's. A large, iridescent scar streaked down her forearm like an animal had clawed her with glowing paint. She had to be what Mrs. Byrne had described as an Amalgam.

"Hey!" he called after her. The redhead turned around.

"Hmm?" she asked. "Do I know ye?"

She looked him up and down in a strange way and Seamus thought she may have been looking for a similar marking on his own body. When she didn't find one, he thought it looked like she instantly stiffened.

"No," he said. "I'm wondering if ye know of a woman named

Jasmine. She should be here. Black hair, beautiful eyes-" He stopped himself, wondering what color her eyes were now. Of course when he knew her, they had been brown. Until that last day...

"Jasmine," the woman said, a nasty grin flashing across her face that Seamus did not like at all. "Oh she's with *Cearbhall.*"

"Who's Cearbhall?" Seamus asked sharply.

The girl relished in his confusion. He tried to maintain a neutral expression, but his patience was waning. She was annoying, there was no other term for it.

"Why, he's our clan leader," she said, again her eyes scanning him for markings. "But *ye* aren't one of us so of course ye wouldn't know that."

Seamus gathered that the Amalgams were much more separated from the "regular" selkies here than he had thought based on Mrs. Byrne's brief description of them. His first impression of this one led him to believe they were certainly more malicious than he had assumed-but not Jasmine. There was no way. She had to still be good.

"Anyway, I might not bother looking for her," said the girl with a flip of her hair. "Cearbhall took her with him and they won't be back for several days."

Seamus' stomach lurched. There was no way he had come this far to somehow miss her.

"Took her where?" he demanded.

"Belfast," she said simply. "To bargain for the stone of the North Sea from Oisin of course."

The irony was almost unbearable. Belfast. Those were the waters he knew better than any other in Ireland, and that was where she had gone. But surely that would take days...no, weeks, to get there. The woman began to swim away, but he wasn't done questioning her.

"Stone of the North Sea?" he asked.

"Oh, I wouldn't discuss that with *ye*," she said with cruel amusement, but did not elaborate further. He thought it unimportant in the larger scheme of information he wanted from her and dropped it.

"How did they get there?" he asked, thinking if he left immediately he might be able to catch up with them.

"The Green Window at Poll na bPéist, ye eejit," she said, all pretenses now dropped. She was clearly as irritated as he was. "Are ye daft?"

"Right," Seamus said, ignoring her insults. "Of course."

He had no idea what the term *Green Window* meant, but he certainly knew exactly what and where Poll na bPéist was. His heart sank as he realized he could have easily hopped off the boat at Inis Mór, gotten to The Wormhole on foot, and never needed to put his brother in danger at all. He said a silent prayer for Aidan's wellbeing.

"Anyway, Cearbhall thinks she's *special*," the girl said as she turned to leave. "And usually when Cearbhall sees something he wants, he gets it." She cackled with self-satisfaction at his dumbfounded expression.

Fury boiled inside of Seamus as he watched the insufferable woman flit back toward the cave from which she had come. What on earth could this mean? The way she had said "Cearbhall thinks she's *special*" made him extremely uneasy. Had she gone with this man willingly?

Suddenly, the gem against his chest began to beat like a heart and he clutched it tightly. No. He couldn't explain how he knew, but if Jasmine had gone anywhere, it had been against her will.

"Hi there," came an eager voice from behind him.

He whirled around and saw another selkie watching him carefully. He was likely only within a few years of Seamus, but had rosy cheeks and an excitable grin that made him look much younger. He shook his head of sandy hair out of his eyes in a manner reminiscent of a golden retriever, and Seamus blinked the excess salt water from his own eyes. "I heard yer looking for Jasmine."

"Yes!" Seamus said eagerly. "Do ye know her?"

"Oh sure!" he exclaimed excitedly, but then his face fell. "But I haven't seen her for a few days. My mam's been worried sick about her, actually. Really took a liking to her since she arrived, ye know?"

Seamus nodded, knowing that while he meant well, the eager child did not quite understand the severity of Jasmine's woes. Did he know about her past...? And he had mentioned his own mother knowing her. How intertwined in selkie life had Jasmine already become? He looked, almost subconsciously, for any marking that resembled what he knew to be the scar of an Amalgam on this new acquaintance. He didn't see one and thought for some reason that made his new friend more trustworthy. Disappointed in his own bias as he knew Jasmine herself was marked as an Amalgam, he sighed. The boy looked at him excitedly.

"I'm Fintan," he said, offering his hand which Seamus took. Surprisingly firm grip for a kid, he thought. Fintan laughed as he maintained his grip on Seamus' hand.

"Jasmine taught me this, actually!" he said, pointing to their intertwined fingers. "The shaking."

"That's class," Seamus said, suppressing a laugh, despite himself. "I'm Seamus."

"Are ye new here? I've never seen ye before," Fintan said, and to Seamus' shock, he then pulled a strand of seaweed seemingly out of nowhere and began to eat it. He offered Seamus a bite which he politely refused.

"Erm-sure," Seamus said. As he had no other leads, he supposed this new companion would have to do. "The woman over there told me that Jasmine had gone with someone named Cearbhall and they've gone through some sort of window?"

"Poll na bPeist?" he asked.

"Aye," Seamus said quickly. "That's the one. It sounded like it was some sort of shortcut-"

"To Belfast," the boy finished his sentence, mouth full of seaweed. "Sure is! I take that route all the time. My fiancée lives out there. Of course we'd love to be together, but when her mam's away (she still land-walks sometimes, ye see) there's no one else to look after her great-great-ahh I forget how many generations it is-granddad. She feels guilty leavin' him. Terribly unfortunate situation. But, once we're married, I'll get her here right away. Much better than the chilly waters of the North down here, ye know? Or I s'pose *"Baltic"* is how they'd call it, up in Norn Iron, ha-ha. I know we've got the powers of adaptable temperatures in our scales, but even so-"

Seamus cut him off as politely as he could, thinking the lad would hardly stop to breathe let alone give him a chance to speak.

"Ah, yes of course, Fintan, I'm sorry-" he said loudly. "Would ye mind showing me the way? I've only been by boat."

Fintan looked confused by this statement, but his expression cleared almost immediately. "Ah so ye land-walk quite a bit, do ye?"

"Aye," Seamus said, not *knowing*, but assuming what it meant.

"Excellent," the boy said, and swallowed the last of his snack. "Let's get going now, then. I'll come along with ye."

"Oh that's not necessary-" Seamus interjected quickly.

"Nonsense!" Fintan said brightly, slapping him on the back. "I just told ye, my future wife's out there. Might as well pay my woman a visit!"

They took off without another thought; Seamus grateful for Fintan's haste, even if he didn't understand the true nature of their mission. As they passed through the veil of Hy-Brasil and back into the gray of the rest of the Atlantic, Seamus kept an anxious eye out for any sign of his brother. But there was no sign of wreckage, and the storm was long gone…he prayed Aidan made it back safely. He was a fine sailor, even if a bit daft when it came to judging weather conditions.

"...And they're all over the oceans, ye see? Otherwise it would take us weeks to get from place to place. Maybe even years!"

"Right," said Seamus, who, though he had not been listening, assumed that Fintan had been referring to the other Green Windows. He vaguely wondered where else they existed, but his main concern being the one that took him to Jasmine, he didn't bother to inquire further.

The swim was elongated by Fintan's excessive chatter, but Seamus found bits of his companion's ramblings to be rather useful. For example, he discovered that Fintan knew quite a bit about the Amalgams and what they were up to-supposedly there was a collection of rare, powerful stones that they were after. They were hidden all over the different oceans of the world and had unthinkable powers once united together. He carefully kept his own pressed to his chest, unsure of whether or not to reveal it to his new companion. The more Fintan told him about the Amalgam's desire for these precious gems, the more certain he was that he was definitely in possession of one.

"Terribly powerful, they are," Fintan said with what would have sounded like a tone of warning coming from anyone less excitable. "But the other selkies-mam and da, too-think it's best they stay hidden. They're sacred, ye know? We're not supposed to be out lookin' for em."

"Why not?" Seamus asked.

Fintan frowned with contemplation before answering.

"Well, the first mermaid, Atargatis, she hid them herself," he said simply, as if this were common knowledge. "The Amalgams tend to think they've been chosen to become what they are-since they're not born this way-and that Atargatis has commanded them to seek the stones and rule the seas."

He glanced sideways at Seamus before continuing.

"But the selkies like us, we don't think so highly of ourselves, ye see? We think the stones are best left alone and nature should run its course. We acknowledge Atargatis as the Mother of us all, but we don't worship her so seriously as the Amalgams do."

He paused.

"Where are ye from, mate? How is it ye don't know any of this?" he asked, but his tone was in no way accusatory or suspicious; merely curious.

"I land-walk mostly," was all Seamus said, recalling the term Fintan had used earlier. But he was now deep in thought trying to piece the puzzle together. He remembered the words of the redhead he had encountered back at the cave and pressed his friend further.

"Fintan, the woman back there told me Cearbhall intended to bargain for one of the stones with Oisin," he said, repeating her words as accurately as he could remember. He gulped, thinking of them in a whole different light now that he knew the significance of the stones. "Ye don't think she meant that-*Jasmine* would be part of this bargain, do ye?"

"No," he said, but his smile faded. "Mam doesn't like me hanging around the Amalgams, ye see...thinks they're not the best influence on me. But I don't think they're all *that* bad of folk. We disagree on the stones, but I've gotten on with them alright otherwise. What could they be usin' Jasmine for as a bargain, anyway? She hardly knew how to swim, mate."

Even as he spoke, Seamus heard the quiver of doubt in his voice and his stomach turned. Before he could inquire further, they arrived at The Green Window, otherwise known to the tourists of Inis Mór as The Wormhole. The sun had officially set, making the normally beautiful natural phenomenon look particularly haunted in the rising moonlight.

"Here we are!" Fintan said, his happy-go-lucky demeanor returned.

Seamus stared into the strange, rectangular shape that was bubbling like a witch's cauldron. How any tourist could look upon the famous Wormhole and see anything other than what was obviously a magical vortex was beyond him now that he knew that this other world, hidden in plain sight, existed.

Fintan, whether out of general politeness or observing that Seamus had no idea how to proceed, kindly offered to go first.

"Right behind ye," Seamus promised.

"Ye might want to take that off," Fintan warned, pointing to Seamus' ripped shirt. "It'd be nasty to get caught on one of the rocks."

"Ah, I sunburn easily," Seamus said, finding that no other excuse came to mind.

Fintan looked at him curiously and then burst out laughing. "Yer gas, Seamus."

He then thrust himself over the edge of the pool, heedless of any tourist that might be peeking over the ledge of the cliffs. He (quite clumsily) dumped his body into the pool of rushing water that greeted him and Seamus braced himself as Fintan's tail scraped the ledge.

"It's easy!" he called. "Ye just need to-"

What it was exactly that Seamus needed to do, he never found out. Fintan was immediately swept up in the bubbling waves and thrust beneath the surface, his arms flailing above his head in either delight or distress, Seamus could not tell. Within seconds, he vanished out of sight.

Seamus shrugged, having no choice but to follow suit. He heaved his body up on the edge of the pool and, deciding there was no proper way to do it, opted to fall backwards into it like a scuba diver. Clutching the gem to his chest where his torn shirt still hung, he felt himself being dragged through the passage like a rag doll.

After what felt like an eternity on the worst roller coaster he had ever been on, Seamus felt the current slowing and suddenly knew it was time to exit, even if he hadn't heard the faint calling of his own name from Fintan beyond the passage. He rolled himself sideways instinctively, landing in a murky bit of water that he saw for a single second before his eyes adjusted accordingly and it became clear once more. The climate of Northern Ireland hit him like a winter's chill, and he involuntarily shivered before regulating his body temperature back to normal.

"It's good craic, innit?" said Fintan brightly. "Quite the rush!"

Seamus laughed, then quickly realized he was not joking.

Thump, thump.

Seamus started at the reminder of the precious stone that hung around his neck. It beat against his chest in the same way it had when he saw the veil that encompassed Hy-Brasil. But this time it was urgent; it was pleading for something. He was sure of it.

While his eyes could adjust for the lack of light in the dark water, his mind had a hard time doing the same. To be underwater in the middle of the night just adjacent to the bay where his own mother had been found dead a decade earlier was not a place that anyone-human or selkie-would choose to be.

He had recognized it instantly, of course, having spent his entire life living just off these shores. The Wormhole had spit him out near the Copelands, but Bangor Bay, he knew, was not far from him, looming in the background like a mountain lion, waiting for its chance to pounce on the child as it had the mother.

"Oisin's place is not far from here," Fintan said, picking up a loose piece of seaweed from the ocean floor.

Seamus' stomach growled loudly and, thinking it would be a long time before he saw real food, decided to copy his friend. He was surprised to find that the snack was satisfying and tasted somewhere between tolerable and quite good. There was a vague sense of revitalization that followed, and he wondered if that had to do with the nutrients of the sea's delicacy or the knowledge that he was one step closer to finding and (hopefully) rescuing Jasmine. He followed as Fintan zig-zagged through the water with ease, having very clearly become accustomed to this route.

"Fintan," Seamus said as the sand began to slope upward, signaling the approaching shore. "Ye said yer parents don't love that ye hang around the Amalgams. But are ye um—on good terms with this Cearbhall?"

"Oh sure," said Fintan brightly. "Don't know him too well but we've always got on, me and him. He asked me to introduce him to Jasmine once he'd heard she was staying with my family, so of course I brought her along with me to the cave ye just saw."

Of course the good-natured Fintan didn't think anything odd or suspicious of the request, but Seamus certainly knew better. Why had Cearbhall wanted to meet Jasmine so badly? Aside from the obvious fact of her beauty and charm, he thought bitterly. Based on his only impression of the Amalgams, he thought Fintan's mam was a bit more wise to their true intentions than her son.

"Here we are!" Fintan called from up ahead. Seamus nearly laughed when he recognized where they were.

They popped their heads above the surface to find an old medieval structure on the water with which he was all too familiar, having been on countless primary school trips to Carrickfergus Castle. Following as Fintan slithered toward the structure, he noticed that for the first time on their journey, his friend's demeanor became subdued. His brow suddenly furrowed and he slowed to a halt.

"That's odd," Fintan said. "It's usually lit up out here."

He then fell completely (and uncharacteristically) silent while Seamus became more alert along with him, swimming as quietly as possible while keeping close to the ocean floor.

Directly ahead of them was an ominous looking gate. There were rumors and legends of course of the haunting below the ancient fortress, but no one cared all that much for Carrickfergus when in comparison to the other grand castles of the Emerald Isle, therefore no one bothered to investigate too deeply. Seamus saw it now in an entirely different light.

Having grown accustomed to the symphony of the heartbeats from both his own chest and the gem that laid upon it, Seamus did not immediately notice that one of them had stopped. With a sudden realization, he reached in a panic for the gem. The light had gone out, and the beat was no more.

"What the hell?" he cursed to himself, a dreadful fear creeping into his chest. What could this mean? Did this mean she was-

"Who are *you?*" came an accusatory voice from behind him that, if he had had legs, would have made him jump.

Instead, he merely flailed and the gem floated from his grasp. The chain kept it anchored to his neck and he quickly drew it in. Shit, had either of them seen it?

Another selkie was there. She wore an accusatory glare charged with fear; her red hair cascading around her shoulders like a sheet of angry fire. Before Seamus could speak, Fintan rushed toward her.

"Aisling!" he said excitedly, pulling into a tight embrace. Seamus realized that this must be the future wife that his friend had spoken of before they left. Noticing her terrified stare in Seamus' direction, Fintan quickly pulled away. "What's wrong?"

"Is he with the others?" she said, pointing at Seamus. "Cearbhall and Camila?"

Fintan looked back and forth between the two of them, brow wrinkled in confusion. "Well, no," he said. "I don't think they're acquainted just yet but-"

"No!" Seamus said quickly, cutting him off from what he was certain would be another lengthy explanation. He looked directly at the woman instead. "I'm looking for that fucking asshole. Is he here?"

"Yes," she said slowly.

"Aisling, what-?" Fintan began to question, but she put up a hand and silenced him.

"Say nothing, Fintan," she said curtly, distrust in her eyes.

She moved toward Seamus, her gaze darting back and forth

between his eyes and the chain around his neck. He could see she was quite young, and although her features were Irish, she strangely had the exact same eyes as someone else he knew.

"Fintan was showing me the way," Seamus said, his hands up in surrender, desperate for her trust. "Because Cearbhall has my woman. Her name is Jasmine. She has beautiful, long black hair… have ye seen her?"

"Jasmine!" the girl exclaimed.

"Yes," Seamus sighed with relief. "Is she alright?"

The girl bit her lip with regret and shook her head. "She's alright, but ye've just missed her, I'm afraid," she said quietly. "I-I sent her through the Window at Bangor Bay."

"Oh damn it to fucking Hell!" Seamus exclaimed, making both the girl and Fintan start in surprise. "Sorry," he added quickly.

"I was trying to help her get away! Cearbhall and Camila had brought her here as a prisoner!" she shot back at him. "And she's still in great danger!"

Seamus stopped, a chill running down his spine. The bargain that the other Amalgam had mentioned crept back into his mind. There was more to fear than Jasmine's simply becoming a selkie.

"Why?" Seamus asked slowly, growing more uneasy upon hearing that this Cearbhall had an accomplice. "Why did they bring her here?"

Aisling looked at him, wide-eyed.

"Jasmine… she's the heir to the sea goddess, the Mother of us all," she said in awe.

"Who-?" he said, his voice trailing off. He looked at Fintan whose expression was frozen in a mixture of shock and awe and he understood to whom Aisling referred. "Ye don't mean she's-"

"Atargatis, of course!" the girl exclaimed. "Jasmine is her direct descendent!"

Fintan gasped, but Seamus shook his head in disbelief.

"No, that's not possible," he said, but even as he spoke them aloud, he doubted the words. How would he know?

"They mean to use her to harness the power of all the stones," the girl continued, eyes flashing with distrust once more. "And I suppose that's yer intention as well." She pointed at the gem that hung around Seamus' neck. In his distress, he hadn't noticed it had fallen out of his shirt.

"Where did ye get one of those?" she asked.

Fintan, having been oblivious to the jewelry until now, looked upon it gravely. He said nothing and Seamus felt a wave of guilt at having not revealed it to him earlier. But how could he have known who to trust right away?

"This is-" but Seamus stopped short. He had no real answer other than the truth, so he came out with it. "It was my mother's."

This statement only seemed to confuse the two of them further, but he did not give either of them time to contemplate.

"Listen, I need to find Jasmine," he said quickly. "That's all I care about right now. Nevermind the stones."

"Yeah? And what's she to ye?" the girl asked fiercely. Fintan took her hand and seemed to mirror her thoughts, all traces of his careless, genial nature vanished from his face.

"Alright," Seamus said slowly, clinging to the little bit of patience he had left as he realized nothing would be accomplished without gaining their trust. "I don't have this stone because I want to keep it. I don't even know what the bleeding yoke is for or what it does. I've only been using it to help me find Jasmine. It-it seems to know where she is."

He finished lamely, hearing how untruthful his own story sounded. But he had nothing else to give. He looked at Fintan pleadingly, hoping his friend could trust him for a few moments longer. Neither of them responded.

"I've told ye, Jasmine is my woman," he continued desperately, unsure of what else to call her. After all, that's what she was. She was *his*, the second he could find her. And then he'd never let her out of his sight again.

"She told me she's promised to a land-walker," the girl said doubtfully. "By the name of-"

"Seamus," he interrupted her.

He prayed with all of his soul that Jasmine had told this girl of him, and not Matt. All hope in finding her was lost if Aisling did not believe him. But could he, a man Jasmine knew for just a few days, have truly replaced her late fiancé in her heart? He felt a sudden, violent surge of jealousy for the dead man.

"That *was* the name," sighed the girl at last, speaking more to Fintan than Seamus. Fintan seemed convinced this was enough, and Seamus' shoulders sank with relief.

"I'm sorry I doubted ye. She told me ye were a land-walker."

"I was," said Seamus simply.

She studied him carefully for another moment. Fintan whispered something to her and she nodded. They both turned to him, apparently agreeing that he was telling the truth as far as they could tell.

"I'll help ye find Jasmine. But I need ye first," she said. "We must help my great grandfather."

"I-" Seamus looked around, desperately wanting to get to Jasmine as soon as possible. He had no allegiance to this girl; no reason to help at all. He knew she could hold him here if she wished, knowing he had no idea where the Window was. But he saw in her eyes immediately that she wouldn't.

"Please," she begged. "I'll need ye both if Cearbhall and Camila are still back there. I promise Jasmine is far and safe away."

"I-" he said, wrestling with his options.

"Jasmine's my blood," the girl said with finality. "I've every reason to want her as safe as ye do."

Seamus did not know how to respond to this, once again not understanding how it was possible. But it did explain his recognition of the girl's eyes, and he knew she was truthful.

"Alright, then," he said. "Show me the way."

They sped through the labyrinth of tunnels below the castle, but Seamus had no time to marvel at the decayed, medieval structure that he had only ever seen from above. There were signs of life here and there, but nothing that would have roused the suspicions of historians enough to investigate further. Besides, he recalled Fintan saying it was only his fiancée and her great grandfather that lived here. Nevertheless, he couldn't help but glance behind him every now and then to ensure no one was following them. The feeling of unease that had clung to him like a shadow seemed to suffocate him further the deeper they wound into the maze.

"Keep that well hidden," Aisling warned, pointing to the stone.

She briefly explained the plan Oisin had derived. It involved giving Cearbhall and Camila a replica of the real stone that he *did* indeed have, hidden safely away, but Jasmine's lack of reaction to the stone had proven its falsehood. Aisling had left at once to see Jasmine safely away, and she had been on her way back to the castle when Fintan and Seamus had crossed her path. Irritated as he was at how narrowly he had missed her, Seamus felt exceedingly grateful toward Aisling for looking after Jasmine so selflessly.

"Did she know?" Seamus asked. "Jasmine, did she know she was the descendent of Atargatis?"

Aisling shook her head in dismay.

"No," she said. "I had no time to explain to her, but the relation is on her father's side. Her mother-my aunt Aine-unintentionally wed the descendent of Atargatis' human child, Semiramis. That'll be Jasmine's father. Because Aine was a selkie, it was the first time the line was able to live as mermaids once more."

"But Jasmine wasn't born a selkie," said Seamus slowly, grasping for answers he couldn't understand. "She was scratched as a child and-"

"I know," Aisling spoke quickly, never slowing as she wound through the tunnels. Seamus was swimming as quickly as he could to keep up with her while Fintan brought up the rear. "That's the part I can't understand just yet. This woman Camila, Cearbhall's accomplice, claimed that her being marked was no accident."

Seamus opened his mouth to ask another question, but Aisling gasped in shock as they approached a grand hall of marble columns.

"Oisin!" she screamed, flying across the room with Fintan in her wake.

The room was bright with the light from their tails that bounced off the dozens of mirrors that lined it. Seamus rushed behind them and saw Aisling was crouched over the figure of a large man who was severely injured. He had a gash across his chest that was glowing in the same iridescent manner that Seamus was familiar enough with by now, but something about it was foreign this time. Rather than shining like a beacon of strength, it seemed to be leaking; emitting a line of smoke from his chest... he realized with horror that this was how selkies must bleed.

"My darling Aisling," the old man said as the young girl clasped his hand. "They have stolen the stone-the real stone. I could no longer command the Ollphéist. My powers are far too weakened."

"No," she whispered. "I shouldn't have left ye-I-"

"Shh," he said, coughing violently. "The Heir of Atargatis is more important than your poor old great-great...me."

The girl looked hopelessly between her grandfather and Fintan while Seamus hung in the background, unsure of what to do. As they were both deeply preoccupied, Seamus looked around warily, and Aisling voiced the question that was burning in his mind.

"Where have they gone?" she pleaded with urgency. "Cearbhall and Camila, are they still here?"

"No," he said. "They narrowly escaped the beast; they have

undoubtedly gone back to Hy-Brasil to unite the stones they already have. And then…who knows what evil they will wrought."

"They won't," Aisling said quickly. "They can't without the Heir. They have no power without Jasmine."

He nodded and sighed deeply, an alarming amount of silver smoke now billowing from his chest. There was little time left, and it was plain from Fintan's expression that there was nothing to be done. He shook his head silently in Seamus' direction.

"Oisin, this is Seamus. He knows Jasmine," said Aisling hurriedly, recognizing there was little time left.

"Oh," was all the old man said, plainly uncertain as to how this information could be helpful as he looked toward the newcomer that stood over his deathbed.

Seamus instinctively reached below his shirt and removed the stone to show the old man. "This—this is one of the stones they seek, is it not?"

The man's eyes grew wide and he looked upon Seamus with a strange mixture of hope and confusion. "It is, son," he said. "How do you come to have this in your possession?"

"It was my mother's," he said confidently, no doubt remaining in his mind. "I didn't know what it was until today."

"Do no evil with this gem," the old man warned. "Do only what you must in order to protect the line of Atargatis."

"I will," he promised the dying man.

What happened next was a miracle to behold, but not the kind Seamus had ever hoped to see. He watched as the old man crossed over from the living world and into the spiritual; his eyes glazing as he went. Oisin took a last deep breath of water and exhausted himself, his head falling gently onto his own shoulder in the appearance of one falling peacefully asleep.

From his mouth trickled a faint, silver fog that was unmistakably the shadow of his soul, ascending to the surface of the water where it disappeared into the waves. His body then slowly began to rise and Seamus recalled the words of the strange witch from Cashel.

"Their bodies are found on the shore, united with the land once more."

He knew what would follow. The man would transform back into his human form and wash up on the shore in the same way that his own mother had been found in these very waters. He chose not to look, and he stood still while Fintan wrapped his arm around Aisling's shivering body.

"It'll be alright," he said quietly. Seamus said nothing at all.

They floated in the room for no more than a few minutes before Aisling gathered herself. Whether it was because she was familiar with loss or simply knew there was no time to grieve, she turned from the others and led them swiftly from the hall.

"Ye heard that Cearbhall and Camila have stolen Oisin's real stone," she said quietly to Seamus as they made their way back toward the gate and into the open water. "But ye have one, and there are still many others. Without them all, and especially without Jasmine, they cannot prevail."

"And ye think they went back to Hy-Brasil?" Fintan asked.

Aisling nodded. "Yes, they will want to gather the stones they have together before setting out to find the rest," she said.

"Jasmine," Seamus said quickly. "I need to get to her immediately."

"We'll show ye the way to The Green Window of Bangor," said Fintan.

Aisling bit her lip and looked at him with uncertainty.

"That particular Window is not always open," she said. "And if it closes while yer attempting to use it…ye'll die."

She finished the sentence she had not been able to say in front of Jasmine before she left. She had known that Atargatis would keep Jasmine safe. But would the Mother of the sea watch over Seamus as well?

A stab of pain, cold as ice ran through Seamus' veins. "Ye said the Green Window of Bangor Bay?"

"That's the one," said Aisling distractedly.

He knew. He need not ask. This was how his mother had died.

* * *

THEY ZOOMED through the open water, dodging the boats as best they could while descending with the slope of the sand. Seamus looked around and felt the pulse of the stone begin to beat once more. He plucked it from his chest and showed it to Aisling and Fintan whose eyes were wide with amazement.

"My God," Fintan said in wonder. "It-it works! The call of Atargatis!"

Aisling looked up from the stone and into Seamus' eyes, remembering her conversation with Jasmine from just hours ago.

"Ye said the stone helped ye find her," she whispered with newfound understanding. "And it's how she can see ye. She's had visions of ye. I thought of them as nothing more than dreams when I thought ye were a land-walker. But this..."

Her voice trailed off and he knew what she meant.

"Thank ye, Aisling," he said. "I promise I'll keep her safe."

They came to a halt as they all instinctively felt they were in the correct place due to the glowing of the stone. Unlike The Wormhole, this Green Window would not be seen. There was a deep rumble from the ocean floor, and the sands below them began to swirl. Seamus knew the passage was opening for him.

It began to pull him in, and before he could call out to either of his new friends, the whirlpool engulfed him entirely and he disappeared.

CHAPTER 24

A WELCOME REUNION

SKELLIG ISLANDS, COUNTY KERRY

My lengthy black hair was caught in my throat. I gasped for air or water-I could not tell which flooded my lungs first as the whirlpool came to a close beneath me. The dark gray of the early morning light was above me, and it didn't look like it was moving... I must be above the waves.

I wiggled my tail and let out a yelp as I felt a surge of pain run straight through my lower body like an electric shock. I looked down into the water to find a thin, wispy line of what could have been either smoke or liquid trailing from a deep gash in my tail; it was unlike any consistency I had ever seen. The color of it was unsurprisingly the same as my scales and scar, and although I was afraid to touch the mysterious substance, I knew it was my blood. I took a deep breath and prepared myself to assess how bad the wound was underneath, but as soon as I touched it, the cut miraculously began to close on its own. Within moments, the scrape had closed entirely and I was healed.

With my physical health now as settled as it could be for the moment, I straightened up and came to a steady bob above the water, beginning to take in my surroundings. Of course Aisling had barely had time to yell after me that I would alight near the Skellig Islands, but this information did me no real service. I had very little clue about these islands other than my vague knowledge that there was a small Christian monastery on the bigger of the two, Skellig Michael.

My poorly formed expectations, however, were far exceeded when I took in the vast landmass that towered above the waves in front of me, looming like a lone castle of jagged stone in the middle of the murky waters of the Atlantic. As I had often thought in recent days, it seemed entirely obvious that there should be magic here. While it was in no way the shining paradise of Hy-Brasil, it was mighty in its own right.

I scanned the perimeter for signs of boats and saw nothing. I assumed tourism was relatively limited here, but I still expected to see *someone*. It dawned on me then that the chill of the air (though it did not bother me) signaled that it was now late autumn; at least a month since I had become what I was. I doubted many travelers chose to come out this way during this time of year.

Nevertheless, the sun was peeking behind the clouds and I could tell it was morning.

Aisling had told me to wait for her, but where? And how long would she be? Cearbhall and Camila could be back in Hy-Brasil already, and they would surely come after me once they had the stones collected together. How long would it take them to track me down? Additionally, I had no desire to drift about for days on end; hiding away from them like a coward. I had already determined that the least I could do was stop them from getting the stones, and help Aisling find her aunt.

Her aunt. My mother.

I reflected on the discovery that she existed but it didn't seem real. How could she be involved in all of this? How could I be a descendant of the original mermaid, Atargatis? There was simply no possibility.

And yet, there was.

I knew that the legend of Atargatis' origins traced back to ancient Mesopotamia. In modern day that would translate to… I thought hard, willing the globe from Raj's office to appear behind my eyelids. Iraq, mostly of course…but also parts of Iran, Kuwait, Turkey, and…Syria. I shuddered with realization of the impossible. My father's family *was* Syrian. And of course I knew my mother had been Irish.

Could it be possible that the mysterious Annie, whose name I could only recall from a once-told memory of my father's, was actually *Aine,* an Irish selkie who had (by pure fate) come to procreate with Faraj Atarga, a descendent of Atargatis herself? Was my parents' union truly the reopening of a long lost line of ancient mermaids?

Camila's words rang in my ear once more and I desperately tried to understand their meaning. She spoke my father's name as if she had known him. As much as I wanted to be as far away from her as possible, my frustration for the unknown was stronger. I needed answers from her.

What had burned me with rage back in the cave came back with a gut wrenching force-Matt's death had been an unintentional casualty in all of this. My stomach lurched as I ached with regret. What had seemed like a freak accident was somehow not, and the man I had loved had been an innocent bystander in the twisted fate to which I had always been destined since my birth. I thought of him now, my heart crumbling beneath the weight of a new layer of understanding.

While contemplating in the depths, I had failed to notice that I was drifting close to the shore. With a sudden jolt of curiosity that was far stronger than all of my other questions, I wondered what would happen if I tried to transform.

Having already discovered that the limitations of the shallows did not seem to apply as I had been told, I wondered if *this* was possible as well. I had never tried, after all. And if I truly were the Heir of Atargatis, I should be able to do...well, anything, shouldn't I? While the queen of all mermaids since the beginning of time had *chosen* to become this hybrid species, surely her ability to become human again could never be taken away?

I tentatively swam closer to the mass of rock, slithering gracefully in contrast to the sharp waves that assaulted me with each flicker of my tail. But where was the shore? I flitted around the perimeter, seeking anywhere that made sense to alight. What would happen if I couldn't do it? And would it hurt?

At last I saw the tiniest stretch of sand and a miniature dock where I supposed boats would park if there were any. I made my way toward it as quickly as I could, fearing I would lose my nerve if I lingered in the distance any longer.

As I got closer to the shoreline, I thought I felt something happening. My tail began to tingle as it gently brushed the sand, sloping upward to meet the chilly air...I could almost feel myself walking again.

And then my hands were digging into the rough sand, dragging my tail behind me like a thirty-five pound dead weight while the waves lapped gently at my lower body that I hardly recognized.

I waited. And waited.

Just as my hope began to slip away, I felt a distinct tingle in my tail. I held my breath in anticipation before the warnings of Sorcha and Lachlan came to fruition.

I gasped in agony. The pain seared white hot as if a fire poker were being dragged down the length of my scales and it was inexplicably excruciating. I wanted nothing more than to dive back into the water and make it go away. I was dying.

"No," I told myself firmly. "*You're not. You are the heir of Atargatis.*"

The pain slowed to a dull burn that felt like I was standing *too* close to a fireplace, unlike the perfectly comfortable warmth I had felt when I first became a selkie. The knives that Hans Christian Andersen had prophesied were also there-digging into my flesh like I was being skinned for cleaning and eating. It was as if my body were rebelling against the unnaturalness of it all, despite having existed with legs for my entire life until I came to this country. I closed my eyes, too terrified to watch.

Why did this *hurt* me? When all of the other selkies made their transition so gracefully? When they popped out of the water and seamlessly grew legs, returning to the other half of their existence on a regular basis as if it were the simplest thing in the world? Why was *I*, the heir to the throne of the seas, so incredibly weakened by the simplest of tasks?

It was because *she* didn't want me to do it. Atargatis herself was forbidding me to abandon what I had been chosen to do.

I cried out again as what I hoped would be the final wave of pain seemed to rip my lower body in half.

I caught one glimpse of my legs-covered in the mysterious, iridescent liquid that I knew to be the blood of a selkie underneath the skirt of fine, green silk.

My world went black again.

* * *

"Jasmine!" I heard the urgency of his voice calling to me from a far distance. But it couldn't be.

I looked out at the water, shielding my eyes from the sun that was now high in the sky. Only then was I certain I was dead, because what I saw could not be real.

Seamus was there, furiously swimming toward the shore in pursuit of me, and I thought I saw... my heart stopped. Trailing behind him and peeking through the water in intermittent waves was the distinct outline of a tail that looked just like mine.

He reached the narrow shore at last and instantly sprinted from the water, his tail melting away as it was seamlessly replaced by his legs that were wrapped in the same mythical kilt of leaves that I had grown accustomed to seeing the men on Hy-Brasil wear. My brain and my body were both frozen. I couldn't speak.

He fell to his knees and took my face in his hands, kissing me fiercely.

"Are you real?" I asked in a voice that sounded far away. I had dreamt of him so many times, I couldn't be sure.

"Aye, Jazz, I'm here," he said soothingly, cradling my head in his chest as I laid motionless on the sand, afraid (or unable) to move my legs. "At's us nai, cailín álainn."

He continued to whisper his tranquil Gaelic into my ear like a lullaby as he stroked my hair, and I began to understand that this was truly happening. But how?

I looked up at him blankly.

"I can't believe you found me," was all I could say as a tear-a real, human tear-ran down my cheek. "I never thought I would see you again."

"I was never goin' to stop lookin' for ye," he said quietly as he ran his finger along my arm and traced the scar on my hand with the same tenderness I remembered from before. "I couldn't let ye go."

"I-" I began, and then I let out a sigh, the totality of my strength drained from my body in the aftermath of my transition. "How?"

He shook his head incredulously, apparently lost for words.

"Professor Brennan, Kiana…all these clues—" he began, but he stopped short, overwhelmed by the details as much as I was. "It's a long story, Jasmine, but I knew ye weren't dead. If you'd been dead, my own heart would've stopped beating with yers."

I let out a small sob, burying my head into him again, when I suddenly observed there was a third heartbeat pounding between us. I looked up at him and noticed something dangling from his neck that I hadn't seen before.

The bright yellow stone looked like a flawless diamond, twinkling with the ancient magic of Atargatis. I knew the pulse I felt was mine. I suddenly understood that this was how I had been able to sense his presence for days on end.

"How did you-" I began, tentatively reaching toward the stone but not yet daring to touch it. "Is this what I think it is?"

"Yes," he said, looking down upon the gem with reverence. He then met my eyes with eagerness that I could not understand. "It was my mother's."

I tried to process, but my brain was lagging like a desktop computer.

"She was a selkie, Jasmine," he said, grabbing me by the shoulders. "I didn't know it until I met ye."

I couldn't believe the words he was saying, and yet-I had seen him alight from the sea and turn back into a man. It was real.

He clutched my arms to support my upper body as it was clear I couldn't walk just yet. He then glanced down at where my tail had been and winced ever so slightly.

"What?" I asked fearfully. "Is it-does it look that bad?"

"They said ye couldn't, being an Amalgam, but if yer the Heir…I wondered if ye could," he whispered. "Are ye in pain?"

So he knew everything, it seemed.

"I am," I said honestly, my eyes squinting in the harsh sunlight that seemed to be scorching my raw legs. "But how did you-"

"Later," he said quietly. "We'll have time now."

The truth of his statement alone was enough to make me momentarily forget all of the terrifying events I had experienced since I had gone through the Wormhole on Inishmore. I didn't know how he was with me again, but he wasn't going anywhere.

"We need to get ye out of the sun," he said, feeling one of my legs. "It's Baltic out here and yet, yer burnin' up somethin' serious."

Of course the sun would hurt me now that I was human. After all, Atargatis was the goddess of the moon. She was doing everything in her divine power to drag me back into the sea. I nodded in agreement, praying that the shade would bring me a moment of comfort if not complete alleviation from the agony.

He gathered me up in his arms in one swift motion, carrying me as if I were light as a bird. Exhaustion descended upon me like a dark shadow as the grains of loose sand fell from my body and back onto the shore. He looked down at me with a smile that seemed to pierce my soul with relief.

I knew where we were going-it was the only option. The ancient monastery at the top of the hill was the only semblance of a fortress that could shield me from the sun. The beehive-like huts were positioned at the top of the stone pathway that I had seen when I approached the shore, and I closed my eyes as Seamus made his way up the side of the mountainous landscape with me in his arms.

"At's us nai," he said some time later, setting me down at last on a ledge within the cool cover of the stone house.

He pressed his lips to my hand, kneeling in front of me as I began to regain my strength. I attempted to move my legs and found that while they were reluctantly beginning to respond to my brain, they remained brutally sore. I stood up gingerly, staggering slightly as a sharp pain coursed through both limbs.

"Alright?" he asked, reaching out to catch me in case I fell.

"Yes," I said truthfully, sensing that the more I moved, the better.

He pulled me toward him and kissed me again-this time I had the strength to reciprocate. I fell right back into the place I remembered, fitting comfortably below his chest as he bent down to meet my lips.

"I missed ye," he said huskily into my hair before moving it aside to kiss me behind my ear. I shuddered as his other hand traced my spine. "But ye nearly feckin' killed me."

Now that both of us were certain I wouldn't break in half, the unspoken need between us returned. His hands, which had held me gently only moments before, now gripped the base of my neck in a borderline possessive manner that was consistent with his behavior in my dreams. He picked me up again and brought me to the ledge beneath the lone window of the hut, pushing me against the wall as he dropped to his knees.

"I think I'll die if I don't have ye right now," he said, his face solemn and without a hint of jest.

I had no objection, other than the dim realization that if I weren't already damned to Hell because of the creature I had become, committing an unholy act such as this within a Christian monastery would certainly seal the deal.

He forced my legs apart with his knee and lowered his head, pulling me closer to him as he wrapped his arms beneath me for the sake of a firm grip. I shut my eyes, desperately wanting to savor the moment I had imagined as it happened in real life.

The frustration that lingered with each awakening from my dreams evaporated in an instant as he moved with purposeful swiftness, leaving no room for sensual delay. His mouth met the warmth between my thighs with an urgent kiss that nearly brought me to the surface instantly, but I held back, running my hands through his dark copper waves.

He explored me selflessly with his tongue for several euphoric moments before slipping two of his fingers inside me, provoking a small gasp that I knew he liked-I could feel him smile.

"Fuck," I sighed.

His emerald eyes seemed to smirk with satisfaction as he looked up at me. He removed his fingers in a swift motion that left me aching for him, but then directly brought his face up to meet mine. He quickly (and rather forcefully) pressed himself inside me without asking permission. I didn't care.

I said his name in the most helpless voice I had ever heard come out of my own mouth. While Atargatis' powers had been so strong that she had mistakenly slain her mortal lover, *I*-the direct descendent of the Goddess of the Sea-was powerless against Man. I belonged to him.

I felt myself approaching a violent, crashing wave as he put his hand on the wall behind my head, the other powerfully grasping the back of my hair. He muttered some sort of Gaelic curse word I didn't catch and I moaned loudly in response. Then I was slipping below the surface, unable to postpone it any further.

"Come for me," he said.

Before I knew it, I was melting into Seamus and him into me. I fell back against the wall as he collapsed into my shoulder, having been reminded of one of the best aspects of being human.

CHAPTER 25

THE RETURN

The possibility that someone might be on the island with us had not occurred to me until the sobering moment that inevitably follows an experience like the one Seamus and I had just shared. I found myself suddenly highly alert as the pain in my lower body that I had been able to ignore in the wake of pleasure immediately returned.

"What if someone sees us?" I asked as I peeked out the tiny stone window, wincing as my legs started to burn again.

Seamus was less concerned than I.

"Can't say I'd care all that much," he said with his eyes closed.

I wished-and briefly considered that-we could stay in our bubble of safe isolation forever. Now that I knew I could land-walk, we could theoretically turn away from this world entirely and revert to the normalcy of what we had known before.

Theoretically, but not actually.

Aside from the fact that it was clear my connection to the line of Atargatis was responsible for the extreme pain and difficulty behind my transformation, I had quite a few other stakes in the game that added to the complexity of my decision.

I knew-especially now seeing Seamus had one of the gems

himself-that I had a job to do. The other Amalgams would be after the remainder of the stones, and I had to find them first, while hopefully tracking down my imprisoned mother in the process.

And lastly, I would drag Camila by her hair into the pits of Hell with me before I let her get away with dropping my father's name the way she had. I would force her to explain to me.

Seamus joined me at the window and seemed to read my mind.

"We've got to go back, aye?" he said, arms crossed as we watched the waves sparkle in the sapphire sea below.

The distinction was not lost on me, and I needed to make it clear that he was not obligated in the way that I was. Selkie or not, *he* wasn't of the line of Atargatis. As much as I wanted him with me forever, he wasn't responsible for the things that fate required me to do.

"Yes," I said simply. "*I* do."

He pulled me into him, placing one firm hand on my shoulder as he cupped my chin with his other. His dark green eyes searched me before he spoke.

"And me as well," he said severely.

"This isn't your burden," I replied in a small voice. "*I'm* not your burden."

He laughed ironically and threw his head back, his auburn waves catching the sunlight through the window.

"But ye are," he said. "I chased yer ghost all the way from Galway and yer daft if ye think I did that only to turn 'round and leave ye once I found ye."

His smile vanished and was replaced by a look of severity.

"No, Jasmine, I'm not allowing ye out of my sight again," he finished.

"Allowing?" I challenged.

"Aye, ye heard me," he said. "Yer my woman and ye do as I say when it comes to matters of yer safety."

I almost laughed, but realized instantly that he wasn't joking in the slightest.

"I love ye, Jasmine," he said, kissing my forehead and making my heart leap the way it had the night I first met him. "I really do."

I loved him, too. How could I not?

"*What* in the name of Manannán mac Lir are ye two doing up *here?*"

I whirled around and saw someone that-while I was glad to see her-completely took me by surprise.

"Aisling!" I shouted as the redhead burst through the tiny doorframe.

In the midst of everything that had occurred since I turned back into a human, I had completely forgotten that she had told me to wait for her. Technically, I had remained on Skellig Michael and therefore *had* kept my promise. She didn't seem to agree with my thought process-she looked alarmed.

"How is this possible!" she exclaimed, gesturing to my legs with a hint of reprimand.

Seamus' eyebrow raised in amusement as I fumbled over my words, explaining myself to my baby cousin.

"I didn't know for sure if I could—" I began.

"Well I s'pose ye are the goddess of the sea, Amalgam or not," she said, shaking her head in dismay as she observed the change in me that all had thought was impossible.

She then made a clucking sound while looking both of us up and down and taking in our disheveled appearances. I raised my hand to smooth my hair but thought better of it.

"Well I'm glad ye've gotten yer ride at the least," she said with an eye roll, and Seamus barked out a laugh at her vulgarity. I had to admit it certainly sounded out of place coming from her child-like mouth. "But Jasmine, I still don't think ye should land-walk if ye can help it. The legends say Atargatis herself would forbid it!"

I massaged my sore legs, confirming her suspicions.

"Yeah, I've gathered that," I said shortly, again feeling the searing pain that reminded me the sea goddess was telling me I didn't belong on land. "Let's get back to the water."

The three of us took off down the rocky path, Aisling telling me all that had transpired in my absence. I was saddened to hear of Oisin, but not wholly surprised. Furthermore, I was able to connect the dots regarding how Seamus had learned everything he knew and felt relieved that I would not have to explain it all to him.

"As for Cearbhall and Camila, they're lookin for the rest of the stones as ye already know…and the other Amalgams know about ye, now. They know they can't do much without ye," she said as we reached the shoreline at last. "I had to stay hidden once I got back to Hy-Brasil. But of course they dunno about Fintan and I-"

"What?" I asked. "You know Fintan?"

"Of course I do," she snapped, irritated by my interruption. I found it hard to imagine the demure, shy girl that I had met just yesterday. "I'm engaged to be married to him."

Deciding I would dissect the familial matters later, I nodded my head in encouragement for her to continue.

"We must go at once," she concluded as we reached the sand. "At great risk to himself-*buck eejit*-Fintan's also been able to find out more about Aine. Yer mam."

"Go on," I said tentatively, my gaze flickering to Seamus for reassurance.

"She's not in one of Atargatis' pools at all," she said excitedly. "She's *escaped*, Jasmine!"

I felt a surge of pride that I could not explain. I didn't know the woman, after all. In my dismantling of my heritage, I had hardly taken a moment to think about who the woman was beyond a mysterious connection to the ancient past. I wondered how I'd feel if…no. *When* I found her.

And now to realize that she had only stayed away from me to keep me safe… I thought about Raj, heartbroken by the mysterious disappearance of his first love. Raising me alone as best he could while juggling a career that demanded he travel the world to get ahead. I wanted nothing more than to speak to him now, and tell him that it had all been for a reason. She hadn't abandoned us at all.

"Do you know where she is?" I asked Aisling tentatively. Seamus squeezed my shoulder tightly.

"No," Aisling said, her face falling slightly. She pointed to the stone that still hung around Seamus' neck. "But I think-now that ye know who ye are-*ye* should be able to see *her*."

I hadn't thought of it, but it seemed entirely possible and even probable now. If the stone could bring Seamus back to me, why couldn't its power also be capable of taking me to her? My mother, the woman responsible for the rebirth of the line of Atargatis.

Seamus removed the necklace and handed it to me. I looked closely into the honey-colored window and shut my eyes as it warmed at my touch.

"*Show me where she is,*" I said to no one in particular. I suppose if I had to guess, I was speaking to Atargatis herself. I don't even know if I said the words out loud.

The world went silent.

I was suddenly floating in a dark sea with a shoreline that was distinctly different from Skellig Michael. There were sloping beaches and an abundance of bright city lights that glimmered faintly in the distance, signaling I was near a bustling metropolis. The air was far more temperate-even with my body's natural ability to adapt to any environment, I could tell it was more pleasant here.

But the smell-I knew it. It was familiar.

I tasted the waves on instinct, knowing that I now possessed wildly superior senses than I had ever had in my life as a human. I immediately recognized it as the very same water that had filled my lungs to the point of near death a long time ago.

It was the same water that had unraveled everything my mother had done to try and keep me safe from the dangerous fate she had unknowingly laid upon me. I looked wildly about in the black water of the night for a redheaded woman lurking nearby, but I didn't need to see her to know. I gasped with understanding and was thrust back to the present.

"Portugal," I said. "She-she thinks I'm still in Porto with my father. She's looking for me."

PROLOGUE

*P*rofessor Liam Brennan absentmindedly rapped his fingers on his desk. The exasperatingly loud clock that the college refused to let him remove due its historical significance ticked away on the wall of his office, driving him to the brink of insanity. Of course he had returned to Dublin, but now that he was here, he felt a lingering sense of regret for his lack of presence on the voyage taking place across the country.

But that was foolish. He knew he had made the right choice in turning away. In fact, he felt more than mildly embarrassed that it took a lad he barely knew reminding him to be a man to get him to see sense. To think that he had even considered risking never seeing his wife or child again for the sake of chasing myths…it sent a shiver of shame down his spine.

Still, there was the adventurer's spirit within him—the one that often battled with the academic persona he outwardly portrayed—telling him he had missed out on the opportunity of a lifetime. He looked wistfully around the room at all of the artifacts procured from his adventures across the globe, thinking that even a simple pebble from the phantom island of Hy-Brasil would have been enough to complete his collection.

And *when*–if ever–would he hear of their success or demise? Would he have to go back to Galway and track down Aidan McCarthy in his signature dingy pub? Or would he simply turn on the news one day to find that two brothers, Seamus and Aidan from Belfast, had been swept out to sea and never seen again?

His thoughts were interrupted by a loud knock on the door that made him jump.

"Professor, do you have a moment for me?"

Given the time in the evening, he should have known it would be *her*. It was an hour that most students wouldn't consider appropriate for visiting their professors. But of course, she wasn't like most students. She batted her long, dark eyelashes at him in her usual mischievous way that presumably worked on everyone else as she entered his office without waiting for permission. She had undoubtedly come to ask for an extension on her *Comparing The Ideals of The Middle Ages and Renaissance* essay, or to make extremely inappropriate comments designed to make him sweat. She relished Liam's discomfort, and she was the bane of his existence.

"Sure, Carly, what is it?" he said, sighing and rubbing his nose with exasperation. He had dropped the pretense of patience for her long ago, but his careless attitude only seemed to encourage her.

She did not take a seat, but rather pranced around his office with her ballerina's grace, gently running her fingers across his possessions in a manner of presumed authority that made his blood boil.

"The essay…" she began.

"Let me guess, you need an extension."

She glanced up at him with deep brown eyes that looked like they belonged to the face of a newborn puppy rather than the countenance of a devious young adult. The trait was extremely misleading, and surely assisted in trapping many others in her web. But not him. Liam found her insincerity revolting.

"I've been working so hard," Carly said, unblinking. "I just need one more day."

He wanted to say no, to tell her that she was a lazy, dreadfully over privileged child whose aristocratic daddy had bought her way into one of the most prestigious universities in the world. He wanted to tell her that she had no business being in the same *universe* as her classmates, let alone lecture halls.

But he couldn't say that, because as much as he hated to admit it, she frightened him.

The truth—and that's all that *should* matter—was that not a single one of the indecent interactions that occurred between himself and Carly Connor were any fault of his own, and he would defend his honor regarding that statement until the day he died. Not only did the sheer existence of the girl repulse him, but he loved his wife Bridget and their precious son Angus dearly. He had never—and *would* never—do anything to jeopardize his family.

No, Liam Brennan was afraid of Carly Connor because one of his oldest friends and mentors in higher education, Raj Atarga, had warned him long ago about students just like her.

"YOU NEED to be careful around your students," Raj said, wagging his finger at him over the coffee table. "As a young professor, all eyes will be on you. Everyone expects you to fuck up, and the temptation will be there. Trust me, I would know."

They were sitting out on the back patio of Raj's house in South Florida, and he was giving one of his fatherly lectures that Liam hadn't asked for after having told him the good news—he had received his first offer for a teaching job. It was a teaching assistant position at a small local college outside of

Cork, but still. It was something. It was the first big step in his career.

He vaguely remembered Raj alluding to an unsavory situation with a student from his past, but if Liam hadn't held his mentor in such high regard, he might have rolled his eyes. In Liam's opinion, Raj had been far too harsh with himself when speaking of her, whatever her name had been.

"But Raj, nothing ever happened between you two," Liam said. "And besides, she was of age. So even if it had, it wouldn't have been the end of the world."

He glanced up at his friend again and saw the distinct shadow of shame cross his face that told him his assumptions regarding Raj's past may have been wrong.

"I made a mistake that I'll regret every day for the rest of my life," Raj said quietly, dropping his voice so there was no chance of his teenage daughter overhearing their conversation. Jasmine was reading on the couch just inside the sliding glass door, entirely oblivious to her father's misdeeds. "I should never have done it, but she was a pretty girl, and I was a lonely idiot."

Liam slumped in his chair, taken aback.

"So you *did* sleep with her?" he whispered, trying his best not to allow the esteemed opinion he held of the man across from him to be warped by this discovery. But it was difficult. He couldn't believe it.

"Once," Raj replied curtly, nodding his head as his eyes misted over in regretful recollection. "And I'll never forgive myself for it. Especially considering what ensued afterward."

"Well, as I said before, she was an adult," Liam replied, trying to justify the transgression aloud. "And of course you were lonely. You've never been married, or even had a girlfriend in the time I've known you."

"Oh, thanks for the reminder, man," Raj said sarcastically, pouring a glass of port for both of them. "Do you come visit just to insult me?"

"No, it's because I need a place to stay when I come to the states," Liam quipped, taking a deep sip of the aubergine liquid that truthfully was a bit too sweet for him. Port had never been to his liking, even when he had gone to school right next to the Duoro Valley, the rolling hills from which the delicate beverage originated. "And hotels in Miami are ungodly expensive."

Raj let out a hollow laugh, but he wasn't finished with his sermon.

"Make no mistake, it wasn't in any way acceptable," he said severely. "And I had no one to blame but myself for the nightmare she became after I did it."

Liam cocked his head. "What did she do?"

"It started off as mild stalking on campus…dropping into my office late at night, leaving notes, all that stuff," Raj replied. "But it evolved into something much worse, and obviously I couldn't do anything about it. One of the most unbelievable things she did was photoshop a picture of us together and put it on my desk before class. It actually looked real, even back in those days. Can you *imagine* if someone on staff had seen that?"

"Yikes," Liam replied, his own stomach turning at the thought. "So what happened? She graduated and left you alone?"

Raj grimaced.

"Ah, I'm so glad you asked, young Liam," he said, the air of wisdom exuding from him in the way it always did when he prepared to bestow a lesson upon his young mentee. "Her delusions about our fake relationship combined with my fear of discovery for being a piece of shit quite literally drove me out of the country."

Liam's jaw dropped. He hadn't been expecting that. "*That's* why you took the post at The University of Porto? Because of *her*?"

"Yes," Raj replied bitterly. "I was convinced she was going to ruin my life. She nearly did, several times. I got tired of the paranoia."

"So you picked up and moved to Portugal?"

"Yes," he said simply. "I kept thinking of Jasmine, and what it would do to her if she ever heard something like that about her father. It would destroy her."

Liam nodded, glancing at the girl in the living room who he knew thought the world of her dad. And then his final bit of curiosity got the better of him.

"What was her name? The student?"

Raj rolled the port around in his mouth as revulsion colored his face. Liam thought he might even spit it out.

"Camila."

CHAPTER 1

NOHOVAL COVE, COUNTY CORK

*H*e was an incredibly selfless lover when it came to using his mouth. Each time—and there had been many, even in the short period we'd been together—his head dropped below my waist, he became a dutiful servant in the pursuit of satisfying me. Of course I never wanted to envision how much *practice* it had taken him to master the art of it, but I appreciated the novelty of it, nonetheless. There were so few men who understood why it was considered a delicacy on the menu of the female experience.

I was rising and falling like the waves on the shore where we rested, undisturbed in the privacy of our isolated oasis.

"*Seamus*," I said his name in the same voice of overwhelmed resignation that I had now grown accustomed to sighing as if I had said it all my life.

He looked up at me, emerald eyes twinkling.

"Are ye pleased, *a stór*?" he asked, slipping two fingers inside of me while I temporarily mourned the loss of his tongue.

He knew how much I loved it when he called me various Irish Gaelic terms of endearment, particularly considering his rich, nearly old-world Northern Ireland accent. I had already become accustomed to his unique speech when just weeks ago I had struggled to understand him. Now knowing his mother's origins as a mystical selkie, a mermaid-like creature of the sea that could have been significantly older than she appeared, I wondered if it were her influence that still made his *"you"*s sound like *"ye"* and prompted his frequent usage of *"aye"*.

As he pleased me over and over, I didn't really care where it came from, to be honest. I just liked it.

"Yes," I replied.

His dark red hair caught the sunlight with a glimmer of auburn as his freckled cheeks rose into a smile of autumn leaves. With his ruggedly handsome embodiment of the most beautiful features of the Irish people, he was so inexplicably attractive to me.

He continued his methodical practice, finding the nerves in my body that threatened to shatter me at any moment. I let my head fall back onto the rough sand, deeply breathing in the salty air as he serviced me. I felt, especially at times like these, extremely fortunate that the curse of being an Amalgam—a mermaid unable to transform back into the human version of themselves—had evaded me despite having been marked by one when I was just a child. That's what they did, after all. Marked innocent, human victims with the mermaid curse that would eventually drag them back into the sea forever.

Even if I had only avoided the curse because I was actually the descendent of Atargatis, the original mermaid goddess of ancient Mesopotamia, and therefore thrust into a world of underwater conflict in which I was obligated to participate...I was still exceedingly grateful that Seamus and I could both change back and forth at will. My tail's transition to legs took several minutes longer than a regular selkie's—including the one who was between mine now—but it was worth the wait.

The familiar wave of ecstasy that Seamus brought upon me each time he made love to me was approaching, and I didn't resist. I allowed myself to be pulled underwater with the current, succumbing to the limp helplessness that sent the addictive heat radiating through my body.

I sighed.

He smirked and rose to meet me, placing a hand on the large rock beside my head. He was, of course, more than ready for me, and although I thought I could die happily where I was, I still wanted him again. I reached up and pulled him down toward me, kissing him tenderly and tasting myself in his mouth.

"*Christ*," he swore under his breath as he pressed himself inside me.

This time I smirked as the uncontrollable chemistry that existed between us ensued, with Seamus giving himself to me while he whispered Irish curse words into my ear that sent shivers of pleasure down my spine. Before I had ever been with him romantically, I had speculated about his nature as a lover in my dreams, and I had been right. When he made love to me, he liked to make me *his*. I let him do it now as he braced himself against the rock with one arm, the other holding my waist flush to the shore.

After another few thrusts of impassioned force, he bent down to kiss me gently, reminding me of his love. I shuddered as he slowly dragged his lips down my throat, sending me to the surface again. I had never had a lover like him—someone who knew what I wanted at all times, even if the desires were hidden in the darkest corners of my mind. Because we had fallen in love with one another so suddenly and deeply, it was intoxicating.

But there was a tiny voice in my head that told me I shouldn't enjoy it as much as I did. My almost-fiancé from my human life, Matt, had been dead now for over a year, and I wondered when the guilt I felt for being with someone else would subside. Especially now, considering I had learned the boating accident that had taken both Matt and my father's lives on the morning I was supposed to get engaged may not have been an accident at all.

Camila, the nefarious Amalgam who claimed it was her right to seek the stones of Atargatis in order to harness the power of the seas, along with Cearbhall–the leader of the Hy-Brasil Irish Amalgam clan–had made it clear only days ago that my late father, Raj, had been a victim of their choosing. How they knew him, I had no idea. I would find out, as soon as I could get a moment alone with the evil woman who I now knew was responsible for ruining my life.

But another factor behind my guilt was the fact that I *didn't* think my life wasn't ruined, despite having lost the two most important people in my world. Matt's death and my subsequent depressive episode had led me to go on the trip to Ireland with my friends where I met Seamus, who I knew now was my soulmate. This new, supernatural existence we shared was just one of many ways that we were bonded. He had gone to the literal ends of the earth to find me after my disappearance, acting on the whim that he, too, thought the Irish selkie blood ran through his veins.

And finally...I had discovered that my mother who had abandoned me as a child had, in fact, only done so out of obligation regarding the mermaid curse. My Irish mother, Aine, was also a selkie. When she had a child with my Syrian father, Raj, who was a descendent of Atargatis, it ignited the ancient bloodline of the mermaid goddess once more. Somehow–and I didn't fully understand it yet–my mother had been imprisoned by the Amalgams in Cyprus for the entirety of my life, and now she had escaped. Now she was looking for me, and I for her.

* * *

SOME TIME LATER, Seamus ran his fingers through my black hair and kissed me on the shoulder before standing decisively.

"We should go, aye?"

We had quickly departed the Skellig Islands when my newly discovered cousin, Aisling, informed us of my mother's escape. Thanks to Seamus bringing one of the stones of Atargatis from Professor Brennan's office, I had a brief vision of my mother in a place reminiscent of my childhood home with my father—Porto, Portugal. I was somehow able to communicate with my loved ones through the stones, and I hoped the citrine that hung around Seamus' neck would lead us to Aine as it had led him to me.

Aisling had hurriedly told us that The Green Window we'd need for the fastest passage to Porto was just as temperamental as the mermaid portal of the seas back in Bangor Bay–it was not always open. But unlike the mysterious whirlpool in Belfast, this one was relatively predictable. The Window was in the sea just south of Cork, and would be open only when the moon was visible.

We knew the closest we could get to wait for our passage without risking being seen was Nohoval Cove, a picturesque inlet near Cork, just east of Kinsale. The sun was setting, momentarily relieving the pain that my connection to the goddess of the moon (among many other things Atargatis was known for) caused me. I had discovered that while my bloodline to her meant I *could* land-walk unlike most Amalgams, it was extremely painful for me to be in the direct sunlight when I had legs. For that reason, Seamus and I had chosen to pass the time in the shady parts of the inlet.

We'd been here for two days, patiently waiting for the sky to clear and reveal the moon. We could likely have already made the full swim to Porto without the underwater highway network within that time frame, but...I hadn't minded how we passed the time.

The final rays of sun hit me as I stood, sending a sharp surge of discomfort down my leg again. I winced, hoping Seamus didn't notice, but he did.

"Jasmine," he said seriously. "I don't want ye to keep hurting yerself. Ye promised ye'd tell me if it was painful."

"I'm fine," I said quickly. "The alternative is much worse, anyway."

The alternative being we didn't go on land and we didn't get to have one another. He had carried me up to the top of Skellig Michael when I was nearly shaking in pain from the sun, helping me find relief in the shade of the ancient huts at the top. Ever since then, he'd ardently watched for any signs of my physical struggle. I thought I'd hidden it pretty well, but apparently not.

"I want ye just as badly, mo chroí," Seamus said, tilting my chin upward to look at him. I rustled his red waves, sending a shower of grains of sand back onto the shore. "I just don't want ye to suffer."

"Really," I said, not meeting his gaze. "It's not that bad."

"Catch yerself on, Jasmine," he said with a raised eyebrow as I stumbled once more. He scooped me up in one swift motion, his green eyes full of concern. I let him do it, despite how helplessly pathetic it made me feel that I could hardly stand.

He carried me to the water and descended into it with me, muttering something about my stubbornness. The moment my feet touched the water, I began to feel the soothing coolness of my transformation taking back over. At last I felt the sweet relief of my legs becoming one, and my body turning back into the form which the goddess of the seas intended for me.

The iridescent tail that I had been so terrified of the first time I saw it was admittedly beautiful. Greenish-silver in the sun, it sparkled like an opalescent version of an emerald as it appeared; each scale crafted with the intention of making me a magical creature of the Irish seas.

"Much better," I said as Seamus melted into the water next to me, his tail that looked just like mine materializing beneath the glass surface. The water was freezing cold, no doubt, given it was autumn in Ireland, but we were protected from it by our supernatural blood.

He touched my cheek affectionately, his muscular, freckled arms gleaming in the amber sunset.

"Atargatis calling ye back to the water," he mused, voicing my thoughts. We began to flit across the surface at a leisurely pace, turning toward the south.

"I hope Aisling wasn't too mad at me," I said, backstroking across the waves.

Seamus smiled. "Aye, well ye're the Queen of the Seas now. Ordering subjects around is something ye'll have to get used to, so it is."

"Very funny."

I didn't care that I was the Heir to an ancient mermaid crown. I didn't want anything to do with it. I wanted to find the stones before the other side could use them for evil, and that was it.

"It's for the best," he continued. "I know ye want to do this part alone."

Despite her strong objection to doing so, Aisling had eventually agreed to my request for her to return to Hy-Brasil and reunite with her own partner, Fintan, who was undoubtedly missing her very much by now. We would see her again soon, but I couldn't allow yet another person to take on my burdens. I was going to first set out to find my mother, reasoning that I had seen a concrete vision of her whereabouts, whereas the matter of the stones was more abstract. I thought—*hoped*, rather—that she might have information on where they were as well.

"Last chance," I said to Seamus as we swam further out into the open water. I pointed toward the general direction of the shores of Cobh.

Seamus didn't even turn to look at me, but his side profile revealed his jaw to be firm.

"I'm not going, Jasmine," he said. "Not without ye, ever."

"Well, you have some messes to clean up back home," I said. "Messes that are my fault."

I looked down at the water, the guilt of having torn him away from his normal life eating at me again.

"No, they're not," he said, his green eyes bright with sincerity. "And we have bigger things to worry about right now, aye?"

Of course Seamus' discovery of his selkie nature was much more of a problematic complication to his old life than mine. Considering both my father and my fiancé were dead, and everyone thought *I* was as well, I had nothing important to return to. He, on the other hand, had a successful career back in London, friends who were surely worried sick about his disappearance during their trip to Ireland, and his brother Aidan and Professor Liam Brennan who were entirely oblivious as to whether or not their mission to send him to the mystical land where the selkies of the Aran Islands dwelled had been successful. I wanted him to go back, at least temporarily, to let everyone know he was alright. To Galway first, and then London.

I thought my chances of returning to my own friends were much slimmer, given I had yet to hear of a Green Window that led to the Americas. Aisling told me point blank that she didn't think there were any until at least the Mediterranean, which meant a journey to Tampa could take a lot more time than I had to spare right now. I thought of Kiana often, of course, considering she had been the only friend of mine who had believed in my survival at any point. I held onto the unlikely hope that she could feel that I was alive in the way that Seamus had, even though she had abandoned the search for me when he hadn't.

But I could see Seamus wasn't budging, and I knew better than to try and force him. Despite the brevity of our time together, I sensed immediately that he was strong-willed. The man would never do a damn thing he didn't want to do...that was certain.

"Fine," I said, and we took a sweeping dive into the depths of the Atlantic.

I inhaled the salty water that breathed life into my lungs, instantly filtering out the filth of land-walker air, as I now called it. There was something so fulfilling about the nutritious ocean to me now, and the tiny slits on the side of my neck thanked me incessantly for satiating them once more.

"This way," Seamus said, reaching for my hand under the waves.

There wasn't much to see beyond endless slopes of sand as we made our way toward the ocean floor, flying at a speed that whipped my hair from my eyes. One thing I *was* looking forward to in Portugal was the variety of oceanic landscapes. I recalled it from my childhood when I lived there with my father, of course, but to see it from this new vantage point would be something different entirely. I couldn't wait to see the rainbow hues of fish and coral, which were now all part of my own environment rather than decorative accents to be observed as an outsider.

"How will we know where it is?" he asked, gesturing vaguely around the dark water.

"Oh, trust me, we won't be able to miss it," I said knowingly, gazing up at the surface to see that the sun had fully set and the sky was black.

The Green Window we sought was hidden within a coccolithophore bloom—a collection of microscopic marine algae. It was filled with calcium carbonate plates called coccoliths, which would make it look somewhat like an underwater cloud. The blooms' role in the removal of carbon dioxide from the atmosphere made them crucial to marine life, but I knew that they could be dangerous. Not to us, of course, but to the humans, maybe. I knew all about them given Raj's occupation as a professor of marine biology, and would be easily able to identify it once we were upon it.

I voiced this to Seamus, and he grinned as he shook his head in admiration.

"I dunno what a brilliant woman like ye is doing with me," he said, laughing. "Ye know something about everything."

"Please," I said, rolling my eyes as he swam in front of me. "Just the byproduct of being a professor's daughter."

My memories of Raj had always been fond, but now they held a deeper significance. Since embracing my nature as a creature of the sea, my recollections of conversations with him had evolved into vital clues essential for my survival. Raj's insights spanned a multitude of subjects—from marine life to geography, mythology, astronomy, and even history to some extent. *He* was the one who had known something about everything. As I embarked on the next phase of my destiny, I knew I would rely on Raj's wisdom more than ever. I only wished he could witness me putting it into practice.

"I think that's it," I said as we approached the swirling, underwater cloud. The seemingly celestial body churned in slow motion directly ahead, its mystical pink foam calling to us.

Seamus led the way and I grasped his arm tightly. I held my breath as the whirlpool enveloped us in its magical substance, the floating violet clouds beginning to noiselessly vibrate in preparation for transporting us to another place. Another sea, another country, another world.

ABOUT THE AUTHOR

A.G. Whitt is the author of the award-winning novel, *The Heir of Atargatis* and its sequel, *I Dream of Iberia.* She lives in Tampa, Florida, with her husband, Ryan, and their rescue Chow Chow, Hiroki.

Follow her on social media for updates on what's next in the *Atargatis* series!

Book 1: *The Heir of Atargatis*

Book 2: *I Dream of Iberia*

Book 3: coming soon…